The Reluctant Commander

Book Two of the Neophyte
Warrior series

A Novel by

Richard Patton

This book is a work of fiction. Names, characters, places, and incidents either are products of the author's imagination or are used fictitiously. Any resemblance to actual events or locales or persons, living or dead, is entirely coincidental.

NEOPHYTE WARRIOR
THE RELUCTANT COMMANDER
Copyright © 2002 Richard Patton
ISBN: 1-894869-57-5
Cover art and design by Martine Jardin

Published by Zumaya Publications, 2002
Look for us online at: www.zumayapublications.com

Cast of Characters

George Washington: Freshly appointed Lieutenant Colonel and second in command of the Virginia Regiment, but the first to encounter the French.

Old Smoke: A Shawnee hunter of the Ohio Valley who was raised by Jesuits in Canada. His uncle Buffalo Hair considers him "too much a white man."

Pariah West/Stump Neck: A mysterious orphan with a yearning to become a savage. A French trader called **Gabriel Menard** (aka **Bushy Bear**) and his Chippewa wife **Bright Dawn** teach him the ways of a shaman.

Robert Dinwiddie: The Scottish Lieutenant Governor of Virginia and an Ohio Company Investor. He talks a good invasion but has not the slightest idea how to deliver one.

Sarah (Sally) Cary Fairfax: The wife of George William Fairfax and the woman Washington does not know he's in love with.

Buffalo Hair: Old Smoke's uncle, a respected Shawnee sachem, and dilettante psychopath. He enjoys torturing captives and owns two black slaves—a girl named **Mud Face** and her younger brother **Deep Water**.

Short Leg: Old Smoke's aunt, a Shawnee matriarch.

Claude-Pierre Pecaudy, Sieur de Contrecoeur: The Commander of Fort Duquesne, a decent man who enlists the aid of friendly Indians to help him butcher English settlers.

Striking Eagle/Sinking Canoe: Old Smoke's youthful best friend and a war lover.

Robert Stobo: A wealthy immigrant Scot and Captain under Washington. He arrives at the battlefield with a horse-drawn carriage, ten servants, and a stash of Madeira wine.

Tanacharison and Monacatoocha: Iroquois vice-regents to the Delaware and Shawnee in the Ohio Valley.

Charles 'Jolicoeur' Bonin: A youthful Parisian whom fate transforms into a French marine under Contrecoeur.

Adam Stephen and Andrew Lewis: Officers under Washington, one a hot-tempered Scot, the other a bear of an Irishman.

Christopher Gist and Jacob Van Braam: One a frontiersman, the other a Dutchman and Virginia officer. Both are good friends of Washington.

Jasper Redfield: A Moravian settler in the Ohio Valley and friend of Short Leg.

James Mackay: Captain of a Carolina Independent Company and Washington's rival for battlefield command.

Coulon de Jumonville: A French nobleman sent on a 'diplomatic' mission by Contrecoeur. His confrontation with Washington will be the defining event of the French and Indian War.

Louis Ecuyer, the Sieur de Villiers: Half-brother of Jumonville and his self-appointed avenger.

Andrew Montour: An Iroquois-French half-breed who, nevertheless, aligns himself with the British cause.

Acknowledgements

I am indebted to the many authors whose writings provided source material for the novel. The books include, but are not limited to: *For King And Country* by Thomas A. Lewis, *Washington, The Indispensable Man* by James Thomas Flexner, *An Old Frontier Of France* by Frank H. Severance, *Ill-Starred General* by Lee McCardell, *Braddock at the Monongahela* (published by the University of Pittsburgh Press), *Guns At The Forks* by Walter O'Meara, *The Journal Of Major George Washington* (published by Colonial Williamsburg, Inc.), *George Washington In The Ohio Valley* by Hugh Cleland, *Delaware-Indian and English Spelling-Book* by David Zeisberger, *Memoir of a French and Indian War Soldier* (edited by Andrew Gallup), *The Most Extraordinary Adventures of Robert Stobo* by Robert C. Alberts, *Christopher Gist's Journals* by William M. Darlington, *Indians In Pennsylvania* by Paul A.W. Wallace, *The Indians of Northeastern America* by Karna L. Bjorklund, *Death And Rebirth Of The Seneca* by A.F.C. Wallace, *The Coming Of The White Man 1492-1848* by Herbert Ingram Priestley, *Pioneer Priests of North America 1642-1710* by the Reverend T.J. Campbell, *Council Fires On The Upper Ohio* by R.C. Downes, and *Old Historic Landmarks Of Virginia And Maryland* by W.H. Snowden.

The Virginia Historical Society, the Western Pennsylvania Historical Society, and the Carnegie Library of Pittsburgh all provided invaluable assistance. The staff of the Pleasant Hills Public Library was always helpful in pointing me in the right direction and in trying (often successfully) to find obscure reference material. I am especially grateful to the staff of the Jefferson Hills Public Library, whose unwavering help and support frequently went well beyond any reasonable call to duty.

Last, but definitely not least, I want to thank Tina H., without whom nothing could have happened.

For our wonders: Tami, Letti, Stefani, Jonathan, Steven, D.J. (or Dean, if he prefers), Dante, Dana, Sam and…so forth…

In memory of Miss Marjorie Scott of Elizabeth-Forward High School and Professor Edwin Moseley of Washington and Jefferson College, who thought I could.

Prologue

In Book One of *Neophyte Warrior*, twenty-one year old George Washington enters the arcane world of British-French colonial politics with a bang *and* a whimper. Appointed Adjutant General of Virginia by Governor Robert Dinwiddie, his first act as a soldier on behalf of the British Crown and, more precisely, Dinwiddie, is to deliver a message warning the French to remove themselves from the Ohio Valley. He does, to a Captain Joncaire at a French outpost on the Allegheny River called Venango. The French reject the ultimatum, surprising no one. After Washington's return to Williamsburg, Dinwiddie informs the young major that he is organizing a military expedition to expel the French from the Ohio Valley by force. A Virginia Regiment is to be formed and commanded by one Joshua Fry with Washington as second in command. Befitting this responsibility, the young major is promoted to the rank of lieutenant colonel.

In the meantime, the French have been strengthening their hold on the Ohio territory. Possession of the forks, where the Allegheny and Monongahela Rivers meet to form the Ohio, will permit them to control the entire North American continent by linking Canada to New Orleans. Captain Claude-Pierre Pecaudy, Sieur de Contrecoeur, leads a force of French and Indians to the forks and drives out a small contingent of Virginians sent there by Dinwiddie to build a fort. Contrecoeur immediately begins work on his own fort, a much more substantial structure to be called Fort Duquesne after the Governor General of Canada.

While Washington and Contrecoeur lay the groundwork for a violent confrontation, the tribes of the Ohio Valley are faced with difficult decisions. Should they choose sides or ride out the impending conflict as neutrals? If they do choose, which side should

1

it be: British or French? The Six Nations of the Iroquois—the dominant native power—favor an alignment with the British. The other tribes of the Ohio Valley—Shawnee, Delaware, Mingo—prefer the limited French presence to the swarming British settlers, who seem always to want yet another tract of traditionally Indian land. Trapped in this stewpot of conflict and uncertainty is a Jesuit-educated Shawnee named Old Smoke. Washington and the Shawnee meet at Venango during the Virginian's first diplomatic expedition, in which Old Smoke's services as a hunter were enlisted. After the failure of that mission the two men go their separate ways: Washington to his uncertain fate as a military commander and Old Smoke to his village on the Ohio River. Upon returning to his village, Old Smoke learns that his uncle Buffalo Hair, a respected Shawnee sachem with a predilection for torturing captives, wants him to enlist as a warrior with the French for the expected confrontation with the British. Old Smoke promises to consider his uncle's request, then learns from his aunt Short Leg that Buffalo Hair plans to butcher a young Ojibwa captive named Cornpicker. Working clandestinely with his aunt, Old Smoke removes Cornpicker from his uncle's clutches and takes him to the fortress settlement of one of Short Leg's acquaintances: a Moravian named Jasper Redfield.

Lurking behind the scenes of overt conflict are more sinister developments: massacre and mayhem on the frontier. Bands of roving renegades, many of them commanded by French officers, mercilessly attack white settlements, sending streams of refugees fleeing over the mountains to the east. One such band, comprised of Indians and French *coureurs de bois,* is led by Stump Neck, a white man turned outlaw. In reality, Stump Neck is a young, mentally disturbed orphan named Pariah West, who was also with Washington at Venango but mysteriously disappeared on the return trip. A Frenchman named Gabriel Menard and his wife, Bright Dawn, find West with a band of Chippewa and train him in the ways of a shaman. After the training is completed, Menard stays on as Stump Neck's contact with the French at Fort Duquesne, thinking that, by doing so, he can exercise a degree of control over the madman. Bright Dawn is not as optimistic. She is convinced Stump Neck will eventually kill her husband and tells him so.

The French have seized the forks of the Ohio without firing a shot and, by doing so, gained control of the waterways accessing most of North America. But the matter is by no means settled. It cannot be; the stakes are too high. Washington is on his way with a regiment of Virginians and expects to join forces with another contingent of Virginians and a regiment of North Carolina Independents at a place called Great Meadows in the Allegheny Mountains. Through their Indian spies, the French are well informed of the invasion and prepare accordingly. Something is bound to happen.

𝕮hapter 𝕺ne

April 20, 1754, Wills Creek, Maryland

The man's name was Hezekiah Bennett and he was a rarity: a Wills Creek farmer who had something to sell George Washington.

"Ya want 'er, Colonel? She's a good animal, make good eatin'," the man gummed as he gestured at the cow.

Bennett had one blackened tooth and a head full of knotted, disheveled hair that he must have trimmed with a hatchet. The tooth grew from the upper gum and was visible between the man's meaty lips even when they were closed. When they were open and speaking, the tooth was a distraction. Lieutenant-Colonel Washington of the Virginia Regiment found himself watching its trajectory, steeling himself for the gush of blood that must certainly issue forth when the tooth punctured the pulpy flesh of the lower lip. To say the man was dirty was to grossly understate his condition and defame the earth. He was one with his environment, patches of which covered his skin, his beard, his shoes, his burlap leggings, his (white?) linen shirt, and the ridiculous red sock he wore on his head. From its smell, it was clear that the environment he carried with him included more than just soil. Some of it had recently departed the intestinal tract of a living creature, possibly the emaciated Holstein standing next to the man, munching the dead grass clumped in the recently thawed mud and leaning against the three-wheeled wagon attached to the swayback gray mare.

"The cow is nearly dead, Mr. Bennett," Washington said from behind the table at which he and Captain Peter Hogg sat at the Regiment's campsite. "It can hardly stand."

"Well, whaddya think I'm sellin' 'er fur? If she was still a good milker, I'd be a keepin' 'er. Besides, it don't matter if she keels over right here, right now. Save ya the trouble 'a killin' 'er," Hezekiah Bennett argued, honestly indignant.

Washington looked at the cow and feared for its life.

"Sir, I am a farmer myself and that cow looks sick to me."

"She *ain't* sick. She's jes' old like me!" the man cackled, an action that was accompanied by an unsightly baring of tobacco-stained gums.

Washington resigned himself to the sale. He needed the cow to feed his troops. Governor Dinwiddie's dictum to his commissary, John Carlyle, that "provisions are plenty in the back country" had proven to be remarkably naive. No supplies from Carlyle or any other source had arrived in Wills Creek and he now had a hundred sixty men to feed after picking up Adam Stephen and his small company in Winchester.

"How much do you want for her?" Washington asked reluctantly. He didn't have much choice.

Hezekiah gave an appropriately contemplative performance, rubbing his chin and nibbling at his lower lip with the obnoxious tooth.

"Five bucks. That oughtta do it," he said finally.

The 'buck,' or one fall buckskin, was the unofficial unit of frontier currency.

"Five buc..." Washington stammered. "That cow is not worth one shilling."

"I'll throw the wagon in free."

"The wagon has only three wheels. And they aren't round."

Seller and potential buyer glanced over at the wagon. The cow, seemingly contented, was still leaning against it, or vice-versa; it was hard to tell which. Made of planks nailed and strapped together, the wheels were ovals with flat spots where the weakest wood fibers had worn away with use. Bennett was aghast with indignation.

"Ain'cha got no carpenters in this here army 'a yers? All ya need is one more wheel!"

Of the hundred and sixty men in the expedition, Washington classified four as carpenters on the basis of their skills with an ax.

5

Constructing a wheel would be a real challenge for these tree-cutters. He was not sure with whom he should be more upset, the comfortable, apathetic colonials on the Atlantic coastal strip whose reluctance to serve had made it necessary to sign up reprobates, or the stubborn, ungovernable, uncooperative malcontents like Hezekiah Bennett who had fled to the western side of the Alleghenies to escape the burdens of civilization.

"I'll give you one buck and I don't want the wagon," was Washington's counter offer.

But Hezekiah Bennett was in a dickering mood.

"Why, Colonel, I'd jes' as soon feed that ol' cow to m'wife 'n kids as sell her to ya at that price. A man's gotta live, ya know. Gotta feed his family."

Bennett topped off his homily with a grin that could have been interpreted as either smug or nonchalant. The young Virginian wondered what kind of woman would permit her man to appear in public in such a wretched condition and decided he did not really care to know. He looked askance at Captain Hogg, whose narrowed lips were mouthing the word 'two.' A quick glance at Christopher Gist and Jacob Van Braam—who seemed to be enjoying his interplay with Bennett—confirmed Hogg's judgment.

"Two then," Washington offered.

"Sold!" Bennett crooned gleefully, pounding the table with one fist. "Hah…Hah, y've made yerself a good deal, Colonel. She'll be good eatin', that cow, good eatin.'"

Captain Hogg stood and counted out the monetary equivalent of two bucks to Hezekiah Bennett, who stuffed it in one pants pocket and departed with the swayback mare and the three-wheeled wagon. Washington noted that Bennett chose to mount the mare rather than ride in the wagon, whose ovoid wheels were so seldom in phase that the wagon bed bobbed and weaved like a rowboat in a stormy sea. He snorted his displeasure for Hogg's benefit, not because the Captain was the source of his frustration, but because he needed something or someone to snort at.

The expedition to the forks had all the portents of a disaster in the making. Not only had he been unable to recruit any but the refuse of Virginia society but, possessing only two wagons and facing the floods and muck of spring, he had been unable to travel more than four miles a day. At Winchester they had arrived exhausted and hungry to find Adam Stephen and the men he had recruited but none of the promised supplies, neither Carlyle's provisions nor Trent's pack horses. They had been forced to impress into service horses, vehicles and food from the local farmers, an activity that did not contribute to the popularity of either George Washington or the expedition.

The next eighty miles to Wills Creek had been worse, with the steep grades of the looming Alleghenies and the dense thickets of mountain laurel to hack through adding to the already substantial transport problems. Carlyle's horn of backwoods 'plenty' was a myth. That, or the proprietors of this abundance were keeping it for themselves. To add to an already acute situation, a rider from Captain Trent brought the distressing news that eight hundred French troops could arrive at the forks at any moment and would Colonel Washington please make a brisk march over the Alleghenies to save the day. But at Wills Creek, as it had been at Winchester, there were no pack horses, and nothing with which to equip them or the expedition they served. While he waited for the expedition's Commander, Joshua Fry, to arrive with the other half of the Virginia Regiment, Washington had decided to approach the local farmers, like Hezekiah Bennett, for supplies. But the farmers had little and sold less. On this part of the frontier they seemed to be little more than a race of near barbaric malcontents with no allegiance to the Crown, Virginia, or anything but themselves. This was no way to run a military campaign.

"Sir, should I close down for the day? There are no more farmers."

It was Hogg. The Captain looked old, tired, and discouraged as he closed his orderly book, a feeling Washington certainly shared.

"Yes, I suppose so. Peter, we still have a few hours of daylight. Have the officers and subalterns come to my tent…"

"Rider approaching!"

He was coming at a good pace from the west, over a small ridge framed by a blurred, orange, end-of-the-day sun. He was without coat or hat. Only a white linen shirt protected him from the elements, which, on this day, were a misty, chilling rain and moderate winds. As the rider approached, Washington thought he recognized the lanky, sinuous figure of Ensign Edward Ward. His heart sank. Ward was supposed to be at the forks completing Fort Prince George.

The rider—it *was* Ward—dismounted from his horse, which was covered by a meringue of perspiration. Ward was gasping for breath and strode directly to Washington.

"Colonel Washington, I have to speak with you, sir," Ward said between wheezes. "The French have taken Fort Prince George!"

In anticipation of the news, Washington's pot had already begun to boil. He paced and stomped his feet on the ground in consternation.

"Damn, damn, double dam..." he muttered, then took the tricorne from his head and pounded the table with it. "Sonofabitch, sonofabitch...son-of-a-BITCH!" he railed with rising intensity as the tricorne was beaten into a shapeless hulk.

At the final imprecation, Washington flung the tricorne in a trajectory he thought to be random, but happened to intersect the udders of Bennett's cow. The animal gave a start and a woeful "Mooooo!"

When he realized what he'd done, Washington apologized.

"Sorry, old girl, I didn't mean to..."

At which Gist, Ward, Hogg, Van Braam, and the several militiamen present broke into an uproar.

"Do you feel better, George, now that you've taken your anger out on this poor cow's teats? How cruel, how cruel!" Christopher Gist chided.

The Colonel acknowledged his foolishness with a snicker but was not mollified. He retrieved the tricorne but did not put it back on his head.

"No, I don't feel better," he moaned. "How can I feel better? On what basis am I supposed to make a sensible decision about this...this...abominable news from Ensign Ward? I have no supplies, no pack horses, no information save his dismal report, and an under-strength force of men who don't even know how to march, let alone shoot at the enemy. I can't inform my commanding officer because I have no idea where he is or when he'll arrive, but I do know there are a thousand Frenchman out there ready to blow my head off..."

"More like six hundred," Ward interjected, "and half as many Indians."

In his tirade Washington had completely forgotten about Ward. He sat down behind the table at which he'd parleyed with Hezekiah Bennett, laid the tricorne on it, and leaned back in his chair.

"All right, Mr. Ward, let's listen to what you have to say. What's your assessment of the situation? Where is John Frazier, by the way? I thought he was your superior officer."

Ward told Washington of Frazier's absence and the reason for it: to attend to his business interests at Turtle Creek. The Ensign was disturbed by this. So was Washington at first, until Ward mentioned the denunciation of the Ohio Company as the root of all evil by Captain Contrecoeur, the Commander of the new French fort to be built at the forks. Then he remembered that his own interest in the company might be perceived—had been perceived by some—as a conflict of interest. He would have to work that out in his mind later.

Ward continued unabated, "…We had no chance, sir. If we'd had the troops to man the fort we might've given them a fight, even without the cannons. But there were only thirty-five of us, not enough to hold off six hundred."

"It's good you stayed the course, Ensign," Christopher Gist offered with his usual aplomb. "It should help to keep our Indians loyal."

"The Half-King was pretty mad, sir."

"And he'll be mad for a while," Gist replied. "But I think he'll stay with us…unless we have a real disaster."

Puzzled by Gist's afterthought, Washington cast a furtive glance at the guide, hoping his words were not intended as a prophecy of things to come. But Gist was blank-faced, as usual.

"Peter, have the officers come to my tent in an hour," Washington said to Hogg. "We need to talk further with Ensign Ward and have a council of war."

* * *

So that all would be comfortable, the war council was held in the clearing adjacent to the tents occupied by Washington, Gist and Van Braam. Night had fallen and the rain-mist had mercifully subsided. A campfire of moist logs burned steadily but not flagrantly in the center of the clearing. During the hour since the Colonel's decision to hold the council, Ward prepared for his journey to Williamsburg with the unpleasant news. The other members of Trent's command—the soldiers, the artisans, the carpenters— filtered into the Wills Creek camp and collectively resigned. At least most of them did. Building fortresses in God-forsaken places and being captured by the French was not their idea of the good life. Then came the settlers, some on horseback, some in wagons, some on foot with their possessions bundled on their backs, all of them hungry, weary, portraits of dejection. It was a sorry procession, a funeral without a body to inter. The corpse—Fort Prince George—was being buried by the French.

The attendees ringed the campfire much as the tribal delegates had surrounded Contrecoeur's council fire in Venango but it was, of course, a smaller circle and the occasion demanded less formality. Tanacharison was seated on Washington's left. He and his Mingo warriors had arrived shortly after Ensign Ward. All the Virginians— militiamen and civilians—were in wilderness garb, none of it military issue. The young Colonel was attired in a simple buckskin shirt, breeches and boots. While the mood of those straggling in from the frontier was one of pessimism, the attitude of those at this council was businesslike. They had to decide what was to be done.

"Gentlemen, may I have your attention," Washington said as he came out of his tent carrying a short stool. While the attendees downed their last brew or stated their final opinion, Washington placed the stool on the ground and sat on it, leaning forward to rest his elbows on his knees.

"I think you all know what has happened. Fort Prince George has been captured by the French and we must decide whether to proceed with this mission or to abort it. If it is decided we will continue, it must be planned very carefully..."

"Sir, how many men do the French have?" asked a voice accented with skepticism.

Washington searched for Abner Singleton, one of Ward's men who, happily, had not been part of the resignation *en masse.* He found the man on his right.

"Sergeant, how many did you say, six hundred French marines

and three hundred Indians?"

"Yes sir, that's as many as I saw."

"Could there be more at Venango?"

"Surely."

Washington waited for further comments but none were immediately forthcoming. He brought his hands to his eyes and rubbed them. A headache was starting to take hold.

"Gentlemen, I think none of you will be surprised to learn that this is a situation I never wanted to be in."

Subdued, nervous laughter.

Lowering his hands, Washington blinked, gazed at the confused-but-eager souls in his charge, and continued, "As you know, this expedition was put together hastily, and I think you can see now why there was so much emphasis on speed. Well, we hurried, and we didn't make it. So be it. Amen. But now we have to face the consequences of all that haste. We have almost eight hundred troops but only a hundred sixty of them are here. That's us. The rest, Colonel Fry's two companies, the reinforcements from Maryland, North Carolina, and New York, and whatever Cherokees Governor Dinwiddie has scared up are…God knows where."

As he spoke, Washington glanced at Tanacharison to make sure he was not moving too fast for John Davison's translation and to gauge the Half-King's reaction. He was rewarded for his trouble with a vacant stare.

"Fortunately, we have the Half-King and his Mingo warriors with us," the Colonel said, nodding in Tanacharison's direction. "I have spoken at length with Tanacharison and can tell you that he is anxious for us to push on and to engage the French. He and his people are very distressed that Captain Contrecoeur and his army have taken the forks and Fort Prince George. But he is satisfied that, given the circumstances, we did as much as we could to oppose the invasion."

The Half-King's true opinion was somewhat less charitable, but the old man would go along with the half-truth for the sake of morale. Thank God for Ensign Ward.

"I've given it a good deal of thought and I must say I tend to agree with Tanacharison, in part at least. I think we must push on to

Redstone Creek on the Monongahela and then give our wayward forces the opportunity to catch up. This is what we've been ordered to do. If we simply wait here or return to Winchester, we might well be ceding to Captain Contrecoeur and his forces the valuable time they need to build their fort and establish themselves. Should our reinforcements be delayed or should Colonel Fry decide to abort the mission, nothing will be lost except a little time and a few inches to our waistlines."

"When are we gonna eat that damned cow ya bought, Colonel?" a voice teased from the back. "Better eat 'er soon or she'll get so skinny she won't be worth chawin' on."

There was genuine laughter. With all that had happened, they still had some spirit left. Bless their shiftless, malcontented souls!

"Actually, I was thinking of making her our mascot…" Washington chided to a chorus of jeers and whistles. He rose to a standing position. The stool was too small for his broad posterior to rest on comfortably for any length of time.

"Colonel, I beg to differ," a quiet but firm voice spoke out. The darkness prevented Washington from seeing the man but he recognized the grating voice of Silas Hobbs, a veteran.

"Speak up, Silas. I'm listening."

The older man hesitated, selecting his words, and then spoke his piece.

"Y've already said this mission was put together too fast. I'd agree with that a hunderd percent. Maybe if we could've got there first it'd be worth the rush, but we didn't. We got no food or pack horses but what we do have is a huge, hairy mountain or two to cross an' all of them frog-eaters in front of us. I think we oughtta sit down for a time an' figure out what we're doin'."

It was the kind of reasoned, sensible argument Washington would have expected from Silas. In fact, he agreed with it.

"Silas, I appreciate your opinion. I've gone over the same ground a hundred times myself. But I have to remind you that Governor Dinwiddie gave us orders to take and hold the forks and, if necessary, throw the French out…"

"Colonel, the Governor is a dear, dear man but he don't know what the hell he's talkin' about. He's a Scotsman, for pity's sake.

Sure, he knows what a mountain looks like, and maybe he's seen a tree or two in his day, but not in the kind of bunches we're gonna have to push through between here an' the Ohio. An' I know for sure he never got himself knotted up in a thicket of laurel slick!"

The Colonel contributed a few belly laughs to Silas's gnarly verbiage, as did everyone but the Half-King, whose understanding of English—even with the benefit of translation—was limited.

"Well, Silas, God knows we've hacked through laurel slick before, and we *will* be sitting down to figure things out with our colleagues when they arrive. I'll promise you one thing, though. If Colonel Fry says we go back, I surely will not make a fuss about it."

He heard a surly grumble from Silas's direction.

"Come on, Silas," Washington teased. "I don't know what you're worried about. A hundred sixty Englishmen with a cow for a mascot ought to be able to lick a thousand frog-eaters, don't you think?"

The guffaw from Silas was rich and resonant.

"Make that a hundred an' sixty Americans," he corrected. "I don't see no Englishmen here!"

The remark elicited another hefty chorus, this time of cheers and applause, which surprised the Colonel. Many of the more boisterous revelers were Scotch immigrants. He had often noted that the officer corps of the Virginia militia seemed to be dominated by Scotsmen of one stripe or another. Some came from the ranks of the vanquished of the 1745 Scottish Jacobite revolt against the British Crown, others from the legions of ambitious Scots seeking their fortunes in the colonies. Hogg, Stobo, Stephen, and even the regiment's physician, Surgeon-Major James Craik, were Scots. What it meant Washington didn't know. Whether he should be concerned he wasn't sure. But their laughter at Hobb's dig at the English was heartier than most. Maybe it was just their way, maybe not. But he found himself strangely pleased by the reaction.

Washington was ready to call an end to the council but found that most of the men were rising and stretching anyway. Silas had already provided closure. Instead, he simply announced, "We'll pull out day after tomorrow. That'll give us time to pack and maybe let our friends catch up. Captain Hogg will organize the departure."

After telling Hogg, Gist, and Van Braam he wanted to meet with them at breakfast to discuss the schedule and the best route to take, Washington approached the departing Ensign Edward Ward and placed a hand on his shoulder.

"Edward, I'd like to see you about nine tomorrow morning. I know you've told us what happened but we need to understand the details and get them down on paper."

"Certainly, sir. I'll be here," Ward replied, nodding his long neck and head two inches above Washington's line of sight. "Oh, did I tell you what the French are calling their fort?"

"No."

"They're calling it Fort Duquesne," said Ward. "After the Governor General of Canada. Captain Contrecoeur told me at dinner. He seems a decent sort, the French Captain..."

Not knowing where to take it, Ward let the thought trail off. He saluted and left, as did the remainder of the officers in short order. Entering his tent, the Colonel lighted the lamp on the table next to his cot. Then he found a mug, went back outside, and poured a modicum of rum into it from a keg near Van Braam's tent next door. He sipped it thoughtfully for a while, considered and forsook making an entry in his journal, finished off the rum with a flourish, and prepared for sleep.

As he lay, quietly letting the rum do its magic, he rummaged through his mind's record of events, sifting and sorting, trying to impose order on chaos. Some thoughts drifted, wanting to become dreams. *Are you there, Sally?* he asked. *Of course I am, George*, she replied. In his dreams she was not another man's wife and they loved openly.

Everything will be resolved when Joshua Fry comes, his own image insisted, oblivious to the abrupt and illogical shift of topic. *I'll inform him of the situation, he'll give me my orders, and I'll obey them.*

But where is Joshua Fry? the image rudely demanded, looking thoroughly perplexed.

Chapter Two

May 12, 1754, The forks of the Ohio

It was an excellent vantage point, this high hill on the south bank of the Monongahela where it met the Allegheny and made the Ohio. It was more than an excellent vantage point, Peter Delaney concluded; it was a looking glass onto an inexpressibly lovely panorama of green valleys, rolling hills, and quietly but tenaciously flowing rivers. *A woman, a lady, like Ireland.* Except for the dense forestation and the chronic overcast it might have been Ireland herself. *But the trees,* Delaney swore under his breath. *There are just too damned many of them, although taken one at a time they can be pretty things.*

As he squinted one eye closed so that the other could sight through the telescope, the émigré from the Emerald Isle complained—perhaps to God—that the scene would be even more picturesque if the four-pointed star that was the genesis of Fort Duquesne had not been branded on its face.

Delaney removed the telescope from his eye and handed it to the other Half-King, Monacatoocha, on his right. Tanacharison and Monacatoocha shared the responsibility of Iroquois rule over the two dominant Ohio Valley tribes. Tanacharison was the Half-King of the Delaware, Monacatoocha the Half-King of the Shawnee.

"Take a look, chief," said the Irishman, stretching and sucking in the cool, morning air of spring. Delaney, a barrel-chested, pale-skinned version of his contemporary and immediate superior, Christopher Gist, had visited the site of Fort Prince George a week earlier and found the militiamen and the Indians constructing it to be in "high spirits." The French Fort Duquesne would dwarf the now

15

defunct Fort Prince George. This did not inspire a mood of celebration in Delaney, Monacatoocha, or the small party of Virginians and Iroquois he and Gist had brought with them.

With the same, unwavering countenance his counterpart Tanacharison had exhibited at Venango, the Oneida chieftain took the strange, round contrivance. But the resolve behind the face was not in evidence. At Venango the French had been the enemy. Delaney and the British were allies. They were in charge. Monacatoocha knew they had to be in charge but he did not like it. This was partly because he suspected the British of incompetence and partly because, as an Iroquois sachem, he was not comfortable relinquishing control. Once waived, power would not be easily regained. Recognizing the weakness of this position, he decided to present a fatalistic visage to his colonial partners. It would be a grudging amiability he displayed but it would not be mistaken for servility.

Unfamiliar with the device, Monacatoocha struggled with the telescope and, after the Irishman had told him to close the eye not pressed to it, was awed by what he saw. Excitedly, he angled it from one position to another, finally settling on a line of sight intersecting the forks. For nearly a minute, he stood with one foot poised on a boulder, staring through the telescope. Then he returned it to Delaney.

"This is nice," he said, indicating the telescope.

"It is that," said Delaney. "Would you like one?"

"Yes."

Delaney put the eyepiece in place again and aimed the telescope at the embryo of Fort Duquesne.

"I'll see if I can get you one in Williamsburg," he said, then chastised himself for conducting business in the middle of a crisis. Buying and selling was an ingrained habit among the traders, one that was difficult to break.

"What do you think of the French Fort?" he asked.

Monacatoocha spread his arms to indicate great size.

"Big," he said. "Bigger than yours."

"It is big," Delaney acknowledged, then said with a smile and an assurance he did not feel, "When we capture this one, we'll make the next one even bigger."

The Oneida chieftain did not respond but regained the telescope and continued to amuse himself.

"Do you see those four areas shaped like arrowheads on the corners of the big square?" Delaney asked. "Those will be the bastions, where they'll mount their cannon…"

Monacatoocha nodded his understanding and handed the telescope back. Sighting through it again, the Irishman studied the construction activities. On two sides of the square that roughly paralleled the Allegheny and Monongahela Rivers, men were setting ten to twelve foot pickets. A stocky officer with *pince-nez* glasses was supervising the construction of the two remaining walls where horizontal, squared timbers were being laid to protect against a land side attack. In front of the land side walls, a squad of mixed French and Indian laborers was digging. A turbid concoction of sweat and grime caked their bodies. There were now two docks: the original landing upstream of the fort on the Allegheny River, around which most of the two hundred canoes and bateaux of Contrecoeur's invasion fleet were still clustered, and a new one near the point of convergence of the two rivers. A trench road connected the second dock to the thirty or forty foot long stockade wall, or curtain, between the north and west bastions.

Giving the telescope back to Monacatoocha, Delaney pointed to the eastern side of the fort and said, "Take a look where the two heavy walls are goin' up, Chief. D'you see those boys with the picks and shovels?"

Monacatoocha squinted, adjusted the telescope, and gave an affirmative grunt.

"That's the side we'll be comin' at 'em from—the east—so those are the two sides they need to be the thickest and the strongest. What them boys are diggin' down there is a trench so that anyone approachin' those two walls'll get theirselves trapped. Makes it a lot easier shootin' someone if he's stuck in a ditch with no cover. Might even put water in there so whoever don't get shot'll be drowned like a rat."

The old man's attention switched from the scene below to Delaney. The burly trader smiled to show he was joking and slapped his companion on the back. Monacatoocha returned the grin and ignored the slap, not quite understanding what was supposed to be funny. Then he went back to the more obvious charms of the telescope.

"No need to worry, Chief. It'll be a tough nut to crack, that fort, but if Colonel Fry gets here real quick, it won't be so bad. Might even be worth thinkin' about a sea side assault against them two flimsier walls," Delaney prattled on, having only a vague idea of what he was talking about but keenly aware of his *de facto* status as advocate of the British cause.

Monacatoocha gave a sudden start, straightened, and peered with heightened intensity at the action below.

"What is it, Chief?" Delaney asked, curious.

Monacatoocha transferred the telescope to the Irishman.

"Soldiers," he said.

Delaney looked again and saw forty or fifty marines in French wilderness garb assembling by the upstream dock. There were two officers: one short, young, and in the same attire as the soldiers, the other tall, middle-aged, and wearing a *Compagnies franches* captain's uniform.

"They look like they're goin' somewhere, Chief. Did you pick out the officers?"

"Yes, they are the ones telling the others what to do," Monacatoocha said stiffly, mildly insulted that Delaney had so little regard for his ability to assess the enemy. "The short one will go with the soldiers. The tall one is Contrecoeur. He will stay."

The Irishman had forgotten that the Oneida chieftain had met Contrecoeur, but was nevertheless impressed by the identification.

"Good eye, Chief," he winked. "You say the tall one with the uniform is Contrecoeur? Wouldn't be any sense him goin' out, now would there?"

Delaney resumed his survey of the small triangle of land he had come to think of as the 'point.' Most of the marines were either milling around or standing at ease but some sort of dispute had arisen among the Indians. A tall, bare-chested one with a long scalplock and black paint on his face was making a fuss. He seemed to be angry about something and was vigorously making his complaints known to an elderly sachem. The two French officers soon spied the commotion and came to the aid of the elderly man. Delaney found himself giggling.

"Chief, look at the big one stompin' his feet an' jumpin' up an' down...by the officers," he said. "What do you make of that?"

Monacatoocha looked.

"I saw him and the old one at Venango. They are Shawnee," he said almost sadly.

"Well, you should know your Shawnee," Delaney said as he placed the telescope in its case and headed away from the promontory toward camp. "Right now, we need to get to Colonel Washington an' tell him there's a company of frog-eaters comin' to greet him."

"Will you tell him he must attack before the French fort is finished?" Monacatoocha asked pointedly.

"Chief, I can't *tell* him to do anything. All we can do is tell him what we seen," Delaney explained patiently.

The Oneida chieftain's face could not have expressed greater concern if his anxiety had been transformed into pigment and painted symbolically on his face. He grasped Delaney's shoulder and brought the trader to a halt.

"I do not want to attack that fort," he insisted, poking his free arm in the direction of the 'point.' "Too many of us will die."

"I don't want to attack it either, Chief," Delaney sighed, shrugging fatalistically. "Believe me, there are things I'd rather do."

* * *

Striking Eagle was livid with rage and would not submit to the pleas from Eye-That-Winks that he settle down and behave reasonably. So he paced, and fretted, and snorted, and scowled for all to see, including the cluster of French marines being assembled to meet the enemy, if 'enemy' was the right word for a peacetime confrontation. It would be an exaggeration to say that all eyes were on him. Only about half were, including those of Eye-That-Winks, whose frustration showed in his folded arms, pursed lips, and rapidly fluttering eyelid. Had Eye-That-Winks been a white man he might not have put up with the tantrum, but as a Shawnee he was bound by Shawnee custom to tolerate spirited behavior in young men, even though he considered this a little beyond the accepted norms.

"I have been digging and shoveling ten days for these *stupid* Frenchmen," Striking Eagle huffed at the senior Shawnee. "I have set their poles in the ground. I have lifted their rocks. I have carried their water…to them I am a horse…that's how they think of me…a horse, to be whipped and prodded, nothing more…"

"They have not whipped and prodded you, Striking Eagle," moaned Eye-That-Winks as the peevish youth circled behind him on one of his frantic forays around the older man.

Being foisted on his own hyperbole only infuriated Striking Eagle more.

"But I have worked hard for these Frenchmen," he shouted, gesticulating wildly with his hands and arms. "They should let me go with them to kill the Englishmen. They told us we could fight the English if we joined them. They did not say they would make slaves of us!"

Eye-That-Winks considered pointing out to his youthful colleague that Striking Eagle could leave anytime he wanted to and was not, therefore, a slave. But he feared that the rash youngster would do just that—leave—and decided against it. While he was considering another, less provocative approach to take with the young giant, he spied Captain Contrecoeur and the shorter-by-a-head commander of the assembled military force walking toward him. He had not met the smaller man but could see by the glow on his plump cheeks that he, too, was relatively young.

"What's the matter, Eye-That-Winks?" Contrecoeur asked.

Eye-That-Winks steeled himself for a lengthy explanation, sighed, and said, "He wants to…"

"Oh, excuse me, Eye-That-Winks, this is Ensign Coulon de Jumonville, one of our best officers. Ensign, this is my friend Eye-That-Winks. He and his Shawnee brethren have joined forces with us."

The two men shook hands and exchanged pleasantries. With his diminutive stature, a compressed grin supported off apple-rosy cheeks, and the hood of his uniform framing his face, Jumonville's appearance was distinctly elfin. By contrast, the impression projected by the other young man present, Striking Eagle, was that of a bear whose honey tree has been chopped down: a murderous, undirected rage against all potentially guilty parties. With the approach of Contrecoeur and Jumonville, Striking Eagle had drifted away and was now standing on the dock with a pervasive sulk possessing his body and soul. *At least he has the good sense to let me deal with the French*, Eye-That-Winks thought to himself.

"Striking Eagle thinks he should be allowed to go with the Ensign," Eye-That-Winks explained. "He wants to fight Englishmen."

Contrecoeur glanced from Eye-That-Winks to Striking Eagle and back again, perplexed.

"But didn't you tell him this is not a military mission but a diplomatic one? Ensign Jumonville will be delivering a message to the British warning them to remove themselves from these lands, nothing more."

Eye-That-Winks knew the mission's purpose and was privately mystified by the French and British practice of sending the youngest and least experienced among them on critical diplomatic errands. But he would not mention his misgivings. It was not his business to tell the French theirs.

"I told him, but he still wants to go. He thinks there will be fighting. He has convinced himself that the British are devils and will attack."

The Shawnee sachem tried to make his exposition a simple statement of fact but his true opinion of Striking Eagle's behavior must have shown through, because a nascent smile began to form on Contrecoeur's lips.

"Let me talk to him, Eye-That-Winks," the Frenchman said. "Call him over."

Eye-That-Winks waved for Striking Eagle to join them, which he ultimately did after demonstrating his displeasure with a series of hostile glares and defiant body language. With his scalplock wrapped in a spiral around his neck and the narrow black isthmus of his nose bridging the twin islands of black pigment covering his lower face and forehead, Striking Eagle could, with the right attitude, have looked fierce. Instead, he came across as merely petulant.

After the young man's reluctant arrival, Contrecoeur paused for a couple of beats before speaking, then said, "Eye-That-Winks tells me you want to fight Englishmen, Striking Eagle. That is good. We can use a man with your enthusiasm, but this is not the right time. Ensign Jumonville's mission is a peaceful one. There will be no fighting."

After Eye-That-Winks had translated for him, Striking Eagle glanced sideways at the marines.

"They have guns," he said.

"They must have guns," the French Captain said. "...as a precaution. They must be able to protect themselves if the need arises. You would not wish them to be eaten by a pack of wolves, would you?"

Striking Eagle conceded the point with a diffident shake of the head. Eye-That-Winks began to see Contrecoeur in a new light. For a military commander, the man had a surprising store of patience.

With a casual glance at Jumonville and Eye-That-Winks, Contrecoeur moved to Striking Eagle and placed his hands on the Shawnee's ample shoulders.

"Striking Eagle, you will get your chance to fight Englishmen. That is, if any of us do. But right now what we need more than your bravery is your strong back. Fort Duquesne must be completed if we are to keep the British out, and only men like you can accomplish such a monumental task..."

Eye-That-Winks and Jumonville caught themselves trying to gauge each other's reaction to Contrecoeur's finely embroidered flattery of the tall youngster.

"Why does he hate the British so?" Jumonville whispered.

The taciturn old sachem wondered if it was worth trying to explain the Shawnee temperament to a Frenchman, then said simply, "He is too young to hate. He is only practicing his hatred so it will be there when he needs it."

As Eye-That-Winks had anticipated, the answer only confused Ensign Jumonville, whose lips parted as if to reply but failed to produce even a grunt. The Ensign then excused himself, saluted his commander once more, and left to muster his charges.

Contrecoeur's lofty superlatives were working on Striking Eagle. No longer was he an enraged bear. He was one step down: a frustrated adolescent. Unaccustomed to speaking with strangers, let alone French captains, he unfolded his arms and let them hang by his sides as he stammered, attempting to verbalize a request.

"I…I do not want to dig anymore," he blurted meekly. "I would like to lay the logs."

Contrecoeur was overjoyed. A compromise had been reached. But Striking Eagle, pressing what he perceived to be his advantage, was not finished.

"But I would like to shoot," the young giant added, stuttering, "To practice in the evenings…"

"Shoot at what?" the French Captain asked, glancing at an equally dismayed Eye-That-Winks for guidance.

Striking Eagle pointed to a clan of squirrels who had taken up residence in the bush twenty or thirty meters downstream of the dock and who were, as was their habit, presently enjoying a community swim in the Allegheny River.

"At them," Striking Eagle answered.

The Captain turned his head, saw the squirrels, and could not imagine anyone wanting to shoot them, even for food. The swimming squirrels, as they had come to be known, were a new phenomenon to the marines and officer corps. The creatures' resolute indolence and love of recreation were a source of amusement and envy to the toiling soldiers. They had almost achieved the status of mascots. He was at a loss for mollifying words.

"I have not shot very much," Striking Eagle explained shyly. "I need to shoot at moving targets…so I can learn to shoot at Englishmen better."

Contrecoeur nodded, relieved. At least the request had a certain logic to it. He was afraid he would be faced with one of the occasional chasms between the white and Indian cultures that no amount of talk, logic, or good will could bridge.

"Striking Eagle, I have a better idea," he said, smiling up at the would-be squirrel assassin. "We have many empty wine jugs that would make fine targets. Why don't you toss them in the river and shoot them as they float by?"

The Frenchman sneaked a glance at Eye-That-Winks. Although the old man's fissured face divulged no discernible opinion, Contrecoeur sensed that he approved.

Striking Eagle thought about the offer and cast a glance of his own at Eye-That-Winks, who nodded once.

"Yes, that would be good," the tall Shawnee replied.

"You'll help us build the fort, then?" Contrecoeur asked, hoping to nail things down.

"Yes, but when you go to fight Englishmen, I go?" Striking Eagle said. It was at once a statement and a question.

He wants to nail this down too, the French Captain thought. Hesitantly, he averted his eyes and said, "Yes, you'll get your chance to kill Englishmen."

With the fires of his smoldering anger quenched by Contrecoeur's disarming civility, Striking Eagle now showed signs of embarrassment. He loped clumsily toward the brush where he'd thrown the pickax, retrieved it, and laid it on the ground in front of Contrecoeur. His face—in spite of the bear grease and charcoal smeared on it—was a portrait of humility.

"I will dig," he said forcefully. "And I will lay logs. But I will fight Englishmen."

Contrecoeur was about to repeat the conditions attached to his promise when Striking Eagle hastily added, "Yes, yes, I know...only if *you* fight the Englishmen..."

The bargain was punctuated by the diminutive but energetic Jumonville who, having formed his troops for departure, returned with another brisk salute.

"We're ready to go, sir," he announced, casting a skeptical glimpse at the freshly contrite Shawnee by his commander's side.

"Very good, Ensign," Contrecoeur said, saluting.

"Will the...gentleman be coming with us, sir?"

"No, Striking Eagle has decided to stay."

Though he tried to suppress outward signs of relief, a pall seemed to lift from Jumonville's disposition.

"Thank you, sir," he said somewhat too gleefully, then rendered another smart salute. "We'll be on our way then."

"God be with you, Ensign," Contrecoeur replied.

The French Captain, the aging sachem and the young giant watched as the marines and their tribal auxiliaries boarded the canoes and bateaux. The plan was to turn the bend at the 'point' and travel up the Monongahela as far as possible, disembark, and seek out the commander of the British forces to whom the ultimatum Contrecoeur had written would be delivered. *It will be a while before they return,* Contrecoeur reflected. Something would happen; he was sure of it. One did not threaten the British Empire without expecting consequences.

"Striking Eagle, I think you will soon get your chance to fight the British. Perhaps very soon," he said almost dreamily as he viewed the boats rounding the 'point.' Hearing no reply from the lofty Shawnee, the Captain glanced in his direction. Striking Eagle was standing, arms folded, as transfixed by the scene as were Contrecoeur and Eye-That-Winks. He appeared quite calm. Though his small mouth was ill-equipped for emotional display, there was not the slightest doubt that he was happy.

Chapter Three

May 25, 1754, Great Meadows

Someone was shouting in Washington's ear to wake up. Wake up? Oh, yes, he was asleep and dearly yearned to stay that way. The three weeks of marching and hacking through the *damned* rain-drenched forest, climbing and unclimbing each of the three *damned* giant mountains—Savage, Negro, and Laurel, and fording the *damned* floodwaters of the Casselman and Youghiogheny Rivers, had exhausted everyone. Had God forgotten how to draw a straight line when he created this part of the world? How he wished he could curse out loud for the world to hear instead of bouncing the expletives off his skull case. God, how his muscles, the entire inventory, ached! Sleep was ecstasy. But he had to wake up. It was expected of commanding officers that their consciousness be accessible at all times. Who had told him that? Lord Fairfax?

Washington rolled over, looked up to see Hogg's young aide, Bibby Brooke, holding a lantern over his head. With him was another man he did not recognize.

"What is it, Bibby?" he asked, squinting his eyes against the lamp's brightness.

"Sir, this is Pete Delaney from Mr. Gist's place," Brooke said, and might have said more, except that Delaney interrupted.

"Colonel, Mr. Gist and Monacatoocha are a mile west of here…"

"Wait, wait, wait…" Washington stammered, thinking a residual dream might be contaminating his awareness. "Say that again."

"Gist and Monacatoocha are a mile out…"

"Monacatoocha is with Christopher?"

A frustrated Delaney fought impatience and tried one more time.

"Colonel, if you'll just let me talk. Mr. Gist and Monacatoocha are watching a company of French soldiers and Indians five miles west of here. They're coming this way."

That got Washington's attention. He jumped from his cot and immediately began pulling his breeches on.

"Why didn't you say so in the first place, man?" the Colonel fumed, his mind still not completely engaged. "Bibby, get everyone out of bed and brief them on the situation. Reveille in five minutes. Mr. Delaney, how many of them are there?"

"About fifty, sir."

Washington released the tension in the boot he'd been pulling onto his right leg and peered skeptically at the Irishman.

"Fifty?" he asked.

"Yes, Colonel, fifty...including Indians."

"That's not very many."

"I guess not, sir," Delaney replied, appreciating Washington's quandary. "But they're armed and they *are* coming this way."

"Do they have cannon?"

"No, I don't think so, but Mr. Gist says we should be ready."

Washington finished pulling on his boots and stood, still perplexed by the small size of the French force.

"Of course we'll be ready, Mr. Delaney," he said, then gestured for Bibby Brooke to leave, adding, "Why don't you get some coffee at the mess tent and get back to Christopher? Tell him I'll be out soon."

After Delaney had departed as well, Washington heard the bugle blow followed by a collective groan from men who had expected a longer night's sleep. He took his time putting his clothes on—fifty invading Frenchmen simply did not inspire a sense of urgency. Half-dressed, he decided to go outside for some fresh air, parted the tent flaps, and stepped out to gaze upon the vast clearing called Great Meadows where they had set up camp two days before. It was early, perhaps 6:00 AM, but already the heat and humidity were weighing heavily on him, making the thought of a pitched battle with the French repugnant. It was a pretty place, Great Meadows, lush green, with only sparsely scattered bushes and trees—a pasture, a respite, an oasis in the endless forest fifty miles northwest of Wills Creek. The morning birds were zestfully celebrating the day, chirping and squawking at the tree line a hundred yards to the south. Some of the men were already out of their tents stretching, cursing the daylight and the bugler who insisted they immerse themselves in it.

He let the words he had written to Robert Dinwiddie float on his thoughts: "A charming field for an encounter," he had said about Great Meadows. He should have let it go at "A charming field," or "A charming field for maneuvers," or for a camp-out, or a hunting trip, or a picnic, or simply to lie flat-backed upon and drink oneself into a stupor. Perhaps Dinwiddie would have called them back by now if his puerile Lieutenant-Colonel hadn't waxed so enthusiastic. What did Dinwiddie expect him to do? Rather than address the question, Washington's half-asleep mind offered up the insightful perception that the Virginia Governor was yet another of the multitude of Scotsmen he had to deal with. It was a British conspiracy, his brain joked. First the British crush the Scots, then they send the detritus of Scottish malcontents across the Atlantic to preside over the colonial malcontents in a war against the recalcitrant frog-eaters! It was perfect: no British casualties and only a few pounds depleted from His Majesty's treasury to buy weapons for the assorted reprobates to play with.

Good Lord, my head does spin in the morning, Washington chuckled to himself. He needed coffee. And he knew the answer to the question his mind had posed before turning to breakfast mush: *Dinwiddie expects me to make the decision whether to attack or withdraw, because he has no idea what to do.* Taking a cue from the growing number of slow risers in his field of view, Washington yawned, stretched, and went back into the tent to finish dressing. Its foolishness had dissipated, but his brain would not relax. Why would Contrecoeur send out an attack force of fifty men when he had more than six hundred at his disposal? Surely he knew that Washington's force—small as it was—exceeded a hundred. It didn't make sense.

Suddenly, he heard the tent flaps rustle and saw an unshaven Christopher Gist enter. The summer sun had burned the guide's skin to a coffee-brown that was almost as dark as the few brown hairs on his head that lived as aliens among the gray. Wearing little more than a cotton shirt, breeches, and a pair of moccasins he'd gotten from the Miami Indians during his travels, Gist was as cool as it was possible to be and still be modestly clothed.

"George, better finish dressing. You wouldn't want the frog-eaters to catch you naked," he said.

Washington finished pulling on his buckskin breeches and sat down on the cot to put his boots on. Gist, it seemed, was always telling him to get ready to do something. If the man weren't old enough to be his father, the habit might be irritating.

"Delaney said there were fifty of them. Is that true?" the Colonel inquired.

Gist was his usual self, taciturn and quizzical at the same time.

"Yes, it's true."

"We should be able to handle that many, don't you think?"

"Sure, sure," Gist nodded, pacing with his thumbs locked over his beaded belt. "Our old friend La Force is with them. Remember him?"

Washington finished lacing his second boot, then rose and said, "Yes, Ensign La Force. The one who took us to Fort Le Boeuf to see Saint Pierre. Is he in charge?"

Gist shrugged as he and the Colonel went back outside.

"I don't know. Could be. They tried to kill my cow, for God's sake! Would have, too, if my Indians hadn't stopped them," Gist declared.

"Ha! So that's why you're here? You want me to send out a company or two to save your cow, like we did two weeks ago," Washington hooted, referring to a detachment he had dispatched earlier to investigate reports of suspicious French activity at Gist's plantation. Then he looked around the encampment. "Didn't you come with Monacatoocha? I don't see him."

"He went back to my place with some of his Mingoes," the guide replied, smiling. "I think he's hoping the French come back. Some of those frog-eaters have pretty fancy hair."

Washington grinned knowingly, tucking the light linen shirt into his pants as he made a mental estimate of the distance to Gist's plantation, which was about a third of the way between Great Meadows and Redstone Creek.

"Tell you what, Christopher. I'll send Captain Hogg and Captain Mercer over to your place with some men. It's about ten miles, isn't it?"

Gist rubbed the three-day stubble on his chin and said, "About that."

"Let's get something to eat. Then we'll decide who else goes," Washington offered. "Do you want to go with them?"

The ancient frontiersmen leered through the stubble and said, "You're getting old, George. I'm going back to Winchester, remember? You gave me a letter for the Governor."

"Oh, yes, yes," Washington replied, recalling his letter complaining of the bleak supply situation and the low pay allotted to the volunteers by the colony of Virginia. He had added the latter complaint after weeks of listening to his men grumble about the working conditions. It would irritate Dinwiddie, but someone back home had to become irritated and the Governor was the most conspicuous target.

The two men hastily proceeded to the mess tent, which, for culinary purposes, was located at the merger of the two small streams, Great Meadows Run and Indian Run. To the northwest, the Colonel spied dark clouds forming and hoped it was neither an omen of things to come or, more immediately, of the weather for the next few days. As he walked, Washington scrolled the events of the last week through his mind, trying to impose order on them. A cavalcade of settlers, traders, and friendly Indians had passed through with a multitude of stories about the French presence at the Forks. There was at once too much information and not enough that was reliable.

"Christopher, what do you think I should do?" Washington asked, thoughtful.

The older man slowed, sensing a need in his friend to discuss his predicament.

"About what, George?"

Washington drew a breath to fuel his exposition. Gist knew as well as he did what their difficulties were, but would require a verbal reiteration of them anyway. It was his nature.

"About the reports we've been getting about the French from all those people who seem hell bent on getting out! Every Tom, Dick, and...Nootimus has his own story. The French are increasing their forces. The French have only three hundred soldiers. The French are on the march. The French have captured Redstone. No, the French haven't captured Redstone! The French are here. The French are there. The French are everywhere! How am I supposed to make sense of it all?"

With less than his usual reticence, Gist responded, "They *are* at my place. That much I know."

"I know that, Christopher, but are they a real threat? You said yourself that your Indians stopped them. What do I make of that? And what do I do with the report I got from Joshua Fry twelve days ago that he's on the way from Winchester with a hundred men? When will he arrive? Are a hundred men enough? I just don't know."

Gist fidgeted with his hair, stared at the tree line fifty yards distant, as if trying to find the enemy he knew to be there.

"You can always go back," he said without conviction. It was a necessary part of the catharsis, the absolution, which Washington was searching for.

"No, I can't," Washington barked petulantly, as if Gist were suggesting treason. "Dinwiddie won't tolerate defeat *or* retreat. You know that. That's why *he's* not here."

Gist, still scanning the tree line, came to a complete halt.

"Dinwiddie is a politician, George," he replied, indulging the beast on his friend's shoulders. "He has to survive. But he's the best of the lot. Can you imagine where we would be without him?"

It was a valid point. No other colonial official, elected or Crown-appointed, had shown as much passion for taking on the French as Dinwiddie had. Half were content to cower in silence behind the Allegheny Mountains. The other half was not willing to be silent in their cowardice and accused the Virginia Governor of using colonial troops for his own purposes. That charge had some truth in it, but the whole truth was much more complex. Only Dinwiddie and a precious few others in the high places of colonial administration recognized that the British colonies could not survive if the French and their Indian allies were successful in seizing an Appalachian frontier stretching from Georgia in the southwest to New Hampshire in the northeast. Gist was right. With all his effrontery, his pretensions of military expertise, his singular naïveté in assuming troops and their military paraphernalia could be moved as easily through the American wilderness as across the theaters of Europe, Dinwiddie *was* the best of the lot. A good man.

"Nowhere," Washington admitted. "Or maybe in Winchester building stockade walls."

They reached the mess tent, which was little more than a large canvas cover supported by saplings and rope. Comforting sounds of men, food and eating utensils in raucous engagement filled the air with a peculiarly martial quality, as if the volunteers sensed something was afoot and were filling their bellies with food and their spirits with aggression to prepare for it. Gist headed for a table where cooks were busily laying out eggs and biscuits in regular formations, quickly sending in reserves as the hungry soldiers depleted the front lines.

"As for your question, George. About what you should do," Gist hurriedly added before rushing headlong to attack the food. "I have no idea what La Force is doing out here. Maybe Hogg can tell us when he catches the frog-eaters who raided my place. Then maybe we'll have a better idea of what to do."

Although he was as hungry as his companion, Washington got only a cup of coffee for himself. He walked toward Great Meadows Run and gazed up at the darkening clouds. It would rain sometime during this day, the twenty-fifth of May. What was he to do, he asked himself for the thousandth time? He did not have the answer nor, as he had just discovered, did the most experienced and trusted of his advisors.

Lacking the tactical sense of an experienced officer, Washington decided to proceed incrementally and wait for clarity eventually to introduce itself. They would continue on to Redstone, but not today. Today he would deal with La Force and his fifty French marines. That was the most logical thing to do and the least risky. He could not possibly be criticized for taking steps to insure the integrity of his fighting force. Could he?

Chapter Four

May 26, 1754, The Clarion River

Gabriel Menard, known to his Chippewa companions as Bushy Bear because of his shaggy exterior, did not like being so close to the British-loving Iroquois, thirty miles east of Venango, looking down at the bearded man wading in the shallow waters of the Clarion River. Though he had no official connection to the Canadian government, military or otherwise, Menard was a loyal citizen of New France and a trader. As such he was frequently encouraged by his government to harass his British counterparts wherever they might be, an avocation he hoped to expand with the unwitting assistance of the madman in the river below. It had been Stump Neck's plan to pass himself off as a hapless trader whose bateau had sunk in the rapids, spilling and strewing supplies—actually containers, boxes and useless paraphernalia—everywhere. The idea was to attract British passers-by—typically traders and settlers—and attack them, kill and scalp most, but let a few escape to spread the word to the British colonies of wanton rape and murder in the Ohio Valley.

Except that this was not exactly the Ohio Valley. That too, for reasons the madman did not bother to explain, had been Stump Neck's notion.

"Where would they be now?" Menard asked his Chippewa companion with the infelicitous name of Rain Worm.

From his semi-crouched stance on the small hill overlooking the south shore of the river, Rain Worm brushed the clumps of knotted hair and mangy turkey feathers away from his bronzed face and pointed upstream to where the river took a sharp turn to the right and vanished into the lush, green foliage. Green was the default color in this mélange of lusty flora; only flowers and a few jigsaw pieces of sky above the tree tops defied the convention. Even the river was an opaque, moss green that refracted the few rays of golden sunlight reaching it into a jaded iridescence.

"There. They should be coming out there soon," he said.

Rain Worm was, of course, basing his judgment on the report of a scouting party that had spotted three keel boats loaded with trading goods a kilometer upstream. On hearing of prey, Stump Neck had put his plan into action, scattering his warriors in the brush on both sides of the river and reverting back to a bearded version of his former white self, Pariah West. The scouts had reported only men on the keel boats. For that, Menard was grateful.

The French trader laid his rifle on the ground to wipe the eye-stinging sweat from his brow and nose. He should have shaved his beard off. It was too hot for facial hair. Only a madman like Stump Neck, whose fevered brain was too busy to recognize sensation, would let whiskers grow in midsummer. While the riverbanks were amply occupied by tall trees, the shade they provided was neutralized by the moisture captured in the dead air around them. It must be like the swamps in Louisiana he had heard about, hot and steamy, but populated by small, harmless fauna instead of brutish alligators.

As if reading his thoughts, Stump Neck shouted, "Gabriel! Gabriel! Catch it. Catch the frog!"

Menard glanced up to see the grinning, bare-chested Pariah West consummating a throw. A small, wriggling object had been lofted on a trajectory toward him. Bushy Bear reached out and caught the thing, felt its amphibian legs kicking frantically in his grasp.

"It's a frog!" called West.

Menard felt warm wetness spread over his gripping palm and quickly released the creature that had just urinated on him. The toad dropped to the ground and scampered away.

"It's a toad!" Menard retorted irritably, for lack of anything cleverer to say. He hastily wiped his hand on some nearby grass.

"Toad, frog, what's the difference? They fly the same," West yelled, cackling an encore as he launched another toad in a high arc toward one of the braves hidden in the underbrush. As the toad fell earthward a hand shot upward and batted it into the river, providing the bellowing maniac with another source of amusement. Still shrieking with demented mirth, West reached down for another toad and flung it into the air. *The crazy bastard must have stumbled onto a whole community of them*, thought Bushy Bear.

The shrill caw of a crow suddenly pierced the air and echoed from the tall tree trunks. Then another, then a third as the agreed upon signal that the keel boats were approaching was relayed from one brave to another. The frolicking Pariah West immediately ceased toad lofting and looked upstream, as did Bushy Bear and Rain Worm. But there was as yet nothing to be seen.

"Gabriel, Rain Worm, are you there? Are you ready?" the decoy cried.

Rain Worm cupped his hands around his mouth and crowed the signal. In like manner, Pariah West quizzed each of the other braves and received the same response. Satisfied, the bait leaned against a boulder and fixed his gaze upstream. Compared to the blaring cacophony of the moment before, the stillness was deafening—only bird chatter, rustling leaves and rippling water disturbed the silence. In the river, West moved to the crippled bateau, which had been strategically placed at the tip of a broad peninsula jutting far enough into the river to diminish the stream's width by half. The stern of the bateau had been filled with water and weighed down with rocks to simulate sinking. West moved toward the blunt bow, sat down on the rocky shore, then took a sharp piece of sandstone and pulled its pointed tip slowly across his chest. Bushy Bear and Rain Worm watched dumbfounded as the shaman's face grimaced with pain and blood oozed out of the centimeter deep gash. Finished, West heaved a ponderous sigh and tossed the stone aside. Then he dipped a finger into the blood, licked it, and raised the scarlet finger into the air for all to see, as if offering them a taste, grinning with grotesque glee as he did so. With the rapture of the moment past, he got down to business, plunging his hands into the river, then using them to spread the blood across his chest and face, and through his hair. Finished, he took up station behind the bow of the bateau and waited for the first keel boat to appear.

It was not a long wait. From their superior vantage point Bushy Bear and Rain Worm were the first to see a blunt prow emerge from around the bend in the river. Then West saw it and lay prone across the bow of the beached bateau. With tedious slowness the keelboat plowed through the water. A man with a pole came into view on the boat's deck, then the rough-hewn log cabin, then another man plunging a pole to the river bottom and heaving his weight onto it. Finally, the second and third keelboats appeared, flanking the first, propelled by their own engines of pole-pushers. At first, because of the distance, all was silent. Then, as the boats closed the distance, Gabriel Menard began to pick up smatterings of conversation. This, and the absence on the decks of any but the men pushing and prodding the boats forward, said that most members of the crews were in their cabins eating, drinking or relaxing.

When the boats were within a hundred meters of Bushy Bear and Rain Worm, one of the polers on the right flank boat, a brawny, orange-haired man, began shouting and pointing at the forest on his starboard side. This was enough to stir the crews from their cabins. Each inquisitive member emerged with his musket and joined his fellows to gawk at the thing. Menard could not see what it was and feared the worst: that the trap had been detected. Then a lightly-bearded man on the lead boat who was wearing nothing but a decrepit pair of breeches spotted Pariah West draped over the sunken bateau and, for a while, diverted attention away from the original distraction. But West's plight could not compete with the fascination inspired by the other thing, whatever it was. Without warning, the boatmen raised their muskets and began firing, which startled Bushy Bear and Rain Worm and even made the decoy's eyes pop open. But after one volley, no more shots were fired. Pariah West calmly closed his eyes and resumed his act.

Things quickly became agitated on the three boats. Men were slapping each other on the back, gesturing with every available limb, chattering incessantly. Gabriel Menard's English was not good enough to follow the dialogue, but it was obvious they had killed something and were pleased with themselves for having done so. The lightly-bearded man then raised his hands and redirected the attention of the crowd to the figure on the sunken bateau.

"Be ready, Rain Worm," Bushy Bear exhorted. "It's almost time."

Rain Worm showed his resolve by raising his musket.

Below, the men were converging on the starboard sides of the boats and preparing to disembark. None had reloaded his musket. Some had even laid the weapons aside, which finally convinced Menard that the trap had not been discovered. The polers scurried back and forth along the port decks maneuvering their cumbersome crafts into position for docking. Several of the men jumped into the quick-moving but shallow water to help push the boats ashore. The lead boat inserted itself into the narrow crotch between West's bateau and the peninsula, at which point the lightly-bearded man tied its prow to the crippled bateau. The two other boats executed similar maneuvers upstream of the lead boat and anchored themselves in place. Even before the boats had been secured, men heaved themselves overboard, some onto the rocky shore, some into the cool, fresh water. All but two rushed toward the spot at which their muskets had fired three minutes earlier, laughing and strutting with the pride of wondrous accomplishment. The remaining two were the light-bearded man with the decrepit breeches and his orange-haired companion, who headed for the prone figure of Pariah West instead.

What followed was a total melee. It was not clear where the first shot came from but Menard was certain one of the Chippewa braves hidden in the brush was responsible. With their muskets empty or unavailable, the crews of the three boats had no chance. The Chippewa guns roared in a thunderous, but brief, fusillade. Those crewmen in the front ranks who had made it onto the shore simply dropped. Their bodies fell beneath the dense thickets of the forest and vanished from sight. Some men at the rear were killed instantly; more were wounded or remained temporarily untouched by the salvo. Menard saw one man on shore scream and grab his jaw, which had been blown away by a musket ball. He and perhaps half of those who had not been killed attempted to scramble back on board the keel boats. The other half scampered into the woods or ran along the shore, terror chiseled into their faces like epitaphs. But it was no use. The Chippewas outnumbered the boatmen two to one and, although some of their guns needed reloading, had all the necessary weaponry. Whooping and shrieking, the Chippewa braves drew their European-made, steel scalping knives and tomahawks and chased their victims down, stabbing and hacking mercilessly, then stripping away the precious trophies of flesh and hair with a slice and a yank, often before the dead-men-to-be had stopped screaming.

As soon as the barrage began, Pariah West was on his feet, tomahawk in hand. Light-Beard and Orange-Hair stopped in their tracks, not sure what was happening. The first to react was Light-Beard, who, seeing West poised on the bow of the bateau with a tomahawk raised menacingly over his head, withdrew a gutting knife from his belt and braced for an onslaught by the bizarre-looking white man. Seeing this, Bushy Bear leveled his rifle, aimed, and fired at Light-Beard, the main threat to Pariah West's well being. Menard saw the red starburst of blood erupt from the man's left shoulder as the bullet entered, effectively removing the threat to his protégé. Light-Beard jerked, dropped his knife and fell to the ground in a loose, awkward heap.

That he was about to be attacked finally dawned on Orange-Hair. As he saw Light-Beard go down, he too reached for the knife in his belt but was too late. Pariah West was on him with a tomahawk blow to the neck, bellowing a credible imitation of an Indian war whoop. The young lunatic was fast becoming a true savage if he wasn't one already. As if to answer that unspoken question, Pariah West grabbed a handful of the dying man's hair and pushed his face into the dirt with a boot to the neck. Making a quick slice across the forehead, he ripped the flamboyant locks from the skull of Orange-Hair. Hooting with infernal delight, the madman held the resplendent trophy high in the air for all to see, angling it so the blood trickling down his arm was easily visible. The demonic smile on the unfinished sculpture of his face told all. Pariah West was exactly where he wanted to be, doing exactly what he wanted to do. He was a man fulfilling his destiny and had a dazzling prize to prove it.

Anticipating a celebration, Rain Worm, whose fire had been directed at the larger party of boatmen, suddenly rose to his feet and ran toward the river, yelping with glee as he went. Bushy Bear followed, fording the stream more cautiously than the raucous Chippewa, who was nearly washed downstream by the brisk current when he tripped and fell but successfully snagged a rock and pulled himself up on the opposite shore. Carefully selecting his route, Bushy Bear made it across well after Rain Worm and Stump Neck had rejoined their colleagues in the brush. The fight—if it could be called that—was over. There was no more screaming. All the boatmen were dead or unconscious.

Save one, Menard discovered—Light-Beard. As he passed the mutilated body of Orange-Hair, Bushy Bear heard a groan. At first thinking it to be Orange-Hair, he turned the body over and saw that the man could not possibly be alive. His eyes stared with vacant unconcern, his head was cocked unnaturally away from the gash in his neck, and the red blood of his ravaged scalp was already congealing.

There was another groan and movement from the other, the one he had shot: Light-Beard. Incredulous, Menard stared at him, knelt down so the wounded man would see him, then simply watched and waited, not knowing what to say or do. Light-Beard's wound was not severe but it was bloody. The bullet had entered under the left armpit, although the large amount of blood made it difficult to pinpoint the exact location. In physical appearance, the man was unexceptional. His raven coal black beard was not a true beard at all, but the consequence of going unshaven for several days. There was less hair on his head, none on his pate, which shone like lacquered maple. After groaning one more time and grimacing with pain, Light-Beard's smoke gray eyes opened.

"How are you M'sieur?" Menard asked like a simpleton.

The man's eyes flickered and then shot toward the source of the ceaseless chatter emanating from the woods.

"Are they still here?" he asked, terrified.

"Yes," Menard answered with genuine remorse. "And so, unfortunately for you, am I. I too am your enemy."

Suddenly realizing the hopelessness of his plight, the man's expression darkened as he asked, "Are you going to kill me?"

"It would be better if you were dead," Bushy Bear said flatly, unwilling to answer the direct question. "Now you will die as slowly as their whimsy prefers."

Light-Beard nodded his head fatalistically and said, "In that case, I'd rather die now. Would you do the honors?"

"M'sieur, I cannot. They would kill *me* if I did…"

"Then let me do it. Where's my knife? It must be nearby…" he said, frantically searching for the weapon.

"M'sieur, it is pointless…"

"My God, man, what kind of a fiend are you? Let me die…please!"

Light-beard raised himself up on one arm—the good one—and reached out to Menard with the other. At first, thinking it to be a threatening gesture, Bushy Bear withdrew but then realized the condemned man was pleading for his life, or for his death. It didn't really matter as long as he could be spared the horrible transition between the two that the savages were so skilled at prolonging and embellishing with pain.

Focused as he was on the tribulations of Light-Beard, Menard did not see or hear the approach of Stump Neck and others of the band until they were nearly upon him. Stump Neck arrived first, stopping near the prone man's head. The conversation between Gabriel Menard and Light-Beard came to a halt. Bushy Bear looked up to see his deranged partner holding a huge set of moose antlers against his square head. Oddly, the antlers did not look out of place, probably because Stump Neck's face did not look human, but more closely resembled that of an animal in a fit of rage. Yet, he was not enraged, but exultant. And he was indeed Stump Neck. All but the physical form of Pariah West had vanished. He had even donned his 'shaman's beads,' a necklace of animal and bird bones, fangs, claws and beaks that he'd made himself.

"How do I look, Gabriel?" the playful sociopath asked.

Seeing the puzzled expression on Bushy Bear's face, the shaman explained, "They killed a moose. That's what they were shooting at."

"And her calf," said a shadowy Frenchman with a Mediterranean complexion and oily hair called 'L'Englise', one of the half dozen *coureurs de bois* who had joined what Menard had begun to think of as 'Stump Neck's Renegades.' The followers of the shaman were not exclusively Chippewa, although the majority of the Indians had been recruited from Bright Dawn's tribe, typically from the ranks of the young, the headstrong, and the restless. As inclined toward barbarity as the Indians, the *coureurs de bois* had another, more worldly, reason for joining: the elimination of the British would leave them in control of the Indian trade.

"They should not have killed the animals," said the somber-faced L'Englise in a guttural voice seeping with sanctimony. "We do not see many moose this far south. It is a *sin* to kill them!"

Menard looked at L'Englise and then at the gory, matted human scalp in his hand and marveled at the limitless power of the human mind to rationalize. Then he turned his attention to Stump Neck.

"Did any escape?" he asked.

"Two," Stump Neck said disinterestedly, then glanced down at Light-Beard. "What's your name?"

"David Casey," Light-Beard responded apprehensively.

"David Casey!" Stump Neck sneered. "An Irishman. I hate stupid Irishmen!"

Menard doubted that Stump neck had any stronger antipathy toward the Irish than any other race. He hated, and loved, any soul luckless enough to be at his mercy.

At that moment, there was a rustling of leaves and nine of the party emerged from the woods dragging the two moose by their tails and hooves, their bovine skulls bouncing lifelessly on the rocky ground. After placing the carcasses in a nearby clearing, they began gutting the beasts with knives and tomahawks and were soon joined by a second wave of Chippewa and *coureurs de bois* who had been busy scalping the dead English traders. All carried scalps of varying brown, black, blond, and gray hues. Some had bunches of the grisly things gripped in their hands like sheaves of wheat. *For the serious scalp hunter, European scalps certainly add considerable variety to a collection*, Bushy Bear reflected with grim irony. Sewn together they would make exquisite quilts.

David Casey gazed with what Gabriel Menard interpreted to be remorseful panic at the dead moose. He was probably thinking he might have escaped if they had not slowed the boats to blast away like a line of infantry at the hapless animals. He could be right, but probably not. The Englishmen would still have been outnumbered two to one and there was no refuge in the narrow, shallow river.

"Are you an Irishman, Casey?" Stump Neck asked in a tormentingly civil tone.

"I'm from Harris's Ferry," said Casey, who was starting to shiver as shock and fear took hold. "I was born in Carlisle. Only half-Irish.

41

My mother was from German stock."

"Germans are stupid too. Stupid bastards can't even speak English," Stump Neck retorted, making it quite clear that all loopholes would be plugged. He knelt down to examine the raw wound where he'd torn the hair from Orange-Hair's head and touched it gently, lovingly.

As the madman examined his kill, Gabriel Menard rose and asked, "Are we going to let this man go?"

Stump Neck shot him a disgusted look, as if he wanted to say, "'Course not, Gabriel. Where's the fun in that?" Instead, he replied tolerantly, "No, Two escaped. That's enough, ain't it?"

Menard lowered his eyes and did not answer. Stump Neck had gone well beyond the shaman training that Menard's wife, Bright Dawn, had instilled in him at her Chippewa village. To his Indian followers the madman was a fusion of shaman and sorcerer. He had taught them that by killing their enemies in ritualistic ceremonies of his design, they would inherit the spiritual powers of their victims. To the Frenchman's chagrin, the madman also seemed to be inheriting Menard's powers and becoming the dominant partner in their alliance, an eventuality that suffused the Frenchman with a chilling dread.

"What was his name?" Stump Neck asked Casey as he petted the ravaged skull of Orange-Hair.

"Angus."

"Angus what?"

"Angus, that's all I know," Casey replied in despair.

"Angus," Stump Neck repeated, trance-like. "That's a Scotch name, ain't it? I like Scotchmen. They're big an' strong an' ugly. Too bad you ain't a Scotchman, Casey."

The last was accompanied by an evil leer directed at the wounded man. Menard was not in the mood for Stump Neck's perverted, taunting, amusements. He shouldered his rifle and made ready to re-cross the river.

"Where you goin', Gabriel?" Stump Neck demanded abruptly, rising to a standing position. His hands squeezed the bare skin of his waist. A challenge radiated from his stony features.

"Back to camp," Menard replied curtly, careful not to let the distaste he felt resonate in his voice. "You don't need me here."

Stump Neck was silent, then glared at Bushy Bear and gave Casey's head a quick kick.

"You shot this man, didn't you?"

"Yes."

"Don't you think you oughtta apologize?" the madman asked, leering.

"If I hadn't shot him, you would be dead."

The leer vanished more rapidly from the madman's face than it had arrived, replaced by a cold, featureless landscape. Any other man would have been grateful, but this one seemed actually to resent having his life saved.

"Maybe," Stump Neck muttered. "Maybe not."

Menard turned to depart, but was again interrupted.

"How come you care so much about me, Gabriel?" the unctuous voice of Stump Neck demanded. "I worry about that. I really do."

Gabriel Menard paused briefly, then took the strides necessary to plunge him into the Clarion River and beyond.

Chapter Five

May 27, 1754, Near the Clarion River

Bright Dawn was trying to be kind to the dead-man-to-be by making for him a beautiful suit of clothes in which to meet his maker. She was worldly enough to recognize that David Casey's maker and her own might not be the same entity. Even if they were, a white man might want to be attired differently than an Indian at such a first meeting. What she could not comprehend was that, for a white man, there was neither a good *day* nor a good *way* to die, though some might be better than others. To Casey, being burned alive in his thirty-first year was out of the running as one of the 'better' ways to die. The prisoner's persistently dark mood and recurrent tears were of great concern to Bright Dawn.

"Why is he so unhappy?" she asked Menard in a private conversation. "He is going to his Great Spirit. Doesn't his religion tell him this should be a source of great comfort?"

Since Casey's religion was essentially the same as his own, Menard felt qualified to answer.

"He would rather die on another day of natural causes, when he is older."

Bright Dawn crowed, almost like a warrior, in disbelief.

"He would rather be left behind in a dark cave where the snakes can crawl into his ears? An old man whining and cursing because he is too feeble to fight the beasts that would consume him? I do not believe it!" she said with willful vehemence.

Menard attempted to explain that whites did not leave their elderly in dark caves to die but instead confined them to their beds, where relatives and friends could gather to watch the fire of life slowly dwindle away, all the while assuring the doomed soul he had many years left to enjoy. Bright Dawn grudgingly approved of this, but was appalled that the dying process was not accompanied by singing and dancing to cheer the bedridden one and ward off the ghosts that would eat his soul. When Menard explained that there were chants and rituals that served the same purpose, she was again mollified. At this point, he was content to drop the subject for fear of compromising the well being of his immortal soul.

As Bright Dawn had instructed, David Casey stood passively outside the Menards' tent while she clipped the fringes on the white buckskin shirt and overalls she had made and draped the bandoleer sashes of intricate beadwork across his shoulders and body. They had managed to halt the bleeding under his arm with mud, leaves, and a piece of an old linen shirt. This medicinal potpourri would not heal the wound, but it didn't have to. Though outwardly submissive, Casey was understandably troubled because he could see Stump Neck's warriors stacking the firewood on the opposite side of the camp and inserting the pole to which he was to be bound into the ground. But he *had* stopped sobbing. That was good.

"Why is she doing this? The clothes will just burn," he squeaked irritably at Menard. Fear had constricted his throat and lent his speech an airy rasp.

"She wants you to look good," Menard explained from his stool on one side of the tent. He was casually watching his pretty wife scurrying about the prisoner, decorating him in her finery.

"Why?" Casey implored.

But Bushy Bear had not been listening. He was busily flirting with his wife.

"What?" he stammered, aware only that Casey had addressed him.

"Why does it matter how good I look? I'm going to die," the prisoner moaned, frantically whipping his head from side to side.

Menard explained that Bright Dawn wanted Casey to impress his God on their first meeting and that she had chosen fringed buckskin because she knew both whites and Indians wore it. That way, it wouldn't matter if he got the white or the Indian God; either would be duly pleased. If he got the white God, she hoped the beaded bandoleer would be appreciated but was afraid that, since white men didn't seem to like wearing pretty things, He might be offended. She hoped not.

Overwhelmed by the absurdity of the explanation and the certitude of his death, Casey's defenses crumbled. The sobbing resumed, accompanied by streams of tears that soaked the black stubble on his chin and neck. Casey flung his head to-and-fro as if trying to decapitate himself, ground his teeth, stretched the muscles of his face and neck until it seemed the skin would crack. He could no longer contain his anguish and fell to the ground, thrusting his knees into his chest and wrapping his arms around them—the only defense available to him—then rocking with a listless undulation.

"Gabriel, I don't want to die," Casey wept. In his introduction to Bright Dawn, Menard had also told the captive his name, and Casey had used it zealously ever since. "What's the point of killing me? They're not angry with me. I don't see hate in their faces!"

Bushy Bear rose from his stool to stand over the pathetic creature that had wrapped itself into a quaking ball. He extended his hand.

"Come, David, this is unseemly. You should not do this..."

The ball moaned and howled defiantly, then in supplication. No discernible speech emanated from it.

"Husband, tell him he must be brave," Bright Dawn said in Chippewa. She too was distraught, Menard knew, but for different reasons. His wife was disturbed by Casey's cowardice, not because she placed great value on bravery, but because she knew he would die a coward's death, the slowest, most agonizing kind, if he behaved like one.

Bright Dawn's eyes lifted to her husband. Her arms were clutched tightly across her chest in unconscious imitation of the writhing thing on the ground.

"Husband, please tell him it does no good to carry on like this. They will have contempt for him. They will not listen to his cries. But if he is brave they will make him a quick death. He must understand this. You must make him understand this..."

Speaking dispassionately in Chippewa, Menard said, "I'll try, but *you* must understand. He has no conception of such bravery. He is a white man, not a Chippewa brave. He has not been taught how to hold back his screams while a knife is plunged through his hand or his face. He has not even been taught that he *should* hold back his screams..."

"Then he should not have come out here. He is not prepared..."

"He is not a coward, Bright Dawn. I saw him today. He was ready to attack Stump Neck when I shot him!"

To his astonishment, Bushy Bear saw that his wife was ready to cry. She bowed her head to avoid his gaze but he could see the wetness in her eyes and the quivering of her chin.

"There is nothing in his experience to help him," Menard said with finality. "Nothing."

Bright Dawn struggled to regain control of herself, muttering, "I do not...I do not want..." Then she looked pleadingly at him and continued, "You must teach him, Gabriel. You must!"

With that entreaty released from her soul, Bright Dawn's control again broke down. She rushed into the tent to suffer her ignominy in private. Menard could not help wondering what had brought on such an emotional state. She had never behaved like this before. Did she really care so much about the life of this man whom she had not known before today? The maiming and torturing of captives certainly was not a new thing in her experience. All the woodland tribes engaged in the brutal practice, even to the point of encouraging their women and children to participate. It was an entertainment, a sport, a social event, no more abhorrent than killing and gutting an animal.

Then why?

He considered peering into the tent to express his concern, but decided against it. It would be better to at least attempt to do what she wanted: teach David Casey how to die well. Menard descended to his haunches, placed a hand on the nearest surface of the cocoon that was David Casey, and prodded.

"M'sieur...M'sieur Casey, we must talk," he murmured, taking care to dip his words in a soothing balm before delivering them.

There was still no coherent response, just a persistent moaning.

"M'sieur Casey, you say you are from Harris's Ferry," Menard said, hoping amiable patter would work where reason had not. "That is on the Susquehanna River, is it not? I have been to the upper branches of the Susquehanna but have never seen it in its fullness. It is an impressive river, is that not so?"

There was a pause and then Casey haltingly murmured, "It's wide, shallow, except when it floods."

Menard warmed to the subject, saying, "I am from Tadoussac, which is at the point where the Saguenay River flows into the St. Lawrence. The St. Lawrence River is so wide there we cannot see across, but it gets even wider as it approaches the sea. Is your Susquehanna so wide?"

"No, not so wide. Not at Harris's Ferry. A mile, mile and a half, maybe, at its widest, all the way to the Chesapeake Bay."

Casey was still sobbing irregularly, snorting and sniffling occasionally, but Menard felt he was making progress.

"What did you do in Harris's Ferry, M'sieur? Did you have family there? A wife? Children?"

"I worked as a wheelwright. It was my father's shop before he died. No, no family left. No wife. You?"

As he spoke, Casey unfolded and sat up, still clutching his knees, resting his head between them.

Menard tried laughter and offered, "My father was a tavern keeper. He spent much of his time throwing drunks into the street. It was an activity that did not appeal to me so I became a trader. As a trader, I spend much of my time throwing drunken Indians out of my trading post. So you see, I have become my father."

Reluctantly, Casey succumbed. A tiny, fragile snigger flew from his lips, a hatchling on its maiden flight.

"I wanted to be on my own, to have a great adventure," he said, now wistful. "I thought being a fur trader would be fun, interesting, a way to make enough money to start a farm."

"Where?" Menard asked.

"Out here...somewhere."

"Do you know farming?"

"No. But I would've learned. It would've been a good place to raise children. Do you have children?"

"No. Lives like ours are not suitable for children."

They talked on quietly, speaking of nothing and everything. For Menard, it was a way to divert Casey's attention away from his fate. For Casey, it was as much a release as a diversion. Finally, Menard decided it was time.

"M'sieur, you know these dreams are all in the past, that there is nothing more for you. N'est-ce pas?"

The doomed man swallowed, nodding his head to show he understood.

"It is important not to dwell on it. And it is well you do not have a wife or children. Do you believe in an afterlife?" Menard asked, not sure he himself did.

Casey nodded again.

"Well then, there is nothing to be concerned about," Menard said, attempting to show a modicum, but only that, of optimism. "You will be one of the saved, I am sure. Best to take a good look at the world around you, breathe deeply, let your senses gather in as much as they can, and think of heaven. Do you understand?"

The Frenchman could tell by the barely audible response that Casey did not want to talk further about his impending demise. Respecting that wish, and in the interest of following his own advice not to dwell on the subject, Bushy Bear searched his experience for topics to small talk about. They discussed love, wealth, politics, adventure, war, and even delved into some of the esoteric speculations of the day concerning who the Indians were and where they had come from. By the time Stump Neck's emissaries came for him, Casey's mood had risen to a state, which, if not lively, might optimistically be called melancholy.

There were two of them, young braves whose names and tribes Menard could not recall. In anticipation of the flames they would shortly be exposed to, they were wearing little more than breechclouts and moccasins. The faces and bodies of both were smeared with black. Each had painted the symbol of his clan on his chest with charcoal and bear grease—one a turtle, the other a wolf's head. In spite of the baleful adornment, neither youth looked at all fierce, merely earnest. They each took one of Casey's arms and raised him to a standing position. He looked beseechingly at Menard, who thought for a moment that all his massaging of the doomed man's spirit had been in vain. But Casey gulped, closed his eyes, and submerged his fear in the rivulets of memory Menard had stirred and which were still flowing through his mind.

"Be brave, my friend," Menard said, grasping Casey's hand in both of his. "Don't cry out when the pain comes. Swallow. Grit your teeth. Bite your tongue. Twist your muscles into knots to kill your perception. Death will arrive sooner if you do."

Casey did not resist as his guards led him across the clearing to the far side of the camp beyond the tents and lean-tos. From the corner of one eye, Menard saw Bright Dawn emerging from their tent, her face red and puffy from weeping. But she was not weeping now as she approached and placed herself in front of him. He could feel the fine strands of her hair teasing his nose as she pulled his arms around her. She pressed her back against his body, at first arousing him but, when he realized it was not her intent, inspiring in him a contentment that seemed utterly alien to the place and time they now occupied.

Silently, as if it were their duty, as if mesmerized by the spectacle of it, they watched as the entertainment began. Standing at the place of execution in a breechclout festooned with porcupine quills and turkey feathers, the madman waited patiently as the prisoner drew nigh. A *coup stick* in one hand and a turtle shell rattle in the other, his visage hidden by a grotesque, black false face with a straggly horsehair scalp piece and a vicious sneer on its bulbous red lips, Stump Neck was a sight to behold. If David Casey had ever nurtured a hope for mercy, the presence of this netherworldly creature dispelled it. The guards stood him on the firewood and, shoving his back against the pole, wrapped his arms around it and tied his hands. Casey's eyelids were closed, his lips slightly, apprehensively, parted.

The drums started. Stump Neck circled the prisoner, dancing and singing his eerie song, waving his *coup stick* and rattle to the beat. The others joined him, their voices whining in not-quite harmony, strengthening, building the song. The dancers brought burning sticks, firebrands and hot coals to thrust into the captive's eyes, sear his legs, and roast his torso. As they tortured him, the Indians taunted with mock concern, calling him 'uncle' and 'nephew' and asking him if he was cold as they warmed his flesh with red-hot daggers. Casey's eyes remained closed but his lips were moving, in prayer, Menard assumed. To himself, the Frenchman whispered, "Good man, good man."

Throughout the performance, Menard noticed Bright Dawn

glancing back at him, then hastily averting her eyes. When the howling of the celebrants reached its peak and Stump Neck lifted a torch to ignite the killing fire, Bright Dawn's gaze dropped to the ground. But it was no use. The brilliance of the flames enveloping the doomed man would not so easily be dismissed.

"Bright Dawn, why are you concerned with this man? He is nothing to you," Bushy Bear murmured, perplexed.

She turned her head to face him and said, "I am not concerned with him. I am concerned with life."

Then Bright Dawn took his folded hands and gently pressed them to her stomach.

"There is life…in here," she explained. Her eyes fixed on him, luminescent against the backdrop of the descending night.

It was while Bushy Bear was struggling to comprehend his wife's message that David Casey used up the last phantasm of his courage and screamed for his merciful God.

Chapter Six

May 27, 1754, Great Meadows

His name was Silverheels and he arrived a half-hour after Gist's departure for Winchester. He was a courier from Tanacharison, who was camped no more than five to ten miles from Great Meadows. Even with his bare skull and red cross-hatched face, Silverheels looked less like an Indian than a European dressed like one. His skull was round, as were his eyes, and his nose, while hooked, was narrow and noble like that of an English gentleman. But he spoke like an Indian, haltingly, as if every word carried with it a profundity of its own, and only by giving each its proper emphasis could his message be understood. His message was simple: He knew where the French company was camped—the one that had been incessantly dogging the Virginians since their arrival at Great Meadows.

In response, Washington had gathered Stephen, Van Braam, Lieutenant Waggoner, and forty men on the evening of the twenty-seventh of May to march out and find the enemy. This, after sending out seventy-five men under Hogg, Mercer, and Ensign La Peyroney to Gist's plantation late that afternoon. Was he overreacting? There was no way to tell. But as he trekked through the thick forest in the dead of night, drenched by a torrential downpour, Washington realized it was not the most intelligent decision he had ever made. Seven men had lost their way and they hadn't even found the Half-King yet, let alone the damn frog-eaters.

But sunrise was imminent. A few, tentative rays peeked at him between the leaves of the tall oaks and maples. Ahead, he could make out a rear view of Silverheels plodding through the mud and underbrush, the fragile potpourri of hair and turkey feathers on his scalp flopping as though it must certainly come undone. As they approached a meadow of tall grass and short fruit trees, Silverheels halted and grunted, "Unh-nh-h!" Then ten or eleven mostly bald, sun-baked bronze heads popped above the thick grass. The exceptions were the two Half-Kings, Tanacharison and Monacatoocha, both of whom had lost the youthful impulse to trim their hair for any other purpose than convenience. Washington was surprised to see the Shawnee vice-regent, Monacatoocha, but only slightly. Indians were always arriving unexpectedly. For them, staying put was anathema. It increased the odds that your enemy would know where you were.

Washington motioned for Stephen and Van Braam to follow as he rushed to the front of the column to meet the Indians. As he was about to speak, Monacatoocha placed a finger to his lips and then pointed toward a trail leading downward into a hollow completely enveloped by the forest canopy. *Be quiet and look over here,* he was signaling. Washington obeyed and motioned for his men to do the same.

"They are down there in that gloomy place," Silverheels whispered to Washington, pointing as Monacatoocha had done toward the dark hollow.

Washington proposed that the Indians send scouts to reconnoiter the French encampment and the area surrounding the glen, which they did. The scouts returned in short order, one of whom made a mud sketch of an oval with the French position in its center and their own at the bottom, barely outside the oval. After talking briefly with the scouts and the Half-Kings, Washington searched for and found Adam Stephen and Jacob Van Braam and called them forward.

"Adam, you take your men to the left of that ravine. Jacob and I will go to the right," Washington whispered, reinforcing his orders by referring to the scout's mud map. "Try not to let them see you. Maybe we can surprise them."

Adam Stephen was a paradox. Naturally hot-tempered and impatient, the young man had nevertheless disciplined himself enough to earn a degree from the University of Edinburgh in Scotland and had been practicing medicine and surgery in Frederick, Maryland prior to joining the Virginia Volunteers. What he had to gain by becoming a soldier was a mystery. To Washington's orders, Stephen brusquely mouthed his understanding and motioned for his company to follow him. As Stephen's men passed by and down the trail, Washington and the Half-Kings conferred, agreeing that the Indians would move out before he did and occupy the far end of the glen, thereby eliminating it as an escape route. While he waited for the two groups to precede him, the young Colonel studied their faces. There was fear in them all, some of it palpable and obvious in frozen, expressionless visages, some of it effervescing as nervous energy and meaningless chatter. He could not speak for the Indians but most of his men had never done anything remotely like this before.

Nor have I, Washington reminded himself, as much to steel his will as to quench any reckless impulses that might still be lurking within him. He had to do well. More importantly, he had to do the correct thing, whatever that might be, if he expected to have any chance at a military career. It was the fear of not being able to judge what the right thing was at a critical moment that dominated his thoughts, leaving little room for lesser matters like life and its perpetuity.

When the last of the Indians had passed, Washington instructed his men by word of mouth to move forward in single file, crouching as they did so for added stealth. Silently he cursed the tomato red uniform of the Virginia militia for its ostentation. Against the green of the sylvan backdrop, they looked like Christmas ornaments. There was nothing a parade of moving red objects *could* be but a column of Englishmen. He stopped to watch Stephen and his men as they crept through the woods on the left semi-circle of the ravine, then glanced toward the Indians on the right. The Indians were almost in position at the far end of the glen. Stephen was about five men away from completing his piece of the encirclement. His heart pounding and his throat dry as burnt toast, Washington led his men up the right side of the ravine onto the stage where his first role as a military officer would be performed.

The first Frenchman he saw was naked from the waist up and washing himself in a pail of water while talking to another who was below Washington's line of sight. Again, he glanced to the other side and was relieved to see Stephen and his company in a neat line, ready to fire. It was then that he realized his side of the glen was more exposed because of the scarcity of trees and brush and the more direct viewing angle it presented to any eyes staring up from below. It was going to be extremely difficult to maneuver his troops to where the ground fell away into the glen without being seen, but it would have to be done if surprise was to be their ally. Passing the word, Washington commanded his men to stay where they were, then cautiously approached the embankment, keeping as low as his ungainly frame would permit.

Before him he could see about thirty men, half of them awake, and only half of these completely dressed in the gray-white and blue of the *Compagnies des franches*. Some were gathered around a campfire downing coffee and biscuits. Others were standing, leaning or lying on the rock strewn terrain that did not look very comfortable and probably wasn't, based on the large percentage of marines arching their backs and rolling their heads to loosen stiff muscles. A young man in a dark blue uniform with red cuffs was resting with his eyes closed, his back against a boulder, a drum resting by his side. Ten feet from him, between his boulder and another, were stacks of muskets and sheathed swords. In front of these were the half-naked washing man and his companion whom Washington had not been able to see but now could. It was the French Quartermaster, Ensign La Force, who had led them to Fort Le Boeuf in December to deliver Dinwiddie's ultimatum. The Ensign was wearing only his underwear, moccasins, and a black tricorne.

The Virginian moved his men forward, imploring them to stay down and out of sight. The rain had stopped but had left the earth saturated and the air over-saturated so that a thin, low-lying fog diffused ghost-like over the spongy soil. Reluctant to crawl along the wet forest floor and relying on the fog for concealment, most of the volunteers approached in a semi-upright position, bent only at the waist, despite Washington's exhortations. Three quarters of them had formed a line and were kneeling in firing position when they were abruptly discovered.

"Regardez! Anglais! Anglais!" a voice cried from the end of the glen guarded by the Indians. Washington searched for its source and found a young French cadet pointing at a sheepish Abner Hazlip to his left, whose nearly upright figure and red uniform could not have been more conspicuous if they had been immortalized on canvas, framed by oak planks, and hung over the door of a tavern. Some of the awakened Frenchmen made a mad dash for their muskets and swords; the others began frantically jostling their sleeping compatriots. The melee in the French camp was in sharp contrast to the ordered row of men and muskets across the glen whose commander, Adam Stephen, had raised his sword and was waiting for a signal from Washington to fire the first volley.

He had to do something, Washington knew, or risk losing the initiative. It had all happened with such lightning speed that there had been no time to think, to ponder the consequences and the alternatives. So he didn't. With only the slightest hesitation, the Commander drew his sword, raised it over his head, and gazed on his troops with a focused intensity that was chillingly unequivocal.

"Ready...aim..." he chanted, then, brought the sword downward with a quick chop and shouted, "...fire!"

The blasts of twenty muskets in near simultaneous discharge produced a deafening roar that echoed off the walls of the glen and galloped like thunder through the forest. It was rapidly followed by an equally intense roar from Stephen's troops on the other side. With a range of only sixty yards and an accuracy to match, the musket was a poor hunting weapon. But in massed fire at close range it was deadly, if for no other reason than statistics: forty muskets aimed in the general direction of a confined body of enemy troops thirty yards distant were not likely to miss everything. With the first volley, five Frenchmen fell. Subsequent volleys were less well executed and less effective, as the anxious volunteers reloaded their weapons and fired without waiting for commands to do so. But it didn't matter. Caught by surprise, a few French marines fought back but the weaponless, undressed, half-asleep majority fled toward the end of the hollow where the Indians lay in wait. And there they died.

The first man killed by the Indians was a diminutive Frenchman in the finely tailored uniform of an officer, who was waving his arms and yelling at the others to follow him to safety. Preoccupied, he did not see Tanacharison approaching until the hatchet wielded by the chieftain penetrated his skull. The Frenchman started to scream but stopped abruptly as the ax split his forehead down to the nose. He slumped to the ground, where the Half-King rolled him over, knelt down over the ruptured head, and began stripping flesh and hair from the dead man's skull. Even with the British-made steel scalping knife it took several tries and several cuts. The Half-King was an old man. When he finally had the gory, mangled trophy in hand, Tanacharison held it up and gave his best war cry: a raspy whoop that made Washington grimace with apprehension.

"No...no...don't...*Sonofabitch!*" Washington cried, realizing with belated clarity what had just happened. Frantically, he hurried down the slippery slope into the glen, slipping and falling twice before the ground leveled off. As best the terrain would permit, he kept running at the Indians, who were too engaged in their grisly sport to pay him any heed.

Finally, frustrated by the lack of response to his cries, he halted and said in a voice crackling with anger, "Stop what you are doing! Do you hear me? I order you to *stop!*"

Tanacharison was the first to react, casting a puzzled look at the chief of the Long Knives. Reluctantly, he let his bloodied hands fall to his sides. The others, save one, immediately followed suit. The exception finished off the scalp he'd been working on, a pretty chestnut piece with long tresses, then wiped and sheathed his knife. All stared at the Virginia officer as if he had lost his mind, a point of view Washington soon came to appreciate when he discovered his hand gripping the hilt of the partially withdrawn sword at his waist. Few had understood anything but the tone of his words but all knew what a drawn sword meant.

Washington hastily re-sheathed the sword and knelt down to examine the Half-King's victim, whose body was lying face down on a partly buried piece of sandstone. He rolled the body over to reveal the features of a man in his thirties with pudgy cheeks that might have been florid if the blood had not left them. Despite the fact that he was clearly ten years Washington's senior, the man had a youthful appearance, certainly more youthful than the Colonel felt at this moment. Washington looked up at the Half-King and his band, all of whom remained standing, tight-lipped and obviously perturbed. Painfully, wisely, the young Commander curbed his tongue.

Amidst the cries of the wounded—most of them French—Washington heard excited voices and the quickening of boots on rock. He rose to meet Captains Stephen and Van Braam and several of the volunteers.

"Colonel, we have captured M'sieur La Force," said Van Braam solemnly. "Would you like to talk to him?"

"Yes, I def…" Washington began, but was interrupted by the stern if faltering voice of the Half-King issuing a proclamation, apparently at him. Swinging his head around, he saw Tanacharison eyeing him critically.

Turning back to his men, Washington asked, "What is he saying? What does he want?"

It was one of his men, Argyle House, who answered, "Sir, he requests that you turn the prisoners over to him because the French boiled and ate his father and he wants to do the same with them."

The Virginian stared in disbelief at House, who blithely shrugged and then cast his eyes to the ground for fear of breaking into an uncontrollable fit of laughter. But Washington was not amused. Waiting for his temper to dissipate, he locked his gaze on Argyle House and said, "Tell him *no!* The prisoners are ours and they will stay with us. There will be no boiling and eating of Frenchmen while I'm in command."

As House, struggling to maintain his composure, was about to relay the message, Washington raised his hand and, with a sigh, added, "No, don't tell him that. Just tell him they are our prisoners and leave it at that." Casting a fateful glance at Van Braam, he said, "Jacob, I would be most grateful if you would stay here and deal with this. I'm afraid my disposition is not up to it right now."

The Dutchman agreed and Washington crossed the glen with Stephen to where his adjutant, the French Huguenot and fellow Virginian, William La Peyroney, was interviewing La Force and the man he'd seen washing before the battle. Tormented by a growing apprehension, he was disturbed with himself for letting anger better him in the presence of the Half-King. Washington was anxious to lay his frustrations at the feet of La Force, whom he blamed for the situation in the absence of other scapegoats.

The chatter between the two Frenchmen—La Peyroney and La

Force—was vigorous and meaningless to the Virginia Colonel. A third French marine was present but was not a participant in the conversation, occupied as he was with finding his clothes. In one arm he cradled a gilded gorget and a gold-laced vest, identifying him as a ranking officer. To establish a modicum of dignity, La Force wrapped himself in a blanket. Except for the dialogue between him and La Peyroney and the labored conversations between English and French speaking officers elsewhere on the battlefield, there was little sound to disturb the natural tranquility of the scene. A mockingbird was prattling high in the treetops, whether to announce the new day or to complain of the heavy cloud of gunsmoke drifting his way was not clear.

"William, I'd like to speak with Mr. La Force," Washington announced to his adjutant.

La Peyroney understood that he was to translate, clicked his heels together with martial aplomb, and said in French-accented English, "Cer-tain-ly, Col-o-nel."

"Mr. La Force, I wish I could say it was good to see you again but under the circumstances that would be disingenuous of me," Washington said, setting the tone for the interview.

La Force was impassive, his expression as stern as it had been at their first meeting. Hesitantly, he cocked his head in acknowledgment.

"Is this gentleman your commanding officer?" Washington asked, indicating the Frenchman with the gorget and vest, a tall, grim man of dubious posture and aquiline profile whose hands were clamped rigidly behind his back.

"No, this is Major Druillon."

Washington and Druillon exchanged polite glances, then the Virginian surveyed the battlefield.

"Which of these men *is* your commanding officer?"

La Force pointed to the man whose skull had been split and scalp removed by the Half-King. With simmering rage and an implacable stare, he announced, "That is our commander, Ensign Joseph de Villiers, the Sieur de Jumonville, and it is *you*, Major Washington, who have murdered him!"

Washington was taken aback by the charge of murder in a

legitimate military confrontation, but he let it pass.

"Mr. La Force, if he is an ensign, as you say, how can he be your commanding officer? This man, for one..." Washington said to La Force but indicated Druillon. "...outranks him."

"The Coulon is...was a nobleman, *Colonel* Washington." Druillon cut in, demonstrating both his knowledge of the rank displayed by Washington's uniform and his contempt for the man wearing it. "and as M'sieur La Force has correctly charged, you have murdered him."

The young Virginia officer was again startled by the accusation of murder, having dismissed the first instance as a slip of the tongue or an error in translation. But the news that Jumonville was a nobleman troubled him: There could be repercussions.

"*Major* Druillon, your commander is a casualty of a military engagement," Washington replied curtly, assiduously avoiding the word 'war.' "You and your men made no move to yield and, in fact, went for your muskets when you saw us. We have every right to defend ourselves. Your charge of murder is absurd!"

"Nevertheless, it *is* murder," Druillon insisted, straightening his posture to stare directly into his opponent's eyes. "You see, Colonel, we are a diplomatic mission and the Coulon was its leader. I believe you have performed a similar function for the British government...last December, was it not?"

As he spoke, the tightly composed Druillon raised his dark eyebrows as a silent query to La Force, who responded with a confirmatory nod. The exchange only heightened Washington's irritation, implying as it did that Druillon's description of Jumonville's mission might not be entirely honest.

"I have served in such a capacity, Major Druillon," Washington bristled. "And I am well acquainted with diplomacy, which does not usually require a company of armed soldiers for its implementation. You are *not* a diplomatic mission, sir. You *are* a hostile enemy force!"

"Nevertheless, we are *not*," Druillon rejoined. "You will find our credentials among the Coulon's personal items or perhaps on...his person."

The certitude of the statement and Druillon's hostile glare convinced the young Virginian that the French Major was speaking the truth, at least as he knew it. Druillon folded his arms and managed to mix in a facile smugness with his fury. Washington sent two of the nearby volunteers, Michael Scully and the Swedish colonial with the tongue-twisting name of Carolus Gustavus de Spiltdorph, to check Jumonville's body and belongings for papers.

"Major Druillon, if, as you say, your mission was merely diplomatic, why didn't you come to us directly and introduce yourselves as we did at Venango? You have been haunting the woods around us, no more than five miles distant, for at least three days and attempted to steal a cow from Mr. Gist's plantation two weeks ago…"

"But we did not steal the cow, Colonel. We left peaceably once…"

"Once what, Major? Once you were chased off the premises? I would hardly call that leaving peaceably…"

Druillon did not flinch, but instead began a slow pacing, and continued, "…Once we became aware that the premises were occupied. As for *haunting* the woods, as you put it, that is our right as subjects of his most Christian Majesty Louis XV, the right and proper sovereign of these lands…"

"We will agree to disagree on that point, sir. The fact remains that your activities could not fail to arouse our suspicions. Only a liar or a fool would argue otherwise. At the very least you are guilty of espionage…"

De Spiltdorph returned, soon followed by Scully, both of whom carried folders of official-looking papers. Washington conferred with La Peyroney, who translated and interpreted the documents. Then he took one of the documents and held it up for display.

"I must apologize, gentlemen," he said to the two French marines. "This is indeed a summons for all British subjects to retire from the lands of his most Christian Majesty, King Louis XV."

Casually, Washington returned the document to La Peyroney, took the other from its folder, and held it up as he had done the first. Then he continued in an accusatory tone, "…and this document indicates that you have, on at least two occasions, sent back reports to your commander, Captain Contrecoeur, on our whereabouts and our movements. What do you say to that, sir?"

At first, neither of the Frenchmen said anything, but merely fumed, Druillon's face turning pink in the process, La Force's darker complexion urging his coloration to a light shade of magenta. With their ears already aglow from Washington's tongue-lashing, both blushed like live hogs in a boiling pot. Druillon resumed his restless pacing, secured his arms more firmly in place, and responded in crisp statements glazed heavily with disdain.

"Of course we have sent reports back to our commander. We are in unfamiliar territory! It is necessary for us to maintain contact with Fort Duquesne, to let them know where we are and to record the roadways, rivers and other features of the terrain we encounter…"

"I am not a roadway, river or a feature of the terrain, sir, and neither is this army," Washington shot back brusquely but calmly, lowering the temperature of the debate a few degrees. "But I will not argue further with you. Mr. De Spiltdorph, please take these men and treat them as our prisoners."

De Spiltdorph led La Force and Druillon to a corner of the glen where the other prisoners were being assembled for transport back to Great Meadows. Lieutenant Waggoner, still checking his figures, arrived with the battle statistics. Ten Frenchman were dead, twenty-one captured, with a loss to the volunteers of one man killed and two wounded. In the last category was Lieutenant Waggoner himself whose wound, fortunately, was superficial. On the face of it, the battle was a clean victory for the Virginians. Yet Washington fretted. He was beginning to understand that there was more to warfare than wins and losses.

The Colonel seated himself on a projecting piece of sandstone and said to Waggoner, "Lieutenant, tell the officers I want to meet with them now…and then have Dr. Craik take care of your wound."

Waggoner murmured his appreciation and marched off. Shortly thereafter, Captains Van Braam and Stephen arrived to join Adjutant La Peyroney at their Commander's front, as did Tanacharison accompanied by his interpreter of the moment, Argyle House. Washington removed the tricorne from his head to give the reservoir of perspiration on his brow a chance to disperse. With growing trepidation, he looked up at his staff, studied their faces, and got to the point.

"La Force and Druillon insist their mission is diplomatic. What do the other prisoners say?"

"Essentially the same thing, sir," Adam Stephen replied curtly. Van

Braam and La Peyroney indicated their agreement with the appraisal.

"Damn!" Washington cried angrily, throwing the tricorne at the ground. "Nothing is ever straightforward on this mission. Even crushing the enemy is…is…"

Without warning, a cloud of gloom descended on his spirit, disheartening him so much he couldn't finish the sentence he'd started. Defeating the enemy was supposed to resolve disputes, not create them, as this victory seemed bound and determined to do. What else could he have done? The French had gone for their weapons, hadn't they? Perhaps he should have called out, demanded their surrender before attacking, but such hesitation could easily have meant more casualties for his side.

Washington looked up at his officers and wondered how much doubt they could read in his face. They would support his position; he knew that. So would the contumacious Half-King, although he didn't think it wise to depend too much on the judgment of a man who wanted to turn the prisoners into food.

"Gentlemen, we need time to prepare," he said, still battling the depression within. "I think once he hears of this engagement Captain Contrecoeur is likely to come after us. Therefore, we don't want him to hear about it. Is that understood?"

Yes, they understood.

"Did we get them all, dead, wounded, or otherwise?"

"Yes, sir," Stephen replied and the others concurred.

"None escaped?"

"None."

Unexpectedly, Tanacharison began gesturing and talking briskly with Argyle House. Washington waited politely for the exchange to end, then focused his attention on House, a question mark in his gaze.

"Sir, he says he intends to send the French scalps to the other tribes as a warning to any who would take up the French cause," House summarized.

"Is he asking for my approval?"

Argyle House thought for a moment and glanced at the Half-King, whose stolid expression betrayed little.

"I don't think so, sir," House mumbled sheepishly.

The damned scalps again. If only it could have been a clean battle of muskets and swords instead of tomahawks and scalping knives, with men dying in a noble endeavor instead of having their bodies hideously mutilated! But he could not afford further offending his Indian allies, as he had intemperately done earlier. Least of all could he risk insulting Tanacharison and Monacatoocha, and if brandishing the French scalps would strengthen the British-Iroquois alliance and bring the Ohio tribes firmly into the British sphere, he could hardly reject the tactic, distasteful though it might be.

"Tell him I agree but that I would ask him not to send his warning until we have returned to Great Meadows."

Argyle House relayed the message, to which the Half-King responded with a rare smile of assent.

With the fatigue of overstressed nerves finally consuming him, Washington lethargically rubbed his eyes and tried to fend off his body's need for restful sleep. There was one more thing that had to be said.

"Gentlemen, I'm sure most of you know this already. If not, then know it now. We may have just started a war!"

No, that's wrong, he thought, staring directly into the abyss. *I may have just started a war.* Just as another French officer, Joncaire, had predicted eight months ago.

* * *

Adam Stephen was literally correct: None of the French marines in the glen had escaped. The better question for Washington to ask would have been: "Are there any French soldiers unaccounted for?" Captain Stephen would not have known the answer to this broader question but it might have provoked him to take a look in the forest surrounding the glen. There, he might or might not have found Sergeant Gilles Mouceau, but probably would have because Mouceau was in no condition to scurry away, suffering as he was from a severe bout of diarrhea brought on by an overdose of the local, unripe apples. The Sergeant had left camp around six-fifteen that morning, taking one of the ceremonial halberds along to probe his way in the dark, just before the Virginians and Indians surrounded the glen. He did not hear them or see them, in part because they were trying to be quiet and invisible, but mostly because Mouceau was a hundred meters distant and preoccupied by his turbid bowel movements. These were awkward and messy to execute from a squatting position behind the chestnut tree whose meter wide trunk he had chosen to protect his modesty, unlikely as that was to need protecting.

A man of moderate size and dexterity, Mouceau had entirely removed his breeches to minimize the chances of their being too close to the target area and was supporting the unbalanced load of his exposed posterior with his hands and arms. It was a tenuous position and, when the sound of the volleys from the Virginia Regiment thundered past his eardrums, literally scared the contents of his lower intestine out of him.

"Jesus, Mary, mother of God..." he cried, vaulting to a standing position. Only then did he realize how ill-advised such a move was when he discovered the warm, moist spattering on his arms and thighs.

"Damn...damn...goddamn!"

With the rags and paper he had brought along and the dead leaves he managed to scrape from the ground, Sergeant Mouceau cleaned himself, pulled his breeches on, and crouched behind the chestnut tree. Cautiously peering out, he could see the sun's morning rays illuminating the cumulus of gunsmoke above the glen and a line of men along its edge, some in hunting clothes, some in tomato red apparel which he assumed to be the uniforms of the British company they had been scouting. After the final irregular rounds of musket fire, the men descended into the glen where the marines of Mouceau's company were camped.

It suddenly dawned on the Sergeant that the British had actually attacked and, from the looks of things, had won a complete victory! What was he to do? It made no sense to surrender although, in a way, that was the most practical thing to do. All his food and equipment were back at the glen except for the halberd. As a weapon, it was virtually useless in modern warfare.

But, on second thought, it would make a good cane for negotiating the treacherous terrain between this spot and Fort Duquesne. Dejected and uncomfortable, Sergeant Mouceau laid the halberd on the ground and waited patiently until he was certain the English attackers were gone. Then he took the ancient weapon in hand, grumbled a curse at the vicissitudes of life, and began the long trek home.

𝕮hapter 𝕾even

May 30, 1754, Chiningue

*I*t is a good game, Old Smoke reflected. *No, it may be an enjoyable game but it is not a good game.* The score was too unbalanced to call it that. Deep Water's team was ahead four-to-one, the difference being the three goals he had scored. A good performance by the youngster is what it was. With his wide, white eyes and grinning teeth set against the ebony of his skin, the black youth looked like some bizarre *manitou* among the eleven Shawnee youth on the field. As one of Buffalo Hair's two slaves, Deep Water was lucky to be in the game at all. The French called the game *la crosse* because of the resemblance of the racket to a Bishop's symbol of authority. This game belonged to Deep Water even though he had been playing at it for only a month, the same passage of time since Old Smoke's return from Contrecoeur's conference at Venango, slightly less than the duration of Cornpicker's absence.

"He is good, isn't he?" Mud Face said, her freckled face beaming with pride at her brother Deep Water's performance.

"Yes, he is very good," Old Smoke confirmed, not yet ready to share his concerns with her or with Short Leg to her left, whose half-moon smile showed that his aunt was also well pleased by the boy's performance. He was certainly not ready to broach the subject with Buffalo Hair who, to all appearances, was another enthralled spectator and Deep Water admirer. But appearances could lie, or at least skillfully dissemble.

"Old Smoke!" Deep Water cried, waving as he once more ran down the well-trodden grass of the field with the wooden ball in his racket. Before Old Smoke could wave back, two members of the opposing team converged on the speeding youth and began clubbing him with their rackets. Surprised by the attack, Deep Water dropped his racket and the wooden ball and fell to the ground, clutching his head. Mud Face's howl of protest was loud and animated.

"Wha…those vicious little savages! Did you see what they did?" she demanded of Old Smoke, pointing an accusing finger toward the scene of the crime. "Old Smoke, did you see what they did? That was *not* fair! That was a wicked, cowardly thing to do!"

There was no time to explain to the inflamed and protective sister that the rules of the game did not proscribe the clubbing of members of the opposing team and that Deep Water probably understood those rules better than she did. Getting no satisfaction from Old Smoke, Mud Face tried her outrage on Short Leg, who shrugged, and then on Buffalo Hair, who dismissed her with a sweep of his quivering arm and remarked, "Be quiet, woman, it is none of your concern," and continued watching the game.

As Buffalo Hair's slave, any expression of rebellion by Mud Face could bring instant or prolonged death down on her. But she could not allow her brother to be harmed and would not allow Buffalo Hair to trivialize her concern. Mud Face prepared to storm mightily onto the field of play.

"No, no, Mud Face…" Old Smoke murmured in her ear, grasping her with strong, enveloping arms and gently pulling her back. "You must not…you must…not…look, he's fine…"

As he spoke, Old Smoke calmly raised one hand and pointed. Still struggling, Mud Face followed the gesture with her eyes to discover Deep Water on his feet again and racing toward the boy who had recovered the ball. With his speed, it was a simple matter for Deep Water to overtake his opponent and, with a whack of his racket behind the knees, bring the startled youth down. But before he crumpled to the ground, the boy's reflexes propelled his arms forward to cushion his fall, which, in turn, lofted the ball out of his racket and skyward. Without breaking stride, Deep Water caught the ball in *his* racket, turned, and charged the enemy's goal where, faced with a single defender of unremarkable athletic prowess, he easily sent the ball back to its proper home, scoring his fourth goal.

Old Smoke and Mud Face heartily cheered their appreciation, as did Short Leg, but with more reserve. Even Buffalo Hair stood and shouted his approval.

"He is a quick one, Old Smoke," the old man said, then dropped his line of sight to take in a rear view of the jostling and bouncing Mud Face. In a confidential tone of voice he added, "It is obvious he and his sister come from the same stock. They are both built to run."

"Yes, Uncle," Old Smoke acknowledged. "Like the wind, as you say. But I don't think your admiration for Mud Face's physique has much to do with running."

For once, Buffalo Hair's wolf eyes revealed nothing but innocent amusement.

"You are right, Old Smoke. And you are wrong also. I do venerate her stride, so you could say my regard for her ass goes beyond lust," Buffalo Hair commented with a sly snicker.

Old Smoke shook his head in disbelief.

"Not far beyond, Uncle, not far…"

As evening approached, the game ended with Deep Water's team victorious, his last goal being the final goal of the match. Happier than he could ever remember being, Deep Water returned to what he had come to think of as his family: Mud Face, Short Leg, Old Smoke and…Buffalo Hair. With beads of perspiration scattered across his brow like rifle shot and his moist, dark hair glistening in the twilight sun, he rushed directly to Short Leg. It was not a slight to Mud Face, Old Smoke knew. In all ways that mattered, Short Leg had become the slave boy's mother.

"Did you see me, Short Leg? I scored four times," he chattered gaily, holding up four fingers.

Short Leg, Old Smoke's aunt, smiled with a mother's warmth and placed her hand on the boy's cheek.

"Yes, you were very good, Deep Water. Wasn't he, Mud Face?"

His sister's grin was nearly as wide as Deep Water's own. She hugged him and said proudly, "You were the best one out there. They couldn't keep up with you!"

It was Old Smoke's turn to pay homage. If Short Leg had become Deep Water's mother, Old Smoke had evolved into an older brother. It had not been intentional. Old Smoke's purpose was protective. With the escape of Cornpicker—an Ojibwa youth who had been

Buffalo Hair's captive—the young black boy no longer had a friend of his own age and status. Old Smoke tried his best to fill that void and to convince Buffalo Hair to let him play with the other Shawnee youths. Expecting resistance, he got a grudging acquiescence from his uncle, which made him both grateful and wary. There would be a price.

"Old Smoke, did you see me? Was I good?" the boy's full lips spoke, demanding praise. Only hyperbole would be accepted.

Old Smoke stooped down to the boy's level, staring deeply into the ivory-on-ebony eyes.

"You were magnificent, Deep Water. As good as I've ever seen."

"Was I as good as you?" he demanded to know.

From the corner of one eye, Old Smoke saw Mud Face and his aunt enjoying his predicament.

"Better. I've never scored four goals," the Shawnee replied. It might be the truth. He really couldn't remember.

Old Smoke reached up and removed the eagle feather and leather band from his head, then placed it on Deep Water's. The boy's hair puffed out like a mushroom as his big brother adjusted the fit and pinned the band in place with the attached bone needle. Deep Water beamed, his eyes straining upward to the champion's crown.

Then they dropped down and with them came the final, inevitable question: "Can I play again, Old Smoke? Please?"

"It's not my decision to make, Deep Water," Old Smoke said. "I think you should ask Buffalo Hair. He let you play today, didn't he?"

Hesitantly, the boy's gaze gravitated to the old man, his master, who had risen to a standing position and was following the conversation. Buffalo Hair was wearing his full regalia of ear and nose ornamentation but, in deference to the oppressive humidity, wore no headdress, only a linen shirt and breeches. He was an odd, perhaps frightening sight with his thinning hair exposing broad patches of scalp and a coarser, alien fluff growing wild and dense on his face. With the tentative steps of the supplicant, Deep Water approached him. Buffalo Hair smiled. Deep Water made a small bow.

"Buffalo Hair, can I play again another day?" the boy asked haltingly.

The old man ran his fingers through the boy's hair, seemingly fascinated by its texture, then slid a forefinger along the eagle feather Old Smoke had given him.

"Yes, of course you may play again," Buffalo hair said, then cast a glance at Old Smoke and added, "What's to stop you?"

To most, the look would have meant nothing, but there was in the lupine face of his uncle an icy undercurrent that sent a chill down Old Smoke's spine. There were only two people who could read his uncle's moods: Short Leg and himself. Casually he looked around at his aunt to find his concern mirrored on her face.

"There's nothing to stop him," Old Smoke said as cheerily as he could for Deep Water's benefit. "Nothing at all."

It was all Deep Water could do to suppress the euphoria within him and maintain the sense of servility proper for his station. But he managed, with his sister's help, to keep his cries of joy down to an excited whisper. The game over, he left with Short Leg and Mud Face for the village as the other spectators were doing. Old Smoke waited, expecting his uncle might need a steady arm to lean on during the walk back. He was therefore not surprised when the old man came to him but was taken unawares by Buffalo Hair's words.

"Old Smoke, I would like to speak with you and to show you something."

"Where, Uncle, at the longhouse?"

"No, at your birth cave."

What could this be about? Had Buffalo Hair concluded that the coincidence of Cornpicker's escape and Old Smoke's sojourn to Venango was not an accident? And yet there seemed to be nothing in his uncle's manner to suggest the kind of ire such a conclusion would surely engender in the old man's fevered brain. There was only an icy detachment, an unstated threat. Was the threat about to be stated?

"Uncle, it is almost dark. Can it wait until tomorrow?"

"You will build a fire."

"The cave is a long way off. Too far for you to walk."

"You will bring your horse for me."

The old man was determined: Any further protestations would be interpreted as disrespect. Old Smoke groaned within and reluctantly resigned himself to an evening with his uncle, then jogged off to retrieve the pinto from its corral just outside the village. When he returned, a half-moon was playing in the heavens accompanied by a chorus of stars. Buffalo Hair was seated on the ground looking up at them, apparently as enthralled as he had been by the *la crosse* match. Old Smoke approached with the horse, a favored pinto, then waited for his uncle to speak.

"They are very far away, aren't they?" Buffalo Hair asked, referring to the skyscape of heavenly bodies.

"Yes, they are."

"Do you know how far? Do your priests know how far?"

The priests were Buffalo Hair's term for the Jesuits Old Smoke and his mother had stayed with during their captivity among the Hurons.

"No, but it is much farther than you or I have ever traveled, or ever will."

His uncle's mood had become reflective, even philosophical, during Old Smoke's absence. He chuckled softly and said, "It is too bad we cannot go there to get away from the whites...and the Iroquois grandfathers."

Old Smoke laughed too. It was a pleasant thought, a universal thought—to be rid of conflict once and for all by escaping to a place no one had ever been. It was a strange thought to visit his uncle's mind, where intrigue, deception, and perversity were the gatekeepers. But perhaps he was being unfair.

Buffalo Hair rose to his feet and, with Old Smoke's help, mounted the pinto. Without speaking further, the young Shawnee took the reins and led the horse in the direction of the cave. Only the plodding of the horse's hooves on the soft earth and the rush of steamy air through its nostrils disturbed the tranquility of the evening.

"They are so different from us, the whites," Old Smoke heard his uncle say, as if to himself. "And yet we are all men. How can that be, Old Smoke? Do you understand it? Do your priests understand it?"

It was a night of surprises: Buffalo hair was actually asking his opinion.

"No, they do not understand it. But there are some whites who think all Indians originally came from a place called Asia..."

"Asia? Where is this place? Is it near the other one—Africa—

where you say Mud Face and Deep Water came from?"

Old Smoke collected his thoughts, tried to remember what the Jesuit Father Bonard had told him about the century old theories of Jose de Costa and Edward Brerewood, men of religion who had been disturbed by the absence of any chronicle of the red man in the Bible. The God of the Europeans apparently had not known of the Indian's existence until 1492, a serious oversight for an omniscient deity.

"No, it's in the other direction," Old Smoke said, pointing at the ebbing sun crowning the western mountains with its subdued orange and red hues. "They think so because the people of this land called Asia look like us."

Buffalo Hair was silent for a moment, then asked, "How do they look like us?"

"Our faces, our high cheekbones. The whites have round eyes, like a raccoon. Ours are narrow, like those of a cat. The people of Asia have similar features."

The silence was longer this time. Finally, Buffalo Hair said, "Hmmm…that is very interesting, Old Smoke. I don't suppose I can walk to this Asia?"

Uncle, you cannot even walk to my birth cave.

"No, Uncle, It is too far and there is an ocean in the way," Old Smoke replied.

"Another stinking lake!" Buffalo Hair exclaimed. "If there is another stinking lake, how did they get here? Did they have ships?"

The young Shawnee decided it would not be wise to try explaining the concept of the Earth as a ball flying around the sun whose surface was covered with a common ocean of water surrounding the several continents. That would be too much for Buffalo Hair's imagination, though he might find it an entertaining yarn.

"They could have come in ships, but the whites think there is a land connection between Asia and here that is yet to be found. They think it may be in the north, where the raw flesh eaters, the *Eskimantiks*, live."

"How do the whites know this?"

"They don't *know* any of it, Uncle. It is called a *theory*. They have seen the similarities between us and the people of Asia and wonder if we were not once the same people. It is called *inductive reasoning*."

"Hmmmph! The whites are always thinking strange things. They would be better off using their heads for more practical matters."

"No, Uncle, *we* would be better off if they used their heads for more practical matters. It is their strange thoughts that brought them here, that created their ocean vessels and their guns and their wealth. These things have given them power. We would do well to study their strange thoughts and make some of our own."

Halfway through his oration Old Smoke realized he was making the kinds of remarks that usually sent Buffalo Hair into a lamentation over his odyssey among the whites and his *alleged* transformation into one of them. This time it didn't happen. The faraway look on the old man's face was something new: Buffalo Hair was actually meditating on his nephew's words. As remarkable as that was, it didn't last.

"I think your priests have deceived you, Old Smoke," Buffalo Hair said with an air of authoritarian finality. "There is no Asia and there are no Asians. They are playing you for a fool."

It was Buffalo Hair's way of re-establishing dominance: Declare a challenge null and void. Whether his uncle believed his own declaration Old Smoke didn't know, but whether he did or not was irrelevant. To be an idea in Buffalo Hair's mind was to be a resident in a longhouse without entrances or exits. He had managed briefly to pry open a vent hole, but the sunlight passing through had offended, and had to be annulled. Unwilling to abide the smug look on his uncle's face, Old Smoke sadly turned his head away and silently led the pinto into the woods bordering his birth cave. Maneuvering in darkness down the rocky trail between giant maples, oaks, and sycamores was precarious, but the moonlight helped guide his way. At the cave, he tied the pinto to a sapling and helped his uncle down. Within minutes, he had a fire roaring in front of the cave entrance, where Buffalo Hair sat in stoic inscrutability on a slab of sandstone jutting from the left wall of the cave entrance. When the flames had stabilized to a hot, mellow radiance, the old man gripped the unburned end of one stick and withdrew it from the blaze. Rising and gesturing to Old Smoke that he needed no help, he entered the cave, using the burning stick to light his way and a hand against one wall to steady himself. Soon, he returned with a leather pouch, which he handed to Old Smoke and then sat down.

"Open it," he said.

Old Smoke did as instructed, finding in the pouch a neatly combed scalp of bronze-colored hair tied into a queue by a blue ribbon. He held it against the fire light, studying it.

"It is French," Buffalo Hair said. "The grandfathers brought ten of them to show to us, the Delaware, and the Mingo. There was a battle between the English and the French in the mountains, near the place the English call Great Meadows. The grandfathers fought alongside the English, and think they can frighten us with the scalps they have taken. They think we will tremble at their ferocity and will follow them like women to the British side."

The sarcasm in Buffalo Hair's discourse was palpable.

"And you do not want to join the British," Old Smoke added, completing his uncle's point.

"No."

"You think we should side with the French?"

"I want the British to go. They are the most troublesome to us."

Old Smoke remembered Contrecoeur's meeting at Venango in April, the one he had attended after removing Cornpicker from the old man's clutches. The arrogance of Monacatoocha, the Iroquois vice regent to the Shawnee, had made Old Smoke reluctantly sympathetic to his uncle's point of view. Monacatoocha's attitude toward the tribes of the Ohio Valley was every bit as imperious as those of the two European powers. But he was too judicious to reveal such an opinion. He nodded his agreement, put the scalp back in its pouch, and returned it.

"How strong are the British?" he asked.

"Half as strong as the French, perhaps five hundred," Buffalo Hair answered, then became more animated. "Your Major Washington is their commander."

Old Smoke sat back in disbelief.

"He is a boy, younger than I am! He knows nothing of warfare!"

"He has asked for a conference with the Ohio tribes. We are sending Summer Duck and Little Muscle."

Old Smoke recognized the names of the two sachems, knew them both to be decidedly anti-British.

"So, we are sending spies instead of diplomats," Old Smoke remarked, knowing the reproof would stir his uncle's ire.

It did.

"Diplomats are always spies, nephew," Buffalo Hair shot back. "Summer Duck and Little Muscle will listen and speak, but they will also count soldiers and cannons. It is in our interest to know such things."

Old Smoke had no argument with this, but found himself wishing he could be among those to meet with Washington, to explain to him the sources of Shawnee disenchantment with the Long Knives and the British. The French Commander Contrecoeur had been willing to listen at his conference. Maybe Washington would too. He did not flatter himself that such a meeting would change anything, but it was always better for men to understand one another even if the inevitable outcome was mutual slaughter.

"There is little to fear from Major Washington and his Long Knives, Uncle," Old Smoke repeated. "If the British were serious, they would send a tested general, not the son of a tobacco farmer seeking adventure."

"When we talked before, you said he learned quickly," Buffalo Hair countered, reached for the pouch with the French scalp, then held it up in exhibit. "In the battle where this scalp was taken Washington gave the order to fire after surrounding the French. It was an easy victory. I would say your Major has done well."

Old Smoke's surprise must have shown in his face, because his uncle's leer lingered teasingly.

"Perhaps he has learned more than I give him credit for. But he is still a boy without experience. I suspect the ease of his first victory will make him headstrong and reckless. At his age, it would be difficult not to be tempted by pride."

Buffalo Hair shrugged and grinned wickedly.

"So much the better for us. Perhaps you will kill him in a great battle and add his scalp to your wardrobe."

"Collecting scalps does not interest me, Uncle. As I've told you many times before, I am a hunter, not a warrior," Old Smoke retorted reflexively, not ready to let his uncle conscript him into the *Compagnies franches* just yet. "I would rather not take sides."

Buffalo Hair's limbs fidgeted randomly like the popping lid of a steaming teapot. As was always the case in his quarrels with Old Smoke, his nerves were starting to percolate.

"I want you to fight with the Frenchmen," he finally managed to insist. "Your friend Striking Eagle has joined them at Fort Duquesne, as you should. They would welcome a man of your skills and articulation."

"I am sure they will welcome any who would die for their cause, but…"

"I want you to fight with the French!" shouted Buffalo Hair, rising shakily to his feet. "Would you shame me? Would you be seen as a coward by your own people?"

"I am not a coward."

"Then why will you not go?"

"I do not enjoy killing. I am not fascinated by death…as you are."

As tired and worn as their disputes were, they still rankled. Old Smoke could feel his heart pumping in his chest. Buffalo Hair was more violently affected. His breath came and went in gasps and snorts and the movements of his arms were wildly irregular, as if they had no strength of their own and were being manipulated by unseen strings. Finally, Buffalo Hair placed one hand against the cave entrance and composed himself.

"I seek only right justice for my beloved cousin. If my desire for vengeance is strong, it is because my grief is deep…" the distraught Shawnee sachem expounded, launching into the usual justifications for his compulsive killing habits. When he had finished gasping for breath, he turned to meet the gaze of his nephew. They were there confronting him, partially hidden in shadows, the flickering firelight dancing on their moist surfaces: the hypnotic eyes of his nephew glaring back at him like miniature candles in the dark. The two men stared at one another for a timeless moment, then Buffalo Hair made his way back to the chair rock and waited for his breath to catch up with his physical exertions.

"Perhaps you are right, Old Smoke. Perhaps I allow vengeance to play on my spirit too much," he said in an airy tone of conciliation. "I am distressed by the thought of the British stealing our land. If I knew they would be repulsed, my anxieties would be lessened. Perhaps I would not feel the need to seek further retribution for my cousin."

It was a veiled threat: If Old Smoke did not join the French, someone would die for the amusement of a wretched old man. But who would it be? Another young captive like Cornpicker? Someone he knew? There was nothing in his uncle's bestial face to tell him. If Buffalo Hair had a victim in mind, he would never reveal the person's identity until the last second. It was part of the game. And with the escape of Cornpicker, the old man's penchant for secrecy had become obsessive. He would tell no one. He would behave as always. He would kill when he got the chance.

Stirring the fire with a dead branch, Old Smoke said, "What you are saying then, Uncle, is that if I do not agree to your demands, you will kill someone."

Rather than scold his nephew's impertinence, Buffalo Hair replied, "Nephew, I am only telling you what you already know—that I am growing old and impatient…"

"You will not kill, then?"

The directness of the question shattered the brittle shell of pretense.

"I cannot promise that," Buffalo Hair said.

Old Smoke tossed the stick into the fire and stood, averting his gaze from his uncle.

"Uncle, I will do as you ask. But I will tell you this. It is possible I too may suffer anxiety if I find, in my absence, that you have not been able to control your own."

Allowing his words a moment to penetrate his uncle's consciousness, Old Smoke let his head revolve slowly toward the old man, then added, "Do you understand?"

Buffalo Hair chose to ignore the question, rising instead to embrace his nephew.

"I am glad we are finally in agreement, Old Smoke. It is not good that we bicker so often."

You could try compromise, Uncle. It is the standard by which civilized men are measured.

Despite their irreconcilable differences, Old Smoke warmly returned his uncle's embrace.

Retreating to arm's length, Buffalo Hair asked, "You will join

Contrecoeur then?"

"I will go to Fort Duquesne and offer my services."

Buffalo Hair paused, looking for loopholes that this revision of his request might allow Old Smoke to jump through. Ultimately he decided that Old Smoke would honor a promise, once made. A major concession having been made by the younger man, small talk became awkward. The nephew once more helped the uncle onto the horse, scattered the burning logs, and selected one with an unburned end. Using it as a lamp to illuminate the trail, he led them back to the rise where the trees stopped and the open field led down to the river. Night had arrived. Day had made good its escape and was no longer visible in the heavens.

"Old Smoke, stop!"

The Shawnee complied and turned to find Buffalo Hair looking wistfully at the western hill the sun had set behind a half-hour before.

"Do you really think there is a place such as Asia?"

"Yes."

"Have the whites gone there too?"

"The whites go everywhere, Uncle. It is their nature, as once it was ours."

$\mathfrak{C}$hapter $\mathfrak{E}$ight

Mr. John Washington
Bushfield, Virginia

Dear Jack,
This is to inform you that I am alive and, except for the hardships here and the hourly expectation of an attack by a superior French force, feeling well. It has been an exciting time. We have had a small engagement, with the result that 12 Frenchmen were killed and 2 or 3 of our own men. Fortunately, I escaped without a wound, although the right wing where I stood was exposed to and received all the enemy's fire. I heard the bullets whistle and, believe me, there is something charming in the sound.

Reports from several of our Indians scouts lead us to believe that a large body of men has gathered at the French fort but we shall, if they delay one more day, be prepared for them. We have already dug entrenchments and are constructing a palisaded fort, which I expect will be finished today.

I am hopeful of your good health and am looking forward to an early reunion.

$$\text{Your Loving Brother,}$$
$$\text{George}$$

Great Meadows
May 31st, 1754

June 2-14, 1754, Great Meadows

On returning from the Jumonville glen to Great Meadows, Lieutenant-Colonel George Washington found it difficult to brood further over the possibility of war. Too much was happening. The several appendages of the expeditionary force were coming together to smite the foe. More accurately, some of the military establishments that had promised to show up with men, equipment, and supplies, actually did. Whether or not they could be molded into a unified fighting force remained to be seen. Washington had hoped to leave that task to Joshua Fry, preoccupied as he was at the moment in supervising the construction of a stockade as a precaution against a French attack and, together with his officers, planning the next move to Redstone.

They arrived in three waves. The first to arrive on the second of June was a force of eighty to a hundred of the Half-Kings' Ohio Valley Indians. As was often the case with Indian allies, they brought their women and children with them, all of whom were in various stages of starvation. Consequently, the Indians consumed more than their share of food, depleting the already dwindling and inadequate reserves. It was a disturbing enough situation that Washington felt fully justified in sending a letter to Robert Dinwiddie emphasizing the critical need for supplies, a letter he had already written a hundred times and was getting tired of paraphrasing.

Although too small an upheaval to qualify as one of the three waves, Christopher Gist returned on the fifth of June from his meeting with the Governor at Winchester bearing assurances of support and the unpleasant news that Joshua Fry was dead.

His head spinning with the ramifications of a dead commanding officer, Washington gaped dumbfounded at the messenger.

"Dead! Colonel Fry is dead? How did that happen, Christopher?"

"He fell off his horse," Gist answered.

"Fell off his horse? You don't *die* from falling off a horse. I do it all the time and I'm not dead," Washington argued, trying desperately to convince Gist and himself that Fry could not possibly be dead.

The unruffled guide shrugged his shoulders and replied, "He was an old man, George, like me. And…well…he's dead."

So the young Colonel finally had to acknowledge that the expedition's commanding officer was dead. Long live the new commanding officer, whoever that might be! At the moment, he suddenly realized, it was he.

Clarification arrived on the ninth of June along with powder and ball, nine swivel guns, and the second contingent of the Virginia Regiment, a hundred fifteen strong led by Washington's former instructor in military science, Major George Muse. The Major approached his former pupil accompanied by the regiment's engineer, Captain Robert Stobo, a slim, striking young man from Glasgow who had made his fortune in Petersburg as an independent merchant and factor. The Captain, in turn, was accompanied by ten skilled servants, a wagonful of supplies, a hundred twenty-six gallons of Madeira wine and a regimental uniform that immediately caught Washington's discerning eye: a coat of excellent blue material faced and cuffed with scarlet and trimmed in silver. A scarlet waistcoat, a tricorne laced with silver thread, and blue breeches completed the elegant ensemble. It was not unlike the one Washington had stored away before the departure from Alexandria, but of finer quality. Military expedition or no, Captain Stobo intended to be a comfortable aristocrat.

After greetings and handshakes had been exchanged, a downcast Major Muse announced, "Colonel, I'm sorry to have to inform you that Colonel Fry is dead."

"Yes, Major, Mr. Gist already told me. He rode in a few days ago."

Visibly relieved, Muse responded with a buoyant, "I am also happy to inform you, Colonel Washington, that Governor Dinwiddie has seen fit to promote you to the temporary rank of full colonel. You will be in command of all Virginia forces until the new commander, Colonel Innes, arrives with three hundred troops from North Carolina."

"Colonel Innes?"

"Yes, Colonel James Innes. He is a Scotsman of good repute."

"Of course he is," Washington replied with a chuckle, not bothering to explain the source of his amusement. There were more

Scots than native Virginians on his staff.

Colonel Innes, said Muse, continuing with Dinwiddie's message, was "on his way." Washington received this news with mixed emotions. He was relieved to hear that some of the burdens of command would be lifted from his shoulders and that three hundred troops were coming, but was mistrustful of a message that left their arrival time open-ended. He felt strongly enough about it that, in his next letter to the Governor, he complained not only about the usual inadequacies—food, supplies, ammunition—but also about this uncertainty. Colonel James Innes, he reasoned, could be commander-in-chief only when he arrived at Great Meadows. *So please, Governor Dinwiddie, encourage the man to advance with the greatest possible dispatch.*

In his next letter, Dinwiddie confirmed Washington's promotion and promoted Muse to lieutenant-colonel, Stephen to major, and La Peyroney to ensign. Washington called a meeting of all the officers to establish pecking order and to plot the upcoming campaign. Aside from the forty or fifty Indians, only half of whom could be called able-bodied, British forces now numbered almost three hundred. The storehouse at Redstone Creek, Washington reasoned to his troops, was still the best place to begin an assault on Fort Duquesne. It was located strategically on the Monongahela River. The heavy artillery—to be supplied by two, as yet fanciful, New York companies that Dinwiddie had enlisted—could only be transported by water to the vicinity of the French fortress. The problem was getting there with three hundred troops, their equipment, and the promised artillery. The Youghiogheny River, situated between Great Meadows and the Monongahela, was less a river than a series of shallow pools connected by plunging rapids and falls. It was therefore unsuitable as means of transportation. The only alternative was to build a road. Yes, the Colonel admitted, many of the traders and settlers fleeing the French advance said it couldn't be done; the terrain was unsuitable. But it didn't matter; it had to be done. Washington's plan was to improve the existing road to Gist's place, regroup, then slice through the intervening sixteen miles of timber and ridge to Redstone Creek. The officers listened attentively to their Commander, groaned inwardly and joked outwardly at the thought of another grinding foray against the obstinate forest and yet another climb over yet another godawful mountain, and eventually acquiesced. Those who arrived with Washington had developed a tentative confidence in their leader. The newcomers were willing to give him the benefit of any doubt they might have. Besides, no one had a better plan.

The third and last wave to arrive—the hundred South Carolina and Georgia Independents—did so on the fourteenth of June. This smartly-dressed, crisp-stepping array of regulars was preceded by a less orderly herd of sixty cattle and a smaller drove of pack horses that emerged mooing and whinnying from the tree line at the eastern end of Great Meadows. They were driven by buckskin-clad men who, in addition to whooping at the tops of their lungs, were making every imaginable noise with their whips, guns, hats, and riding paraphernalia to keep the animals confined and moving. The sight was one Washington knew he would not forget. It was a new way, possibly the only way, to move large numbers of herd animals across this vast, often unfriendly, always contrary land: frighten them constantly and mercilessly into a controlled stampede.

At the end of the procession of Independent troops a carriage emerged pulled by two horses and trailing a third—a white stallion complete with saddle. Once into the clearing, the carriage stopped. The soldier serving as coachman stepped down, unhitched the white stallion, and opened the carriage door. A tall, rigid man who Washington assumed to be James Mackay, the Commander of the Independents, emerged brushing the wrinkles from his uniform and shouting to a nearby officer to halt the caravan and put the troops in an orderly state of ease. Mounting the stallion and taking a moment to thank his coachman, Mackay promptly nudged his steed in the direction of the awaiting Virginians.

Washington had decided his first meeting with the Captain of the Independents should be on horseback and in the presence of other officers. He chose Hogg, Muse, Stephen, Stobo, and Adjutant La Peyroney for that purpose; all but La Peyroney were mounted. One of Dinwiddie's recent letters had stated—nay warned—that Mackay had a King's commission. Washington should therefore demonstrate "suitable regard" for the Captain and would be held responsible for "any ill consequences of an unhappy disagreement." Washington could not help wondering why the Governor of Virginia felt compelled to urge his field commander to grovel at the feet of a stranger. He was about to find out because the straight-backed commanding officer of the Independents, his blunt chin and razor-thin lips thrust grandly forward, was at his side.

"Mr. Washington," Mackay said in a mellow baritone, his nostrils elevated and flaring. His enunciation carried with it a less than subtle note of disdain.

"Captain Mackay," Washington returned, saluting.

The haughty Mackay slowly scanned the encampment, his gaze finally coming to rest on the partially completed stockade Washington had ordered built as a precaution against a French attack.

"Is this to be a permanent fortification?"

The Colonel explained the stockade's transitory function and that the permanent base was to be at Redstone Creek, where a storehouse for weapons and supplies already existed. But Mackay remained fixated on the stockade.

"It's too close to the trees," he said, pointing to the southeast tree line. "An attacking force could pepper you with musket fire from that cover indefinitely without exposing itself. You've lost the advantage of the open field. The stockade should be moved back at least fifty yards into the open grassland."

Having finished offering unsolicited advice, Mackay kept his eyes on Washington. It was not exactly a glower or even a hostile stare, but the effrontery in the man's manner was obvious. The Virginia Colonel, percolating with inner agitation, struggled to check his temper.

"We will camp over there," Mackay announced bluntly, pointing to the gently sloped southwest section of Great Meadows and then spurring his horse in the same direction.

"Captain Mackay, we must speak. It is essential that we co-ordinate our activities…"

The Captain glanced back over his shoulder and said, "I will let you know when I'm ready, sir. My men are weary. We need to make camp."

"Captain, you must at least take the time to understand our plan for moving the base of operations to Redstone Creek. Otherwise, there can be no co-ordination between our forces. And we need to know how many of your men can be freed for the construction of roads..."

"As I have said, my men are weary," Mackay interjected curtly, then shook his head with feigned forbearance. "As for activities beyond their military duties, my men cannot be used unless they are paid a shilling per day."

"And where, Captain Mackay, do you expect me to find such wealth?"

"I don't, sir. I am merely informing you of the rules of our service, nothing more," Mackay replied.

Throughout the conversation the Independent Captain held his horse at a steady speed, a tacit gesture of dismissal. It was the final straw. Fuming, Washington whipped the sorrel and galloped to intercept his provocateur.

"Sir, we will speak now!" Washington cried, reining in his horse ten yards from the Carolinian.

Mackay halted, then turned to face the Virginia Commander. Scorn pervaded his attitude and posture but Mackay decided momentarily to set it aside and speak calmly—instructor to student. He had a point to make.

"Mr. Washington, we are an independent company, not a colonial militia. While we are citizens of South Carolina and Georgia, we are, nevertheless, members of His Majesty's armed forces. As such, we cannot—I *will not*—accept orders from a militia officer of any rank. Do you understand?"

Washington understood, but had his own point to make.

"Sir, there can be only one commanding officer of this expedition and, for the moment, I am he. You *will* obey my orders..."

"I will *not* obey, sir," Mackay insisted with an attitude bordering on contempt. "We will discuss the co-ordination of our activities, as you have requested. But as an officer of the King, I am not your subordinate. You are mine. Should matters arise which affect both our organizations, my orders will prevail. I ask again: Do you understand?"

The two men locked stares, the one projecting a pompous arrogance, the other quaking with anger and mortification. Even the sorrel under Washington could feel the tension in its rider. The horse pranced skittishly on the trampled summer grass, sensing a threat but unable to identify it. When Washington turned the animal about and dug his heels into its flanks, the anxious sorrel responded with enthusiasm. They were fleeing the danger; *it was good.*

His face flushed and his stomach wrenching with nausea, Washington trotted the horse past the line of officers he had brought with him and now wished he hadn't. Thankfully, their eyes were downcast and would not meet his. He could feel the fury within him intensify, then build to a crest as he tasted the bitter humiliation. Blinded by exasperation, the Commander was almost to his tent when he discovered La Peyroney behind him. The Adjutant's face was also red and flushed but for a different reason. He had been running.

"William," Washington said, barely managing to put his anger in check.

The new Ensign squirmed, searching for English words to soothe his superior's vexation. A recent immigrant to Virginia, La Peyroney had come from a family of notable, if poor, French Protestants, and looked like a stereotype of one: plain featured, sandy hair, possessed by a chronically underfed look.

"Sir, is there anything I can do?"

Washington did not reply, merely huffed as he removed his coat and entered his tent. La Peyroney followed at a distance.

"That bastard! That bloated, insolent, overbearing sonofabitch!" the Colonel bellowed, flinging the coat onto the cot at the far end of the tent. "Who the hell does he think he is? Who does he think we are? His slaves?"

Stunned by the language but not entirely surprised—others had told him of Washington's famous temper—La Peyroney hoped the questions were rhetorical because he had no intention of answering them.

Seeing the Ensign's uneasiness, the Colonel gripped him by the arms and, hurling the demon from his breast, said, "I'm sorry, William. I know you're a religious man. I promise to keep my remarks clean and to wash my mouth with soap when you're gone."

Washington followed up with a snicker, which the Ensign emulated with a taut, prim grin. Then the Virginian sat down on his cot and leaned forward, bracing his hands against his knees.

"William, sit down," Washington said, indicating a chair at the foot of the cot. La Peyroney complied. After gazing quizzically at the Ensign for a moment he went on: "You've been a soldier before, William. I wonder if I could ask your advice?"

He had indeed been Chevalier La Peyroney in France, so the Adjutant replied, "Yes, certainly."

"I have a problem," the Colonel began, then laughed again. "Actually, I have several problems. Captain Mackay is only the latest. But I'm not worried about him. He's an irritant, nothing more. If he doesn't want to co-operate he can go to…the devil."

Washington paused to assess La Peyroney's reaction and found the man unruffled, listening intently.

"I need to know how to pull this all together, William. I don't know half the officers, not personally at least. I need them to be with me," the Colonel told his friend, beseeching with hands and eyes as well as words.

"You will know them, Col-o-nel," La Peyroney assured. "Already we have fought with you against the French. There is a bond men form when together they face the possibility of violent death. When the others have fought with you, we will be a true army."

"What if we lose?"

It was La Peyroney's turn to laugh and respond with: "Then it does not matter if we are an army. We will be dead."

Yielding a polite snicker, Washington quickly became serious again. "The move to Redstone Creek. I've stayed up nights thinking about it, William. Is it the right thing to do? I think it is. I think we cannot operate successfully against the French from a pasture in the middle of nowhere, but I can't be sure. How can I get the sense of it? How can I know?"

"You can't."

Nonplused by the reply, Washington stood and pointed in the direction of the troop encampments and asked, "If I can't know, how can I convince them?"

"You can never know absolutely, but that is not important. What *is* important is that they think you know. You must speak to them forcefully and confidently as you have already done. You must convince them that your judgment is correct. If you can do that, half your problem is solved."

Throughout his discourse, the plain face of the Ensign maintained its stoic composure. His advice contained no homilies or appeals to right behavior, only a near Machiavellian commentary on what would work. It was an odd argument for a religious man to make. At this point Washington realized he did not fully understand William La Peyroney and that it was probably not a good idea to try. The Ensign, after all, was a Frenchman who was willing to kill Frenchmen. It might be unwise to probe too deeply into the motives of such a man.

"So, I should pretend?"

La Peyroney considered the question, then replied, "Pretense if you like, but you could think of it more...auspiciously...as creating a perspective of optimism."

"It's still pretense."

"Yes," La Peyroney admitted.

The Colonel strolled thoughtfully to the entrance of the tent, looked out, then returned to face La Peyroney.

"And how do I solve the other half of my problem: making the *right* decision?" he asked.

"By having excellent judgment, of course."

"Can you tell me how to do that?"

"No."

"That's the hard part."

A puzzled look came over La Peyroney's face.

"That's the *difficult* part," Washington rephrased.

"Ah...yes...*difficile*...difficult. Yes, yes, that *is* the hard part."

Conversing with a friend loosened the knot Mackay had tied in the young Colonel's nerves. They spoke of acquaintances, family, life, avoiding any talk of La Peyroney's past existence in France. Washington could not help reflecting on the other immigrants like La Peyroney he had met, many of whom were with him: Van Braam, the comically constructed Dutchman, Lewis, the huge Irishman, de Spiltdorph, the blond Swede with the violent grace of the Scandinavian, and, of course, the willful and ubiquitous Scots. In many ways, they were all malcontents of one stripe or another, as his own ancestors had been. They and their descendants would ultimately mix with the already potent ingredients of British and

German already simmering in the pot and create some kind of stew. But what would it be? Mixing eggs and milk always made an omelet, but what would a concoction of disgruntled English, German, Scotch, Irish, Scandinavian, Dutch and French produce? God only knew how many other peoples would come here seeking their fortunes or running for their lives. Who would they become? Some new race, perhaps, without a clear memory of its origins but with a vague sense of purpose.

The Colonel offered his Ensign some of the Madeira wine Robert Stobo had been so kind to present him as a gift. La Peyroney, as a Frenchman, accepted it with grace and enthusiasm. The visit and the casual conversation were exactly what the young Colonel needed. He acknowledged as much and thanked La Peyroney when the Ensign finally departed. Alone, Washington found the incident with Mackay lingering in his mind like a sore that would not heal. But he could now view it dispassionately and concluded that, although his own actions could be criticized, Mackay's were intolerable. Reluctant but resigned, he sat down at his desk with quill and paper to write Dinwiddie a letter about Mackay's behavior. No doubt the Governor would, in return, excoriate Washington for letting the situation get out of hand but it didn't matter. The Governor would be dutifully informed. The letter went quickly. It was not difficult to find words to describe Mackay's extraordinary behavior: "I can very confidently say that his absence would tend to the public advantage," he wrote, careful to avoid overstating his case. Finished, he placed the letter in an envelope, sealed it, and prepared it for posting. While he was in the mood, he decided to finish the account he'd begun in his journal of the encounter at the glen. In fifteen minutes he finished, scanned the summary for accuracy, and set the journal aside.

Drowsy from the wine and the strain of confrontation, Washington loosened his blouse and breeches and lay down for a nap. Normally, sleep would have been impossible in the bake-oven environment of a tent in midsummer, but he would think of Sally Fairfax until exhaustion overcame him. That would allay the discomfort; it always did. Though Sally was the wife of his best friend and next door neighbor, George William Fairfax, Washington felt no guilt. He did not know that what he felt was love.

She was in the flower garden at Belvoir, wearing an apricot lawn dress with a quilted petticoat and a straw milkmaid hat tied by velvet green ribbons. With a bouquet of freshly picked daisies in her arms, she was walking briskly away, but the suggestive glance she cast at him over one shoulder told him she would soon be back...

$\mathfrak{C}$hapter $\mathfrak{N}$ine

June 16, 1754, Great Meadows

he parade from Great Meadows was an all-Virginia spectacle: a double column of men, half of whom were bare-chested and armed with nothing but axes. Tanacharison and his people weren't yet ready to leave, Monacatoocha was in Logstown with his warriors and the ten French scalps trying to intimidate the Ohio tribes, and Mackay would not be coming. That much was clear. But the nine swivel cannons George Muse had brought would be coming and for that much Washington was grateful. The cannons were the closest thing they had to artillery.

In a final attempt at co-operation Washington sent a messenger to the Captain of the Independents with the password and countersign. Mackay refused to accept them. He would stay at Great Meadows while the Virginians slashed their way to Gist's place and from there to Redstone Creek. As far as Washington was concerned, Captain Mackay could go to Hades. The young Colonel permitted himself the dubious luxury of mouthing the words "Go to Hell" in the general direction of the southwest meadow, where the Independents were bivouacked. *But, come to think of it*, he sniggered inwardly, *the Captain will only be able to reach the netherworld if he pays his soldiers a shilling per day to take him there.* Mackay would be saved from eternal damnation by his own Scotch miserliness.

Still, Washington could not help envying Mackay. The Captain commanded a regiment of regulars, something the Virginian had always wanted to do. That morning, while the members of the Regiment were loading their equipment, feeding their animals, and forming themselves into a lumbering cavalcade of nondescripts,

Mackay was leading the Independents in the light infantry drill. Dressed in formal, green-faced, scarlet uniforms and high top, Canadian-style leather leggings called 'mitasses,' the Independents formed into two platoons, one to fire while the other reloaded, then the converse. The loading of charge and ball was only a simulation—ammunition was too scarce to waste—but it was a magnificent performance nonetheless. At the sharp, terse commands of Mackay and his officers, each man of the firing platoon dropped to one knee, aimed and fired in perfect unison while the men of the other platoon ticked clock-like through the reload sequence with a symmetry no less precise. It was a thing of beauty, more so in silence than it would have been in truth: a mime play, a portrait in motion, a ballet of violence.

As Washington watched the Independents march from the field to the beat of their adolescent drummer, he saw Robert Stobo and his entourage of servants approaching from another angle. Noting Washington's preoccupation with Mackay's smart-stepping regulars, the lean, elegantly-statured Stobo rode up beside his Commander and said, "We're not all the stubborn jackasses the Captain likes to make of himself, sir."

His reverie disrupted, Washington replied, "What?...Oh, no, no... In fact, I was just admiring Captain Mackay's troops..."

"They *are* well-trained lads, Colonel. I'll give 'em that..."

"I would have to disagree with your judgment, Captain," Washington interrupted, teasing. "You may not all be stubborn, but I've never met a Scotsman, from Robert Dinwiddie to Peter Hogg, who wasn't disagreeable in one way or another."

Stobo sat back in his saddle, playing the fool, and replied, "Why, Colonel, how can you say that? I, for one, am the most even-tempered lad you'd ever want to meet..."

"Suppose, Robert, I ordered you to send nine of your servants and half your Madeira back home?"

Stobo was aghast.

"That would be completely uncalled for, sir! I've paid for them all m'self, and for the horses and wagons that brought 'em to this God-forsaken place. There's no need..."

"You're quibbling with me, Robert..."

"Sir, I'm not quibblin'. I'm merely pointin' out that…"

"You're *quibbling*, and you have the temerity to tell me there is no ill-humor in you! Do I make my point?"

Stobo's full lips broke into broad smile of perfect teeth.

"Yes, Colonel. You have indeed made your point."

But Washington was not finished having his fun.

"Incidentally, Captain, I thought the men of Scotland were supposed to wear kilts," he said with mock seriousness. "With all the Scots in this army, I have yet to see a single kilt adorning anyone's fine figure, yours included. Why is that?"

Stobo leaned forward gripping his saddle horn, frowned, and replied, "Well, y'see, it's this country, sir. The citizens just don't understand…"

"Don't understand what?"

"The taverns, Colonel, the taverns," the Captain answered with a scowl. "We can't wear kilts into the taverns."

Sensing a punch line, Washington played the straight man.

"And why can't Scotsmen wear kilts into taverns in this country, Captain Stobo?"

"The big, burly gentlemen at the bar, sir," Stobo replied, again breaking out the toothy smile. "They always want to do one of two things: Knock us about—and they could get badly hurt tryin' such a thing—or buy us a drink and coax us up to the barmaid's quarters. They definitely *will* be sufferin' in agony if they try that!"

Both men enjoyed the joke so much that their clamorous laughter frightened the horses and deflected the eyes of passing Volunteers in their direction.

"And besides…besides, Colonel," the breathless Stobo stammered, "We wouldn't want to tempt the savages to be cuttin' off more than our scalps, now would we…Hah!"

More boisterous laughter caused more stares to be directed their way, but the horses finally realized nothing was amiss and merely snorted in complaint. The passing wayfarers who saw the two revelers enjoying themselves for no apparent reason included Christopher Gist and William La Peyroney, who were riding alongside the winding columns of Volunteers. Gist's puzzlement was framed on his face. La Peyroney may have felt a similar perplexity, but it didn't show.

"Gentlemen, is our army such a comic sight?" Gist stopped to ask. "What's so funny?"

"Nothing, Christopher, nothing," Washington declared, trying to control himself.

"What d'you mean *nothin'*, sir?" Stobo guffawed, intentionally misinterpreting Washington's statement. "Are a Scotsman's private parts to be reckoned as *nothin*? I, for one, would dearly notice their absence. It's a harsh man you are, Colonel…a *harsh* man…"

After the source of the merriment was explained to Gist and La Peyroney, all four men crowed with glee. Then, still trying to catch his breath, Stobo said, "But to answer your question, Mr. Gist: No, I wouldn't say there's much that's comic out here, not much at all, except maybe for that pathetic little thing over there."

As he spoke, Stobo pointed to the fifty foot circular stockade of split oak logs planted upright in the ground a hundred yards to the southeast. At that distance, the stockade and the fifteen-foot square log storehouse in its center did not look like much. Tanacharison himself, who had seen many of the French and English forts on the Appalachian and Canadian frontiers, referred to it as "that little thing in the meadow." Among the men who had built it, there had been some tongue-in-cheek wagering on how many Frenchmen it would take to push it over.

"Gentlemen," Stobo proclaimed solemnly, placing his hat over his heart and bowing his head. "I think it's time we gave our wee fortress a name, don't you?"

"A name?" Gist scoffed. "It's too insignificant to have a name."

"Aye, she is a tiny lass. But, God help us, we may one day have to fight behind her walls," Stobo reasoned. "She'll be a lot friendlier if we can call her by some decent name. Otherwise, she's just a sorry waif."

"Fort Prince George is out. That would be bad luck," Washington offered, then challenged, "What then? Fort Dinwiddie? Fort Fry?"

Christopher Gist shook his head, said, "Too grand. A pathetic little fort should have a pathetic little name, like Fort *Ad Hoc* or Fort Last Resort."

"I have it…I have it…" Stobo said, suddenly exuberant. "I can think of only one reason ever to cram our three hundred wretched bodies into that cramped little hovel…"

Stobo waited expectantly for their imaginations to place bets.

"Fort Desperation?" Washington tried.

Stobo shook his head.

"Fort Hopeless? Fort Forlorn?" proposed Gist.

"No…no…there's too much gloom in you, Christopher. Here's a clue: Who is the fine lady we know as Invention's mother?"

"Necessity!" Gist exclaimed. "Fort Necessity!"

Stobo raised his arms triumphantly.

"Exactly!" he affirmed.

It was agreed. The little stockade, for posterity's sake, would be called Fort Necessity. It was a name suited to both its stature and purpose: *To be used only in the event of an emergency.*

The shy La Peyroney had a final, unintentionally cryptic word to say: "Let's pray necessity is not too demanding."

Because he said it with a timid smile, the others politely grinned back. It was then that Southy Hazlip, one of the Volunteers charged with maintaining the wagons, walked up with a hot, irritated expression on his ruddy, Celtic features. Saluting Washington, he announced, "Sir, one 'a the wagons broke a wheel."

"Southy, we aren't even out of the meadow yet," the exasperated Colonel replied.

Southy shrugged fatalistically.

"Do we have a spare wheel?" Washington asked, wishing now that he'd bought Hezekiah Bennett's three-wheeler for spare parts.

"No, we'll have to fix the broke one. Take maybe an hour."

It was a minor setback but an inauspicious omen. As Hazlip returned to his wagon, Washington turned to his colleagues.

"Back to reality, gentlemen," he said in a tone of troubled resignation. "Redstone Creek is a long way off."

June 25, 1754, Gist's Plantation

Washington's body and spirit were utterly exhausted. Arriving at Gist's Plantation after the arduous trek from Great Meadows, he had hoped for a respite to recover his strength. But his invitations for the Ohio Valley chiefs to meet with him at Gist's place—a collection of log buildings and storehouses at the foothills of Chestnut Ridge—had borne fruit, of a sort. As he searched the assembled faces of the delegates on this, the third day of the conference, he found disinterest, suppressed hostility, and, in the case of the eight uninvited Mingoes from Fort Duquesne, open confrontation. It was obvious that this octet of swarthy, saturnine savages had no other purpose than intelligence gathering for the French. Although Washington would have liked nothing better than to boot their arses out of camp and down the mountain, the rules of Indian etiquette would not permit it.

Weary and discouraged, the Colonel was nevertheless impressed by the diversity and outright strangeness of the delegates who, excluding the Mingo spies, were about thirty in number. They differed not only in dress and ornamentation but in attitude. The uncommunicative Shawnee delegates were almost as doleful as the Mingo spies, but were at least attentive. Two Delaware sachems, Shingiss and Delaware George, vowed eternal fealty between their people and the British, but only if no one else knew about it. Having rested at Great Meadows, Tanacharison and his braves were happy to travel the thirteen miles of newly-widened road to attend the conference. Among them was a handsome Mohawk with the quixotic name of Moses the Song, a brother-in-law of Monacatoocha, who was mysteriously absent. Of course, the Virginians were expected to feed the delegates.

By far the most bizarre of the attendees was the man standing at the south pole of the circle of delegates and serving as Washington's interpreter. His name was Andrew Montour. He had arrived with Muse and the second wave of the Virginia Regiment along with his friend and associate, the loquacious and boastful George Croghan. As he watched and waited for Montour to finish translating the portion of the speech he had just delivered, Washington could not escape the feeling that the man was not real. A rational god would not have created an Andrew Montour.

The son of an Oneida Chief and a French-Indian mother who taught her son that Christ was a Frenchman who had been crucified by the British, Montour nevertheless chose the English side, perhaps reacting against his mother's gross tabloid interpretation of the biblical story. Montour was a patchwork of white and Indian characteristics. He looked like and, when not drunk, behaved like a quiet, somewhat shy white man. Preferring brightly-colored European clothes, he dressed himself like a ragamuffin, never deigning to tuck in a shirttail, and bedecked himself with necklaces, bracelets, and brass pendants that hung from multiple, Iroquois-style ear slits. A forehead colored red and a face encircled by bear grease paint completed the disguise of his European features. Andrew Montour's appearance was more than enigmatic: It bespoke of a man who did not know, could not decide, or preferred to conceal, who he was. And yet he was highly intelligent, was fluent in French, English, and numerous Indian tongues, and was a respected advisor in both white and Indian circles of power. There was no doubt about it. Andrew Montour was a figment of Washington's imagination, but one he would have to respect until the hallucination dispersed.

For some reason Montour had stopped talking and was looking at Washington. *Oh, it's my turn.* He quickly inhaled some proselytizing air.

"My children, we must hold fast to the chain of friendship which binds us," the Colonel began, intertwining the platitudes and metaphors of sundry previous speeches into the plush rhetorical style the Indians loved to taste, if not always to swallow. Then he glanced askance at the Mingo spies and warned, "Those who do not join us will be responsible for the consequences..."

If there was any doubt whether the Mingoes had been listening it was instantly erased. Their expressions changed from mysterious to openly hostile. Washington noted several angry glares directed his way. *Well, gentlemen,* he thought, *you can't expect to come here, eat our food, spy on us, and not be subjected to the occasional insult.*

He ended the speech with an appeal that the Indians bring their families under the protection of his arms while their warriors and young men unite in the common cause against the French. Then he joined Montour and Croghan in distributing the few gifts they had managed to haul over the mountains with the second contingent of the Virginia Regiment. After making a few mandatory social calls, Washington let the more talented and better known Croghan assume responsibility for the amenities and took a stroll with Montour.

"Well, how did I do, Andrew?" he asked.

The European face peered out at Washington through its bear grease frame and between the random strands of wavy brown hair covering it like camouflage. Taking a deep breath, Montour said, "It was a good speech, Colonel. I took the liberty of fixing it where I thought improvements were called for. I hope you don't mind."

Washington gestured his approval.

"But you have to realize," Montour continued, "that these people have eyes and ears and stomachs just as you and I do. They can see you have only twenty-six cattle left and that your horses are worn out. Their stomachs are not impressed by parched corn and lean beef..."

"We do what we can, Andrew. I have to feed our men too..."

"That's not the point, Colonel. It's not the point at all," Montour implored in a tone annoyingly close to desperation. "The chiefs have been to the forks. They've watched soldiers march and prepare for war. And they've enjoyed the food and liquor of a well-supplied French garrison..."

"Is that all their loyalty depends on—which side can fill their bellies the fullest?" Washington snapped caustically.

Montour took a step back, his Indian temperament bristling to the surface.

"That's not fair, Colonel. No matter what happens, you and I can go back to Williamsburg. They can't. They have to make peace with the victor of this...war, whoever that might be. Or, as you've said yourself, suffer the consequences."

Washington knew Montour was right and instantly regretted his rash declaration. His was such a frustrating command, with so much potential for success if only things would go right! *If* only Innes would arrive in time to make a difference. *If* only the New York regiments would get here with their much needed artillery. *If* only John Mackay would co-operate. *If* only John Carlyle would keep his promises to send supplies and equipment. There was an overabundance of *ifs* plaguing this mission.

"I'm sorry, Andrew. There's too much on my mind, I'm afraid," the Colonel apologized, then remembered La Peyroney's dictum to present an optimistic front. "John Carlyle assures me that supplies are on the way."

What Carlyle had really said in his latest communication was that he hoped he could find enough money to cover the Volunteers' back pay and would soon have enough flour to fill a few wagons. Responding to a request for tools, Carlyle had encouraged Washington to make his own from whatever iron could be scrounged around camp. What did the man expect him to do—set up a forge while he prepared for battle? It was madness.

Either out of politeness or lacking a sense of irony Montour declined to respond. Instead he changed the subject.

"The road seems to be coming along well, Colonel," he said laconically.

"Yes, Captain Lewis and his men have completed eight miles of it. There's that much more to clear before we reach Redstone, though."

Montour nodded, became silent and stared off in the direction of the twenty-six cattle grazing in the hilly pasture next to Gist's main building. Washington wondered if he was performing some sort of mental calculation of the nourishment needed by men felling trees, blasting rock, and laying corduroy spans over swampland versus the nourishment contained in the four-hoofed packages lazily lounging in the pasture. Whether the equation balanced or not was not at all clear. But Montour could not help him with that problem.

"Do you think they'll stay, Andrew?"

He meant the Indians, of course.

Without looking at his strolling companion, Montour answered, "Some will. Some will disappear overnight. Others will seem to be co-operating and then not return on some errand you've sent them on. It all depends on how they feel about your chances."

"I haven't seen Monacatoocha for a while. Have you?"

"No...I haven't," Montour replied without embellishment. It was difficult for either man to believe the Oneida chieftain had abandoned them, even harder to discuss the possibility.

"Colonel, have you ever been under attack?"

Montour framed it as a simple question but Washington's first reaction was to see it as an aspersion on his military experience. He was about to claim the Jumonville glen incident as an example but realized it did not qualify: He had been the attacker there, not the besieged. The only time he had ever felt himself under attack was by the impersonal forces of the hurricane that had assaulted the ship in which his half-brother Lawrence and he had sailed to Barbados. They survived the hurricane but the tropical weather had little beneficial effect on Lawrence's tuberculosis—he died the following year. But this was not what Montour meant either.

"No, I've never been under attack," the Colonel admitted, knowing Montour was about to give him some advice.

"Resisting a siege is in principle a simple matter. It takes only food, water, ammunition and protection. If you lack any one of these the enemy will simply camp himself on your doorstep and wait for you to come out, which you will...eventually. Because of this, withstanding a siege takes more fortitude than bravery and cannot be done without planning."

"Andrew, I appreciate your advice but our plan is to prepare for an attack on Fort Duquesne when our troops and supplies arrive..."

"And if they don't, Colonel, what will you do then?" Montour wanted to know, his iron gaze striking the Colonel like a hammer blow. "What if the French attack with superior numbers and firepower as we hear almost every day they have the power to do?"

Montour paused, glancing away as if to settle his passions, then turned his gaze—less fervid than before—back to Washington.

"I think it's time to give serious thought to a plan for retreat, Colonel. I'll do my best to convince the Indians to stay but it's dangerous to push on blindly. You should at least consider it."

"But if we retreat, the Indians will abandon us."

"Yes, they will," Montour replied without hesitation.

The Colonel waited for Montour to present further arguments to reinforce his position or to leave a crack in his logic that Washington could exploit to his advantage. But Montour gave no further explication; he was not playing that game. The man with the bizarre facade had in fact the stronger sense of reality.

"Can I depend on you and your men?" Washington asked, referring to the eighteen frontiersmen Montour had brought with him to serve as scouts and rangers.

"I'll stay," Montour said. "If the men decide to leave, they'll be the last to go."

It was as much of a commitment as he could expect. Montour's free-spirited fur traders and woodsmen were almost as ungovernable as the Indians. The two men took their leave of one another. Washington stood quietly mulling over his alternatives, then watched as the cook and his helper led another precious cow away to be slaughtered for the evening meal. It was a depressing sight.

Chapter Ten

June 27, 1754, Chiningue

"Look, Old Smoke," Deep Water shouted, dropping his fishing pole into the canoe as he pointed a wavering finger at the sky east of the Shawnee village.

When Old Smoke first beheld the black-like-coal smoke rising above the forest canopy he gasped, fearful that the village was on fire. But then he gauged the distance to the smoke and the amber glow beneath and realized it was not. When he scanned the riverbank and saw the flotilla of elm bark canoes moving from the north shore and heading east he knew what was happening.

"Are our houses burning?" Deep Water asked, his glassy eyes dancing in their sockets like jumping beans.

Old Smoke pulled in his fishing line, then placed it and his fishing pole next to the day's catch of bass, trout, and carp. The latter, the most plentiful in the river but repellent to humans, would be dried and fed to the horses.

"No, the grandfathers are leaving," Old Smoke said, showing Deep Water the canoes he had spotted. "They're burning their own village."

Although he was a slave, Deep Water's allegiance was with the Shawnee. He was aware of the festering animosity between his tribe and their overlords, the Iroquois.

"That *is* good, isn't it?" he said with naive glee.

"Tomorrow it will be good," Old Smoke said enigmatically. "Today it is not. Get your paddle, Deep Water, and help me row to shore."

Bewildered, the young black boy shelved his curiosity and did as he was told. Surveying the local scene as he rowed, Old Smoke noted clumps of gawkers on the shoreline and among the other fishermen who had been quietly enjoying a lazy afternoon on the flat, green surface of the Ohio River. Whatever recruits he could assemble would have to come from the shore gawkers. If events transpired as he feared they might, there would not be enough time to coax the fishermen in. Catching sight of two turkey buzzards making figure-eights in the sky, he wondered if they were merely curious or were contemplating their next meal.

As soon as the canoe struck the bed of sandstone pebbles that comprised the shore Old Smoke leaped out and beached it. Why was he the only one who saw the danger? Had his people been subservient to the Iroquois so long they could no longer think of their own, independent interests? If his interpretation of the Iroquois evacuation was correct and they were departing Chiningue to support the British, he knew they would burn not only their own homes but also those of any tribe they perceived to be a potential enemy, like the vexatious Shawnee. At least they would try.

"Deep Water, go to the longhouse and tell Short Leg and Mud Face to get everyone out of the village," Old Smoke shouted at the perplexed youngster.

"Why, Old Smoke, what's the matter?" Deep Water stammered.

"Just do it," Old Smoke said with quiet intensity. "I don't have time to explain...Please."

Knowing Deep Water would obey, Old Smoke left him and began searching for candidates to help him defend the village. Most of those present were women and old men gutting fish, laying them out on racks to dry and engaging in the kinds of activities Shawnee braves and sachems considered beneath their dignity. And most of these were blithely enjoying the unexpected entertainment provided by the blaze next door. Old Smoke spotted a group of adolescent boys crafting fish hooks and poles and ran toward them.

"Thick Belly, Seven Trees, I need your help. Get some horses and follow me."

Thick Belly, a short, squat thirteen year old with the same, sallow complexion as the fish spread out on the rack behind him, replied, "What do you want *us* for, Old Smoke? We're busy..."

"Right now," Old Smoke implored, the urgency in his voice unambiguous. "The grandfathers are coming to burn our village."

Without waiting to see if his entreaties had stirred the youths into action, Old Smoke turned and streaked for the corral. There he took and mounted the first horse he could find, a dappled gray mare. Leaning forward to steady himself, he dug his heels into its flanks. Startled, the animal tensed and then shot forward, sensing the urgency driving its rider.

There were only two good paths between the Shawnee and Iroquois settlements at Chiningue: the one along the riverbank above the rocky shore and another through the woods farther north. Because it was more direct, Old Smoke took the woodland route, reasoning that whatever Iroquois were coming to burn the village would want to rejoin the rest of the fleeing tribe as soon as they had demonstrated their bravery. The woodland route would be quicker and furnish more concealment. Using the gentle touch of his palms on the gray's neck to steer, Old Smoke passed the northern wall of the stockade fence surrounding the village and headed into the woods. Because the path was narrow and strewn with rocks and surface roots, he had to slow the horse to a canter as he searched for signs of intruders. They were not long in coming. He heard the shrill war whoops before he actually saw the band of Iroquois youth running toward him, their torches raised overhead.

Old Smoke heaved a sigh of relief as he realized that, although they numbered at least twenty, all on foot, they were all boys and, except for the torches, were weaponless. It was not an organized raid and had the look of a rite of passage, something to absorb adolescent aggressiveness while parents attended to the more pressing business of evacuating a village. But his relief was not complete. It suddenly dawned on him that, in his haste to head off the arsonists, he had forgotten to bring a weapon. With calm but hurried deliberation he dismounted and found a dead oak branch. After hastily trimming it to suit his needs he remounted the gray and, wielding his new club, cautiously approached the shapeless phalanx of would-be warriors. By this time the youths had spotted him and slowed to a guarded walk themselves. Their leader—or at least the point man—was within twenty meters of Old Smoke before he came to a reluctant halt. The boy was mostly naked, his body covered in a war paint veneer that included black eye circles on an otherwise crimson face and, except for a rude disposition, reminded Old Smoke of Striking Eagle.

"Go back," Old Smoke said, tightening his grip on the club with a theatrical flare.

He could see doubt in their frenetic faces. They hadn't expected to be challenged in this sojourn to glory. But fear was not a part of their vexation. Their high-strung restlessness probably came from working themselves into a frenzy around a bonfire until their spirits were overwhelmed by rage and their minds drained of reason. Beneath brows arched in grim resolve Old Smoke looked down at this pack of boys-become-beasts. A knot of fear squeezed at his stomach. If they dragged him from the horse they would kill him. Therefore, he must stay on the horse.

The tall youth who looked like Striking Eagle made a move to Old Smoke's left.

This way, horse.

The Shawnee nudged the gray in the same direction and easily checked the boy, who collided with the horse's right shoulder and fell to the ground, mortified and dazed, but otherwise unharmed.

"Go back, there is nothing for you here," Old Smoke declared with icy determination.

Two other youths took the opportunity presented by Old Smoke's leftward stratagem to dash around his right flank. Old Smoke saw them and doubled back, noting with a thrill of satisfaction that the horse and he were now one. He had only to flex his thigh muscles and lean one way or the other to make the mare respond. This time there was more violence. The pair had gotten a head start so the Shawnee was forced to give chase. Easily closing the gap, Old Smoke rode right into the trailing boy. One of the horse's hooves tramped on the boy's foot and sent him squealing into the brush. The other boy he simply clubbed and sent sprawling to the ground.

Hearing the whoops and cries of the remaining youths closing in on him from behind, Old Smoke retreated thirty meters and took a quick glance to see if help was coming. *Nothing yet.* Turning the horse, he charged the oncoming horde, picking the front runners as prime targets. The lead boy caromed off the horse's flanks but the next managed to grab hold of the Shawnee's breechclout and swing himself partially aboard. Old Smoke doubled his fist into a ball and struck the boy underneath his right ear between the jaw and the neck. The youth immediately crumpled to the ground, unconscious.

Old Smoke continued retreating and attacking, preventing his opponents from re-forming into the coherent if untidy salient they had once been. But it could only be a holding action. Some of the youths were bleeding, others limping, but none—even the one he had knocked unconscious was back on his feet—had been put out of commission. And his successive retreats had forced him back to the edge of the woods, with the village only fifty meters behind.

As he prepared for his next charge, wondering fitfully what had happened to Thick Belly and Seven Trees, Old Smoke heard another cacophony of agitated voices. Not war whoops, just a chorus of voices with a strident edge to them. The dull roar came from his rear and was growing in intensity. Before he could determine the source of the commotion, he saw the first signs of true fear dawn on the faces of the Iroquois youths he had been sparring with. Risking a break in his surveillance, he turned to find what appeared to be the entire citizenry of the Shawnee village approaching on a broad front with a disheveled and irascible Buffalo Hair leading them. Consisting mostly of women, children, and old men wielding farm implements, stones and makeshift spears, the crowd included a few of the younger men and boys who had not gone out for the day's hunt or who had already returned. It was undoubtedly these citizens, especially those with muskets raised and leveled, who were responsible for the masks of stark terror now twisting the faces of the Iroquois.

Old Smoke seized the moment to parade before the raiding party like a war chief reviewing his braves, except that his purpose was to instill fear, not courage. Still rabid with the bravado inspired by their war dance, the youths glared from Old Smoke to the crowd, reluctant to abandon their glory quest.

"Put the torches down. Return to your people," Old Smoke implored, coloring his voice with empathy—a big brother advising his siblings. "There is no shame in going back. If you don't, you will surely die."

Stating the obvious had a chilling effect on their attitudes.

Whatever hostility remained in the collective will of the Iroquois dispersed into thin air like mist from a waterfall. The first to waver was the one who looked like Striking Eagle. Keeping his torch as a final, futile act of defiance, he turned and, at first, strolled casually away, as if he had simply changed his mind about the whole thing. The others followed suit. Soon the stroll became a jog and the jog a footrace, until the Iroquois were in full retreat. Not a single one looked back. The crowd jeered and cheered in a dissonant clamor of outrage and joy. The grandfathers were gone. *Good riddance.*

Old Smoke dismounted the gray and made his way to its front.

"Good horse. Good horse," he whispered softly into its ear as he patted and caressed its sweaty jowls. The gray snorted anxiously, then settled.

Dressed in nothing but a bear fur robe and moccasins, a grumpy Buffalo Hair strode ahead of the crowd, barely acknowledging Old Smoke as he passed, his fist in the air and a menacing expression on his hoary face.

"Wretched, foul-smelling issue of *Malsum*, the devil *manitou!*" he grumbled in a resonant but unmelodious bass. With his inclement disposition and affronted dignity, Buffalo Hair could have been the god *Menabozho* himself, rudely awakened from a comfortable night's sleep behind the farthest mountain.

"Putrid maggots of the sand fly!" he shouted, shaking his raised fist at the retreating Iroquois. "Stinking offal of the *pukwudjinnies.* I spit on you! Do you hear? I spit on you!"

Which he did, or tried to. His lexicon of woodland spirit metaphors exhausted, Buffalo Hair joined Old Smoke and the circle of admirers that had begun to gather around him.

"Uncle, you look like you just woke up. Were you asleep?" Old Smoke gibed.

"I am an old man. It is my privilege to sleep," Buffalo Hair replied with no moderation of his ill humor. He did indeed look old and tired without the splendid paraphernalia he normally wore in public.

"The path by the river. Did anyone…"

It was not Buffalo Hair but his aunt, Short Leg, who answered, "When Thick Belly and Seven Trees saw where you were going, they decided to scout the river trail. Not many were coming that way. They were easily chased off.''

It was the first he had noticed his aunt, who was not so much smiling at him as beaming with pride. With her were Deep Water and Mud Face, who *were* smiling, Deep Water from beneath Old Smoke's eagle feather, the trophy Old Smoke had awarded him for *la crosse*. *Have I ever seen a smile between Short Leg's broad cheekbones or is smiling a talent her face has forgotten?*

The crowd was pressing close. They wanted to congratulate him, praise him, tell him how bravely he had behaved against the Iroquois raiding party. It was a new experience for Old Smoke. He had never been a hero before. Oddly, the only person not in a festive mood was Buffalo Hair, whose disposition seemed somehow out of kilter. Why he should even notice his uncle's aberrant mood Old Smoke could not adequately explain to himself. How a man of such extreme contrasts—respected diplomat and recreational murderer—could present to his fellow man anything resembling a normal personality defied the natural laws of human behavior. The old man was a physical and spiritual freak. Despite this, the Buffalo Hair personage was an established, identifiable quantity and this was not quite it. He seemed ill at ease with the throng of admirers now clustering around Old Smoke. He would inject himself into a conversation, be politely rebuffed, sulk, and try again. Then Old Smoke understood: Buffalo Hair considered it to be his place, not Old Smoke's, to receive adulation. The old man sensed and dreaded the loss of authority it might portend. His uncle was used to controlling a situation, not being controlled by it or by an often-disagreeable nephew.

There might be an advantage here.

Old Smoke continued to enjoy the moment, assiduously avoiding any contact with his uncle. He wanted, expected, the old man to come to him. He watched with amusement as the Shawnee boys rushed forward, launching their rocks, sticks, and arrows at a foe that had vanished ten minutes ago. When Deep Water, proudly sporting Old Smoke's eagle feather, began mimicking their actions, Old Smoke grabbed the nimble black boy and raised him overhead. The crowd cheered. Deep Water, surprised and flustered, could only express his awe with a wide, white grin.

Good. Good. Deep Water is no longer a stranger. Good.

After he lowered Deep Water, Old Smoke saw his uncle approaching, stern-faced and wary.

"Nephew, it is time for you to go," Buffalo Hair said, expecting an argument.

"I agree. It is time," Old Smoke replied, not deigning to give him one.

But before I go to join the French, Uncle, I will speak with Short Leg. She will be my spy. And it is you she will watch.

June 28, 1754, Gist's plantation

He came in the late evening, a hot, sultry one, with overcast so heavy the moon was no more than a blur of luminescence behind a drab scrim of clouds. His name was Gokhoos, he said through Andrew Montour, who, with Washington and a few of the officers and frontiersmen, was enjoying rum and raucous conversation around a small campfire. Gokhoos wore only a breechclout and moccasins and was breathing hard.

"Monacatoocha has burned his village at Chiningue and is taking his people to Redstone," Andrew Montour said, translating the words of Gokhoos.

So, Monacatoocha did not abandon us, Washington observed. It was good news but not the kind that would require sending a runner to him in the middle of the night. *Why is Montour so tense?*

"Is there more?" Washington asked diffidently.

"Gokhoos says they docked their canoes near the forks and doubled back to the French fort. Contrecoeur has his reinforcements and is about ready to leave."

"How many?"

"Eight hundred soldiers and four hundred Indians, mostly from the northern tribes. They have two to three hundred boats to carry them."

Twelve hundred! That was nearly four times the number of fighting men he had.

"When?"

Montour posed the question to Gokhoos, who made a gesture at the sky and a fitful reply to the translator. Their curiosity aroused, several of the men around the campfire gathered around the animated messenger.

"Soon, he says. Maybe tomorrow, maybe three days," Montour responded without further elaboration.

By this time, most of those enjoying the evening's respite knew something was afoot and were listening attentively. Among them were William La Peyroney and Robert Stobo.

"William, send a runner to Captain Lewis and tell him to bring his men and equipment back in the morning. Robert, do you think you could find the words to persuade Captain Mackay to come over? We need to have a war council."

"I'll use my best brogue, and maybe a selection of Gaelic curses. Would you prefer that I deliver them in Scotch or English, Colonel?"

As he was enjoying Stobo's sarcasm, Washington suddenly realized he had sent all the teams of horses, except for those Lewis was using for road-clearing, back to Great Meadows to wait for supplies from Wills Creek. It would be several days before they could be returned and loaded with the nine swivel cannons plus powder and shot. They had to have the cannons: A defense against twelve hundred of the enemy would be impossible without them. Washington cursed his lack of foresight and looked to see if Montour was gearing himself up to deliver another barrage of criticism. But the strange half-breed was still conversing with Gokhoos and seemed to have other things on his mind.

"I think you all understand what this means," Washington said, turning his attention to the anxious faces surrounding him. "We will not be pushing on to Redstone."

Hush. Chatter. Then another hush.

"What are we goin' to do, Colonel?" an ensign from Hogg's company inquired uneasily.

He didn't know.

"We'll discuss it at the war council in the morning. Pass the word to the other officers to be there, and to get a good night's sleep," Washington said with as much confidence as he could muster.

But his true reaction was dangerously close to despair, a reaction that sent a cold shudder down his spine. It was not a lack of courage that gripped him—Washington had more of that than a sensible man would want—but a recognition that he might actually fail. As a leader, he felt inadequate. He had been indecisive and, in the end, confused. Those shortcomings could not be remedied overnight. But he might, if he wrapped his thoughts around the character he had chosen to play, give a tolerable imitation of a leader. The first person he had to convince was himself. It would be a challenging performance.

June 28, 1754, Fort Duquesne

Despite the fuss being made by Captain Louis Ecuyer, the Sieur de Villiers and older half-brother of the slain Jumonville, Contrecoeur could not keep his eyes off the least likely pair of comrades he had ever encountered: the dwarf, Jolicoeur Bonin, and the giant Shawnee who called himself Striking Eagle. Standing on the shore of the Allegheny River downstream of an assembled force of six hundred marines and a hundred Indians loaded into canoes and bateaux, Bonin was launching empty wine bottles into the water for the big Indian to shoot at. It had been Contrecoeur's own suggestion, of course, an alternative to letting him exterminate the swimming squirrels one by one. But the Commander of Fort Duquesne had expected the Shawnee eventually to lose interest. He hadn't, and Contrecoeur had encouraged Bonin to take the young man under his wing and simultaneously calm him down and teach him how to fire a musket with some degree of accuracy. Bonin had succeeded in the latter but not the former and had, in the process, become Striking Eagle's friend. They had even managed to learn bits and pieces of each other's language.

"Captain Contrecoeur, you *must* give me command of this campaign," the enraged and frustrated Villiers insisted with set jaw and clenched teeth. "It is my right. I am the brother of the Sieur de Jumonville!"

As Villiers spoke, La Salle the terrier detected a threat to his master, and yapped incessantly at the unfamiliar Captain. From his sentinel position at Contrecoeur's feet, La Salle was prepared to bark at any creature, large or small.

Villiers outranked the battalion's designated commander, Le

Mercier, and, since the northern Indians he had brought from Canada were loyal to him alone, there was more than an ample rationale for transferring command to him. Contrecoeur was inclined to accede to Villier's demand. He was, after all, 'le Grand Villiers,' a genuine hero who had already fought one war against the British in Acadia and had been with the Celeron de Blainville in the 1749 expedition down the Ohio River. That famous sojourn was the basis for the French claim to all lands 'drained' by that westward-meandering stream. Captain Villiers definitely had the credentials, but Contrecoeur was concerned that he might not have the good judgment to lead *this* expedition. Diplomacy in such matters was always a tortuous maze; it could entrap one side as easily as the other.

Contrecoeur glanced at the stout Le Mercier, who, with another officer assigned to the mission, Captain Charles-Jacques Lemoine de Longueuil, was standing on the dock next to the escapee Mouceau. Le Mercier's attention, like that of everyone but Villiers and now Contrecoeur, was focused on the skeet shoot being conducted by Bonin and the magnificent Shawnee.

"Francois, could you come over here..." Contrecoeur began. He was interrupted by the blast of a musket, the sound of shattering glass, and a roar of admiration from the marines waiting restlessly in their boats. Striking Eagle had once more hit his target.

Le Mercier heard the truncated call and came over, accompanied by Mouceau. The Sergeant was uneasy in the presence of so many captains. The rank of Captain being the highest attainable in the *Compagnies franches de la Marine*, the enlisted soldier could never be entirely sure of the proper pecking order in the officer corps.

"Yes, Captain," Le Mercier replied.

Contrecoeur unconsciously drew himself to his full military height.

"Francois, the Sieur de Villiers has requested that he be placed in charge of this expedition. I am sure you can appreciate his reasons. Nevertheless, you have been appointed its commander and I am reluctant to grant his request without your concurrence. Is it acceptable to you?"

Le Mercier presented a curt bow to his cousin Villiers and

replied, "Of course. It is my pleasure to serve the Sieur."

And that was that.

"Captain Villiers," Contrecoeur said, extending his hand and gripping Villiers'. "You are in command, sir. However, I have one request to make before you depart. May we please review the Sergeant's story one more time? To make sure we fully understand the circumstances of your brother's death and do not act precipitously?"

It was as polite a plea for caution as Contrecoeur could make but Villiers' glacial glare left no doubt as to his emotional state.

"Of course, Captain. It is always wise to review the facts," said Villiers with a cold stare, setting his jaw so firmly that Contrecoeur could see a wave of muscles rippling all the way back to his neck.

Mouceau went through his chronicle with an efficiency and embellishment born of repetition. As he listened, Contrecoeur remained unconvinced that Gilles Mouceau was telling the whole truth about Jumonville's death. It wasn't that he thought the Sergeant was deliberately lying, but his experience told him that the human mind had a remarkable capacity for creating tidy, coherent recollections from ambiguous circumstances. This man's mind had been influenced by secondhand accounts of Jumonville's gratuitous murder related to him by Indian spies. The story they told was that Jumonville and his diplomatic retinue had laid down their weapons and were pleading for negotiations when the British, who had surrounded them early in the morning of the twenty-eighth of May, summarily fired, killing ten, including the Sieur de Jumonville. What was suspicious about Mouceau's narrative was the assertion that the British Indians, the Iroquois, had tried to prevent the massacre. Given the chronically deplorable state of French-Iroquois relations and the dead Marin's arrogant behavior toward representatives of the Six Nations, such compassion from Tanacharison and Monacatoocha was unlikely. There was also the question of whether Mouceau could actually have seen the events at the glen. If he had, how had he avoided being seen himself? And if, in the act of evacuating his bowels, he had been startled by gunfire, how did he get to the scene of the alleged massacre in time to see anything but dead bodies, especially if he had first taken the time to tidy himself and pull his breeches up? Surely he hadn't rushed to the scene of infamy without his breeches!

But that was not the way Villiers saw it. Upon hearing the news of his half-brother's death, *le Grand Villiers* had hastened to Fort Duquesne from Chataqua with food, liquor, twenty marines, a hundred thirty Indians from a half dozen northern tribes, and a burning passion to avenge his sibling's murder.

"Sergeant, you are sure the English attack was unprovoked, that the Sieur de Jumonville was unable to return fire and had in fact surrendered when the English killed him?"

Mouceau had been asked the question so many times that his first reaction was a weary resentment. But the insistence of the query and Contrecoeur's indomitable gaze unsettled him, causing him to examine more closely the account he had convinced himself was true. Nervously, his eyes darted from one to the other of the three captains interrogating him. Then came another musket blast, a chorus of broken glass, and vocal cacophony.

Mouceau jumped as if he had been shot instead of the wine bottle.

"Yes, yes, Captain…of course," he stuttered, expelling from his thoughts the spurious notion that his recollections might be flawed. "That is exactly the way it happened…exactly."

Contrecoeur searched the Sergeant's face for signs of deceit, saw only an anxious marine, and decided he had no recourse but to embrace the version of events the man had recounted. The English had behaved abominably. They would be punished. But it would have to be done in a civilized manner according to the accepted norms of behavior between nations. For posterity's sake, and for the consumption of the non-combatant European nations who would eventually be called upon to mediate the dispute, Captains Contrecoeur, Villiers, and Le Mercier had drafted a statement of intent the night before. In essence, the statement justified retaliatory action against those responsible for the murders of Jumonville and his entourage, but proposed friendship between the opposing nations of Great Britain and France once the English had been taken to the woodshed for their punishment.

"Captain Villiers, you will abide by the principles delineated in our prepared statement for this mission and any that may follow,"

Contrecoeur said, trying for a satisfactory combination of faith and skepticism in Villiers' ability to curb his wrath for the greater good.

Villiers' response was icily calm: "Of course, sir. We will behave with the utmost propriety."

The three Captains and the Sergeant jumped as another musket blast shattered another floating bottle. It reminded Contrecoeur of a promise he had made.

"There is one more thing, Captain," he said, addressing Villiers, then pointing at Striking Eagle, who was reloading. "You will be taking that gentleman with you along with his undersize companion, M'sieur Bonin. Have you any objections?"

Struck dumb and tongue-tied by the unexpected addition to his roster, Villiers could only mumble, "Mm...I..." before Contrecoeur turned abruptly to Le Mercier and said, "Captain, please inform those two that they will be going with Captain Villiers."

Cupping a hand over his lips to hide his reaction, Le Mercier did as his Commander ordered. Jolicoeur Bonin acknowledged the order with a nod and a salute to Contrecoeur. The reaction of Striking Eagle was more explosive. He jumped into the air, screamed a series of what could only have been Shawnee war whoops and then, musket still in hand, dived into the water and began swimming toward the fleet of canoes and bateaux. The throng of marines gazed on in awe. They could not believe a man holding a musket could swim so fast but there he was, churning through the water powered by only one arm. On reaching his destination—an empty canoe—Striking Eagle tossed the musket aboard, then himself, then yelled and gestured at Bonin to join him. Jolicoeur accepted the invitation with a hearty laugh but strolled to the dock the canoe was lashed to instead of swimming over. By this time, Villiers had regained some of his senses.

"Sir, I don't need them," he pleaded.

Had Villiers' composure been fully recovered, he might have taken greater notice of Contrecoeur's unctuous, ingratiating manner as the Commander said, "Think of it as a favor to me, Captain. He wants to kill Englishmen and I think he will be very good at it. He has not missed a wine bottle in two weeks."

Villiers glanced from Contrecoeur to the copiously energized

Striking Eagle and back again.

"He wants...to kill Englishmen," Villiers responded insipidly, not sure what emotion to attach to the statement.

"Yes, he does, and it is extremely important to the well being of Fort Duquesne that he be given the opportunity to do so," Contrecoeur said with a straight face.

Villiers stared blankly at the Commander, uncomprehending.

"We are almost out of empty wine bottles, Captain," Contrecoeur said with a revealing grin. "I don't want him to start shooting at the full ones."

Chapter Eleven

June 29, 1754, Gist's plantation

It was going to be another of life's cruel lessons, Washington concluded, as he climbed down from the sorrel to examine one of the nine swivel guns in hopes of finding a way out of the dilemma. A lesson with all the pedagogical value of a lightning bolt up the arse. He could sense it. It had the rough, ephemeral texture of a stillborn truth, one of God's waggish pranks, a problem, which, in all other circumstances, would not have risen to the status of the trivial but, which, here and now, was absolutely life threatening. Was it something a more experienced commander than he could have anticipated or was it simply a whim of fate, like a boulder hidden far enough below the water's surface that it made no ripple, yet shallow enough to tip over any boat passing by?

"Colonel, without the teams we can't move the swivel guns *or* the powder *or* the shot," said Peter Effleck of Hogg's company, his sharp, stubbled chin thrusting forward to emphasize the finality in his words. "An' we ain't got enough pack horses to carry 'em either."

That was the difficulty in a nutshell. They needed the teams but the teams were at Great Meadows waiting for supplies. So now there was no way to move the swivel guns if they were forced to retreat.

"We have to have the swivel guns, Peter," Washington pleaded, trying to turn his wishes into horses.

"I know that, sir. I'm aware 'a that, sir," Effleck explained patiently. "If we stay here, there's no problem. We'll just mount 'em on the stockade."

Washington looked at the new stockade to see how it was progressing. At that morning's war council, a tentative decision had been made to build a stockade around the storehouse using Gist's rail fence. As he watched Lewis's men raising the structure, Washington could not rid himself of a nagging doubt about the wisdom of fighting on this ground. That and the fragility of the rail fence were among his greatest concerns, which seemed to be multiplying by the hour.

"But we may not be able to stay here, Peter. We have to plan ahead, just in case. The French could be here tomorrow, before the stockade is finished."

Effleck shook his head in abject despair, then said, "I can't see any way to do it, Colonel, until the teams come back."

Washington lifted the muzzle and sighted down the barrel of the swivel gun. It did not look like much: three feet long, a hundred to a hundred fifty pounds, but it could hurl a half-pound ball two hundred yards or more, which was a damn sight more than a musket could throw with anything resembling precision. They had to have these guns.

"Can't we rope them and pull them behind us?"

Effleck's head resumed its negative gyrations.

"What do you wanta do, Colonel, drag 'em by the muzzles or the mounts? Whichever ya drag 'em by, the other ends are gonna be battered to a pulp. If ya damage the muzzles, ya won't be able to fire the damn things, an' if ya damage the mounts, you can't set 'em up. A swivel gun's no good unless you can mount it. You can't fire it like a rifle and you can't sit it on the ground like a mortar. It has to be mounted."

Effleck was right, of course. The mounting post in the breech of each gun had to be functional to secure it to a block, stump, or post. Otherwise, the recoil would send the gun flying off in some God-forsaken direction. Washington had a vision of a swivel gun caroming off walls and hillsides like a frightened pig trying to escape a band of hungry soldiers, found himself laughing, then began wondering which he was suffering from, exhaustion or lunacy, wishing for the latter.

"There has to be a way, Peter. Think hard. I'm depending on you."

Even as he said it, Washington could see the creases in Effleck's

119

forehead narrow into fret lines. The Colonel knew he was unloading a great deal of responsibility onto the shoulders of an enlisted man like Effleck. But he had to unburden himself of some of the responsibilities that had naturally fallen on him as a commander. There were too many of them.

Effleck scratched his head, then offered a languid, "We *could* strap 'em to our backs, sir. Take turns carryin' 'em."

Oh, God, strap those things, pack horse style, to men's backs? They might make a hundred yards in a level walk and there was no such thing as a level walk in these mountains.

"Keep thinking about it, Peter. There has to be another way," Washington repeated feebly, then lifted himself back onto the sorrel. "In the meantime, get the swivel guns up to the stockade. We may have to use them soon."

"Can I get the ladies auxiliary to help me, Colonel?" Effleck asked with a crooked glance at Mackay's Independents, who had just arrived and were gathered on the porch of Gist's main building. Most were attending to their weaponry or engaged in idle conversation with each other; none was doing a lick of work otherwise. The twinkle in Effleck's eye and the cynical undertone in his voice belied the lightness of his words: He was not amused.

"We'll deal with that later, Peter," Washington said, then immediately nudged the horse away. Allowing Effleck to sidetrack him with a list of complaints about the chronic indolence of Mackay's troops would be neither prudent nor timely. But the handwriting was on the wall. A seed of resentment among the poorly paid Virginia Volunteers, who, unlike Mackay's men, were expected to be both soldiers and manual laborers, had been planted in fertile ground. It would grow.

In his anxiety to get away from Effleck, the Colonel discovered he did not have a specific destination in mind. But it didn't matter. There were so many problems to think about and oversee it would take him all day to work through the entire list. Then it would be time to start over. In his mind, this was the essence of leadership: attending to the various components of the machinery under his charge, making sure it was well lubricated and functioned properly. He had not learned to step back, detach his mind from the hounds giving chase, and simply think. To the young man who was the *de facto* Commander of the Virginia Regiment that would have seemed a waste of time.

Finding himself headed for the stockade construction site, Washington looked for and found Robert Stobo, the regimental engineer, who was supervising the activities of approximately fifty men. Most of them were naked from the waist up and scantily clad from the waist down except for leather boots to support their ankles on the rough terrain. Only a few wore the leather breeches favored for marching through thick brush. None of the tomato red Virginia Regimental breeches were in evidence.

"How goes it, Robert?" Washington asked the man from Glasgow and Petersburg.

As an officer, Stobo insisted on wearing at least a coarse linen shirt, as Washington himself did. But Stobo's was unbuttoned, its sleeves rolled up in an attempt to throw off the oppressive heat and humidity of Appalachian summer. Despite the attempt, perspiration poured from his classic brow down and around the mirthful, elegant face.

"Three, four days, Colonel. Do I have that much time?" Stobo responded, found a relatively dry section on his sleeve, and raised it to his drenched forehead.

"I wish I knew."

"No further word of French movements?"

"No."

The Scotsman nodded and resumed his activities while Washington looked over the fruits of his labors. The stockade would be similar to Fort Necessity in construction: vertical poles sunk into the ground to form palisade walls. Unlike Fort Necessity, it would be rectangular with horizontal supports that would also serve as gun rests once loopholes were cut between the posts. Stobo would probably mount swivel guns in the four corners of the stockade and build platforms to access them. The other swivel guns would be placed wherever they were considered to be tactically most useful.

Washington concluded that there was not much more he could do except volunteer his back and his labor, and that would be neither seemly nor practical. As he guided the sorrel back down the hill he felt the envelope he had shoved into the top of his breeches that morning twisting against the skin of his hip. Then he remembered the elation he had known at reading the letter it contained. It was from Sally and had been concealed in a letter Mrs. Carlyle had written him, which itself had been enclosed in John Carlyle's letter suggesting that the Virginians find some iron around camp to forge the tools they needed. Such furtive communications were possible because Mrs. Carlyle was the sister of Sally's husband, George William Fairfax. Washington considered it doubtful that Mrs. Carlyle had read Sally's letter. It was filled with...what was the gentlest word...indiscretions? It had to be destroyed, but not before he read it one more time.

* * *

Once on the road Lewis's men had cut, he let the sorrel accelerate to a moderate trot. Though he would have liked to do so, he could not bring the horse to a full gallop because the trees that had been cleared to make the roadway were cut twelve inches from the ground, just enough to allow the wagons to pass but not much more. One of Lewis's wagons had, in fact, been 'stumped' that morning. The phenomenon known as being 'stumped' happened when a wagonmaster who had successfully negotiated his way into a pasture of tree stumps discovered he was unable to successfully retrace his path.

Washington brought the sorrel to a halt at the crest of a hill sufficiently free of plant growth for him to see out over the endless forest. The forest and the mountain ridges it covered did indeed look like a series of interlocking green fingers, or a boundless succession of swells in an oceanscape frozen in time. He wasn't sure which of the customary analogies he liked best—probably the oceanscape but only because Lawrence had once arranged for him to enter the Royal Navy at fourteen, as a midshipman. He had often wondered if that branch of the military might have been a better career choice. He chuckled wistfully as he recalled the Fairfaxes and their surreptitious involvement in the affair. Lawrence had told him to meet with William Fairfax, manager of the Great Lord's estate and George William's father, in Fredericksburg. In the message, Lawrence had urged his younger sibling to avoid telling his mother of the meeting for reasons they both understood: Mrs. Washington would have demanded to know what Lawrence was up to before he was ready to say. At the meeting, Fairfax presented George with a letter from Lawrence indicating that he could have an appointment as a midshipman in the Royal Navy if he wanted it. Lawrence was his idol; George could not say no. Then Fairfax gave George another letter from Lawrence addressed to his mother. Lawrence was as averse to speaking with his stepmother as were most temperate people. Despite Lawrence's gingerly chosen words, Mrs. Washington ultimately vetoed the idea, creating in the adolescent George a keen sense of disappointment, an even stronger sense of relief, and a not entirely cynical appreciation of his mother's pertinacity.

Washington reached inside his blouse and pulled out Sally's letter. Tenderly, he removed it and put the envelope back inside his shirt. There were two complete pages. The handwriting itself sent a wave of pinpricks coursing across the skin of his abdomen. He did not read the letter as much as feast his eyes on the angelic script and the ripe phrases it painted, like rosy-cheeked cherubs, throughout the text: "...our secret reminiscences...", "forget not the hours we have passed together..." Intentionally clouded in a mist of circumlocution, Sally's words could still scandalize. What could she have been thinking to put such revelations down on paper? Even Mrs. Carlyle's letter, replete as it was with plaudits to his patriotic mission, had embedded within its shifting context the tempered warnings of a concerned friend. Maybe she *had* read Sally's letter.

This was the one aspect of Sally's letter that displeased him, even to the point of anger. Her indiscretions had to stop. There were too many people who could be hurt by them, not the least of whom were she and he. Lord Fairfax would have been livid with apoplexy if he had scanned even a line of Sally's letter. And George William, his friend, Sally's husband, the Fairfax son whom Washington had displaced in the hearts of the Fairfax gentry during the boy's stressful fifteen year exile in England: How would *he* react? But what could the young commander say to the woman who had so thoroughly bewitched him? Tell her not to write? Demand that she be more temperate, more circumspect, in her use of language? But if he asked this of her, she might actually comply, and that was perhaps the most dreaded of all possible outcomes.

There was only one thing he could do: dispose of the letter as he done with all the others, hoping that its absence would in itself be a sufficient proof of never-existence. Slowly he folded the letter and replaced it in the envelope, murmuring its contents to fix them in his memory. Meticulously, he began tearing the envelope and its treasure to pieces, first down the middle, then stacking the two halves and tearing again down the middle, repeating until no fragment was larger than a stamp. Holding the detritus in one hand, Washington rode the sorrel into the woods adjacent to the road, dismounted, and made his way to the edge of a briar patch hemmed in by laurel. Raising his hand and sweeping it in as wide an arc as possible, he released the remains of Sally's missive and watched its vestiges flutter like autumn leaves among the thorns and laurel branches. Suddenly, as if to prove that no place was safe from prying eyes, a rabbit darted out from beneath the briar patch, startling the heartsick Virginian. *Well, rabbit, if you're the only one who sees this letter, I have no complaint.*

His clandestine mission completed, Washington clapped his hands together to make sure no paper had stuck to them and glanced up to find that the sorrel had drifted to a spot where a hole in the canopy of leaves overhead let the sun's rays penetrate all the way to the forest floor. The effect was both breathtaking and serene: a shower of pure light washing away the darkness, revealing the preternatural glories hidden beneath the distant green ceiling. The horse was standing in the center of the illumination, bathing itself in the cascading beams of raw brilliance. Washington approached quietly, not wanting to disrupt the animal's moment of repose. Gently, he patted its shoulder to let it know he was there. Then he felt what it felt: the soft heat of the sun's rays caressing his shoulders and neck like the fingers of God.

In the traditional sense, George Washington was not a demonstrably religious man. He had no patience with a god who, like a pampered child, would rain terror down on his subjects if he found them wanting in zeal or character. God was man's creator, was He not? If men were not perfect, much of the blame must be laid at His gate. But neither was the young man a typical product of his age, a partisan of the fashionable theology of the day, Deism, which held that God had created the heavens, the earth, and man, but had, in a fit of pique, like a reluctant father, walked out and left his brood to its own devices. To a parochial Virginia farmer, such a philosophy was noxious and nonsensical. Would a planter sow his seed and then not exert himself to insure it would grow to fruition? Not likely. But if this were God's true nature, it would be better for man to deceive himself and indulge his imagination with fancies of a more compassionate parent. Civilized man could not remain civilized if he knew with certainty that he was nothing more than a cosmic orphan clinging to an insignificant shred of flotsam in an infinite sea.

His was a religion of the first born of a second wife, conceived of the meditations of a child whose uniqueness distanced him from his older half-siblings. To George Washington, God was to be respected but not as a friend. A friend's judgment could be flawed by sentiment. God had something in mind for him. He had no idea what it was but he knew with a passionate certitude that he had been selected even if his intellect insisted it was nothing more than whimsy fed by arrogance. But the signs of God's oversight were clear: his virtual adoption by Lord Fairfax, the most influential man in Virginia; his survival of smallpox, musket fire, and the frigid waters of the Allegheny River; his rise to the status of surveyor and landowner at the age of nineteen. To be sure, much of this could be attributed to his own character and, to be fair, his family's position in the Virginia aristocracy. But if someone had suggested that George Washington was invulnerable, he might make a rational argument against such a laughable proposition, but would secretly believe in it. God would do that for him, God with a small 'g', an uncle, a mentor, a being he could speak frankly to or even admonish, but God nonetheless. God his protector. God his mystical accomplice. God whom he could revere but not adore.

Washington adjusted his body so that his line of sight paralleled the dazzling radiance enfolding him, seeking its source.

Why are you doing this? His mind asked, some of the words · spilling onto his lips.

Silence, of course. God doesn't speak.

Again: *Why are you doing this?* To make sure God knew his

displeasure.

I do what you want. I follow the path you've set before me but I find nothing but confusion. How can this serve either of us? You must set me right, give me guidance. Do you want me to fail?

Once more for emphasis: *Do you want me to fail?*

Maybe God did want him to fail. Maybe it was necessary. But he didn't want to fail.

If you allow me to fail, I may become demoralized and abandon this...this...quest...

Even as the words played in his brain, Washington knew it was a lie and that God would see through it. He could no more abandon his destiny than his right hand. Grudgingly, he accepted failure as a possibility and proceeded to his next complaint.

This woman that you've...No, no.

He tried again.

You know what I feel for Sally Fairfax. Why did you let this happen? It complicates everything and there is no point in it. She is in every thought I think and every dream I dream. There are times when I think you cannot be a serious god, that you must be a simple buffoon who enjoys nothing better than toying with his creations...

"Colonel, Colonel Washington!" called a voice from another universe. It was Southy Hazlip, Washington saw, running urgently toward him, popeyed and breathless. Anticipating a need to return, he took the horse's reins in one hand and faced the messenger.

"What is it, Southy?"

Hazlip waited until he had stopped running and, between gasps, replied, "I didn't know where ya was, sir. Somebody said they saw ya headin' down the road..."

The Colonel did not bother with a reproach. Instead, he gave Southy a foul look that could mean only one thing: *Get to the point.*

"Another runner came, Colonel. The French've started movin' south with lots of men, boats, and artillery," Hazlip finally babbled.

Washington's eyes rolled upward at the heavens but he decided against sending an appended complaint.

"Take my horse, Southy," he said, handing the reins to Hazlip. "Tell the company commanders, Captain Mackay, and Lieutenant La Peyroney we need to have another war council."

Southy Hazlip reluctantly accepted the reins, uncomfortable with the thought of riding while his Commander walked.

"I need to walk back, Southy," Washington explained with a curt smile. "I have some thinking to do."

* * *

They weren't really having an argument, but since it was James Mackay's nature to be contentious, he was having one all by himself.

"We can't stay here," he insisted as he strutted across the porch Southy Hazlip had just cleared of Mackay's indolent Independents. "With twelve hundred French and Indians on the field, we must now consider our forces to be on the defensive. Even if the stockade is finished today—which I doubt—and even if Mr. Stobo has built an impregnable fortress—which I also doubt…"

"Oh, an impregnable fortress she won't be, Captain. That much I can assure you," said Stobo from his perch on the porch railing. He briefly considered taking offense at Mackay's criticism of his work but decided it wasn't really criticism but truth that Mackay spoke, albeit in a tone unsuited to persuading an audience.

Mackay acknowledged Stobo's remark with an abrupt nod of the head and continued, "…and even if the stockade provides us with an adequate defense here, the French can merely bypass our position and go on to Great Meadows."

Mackay, whose pacing had taken him beyond Washington on Stobo's right and who was now facing away from his listeners, paused pregnantly, turned around, and struck a noble pose an artist might have suggested he assume for posterity's sake.

"I don't think I need to elaborate on what *that* would mean, gentlemen. We would be cut off from Wills Creek! The French would have us! No further discussion is necessary. We must leave here at once and return to Great Meadows. Not only will such a move improve our defensive position but it will also stretch French supply lines and make them vulnerable to the kind of attack for which our Indian allies are so well known. I might also remind you that our Indian allies *are* returning to Great Meadows, a fact which renders our continued presence here something of a military absurdity."

As he shook his head in disbelief, Robert Stobo scanned the officers of the Virginia Regiment to gauge their reaction to James Mackay's latest tribute to his own importance. Washington, angered and abashed, diverted his gaze away from the proceedings and seemed to be staring at the cattle grazing in the pasture nearby. *He must be feeling quite stupid for bringing us here*, Stobo thought, then continued his survey. Muse, Van Braam, La Peyroney, and Stephen were gathered around a table in various stages of apparent indifference. *They probably agree with Mackay but don't want to give the pompous ass the satisfaction of knowing it.* Andrew Lewis was also seated at the table but his disposition and the knowledge that the ground often shook at his passing rendered him incapable of appearing indifferent to mere mortals. The final Virginia officer, Peter Hogg, as bare-chested and dirty as the enlisted men, did not seem so much indifferent as detached. Sitting on the edge of the porch opposite Stobo, the elderly but athletic Scot was busily whittling on a stick of maple wood with a deer knife. What Hogg was carving Stobo couldn't tell; it retained the appearance of a stick of maple wood despite the pile of chips Hogg had built up.

"Captain Mackay, I think we all understand our vulnerabilities here," Washington replied, his face flushed. "But there are problems to overcome. The cattle have to be driven and we will have to haul the supplies, including the swivel guns, with only the wagons and teams in camp right now. And I don't think I need to point out to you, sir, that Chestnut Ridge lies between us and Great Meadows…"

Easy, Colonel, that one almost cost you your temper, thought Stobo as he watched his Commander's neck and jowls grow taut with repressed indignation.

"That, sir, is not *my* problem," Mackay retorted icily, then launched his body on what would become an orbit of the table. "That is *your* problem. I did not bring your regiment to this place, nor the cattle, nor the swivel guns. I will have enough difficulty explaining to my men why they have to march back to Great Meadows only one day after leaving *there* to march *here*…"

The two Commanders were talking to each other in 'sirs.' It was not a good sign.

"That *would* be a pity, Mr. Mackay. A real pity to demoralize your men like that," someone with a rich bass voice said. Stobo could not at first identify its source but then realized it belonged to the normally subdued Peter Hogg, who was still whittling but remained otherwise immobile. "But I'll tell you what, Captain. I think it wouldn't be too difficult keepin' your boys entertained by strappin' a few swivel guns to their backs. Helpin' out in the common cause, so to speak…"

"That would be impossible, Mr. Hogg, as you already know…" Mackay said, stiffening.

"And why is that, Captain?" Hogg asked pointedly, finally turning his face toward Mackay. "In Bonnie Prince Charlie's army we all got up at the crack of dawn with our swords and muskets at the ready. There were no slackers, no British lackeys pretendin' to be Scotsmen…"

If Mackay was offended by the implications of Hogg's remarks, he didn't show it. Stobo was unaware whether or not Mackay had fought on the British side against Charles Edward Stuart, known to his followers as Bonnie Prince Charlie and to his enemies as the Pretender, when that nobleman had attempted to seize the British throne in 1745. But he was certain the Carolina Commander's loyalties lay in that direction.

"So, Mr. Hogg, you wore a blue bonnet and a white cockade, did you?" Mackay murmured with bemused nonchalance, referring to the symbols of allegiance Prince Charles's followers had worn.

"I fought *with* the Prince, the rightful heir," Hogg corrected.

"And lost."

"Not my self-respect, like those who followed Billie the Butcher did."

Mackay completed half his orbit of the table and was now standing with his back to the others. Like all Scotsmen of his generation, he was familiar with the appellation *Billie the Butcher,* the Jacobite name for William, Duke of Cumberland, son of King George II, so given because of the Duke's policy of systematically exterminating the defeated Scots after the Battle of Culloden Moor. The decisive battle of the second Jacobite rebellion, Culloden was largely a fight between Scottish clans, many of whom had fought with the British. But if Mackay had been on the side of *Billie the Butcher,* he wasn't going to let himself be provoked into saying so here and now. As if in prayer, he held his hands in front of him, the fingertips of opposite hands brushing lightly together.

"Are you angry about something, Mr. Hogg?" he asked airily. "If Bonnie Prince Charlie had won at Culloden Moor instead of the Duke of Cumberland, he would now be the British sovereign and George II would be in exile somewhere. Does it really make that much difference to us? I don't think so."

"Well, my own pars'nal opinion is it's always the occasional good thing to beat the pants off the British," Andrew Lewis, the Irishman, chimed in with impish good cheer. He was rewarded with a flurry of chuckles, even a hint of a grin from Mackay. The only one who didn't seem to get the joke was Washington.

"You may be right, Captain," said a better-humored Hogg. "But so is Andrew. The British do deserve a lickin' now an' then the way they set brother against brother..."

"Ah, but that's where you're wrong, Peter," Mackay retorted, his King's English suddenly basted with a highland sauce. "Y've heard the term 'divide and conquer', have you not? The British are the greatest practitioners of the art of conquest in the whole world. Do you expect 'em to abandon the tools of the trade?"

"I would hope their good Christian consciences would keep 'em from conquerin' anyone," Hogg retorted somewhat piously.

Mackay leaned over his sparring partner, bringing their locked eyes close enough that each could have counted the beads of perspiration on the other's brow.

"What about the savages in this country, Peter? Do you not think that what we intend to do out here is fully in the way of conquerin' an indigenous people? If you don't think so you're a bit of a silly fool."

"Maybe what Peter should have said is that he would hope the Christian British would forswear the conquest of other Christian peoples, like the Scots," Robert Stobo said.

Mackay had not expected a comment from anyone but Hogg but must have anticipated the remark itself, because he had an answer. He resumed his orbit, working his way around the table to Stobo.

"Well now, Robert, so you say Christians shouldn't conquer Christians. Is that right?" Mackay queried, his demeanor, his gait, the smile on his face unbearably smug. All remnants of his practiced

British dialect were gone. He didn't wait for an answer.

"Did you know, Robert, that the south islanders and the north islanders of the place we call Britain have been at each other's throats for a long time, way before either could properly be called a Christian, good or otherwise? Did you know that our Scottish ancestors used to paint their faces and bodies, just like our pretty savages do here? What do you think 'a that?" Mackay demanded with a wry grin and arched eyebrows so firmly defined they seemed to be cantilevered off his forehead. "Imagine these lovely beasties in full battle regalia with their war paint, their battle axes, their shields, and their wild hair growin' from the tops of their heads to the soles of their feet so they don't need but a few animal skins and furs draped over their shoulders and stuffed in their tender places to keep warm. Why, they were the fiercest, ugliest, most God-forsaken, bad-tempered man-creatures God ever put on this earth! Theyd've scared the livin' bejesus out of any of the hairless savages in this country, includin' Andrew Montour. And Christian charity was definitely not one 'a their virtues. Do I make my point?"

Stobo, who had been relaxing with his feet up on the rail, dropped them to the floor and faced the quarrelsome Commander of the Independents.

"You *could* be making one of two points, Captain. One: As good Christians, we should not be pilferin' what rightly belongs to the Indians, or two: We should indeed be pilferin' as much as we can in order to spread civilization and the good word to the heathen savages. Which is it?"

If he noticed the undertone of sarcasm in Stobo's voice, Mackay preferred to ignore it. He was all good will and laughter—a snigger too far out of character to be credible—and laid a brusque pounding on Stobo's shoulders with unexpectedly powerful hands.

"Y've got a good head on your shoulders, Robert," Mackay said, then draped his left arm around Stobo and turned to find Peter Hogg. "Tell me truly now, Robert, you didn't fight for... *with* the blue bonnets like Peter here, did you?"

"Captain, for your information, Peter is not the only one whose loyalties were with Prince Charles," Adam Stephen interjected without lifting his gaze from the table. "So were mine."

Stephen spoke calmly, evenly, which was unusual for him. His typical conversational style was somewhere between sardonic indifference and impassioned cynicism. But in this instance he wanted to be taken seriously. It was a simple matter of honor. He did not think it fair that Hogg should be the sole recipient of Mackay's acerbic barbs.

"Good God, what is the matter with you people?" Washington suddenly shouted, throwing his arms in the air. "You're talking about a fight that's been over for nine years! What difference does it make who was on which side? It's done and it is of no consequence to the here and now. We have to get about the business of making an orderly departure from this place and we don't have much time to do it. I would appreciate it if you would all keep that in mind and save your blood feuds for a less trying moment!"

Because George Washington despised his own hot temper and tried to suppress its public exhibition, no one had noticed the gradual deepening of the Colonel's complexion or the struggle his lips were making to remain sealed and prevent his head from exploding like an artillery shell. As the only native colonial present, Washington did not fully appreciate the context of the debate and, as the Commander of the Virginia Regiment, had higher priorities. The tremor of exasperation that had just shaken him relieved the mounting pressure engendered by what seemed to him a pointless dispute. Everyone was surprised by the outburst but none more so than James Mackay who, for once, was uncertain how to react. Whether through habit or conscious design, he soon fell back into his self-appointed role as the sole representative of His Majesty's Forces in America.

"Mr. Washington, your impatience is understandable and you've made your point, but there is no need to be abrasive..." Mackay said calmly, all traces of his highland lilt extinguished.

"Mr. Mackay, in light of our current predicament, impatience is virtue herself and abrasiveness her noble champion. Please go to your men and prepare them for a prompt departure..."

"Sir, I thought I made it clear I will not accept orders from a provincial officer and, furthermore, I do not like your tone," Mackay protested with a stiff back and elevated chin.

"I don't give a damn if you like my tone or not. And if you don't like my orders, then make some of your own," Washington fumed, stepping closer to Mackay to emphasize his size advantage. "Rest assured, Captain Mackay, the Virginia Regiment is leaving. Unless you are prepared to take on an army of twelve hundred all by yourself, you would be well advised to join us."

It was an odd disagreement in light of the fact that Mackay had been the one insisting on a return to Great Meadows in the first place. Robert Stobo found himself admiring his commanding officer's ability to turn the tables in his favor, not with any particular rhetorical skill, but through sheer will power. This hulking young man might actually make his mark on the world some day. James Mackay was not cowed by the bigger man's belligerence and, as a professional solder, was not accustomed to yielding to the demands of lesser officers. But with victory denied, the Captain appeared ready to beat a strategic retreat.

"I bid you good day, sir," he said with a curt bow. As he passed the other Virginia officers, he acknowledged each with a sharp snap of his head and a stiff smile. He saluted no one.

"Gentlemen, please go and prepare your companies for departure. I want to be out of here before noon," Washington said, his anger dissipating. Running his fingers through the disheveled locks of his auburn hair, he added, "George, William, will you come with me, please?"

The two officers dutifully joined the Colonel, as did Jacob Van Braam. The rest—Stobo, Hogg, Stephen, and Lewis—gawked timidly at each other for signs of comprehension and drew into a cluster, each hoping that at least one of the others might better understand what had just transpired than he did. The expedition, a monument to poor planning and hasty execution, had just taken a decided turn for the worse and there was nothing to do but retreat and regroup. Despair did not yet loom large in their minds, but it was evident in the lassitude of their movements and the downward angle of their collective gaze. They sought refuge in small talk.

"What's the answer to the question, Robert?" Peter Hogg asked with an inflection suggestive of nothing more than mild curiosity. "Whose side were you on in forty-five?"

"I don't take sides," Stobo answered, then continued with what had become his stock response. "One of my noble but imprudent ancestors fought for the first Charles Stuart and got hung for his trouble. Then they sliced him into pieces and distributed the *hors d'oeuvres* to all who wanted 'em. Since then, my relatives and I have tried to avoid politics and politicians."

The others quietly accepted Stobo's rationale. The previous hundred years had been a turbulent period for Scotch-English and Irish-English relations.

Andrew Lewis said, "I do think the Colonel has a point, though. We need to keep our attention here, not across the sea!"

"You're right, Andrew," Adam Stephen chuckled. "And it's our own fault! The damned Scots should have known better than to put their country on the same island with the English."

All received the comment in good humor except for Peter Hogg, who replied, "Are you sayin' that the Scottish lamb shouldn't be lyin' down with the British lion?"

"It's a joke, Peter. I'm sayin' nothin' of the sort, just pullin' our legs, nothin' more," Stephen replied.

"And where would *you* put Scotland, Adam?" Hogg demanded, not yet appeased.

"Oh, I don't know. Maybe here, where we are right now," Stephen answered, maintaining his conciliatory tone. "It's got enough hills to keep your legs from turnin' to mush. And it's pleasant enough..."

"Pleasant! Are you daft?" exclaimed Andrew Lewis, staring up at the tall forest surrounding him. "Look at all these trees! So many of 'em you can't even see the sky half the time. And when you do, it's usually gray!"

"It's also a few thousand miles from Great Britain, Andrew. How far is Ireland, a hundred or two? To my mind, bein' halfway around the world from the English gives this land a rare and lustrous charm."

Lewis scratched his head, then bellowed, "Well, you have a point there, Adam."

"What are you suggestin', Adam? That the Scotch and the Irish come over and inhabit these woods?" Stobo asked playfully, gesturing toward the forest and mountains with a broad sweep of his arms.

"I can't speak for the Irish, but there's one or two Scotsmen here already. Us, for instance."

Stobo started counting the Scottish émigrés on Washington's staff. There were himself, Adam Stephen, Peter Hogg, William Poulson, Dr. Craik...

"Does the contrary Captain Mackay count?" he asked.

"He's here. He counts," Peter Hogg replied to the delight of everyone.

It was to be their final moment of relaxation before the long haul back to Great Meadows, a shared daydream, a fine fantasy, an escape into a future as yet undefined. They talked about building homesteads, farming, raising families, dealing with the Indians, but mostly of placing them and theirs outside the reach of civilized institutions like British law and colonial governments. Like all immigrant Americans, they had come to escape *something*. The first wave had come in the sixteen-hundreds. Theirs was the second wave and included not only the disenchanted of the mother country but the malcontents whose fundamental dissatisfaction was with civilization itself.

But Andrew Lewis was skeptical.

"We can't build a country here," he announced, thoroughly discouraged.

"Why not, Andrew?" someone asked.

Lewis the road-builder looked up to the roof of the forest, around and into its depths, then shook his head and frowned.

"Nobody can. I already said it: There's too many trees," he said, all hope abandoned. "Ain't enough men in the world to cut 'em all down. There's just too damn many trees."

@hapter Twelve

June 30, 1754, The Monongahela River south of the forks

he day was hot to start with. It seemed steamier than usual because of the sun's reflection off the placid surface of the water and the stifling humidity it created as a result. With supple grace, Villiers' flotilla of canoes and bateaux moved southward thirty miles from Fort Duquesne, its engines—the men who served as polers and paddlers—maintaining a workmanlike pace. Enthusiasm had dissipated somewhere in the first ten miles and, along with it, the hue and cry of an invading army looking for its first kill. The enthusiasm would return with the first sighting of the enemy. For now, heat and boredom were the enemies, and many of the marines and Indians had decided to attack them with the most potent weapons available: rum, wine and, for the officers, brandy.

"Hey, Jolicoeur, you look pale," a half-naked marine with lips like dried prunes shouted from the starboard bateau. The marine was joined by his leering, half-naked boat-mates, who were watching Jolicoeur Bonin and his boat-mate, Striking Eagle, with unusual interest.

"Just a little tired. That's all," Jolicoeur responded. "We should teach the dogs to pull the boats like they pull the snow sleds. It would save us the humiliation of dying on the way to battle."

Like everyone else, Jolicoeur wore little more than breeches and moccasins. Unlike everyone else, he had covered his head with the blue knit cap in an attempt to shield his skull from the baking sun. He knew he looked slightly ridiculous, but that was consistent with his unofficial position as regimental jester, and he didn't mind.

The diminutive *canonnier* had decided the time was ripe for

Striking Eagle to become more intimately acquainted with French wine jugs than as targets for musket practice. As a Frenchman, Bonin expected to drink his new friend under the table, but he did not adjust his thinking to their relative sizes. Bonin was a dwarf, Striking Eagle a giant. Consequently, after two jugs of wine had been consumed, Bonin found he could no longer dip his paddle into the river without risking a fall overboard. Striking Eagle, by contrast, continued to row with the same potency he had started with at the forks.

"How do you like the wine, M'sieur Eagle?" Bonin asked, trying to rotate his head to face his companion at the rear but finding the action disorienting. He settled for a sidelong glance.

"It is good," Striking Eagle replied, then punched his stomach and belched. The sound of the belch and the sight of his boat-mate thumping his stomach to produce it made Jolicoeur want to retch. But he managed to restrain his stomach's inclinations by facing forward and focusing on his function as paddler of the fore deck. Fortunately for him, the paddler of the aft deck produced ninety percent of the thrust needed to stay abreast of the fleet.

Word of Jolicoeur's wretched condition spread rapidly. Although Striking Eagle's efforts allowed them to keep pace, they could not outrun the other boats. The unhappy result of this was that a steady procession of canoes and bateaux came alongside, their occupants offering wine to Bonin and casting unkind if harmless aspersions on his manhood to the endless delight of everyone. Everyone, that is, but Jolicoeur, who was not in the mood, and Striking Eagle, who didn't quite know what it meant to be drunk. Jolicoeur was weighing the agony of punishment against the joy of vengeance for battering a particularly obnoxious grenadier over the head with his paddle when a cry from the lead bateau reached his ears. Shifting his gaze forward, he saw the marine who was serving as pilot of Villiers' bateau pointing toward the eastern shore. Then he saw what the pilot was pointing at: the British storehouse at Redstone Creek, a tall, overlapping log structure with no windows sitting on a shallow plateau above a rocky riverbank. It was framed by a stand of oaks, maples and beeches to its rear and, in front, by a field of grass that showed signs of trimming but had grown back to a height of thirty centimeters or thereabouts. Bonin could detect no signs of life inside or outside the structure. But Striking Eagle could.

"Over there, over there, Jolicoeur," he chattered eagerly. "Look, do you see them? Iroquois!"

Bonin followed the line of Striking Eagle's outstretched arm and pointing finger to the edge of the forest at the left of the storehouse. At first he saw nothing but then spotted two, then three black faces peering from behind tree trunks. Now knowing what to look for, he found several Indians deeper in the woods.

"How do you know they are Iroquois?" Jolicoeur inquired.

"I know two of them. They are from Chiningue."

Bonin remembered that Chiningue was the name for the Indian settlement the British called Logstown, ten miles downstream of the forks.

"You recognize them even with their faces painted black?" Bonin asked querulously.

Striking Eagle stared at his boat-mate, uncomprehending.

"A man is more than his face, Jolicoeur," he explained. "He stands, he walks, he runs. All of these tell you who he is. The big one in the middle, do you see? The one who stoops on his knee. His name is Long Man. See how he stretches his leg in front so it will not block his aim. It is easy to know who *he* is."

Bonin glanced at the spot indicated by his friend. Sure enough, a black-faced Indian was kneeling on one knee with the other leg thrust forward to permit him an unobstructed view along the barrel of his musket. It was slightly unsettling that the musket appeared to be aimed at him.

"It would be easy to know you too, Jolicoeur," the big Shawnee chortled. "You are too short to be a man and too wide to be a boy."

"Ha, ha, M'sieur Eagle. That is very funny, I suppose," Bonin said with a smile, wondering if, in calling him *wide*, Striking Eagle meant *husky* or *fat*. Self-consciously, he sucked in his waistline.

By this time, the crews of Villiers' bateau and several others had caught sight of the partially concealed Indians ashore. Seeing that they had been spotted, the Iroquois fired off their muskets in the general direction of the flotilla and then scampered into the woods. Several desultory rounds of musket fire exploded from the flotilla in response, but to no avail. The exchange had been a waste of ammunition on both sides.

As each canoe and bateau landed, its Indian passengers leapt out, whooping and screaming, and made for the woods. To maintain a semblance of order, Villiers and Le Mercier dispatched several officers to tag along with their Indian allies. The remaining companies of marines were assigned the tasks of breaking into the storehouse to search for Englishmen or unloading the bateaux. Villiers, Le Mercier, de Longueuil, and their subalterns conferred in the shade of a tall sycamore clutching the edge of the plateau where it fell away to the riverbank. Since the Indians were already chasing the Iroquois and there were more marines than tasks to occupy them, the remainder of the assault force stretched out on the beach, stood around talking and drinking, or gathered at the shore to skip the flat, sandstone rocks littering the beach over the sleek surface of the river. As soldiers of all armies do most of the time, they waited for something to happen.

Jolicoeur Bonin and his Shawnee companion joined the group of marines watching the stone-throwers. To the cheers and applause of his cohorts, a slender, wiry man with a hooked nose overflowing with nostril hair successfully skipped a rock seven times before it finally succumbed to drag and gravity. Jolicoeur dutifully clapped his appreciation as well, then sat down to relax.

"Do you want to go hunting for the black faces?" he asked, thinking his friend would jump at the chance.

"No," a bored Striking Eagle groaned, leaning on his musket. "It would be good to hunt Englishmen but those ones are only Iroquois."

Jolicoeur removed his blue cap and laid it on a bed of rocks to rest his head on.

"I'm going to try to sleep," he announced, meaning that he wanted a chance to recover from the effects of too much wine. He had just dropped off, nurturing erotic visions of the three buxom officers' wives who had given him the *nom de guerre* 'Jolicoeur' or 'Sweetheart', when he realized he was being shaken. He opened his eyes to find the big Shawnee kneeling over him.

"Jolicoeur, are you awake?"

"No more," Bonin answered, rubbing his eyes. H

"Would you like duck for dinner?"

When his vision finally cane into focus, Jolicoeur saw the line of mallards twenty meters offshore that a grinning Striking Eagle was scrutinizing like a Montreal poulterer.

"Go ahead, shoot one. I don't care," he mumbled, quickly replacing the blue cap on his head.

"No, no, I need your help," the Shawnee grumbled, resuming his badgering of the smaller man. "I need you to frighten them."

"What?"

"I need you to shoot over their heads…to make a big splash," Striking Eagle explained, his grin broadening.

Bonin gazed at his tall companion, then at the ducks, and decided to avoid further aggravation by cooperating, even though he did not understand the motive behind the Shawnee's request. After loading powder and ball into his musket, he struggled to his feet, aimed, and fired. Penetrating the water two meters behind the luxuriating mallards, the ball kicked up a spray half as high and achieved its objective: The ducks complained mightily in a single, collective quack and took to the air, assuming a flight path directly over the beach. Striking Eagle pointed his musket at the lead mallard and fired. The duck stalled as the others darted by, then fell to the ground near the base of the plateau, its wings still flapping. The Shawnee rushed to it, struck its head with the blunt end of his scalping knife, and returned victorious to a second round of cheers and applause from the marines.

"Amazing," Bonin exclaimed, stupefied. "Why didn't you just shoot it in the water?"

Walking to the canoe, the big man responded, "I would have to swim out to get it if I did that."

"But what if they flew the other way?"

Striking Eagle's undersized mouth grinned puckishly.

"It is more fun to shoot at them while they are flying. Besides, that is why I told you to shoot at the water behind them, so they would fly this way."

Amazing, Jolicoeur thought to himself, *that a man who has shot at nothing but wine bottles and has so little capacity for reason can achieve a feat of such skill and judgment.* And he had done it with a single shot from a weapon not known for its accuracy. It must be what was referred to in wolves and mountain lions as 'cunning.' The diminutive Frenchman mouthed a small prayer of thanks to his Catholic god for giving the big Shawnee to him as a friend and not as an enemy.

While Striking Eagle was stuffing the duck into a hunting pouch retrieved from his belongings in the canoe, a rustle of activity burst forth at the edge of the forest. The two companions turned to see five of the French Indians leading a young brave by a rope tied around his neck. The youngster could have been no older than Striking Eagle and, except for ornamentation in his ears and nose and intricately painted designs tattooed on his face and torso, wore nothing but a breechclout and moccasins. These and the roach cut jutting like a clothes brush from his skull would have made him look utterly ferocious had it not been for the small, darting, rodent eyes that proclaimed only abject terror.

"They will torture him, then they will kill him," Striking Eagle said bluntly.

"How do you know?"

"Because they are from the north: Hurons, Abenakis, Ottawas. They hate the Iroquois even more than we do."

Bonin accepted the explanation. He had heard before of the animosity between the Six Iroquois Nations and the tribes of the lake regions. There were some who said that, had the Europeans not come to North America, the Six Nations would exert the dominant military and political power on the continent and would have been hated in proportion to that power. The northern tribes hated the Iroquois more than most because they had only recently tasted the bitterness of being driven from their homelands south of the Great Lakes and the St. Lawrence River. It was a hatred the French had played liberally upon to persuade those tribes to come south and fight their enemies and the allies of their enemies: the British.

As Jolicoeur watched, the captors led the captive to the storehouse, where a sullen Villiers, a paunchy Le Mercier, and a diffident de Longueuil were standing.

"Perhaps they will not have to hurt him. Perhaps he will tell my Captains what they want to know and they will let him go," the optimist in Jolicoeur said, searching for confirmation in Striking Eagle's face. He did not find it.

"Your Captains do not own him," Striking Eagle said with untypical fatalism. "The Hurons own him. They are not known for their mercy."

It was an odd statement for a man whose every waking instant seemed to be consumed by the thought of killing Englishmen. Mercy was not a quality Jolicoeur would have thought his friend possessed in perceptible quantities.

"You have had a bad experience with the Hurons?" he asked.

"They attacked our village when I was very young. My father was killed before they were driven away. A friend of mine and his mother were carried off."

The equanimity with which Striking Eagle spoke caught Jolicoeur unawares. Given such a tragedy in Striking Eagle's past, Jolicoeur would have expected his friend to be overwhelmed by a passion for vengeance. Yet here he was dispassionately discussing the death of his father and the loss of a friend to a Huron attack.

"You do not hate the Hurons for what they did?" Bonin inquired delicately.

The Shawnee paused to think. He had never before been confronted by such a question.

"Yes, I hate them," he answered, with a conspicuous lack of ardor.

"But you are not angry! And yet you despise the British who have, to be sure, cheated your people, but have never harmed you personally."

The tall youth folded his arms and gazed at the Frenchman from beneath brows furrowed by uncertainty.

"You *want* me to like Englishmen?"

"No, of course not! I just want to understand. You want to kill Englishmen, or so you tell me every day. But you are willing to excuse the Hurons for what they did. It does not make sense."

"What does it mean, *excuse?*"

"It means you do not care to seek revenge."

"But that is wrong! I *will* have my revenge," Striking Eagle explained patiently, as if speaking to a child. "But I cannot be angry with all my enemies at once. There are too many."

"And now is the time to take revenge on the British?"

"Yes."

"Why? What makes it the right time?"

"There are many things…" Striking Eagle stammered.

Jolicoeur Bonin could see he was disrupting the big Indian's composure but pressed on, curious to learn more about a way of life in which anyone outside the tribal unit was an enemy by predestination and outrage was governed as much by opportunity as by wrath.

"…I don't think we should talk about it anymore," Striking Eagle muttered vexatiously. The queue of hair spouting from his skull writhed like a nervous snake as he added, "Why are you asking me these questions? What does it matter about the Hurons? When it is the right time, my people will have their revenge. But we are all fighting the British now. Is that not so?"

Bonin was impressed by the logic and amused by its simplicity. *Kill* the English now because it is the right time and we are all, French and Indian, in the mood for battle. Pure, unfettered aggression, unadulterated by arcane notions of chivalry. It was marvelous!

"You are right, M'sieur Eagle. We will not talk of it further."

But Striking Eagle was not quite ready to wind down entirely.

"There is too much going on in your head, Jolicoeur," the Shawnee scolded, pointing to his own skull. "You remind me of my friend. He too is fond of asking questions that have no answers, like you."

"And who is this friend?"

"His name is Old Smoke. He is the one I told you about, the one who was taken by the Hurons."

"But how can you talk to him if he was taken by the Hurons?" the confused Frenchman asked.

"They let him go after his mother died. They said she was a saint, the Hurons and the French priests…What are they called?"

A germ of interest awakened somewhere in the memory of Jolicoeur Bonin.

"The Jesuits? This Old Smoke and his mother were with the Jesuits? Do you know…where?"

Striking Eagle shook his head. The writhing snake of his hair mimicked the motion.

"I do not remember, but he will be joining us soon. You can ask him then why he wants to kill Englishmen instead of Hurons," The Shawnee said, flaunting the sarcasm. "He will have better answers than I do and may even have some stupid questions for you."

Bonin laughed and was preparing to ask a few more stupid questions when he saw his friend's attention suddenly diverted elsewhere. With a nod in the direction of the storehouse, Striking Eagle said, "Your Captains are calling us."

It was, in fact, only Le Mercier and de Longueuil who were shouting and making their way down the steep slope from the plateau. The Commander, Villiers, remained at the storehouse chatting with two of the servants he had brought with him. Once on the riverbank, the paths of the two Captains diverged, de Longueuil heading for a group of marines and Indians farther upstream and Le Mercier strolling toward the gathering of rock-skippers of which Jolicoeur and Striking Eagle were honorary members. With his *pince-nez* glasses perched on the tip of his nose, the overweight Le Mercier looked like a schoolmaster on a Sunday outing as he tip-toed over the rocks, trying to avoid injury to his tender, moccasin-clad feet. On arriving, he stood upright, legs slightly apart, hands on hips—a relaxed but authoritative pose.

"I'm sure you'll all be glad to hear that we are moving out," he said, peering at them over the *pince-nez* and offering a friendly if forced smile. Le Mercier was not a gifted speaker. A few murmurs rose and fell and the Captain muddled on: "The prisoner has told us that a force of four hundred British soldiers is twenty kilometers east of here at the cabin of one of the English traders…"

Out of the corner of one eye, Bonin could see the French Indians leading the disconsolate prisoner into the woods south of the storehouse.

"Until yesterday they were building a road to this place, which they call Redstone, undoubtedly for the purpose of launching an attack on Fort Duquesne. But they have stopped and are now retreating, probably because their spies have told them of our movements. We are *three times* their number!"

Le Mercier stopped for a pregnant pause to let it sink in that the British would be overwhelmed. It was good practice to let potential deserters know that a glorious victory was in the offing; defeat and its anticipation tended to thin the ranks. When the Captain resumed his exposition, his expression was noticeably more self-assured, verging on smug. The good part was coming.

"But we must catch them first," said Le Mercier, enjoying himself as he revealed the plan. "And to accomplish that we must move quickly to prevent their escape. And to accomplish that…"

Another pregnant pause with raised eyebrows and an enigmatic grin.

"…and to accomplish that we must travel lightly. So, we will be leaving the wagons and cannon behind…"

The Captain went on to say that the reserve provisions would be kept in the storehouse along with the wagons and artillery, to be guarded by a small detachment—*Are there any volunteers?* —to be chosen by him. While the paunchy Captain was talking, Jolicoeur Bonin noticed Villiers poised rigidly at the top of the embankment, overseeing the proceedings, his thin lips compressed into a tight, horizontal line. It was the chiseled-in-stone face he had worn since the departure from Fort Duquesne.

"Why is your captain always so angry, Jolicoeur?" the Shawnee whispered.

"It was his half-brother who was killed by the British."

"Still, he should laugh. He will be killing Englishmen soon. He will have his revenge."

Bonin took a quick glance at Striking Eagle to see if the Shawnee's curious juxtaposition of laughter and death was accompanied by an expression of wry humor. It was not.

"It is a matter of honor. Captain Villiers will not be content until this Washington and the others who killed his brother are captured."

"And he will be angry until then?"

"He'll try to be angry until then."

Striking Eagle shook his head in disbelief, saying, "I would save my anger until I could make use of it."

"You are not a Frenchman."

After answering questions and identifying the men who would stay behind, Le Mercier told the remainder to form into two columns at the storehouse and await further orders. Jolicoeur Bonin and Striking Eagle pulled their canoe completely ashore and extracted their belongings: a haversack which the small Frenchman strapped to his back, and Striking Eagle's deerskin bag fitted with a long strap for supporting it from his forehead. The Shawnee removed the hunting pouch with the mallard from the canoe and stuffed it into the bag. Then he tossed the bag onto his back and adjusted the strap for a good fit with his scalp. Both men rested their muskets, barrel front, on their shoulders and climbed the embankment to the storehouse, where they joined the second of the two columns forming up.

As he and the others waited for their marching orders, Jolicoeur had time to reflect on the unexpected twists his life had taken since his initiation into manhood. Three years before, at eighteen years of age, his only plan had been to join an uncle at La Rochelle near Paris to seek his fortune—or at least a well-paying job. But on arriving he discovered that his uncle had died, and took the advice of an officer he had met on the road to seek employment with the military establishment on the Isle of Rhee, a recruiting station of sorts. After working there for a year, he developed an urge to travel and became a recruit for service in Canada, a place he had never heard of as a child in Paris.

How very different his life would have been if his uncle had been alive and well! He would probably have spent his entire existence as a clerk in some insignificant business establishment and would never have experienced this magnificent land! The woods before him for instance. There was nothing so grand and foreboding at home. Men had become lost in these woods and never returned. Rural France was a cow pasture by comparison, where a traveler needed only to find the nearest church steeple or a gaggle of local geese to re-orient himself. On a day like this one, the woods would be hot and sweaty as well as grand and foreboding, so Jolicoeur removed the blue cap and stuffed it into his haversack. *At least we will be out of the sun during the march!*

When the Captains did not arrive in short order, Bonin, Striking Eagle, and the others removed their packs and sat down to relax on the dry ground. Striking Eagle, resonating with nervous energy, found he could not relax and was soon on his feet again pacing, throwing his scalping knife at innocent trees, and irritating everyone who would have liked to do nothing for as long as possible. With his eyes, Jolicoeur signaled the Shawnee to calm down, but only succeeded in converting Striking Eagle's anxieties into speech.

"I am glad we are not taking the cannons!" the big Indian announced suddenly and decisively.

"Why?" Jolicoeur asked.

"It is not…a good thing for men to explode their enemies into small pieces. It is not…" the Shawnee stumbled, searching for the word in his companion's language.

"Decent? It is not decent?" Jolicoeur offered.

Striking Eagle quickly embraced the suggestion. "Yes…It is not decent…"

Bonin wondered if this was to be another example of unexpected humanity from his friend. It nearly was.

"A man who dies from cannon fire does not know his killer. He should know him. It is his right. To kill a man with a cannon is cowardly. It is more decent," Striking Eagle pontificated with perfect seriousness, "…to cut out your enemy's heart as he stands bravely before you."

The Frenchman could see it would be necessary to have further conversations with his friend on defining a mutually agreeable concept of decency. But not now. The Captains were coming, no doubt to move them out. What was that prayer he had uttered less than a half-hour ago? *Thank you, Father, for giving this man to me as a friend and not as an enemy.* He would have to write it down, that prayer, or sear it into his brain as a liturgy to be recited during moments of peril.

Chapter Thirteen

July 1, 1754, The road to Great Meadows

It was not the first time he had tripped and fallen to the ground—half the weight of a swivel gun was still a heavy load— but it was the first time the cannon had struck him during its fall. Thomas Patton cried out in anguish and grabbed his right ankle. The man at the other end of the gun, John Ramsey of George Mercer's company, set the breech end of the gun on the ground and came to Patton's aid. So did their marching companion, Ezekiel 'Zeke' Richardson, but only after he abruptly dropped the swivel gun he was carrying into a ditch lined with grass and weeds. Richardson was a hulking backwoodsman and farmer from the Shenandoah Valley and had carried heavier loads than this one on his callused shoulders.

"Let's see it," Ramsey said, kneeling down.

Thomas released his grip on the gun, removed his boot, and let Ramsey roll up the leg of his breeches. On the right side of his ankle was a swollen, purplish-blue welt an inch in diameter, but there was no break in the skin, no bleeding. Richardson took the skin around the bruise between his massive fingers and massaged. Thomas winced and let out another brief cry of pain.

"Nothin' broken," Richardson concluded.

"Try walkin' on it," Ramsey coaxed. He was an amiable but cynical man with a perpetual frown and whiskers that never quite made it to beardhood but never vanished entirely. His amiability was reserved for his enlisted cohorts. He had never much cared for officers—a point of view that had been considerably reinforced by circumstances. Having to participate in lugging a cannon over rugged terrain was one such circumstance, even though the militiamen had drawn lots to determine which of them would carry the clumsy weapons. The officers, of course, were exempt.

Thomas Patton slipped his shoe back on and took a few steps, finding that he could walk, albeit with a limp. As he was testing the ankle, the members of Mackay's Independents passed by in double file, looking their usual crisp, military selves. Some waved sympathetically; others were more reticent. Ramsey would have none of it.

"If y're so damned worried about the boy, why don't ya take his end 'a the damned cannon?" Ramsey shouted, removing the patch of burlap he used to prevent his scalp from frying so that he could chase after one man. The surprised soldier hastily retreated under the assault. Ramsey quickly restored the burlap to its protective position on his head and neck. The road back to Great Meadows was the most efficient route and the only one the wagons could take, but the absence of a leafy roof above their heads left the men exposed to the sky and its fiery resident, the summer sun.

"Sons of bitches," Ramsey spat. "Bastards! Lazy, son-of-a-bitchin' bastards!"

"John, there's no need to curse," Zeke Richardson sighed as he adjusted the straw hat on his bald head for better shielding. He knew that purity of speech was not likely ever to become a John Ramsey virtue but hoped optimistically for a degree of moderation. "It's not their fault. Some of those boys would like to help, but they have to stick to the rules, and the rules say they can't. They got no choice."

Ramsey glanced sharply at the man from the Shenandoah, looking for an argument, but found Richardson's countenance so pacific, so serene, that he couldn't make it work. Arguing with someone who always replied in calm reasoned tones was frustrating. John Ramsey preferred knock-down, drag-out shouting matches as a way of releasing cumulative stress.

"A-a-ah!" Ramsey complained, turning his head away.

To make things worse, Richardson patted Ramsey on the back and muttered, "Good man." Then he said to Patton, "How is it, Tom? Can you carry the cannon? We'll ask the Colonel for someone else if you can't."

"Yeah, it's all right. I can do it," Thomas replied, not wanting to relinquish his first real responsibility. The young man felt an orphan's need to impress everyone, especially his mentor, Washington. "We don't have far to go, do we?"

"No."

"Then I can carry it," Thomas said, trying but failing to inject enthusiasm into the statement.

"Good boy, good boy," Richardson said, inflicting his spine-rattling back pats on Thomas as he had done on Ramsey. While Thomas appreciated the words of encouragement, he did not care to be called 'boy.' But he knew Zeke Richardson intended no slight. The huge, pear-shaped, backwoodsman spoke to everyone in friendly but patronizing inflections. It was as if his size and strength set him apart from mere mortals, who might break if he treated them too roughly or cry if he spoke too harshly to them. This god-like demeanor was not matched by a divine shape, however. Though lack of food had diminished them all somewhat, the rolls of flesh stacked at Richardson's waist line and the creases between his major body parts—armpits and the like—were dripping with sweat and glowing rosy red from constant battering. Had Thomas Patton ever seen a walrus, he might have compared the figure of Zeke Richardson to the hairless, lumbering sea beast and wondered how long his companion's body fat could sustain him without food. A good while, Thomas might have concluded. Richardson received the same inadequate rations as everyone else and had still chosen to carry a swivel gun himself rather than attempt to co-ordinate his movements with another human being. Of all the swivel gun porters, Richardson seemed to suffer the least.

Thomas took his place at the front of his and Ramsey's cannon and stooped down to grasp it behind his back so that he was facing forward as the bow of the cargo ship he and Ramsey would become. Ramsey took his place at the stern and—on three—they lifted their cargo to waist level and re-joined the ragged line of marching Virginia Volunteers who were struggling up the western slope of Chestnut Ridge. Zeke Richardson hoisted his cannon onto his broad, fleshy shoulders and followed. To minimize the irritation to his ankle, Thomas Patton found it best to lay his injured foot down ball first, giving him a distinct limp. But it kept his focus on the job at hand instead of on Ramsey's incessant sniping.

"It's a hell of a thing, Zeke," said Ramsey, offering the bait.

"What's that, John?" Richardson replied, trying, like Thomas, to expend at least half his mental energy placing one foot in front of the other.

"This expedition. This army. I have to say I'm dis'chanted with the whole thing. What the hell we doin' out here, anyway? We oughtta go home."

"We came here to defend Virginia, to boot the French out," Richardson said dutifully, then added as a teasing afterthought, "and to claim our share of Dinwiddie's two hunderd thousand acres."

"That's right," Ramsey nearly shouted, rolling his head in a wide circle because he couldn't use his arms to express his ire. "That's right. We came out here to be soldiers. An' what the hell are we? Goddamn mules, that's what!"

Richardson snickered at the metaphor, then became serious.

"What would you have us do, John? Throw the cannons away and retreat without a fight? You want to give up your piece of land that easy?"

Ramsey crept alongside his larger companion and lowered the timbre of his voice.

"I don't know if you noticed, but we ain't gonna win! There ain't gonna be no land to divvy up! Look at this mis'rble army," Ramsey whispered with a surreptitious cock of his head toward the procession. "Ain't nobody in it knows anything about fightin' a battle, 'cept maybe that sonofabitch Mackay, and' he ain't gonna dirty his hands helpin' *us*. Christ, Washington is only…"

"John, please watch your language," Richardson scolded.

"…Washington is only twenty-two years old," Ramsey continued. "Ain't much older 'n Thomas. What kinda commanding officer is that? He ain't got no trainin'. He ain't got no experience. Christ, he ain't even fought a battle yet…"

"Yes, he did!" exclaimed Thomas, defending his mentor. "He fought a battle last month, and won. I know. I was there."

"Ya call that a battle?"

"How do you know? You *weren't* there."

Which was true. Ramsey had been with the detachment sent by Washington to Gist's place while the Colonel and Adam Stephen had been shooting Frenchmen and starting a war.

"I heard it was a turkey shoot," Ramsey said. "Don't need no general to win a turkey shoot, Thomas. Don't need no pluck, neither."

Unable to respond effectively, the younger man put on his most disagreeable face, flashed it at Ramsey, and turned his head to the front, muttering, "Don't talk about what you don't know, John. The Colonel's a good man…"

Thomas would have liked to say more, mount a stronger defense, but was again at a loss for words. Following Ramsey's lead, he jumped into the right column, just ahead of the pack horses and cattle at the rear of the parade. Zeke Richardson took a place in the left column. Just before making his move, Thomas spotted Washington's sorrel five rows back, loaded with ammunition packs.

"Y'see that, John? That's the Colonel's horse. He's walkin' just like us."

"He ain't carryin' no cannon," Ramsey scoffed.

"He's a good man, John. Why do you want to get on him so?" Patton retorted.

"My barber's a good man too, son," Ramsey said, chuckling. "Nice fella. Just a gnat's knee over five foot tall. Good height for cuttin' hair but I sure as hell wouldn't hire him to be my bodyguard."

With an edge in his voice, Richardson peered at Ramsey from beneath his straw hat and said, "John, we know you don't like the Colonel…"

"It ain't I don't like the Colonel…"

"Well, then, you don't think he knows what he's doin'."

"That's right. He don't know what he's doin' any more'n the rest of 'em do. An' he ain't tellin' us the truth about the supplies, either. They ain't comin'. I'm tellin' ya, they ain't gonna be there."

Thomas gritted his teeth and bowed his head, wanting to say something positive but lacking the skills to present his case. The officers, including Washington, had been telling them that supplies from Wills Creek would be waiting at Great Meadows when they arrived. If they weren't…but Thomas could not bring himself to project his imagination beyond such a dreadful prospect.

Richardson must have noticed Patton's dismal mood because he said, "Don't worry, Tom, the supplies will be there. At least some of them."

"Ain't none gonna be there, Zeke," Ramsey reiterated annoyingly.

Responding to Patton's skeptical gaze, Zeke Richardson shrugged his shoulders as best he could with a cannon weighing them down and said, "Can't talk to a stubborn old mule."

"Hummpph!" the stubborn old mule brayed.

Contrary to Zeke Richardson's encouraging words, there remained six or seven miles of travel to Great Meadows, farther than Thomas would comfortably have resigned himself to had he known. But he didn't know. So when they reached the crest of Chestnut Ridge, passed within a mile of the place where Jumonville's command had been attacked, and traversed the series of undulating hills between Chestnut Ridge and Great Meadows, Thomas took each obstacle as a sign that the journey was nearing its end. Except for random complaints and cursing from John Ramsey, there was not much to be heard from the marchers but heavy breathing and the crunch of boots on sod and rock. They were too tired for conversation. When finally the confined roadway expanded into the spaciousness of Great Meadows, Thomas found himself surprised, even unbelieving. But before he could revel in leisure, Thomas saw Washington, Mackay, and a few of the other officers returning with dejection on their faces, Washington looking particularly despondent. The Colonel and Mackay then halted while the remaining officers gathered their men around the two commanders. Washington raised his hands for silence and began to speak.

"I can't hear what he's sayin'," Thomas said, dropping his end of the swivel gun to the ground. "I'm gonna get closer. John, Zeke, are you comin'?"

"Yeah, I'll be right with you," Richardson said. Then, noticing that Ramsey had dropped his burden and seated himself comfortably against the trunk of a pin oak, he added, "You're not comin', John?"

"No, I already know what he's sayin'. He's gonna tell us there ain't no supplies."

Richardson unloaded his swivel gun and gave each shoulder a

good rubdown with the opposite hand.

"John, you're an old reprobate. How do you get yourself out of bed each morning with such a black outlook? It must hurt somethin' awful."

Ramsey shifted the burlap to cover his forehead, then gazed plaintively up at the bigger man and said, "I ain't no reprobate, just realistic. What if I'm right? What if there ain't no supplies? What if we got no chance 'a winnin'…like we ain't? Can you give me a good reason why I should stay here, Zeke? I mean a good reason, not just 'for old Virginny' or somethin half-witted like that? A good reason. Why should I stay here, Zeke?"

The two men stared intently at one another, each keenly aware of the implied threat Ramsey had just uttered. Richardson stood perfectly still, reluctant to reply to the treasonous implications of Ramsey's statement. Finally, he did speak.

"You find your own reasons, John. And God save your soul."

Patton and Richardson left Ramsey to dwell on his fevered ramblings and went to join the crowd that was gathering around Washington, Mackay and the officers of the Virginia and Carolina forces. Washington was speaking. Oddly, or perhaps characteristically, the status-conscious Mackay always seemed to defer to the younger Virginian when there was bad news to be told or unpleasant decisions to be made. The Commander of the Virginia Regiment was no more gaunt and malnourished than anyone else, but there was a sallowness in his complexion that set him apart. Dark circles hung heavily beneath his eyes, pressing his lips into an immutable frown. At twenty-two years of age, Colonel George Washington looked old. As he talked, his eyelids fell to disguise the shame and anxiety in his face as he told them that no supplies and no troops had arrived. Then he told them that Tanacharison and his retinue had broken camp and disappeared—which they *hadn't* known—and that, although Andrew Montour remained, his backwoodsmen had gone—which most of them *did* know. There was no discussion of Monacatoocha. The Oneida chieftain who had made such a bold statement of his British sympathies by burning his village and moving his people east had simply not shown up. There was nothing to talk about. It was a bleak picture Washington was painting.

The commanders ended the meeting by instructing their men to make camp. The Virginians were also to be prepared to begin strengthening Fort Necessity's fortifications immediately, with Captain Robert Stobo in charge. The groans were few; they all knew the French were coming and what that meant. Lethargically, Thomas Patton and Zeke Richardson turned to retrieve their swivel guns only to discover that the spot where John Ramsey had perched himself against the pin oak was vacant. Fearing the worst, the two men searched frantically for their companion among the troops and within the woods adjacent to Great Meadows, but to no avail. John Ramsey was gone.

As if to mock the expedition's plight and Ramsey's desertion, several wagonloads of flour arrived two hours later, along with the news that two New York companies had reached Alexandria and would soon be on the way with heavy cannon, ammunition, and foodstuffs. But there was no jubilation: The hungry, overworked warriors at Fort Necessity had heard it all before.

July 2, 1754, Jumonville's glen

It would have been well if the Recollect monk who was the chaplain of the expedition could have given the prayer, but the good father had collapsed after a few miles of forced march in the sweltering humidity and had to be sent back to Redstone.

Not all of the bodies strewn about the rocky floor of the glen were absent their scalps, but enough were to make it clear that the Iroquois allies of the British had participated in the massacre. This was a departure from the story told by Sergeant Mouceau. The Iroquois had clearly been willing participants, Le Mercier ruefully concluded as he stood next to his tormented and ashen-faced Commander. At least as unexpected as the Iroquois involvement was the fact that some of the bodies had not been scalped, suggesting that the British had at least attempted to exercise a limited degree of control over their Indian allies. But it was of no consequence. In violation of the norms of civilized behavior and battlefield etiquette, the British had failed to bury most of the bodies. It was perhaps a small thing, but one that mattered to men already enraged by British perfidy. As it was, the disorderly display of death only served to confirm the preconceived notions of the officers and men of the *Compagnies des franches* and strengthen their resolve.

"Bury them," Villiers muttered to Le Mercier, barely moving his lips. "I will say the prayer."

Le Mercier saluted his Commander, replied with a terse "Yes, sir," and began retracing the path he and Villiers had followed to the scene of Jumonville's murder. Villiers, plunged into a deep melancholy, remained at the death scene—Le Mercier assumed for the purpose of communing privately with his dead brother's spirit. As a man who would never be mistaken for an athlete, Le Mercier trod carefully over the stony ground, finding the boots he had donned for the march to be as cumbersome as moccasins were unsupportive. Looking around, he could see that the glen was a pretty place, probably at its best when the sun shone through the breaks in the foliage and illuminated the ground below. That was probably why the Sieur de Jumonville had chosen it as a campsite and why, in Le Mercier's judgment, the young man had made a grave error. As the regimental engineer, Captain Le Mercier had an eye for good ground and this was not good ground. A capable commander simply did not place his troops in a hollow between two dominant hillcrests shrouded by trees. It was a death trap. But he would not bring his conclusions to the attention of Villiers. The man had enough on his mind without being told of his half-brother's incompetence.

But perhaps he was being too judgmental. As a diplomat, Jumonville had no reason to anticipate an attack. Still, as a soldier, he should have been prepared for the worst. His command, with its estimable contingent of armed marines, did not have the look of a peace mission. Le Mercier was also well aware that Jumonville and his men had tracked the movements of the British and carried information about them back to Contrecoeur—hardly an activity that could be characterized as diplomatic. The Sieur had been careless, or naive, or whatever young men the world over are the moment before they are forced to face the reality of death.

Before his line of sight was blocked by hanging branches, Le Mercier turned to check the status of his Commander. Villiers was wandering randomly, perusing the arena of destruction, his arms folded and his face a mask of detachment—a policeman looking for clues. His eyes drifted to the left ridge, then moved to the right, then fell back down to the floor of the glen.

He knows. He knows his brother's error.

The portly Captain left Villiers to his restless ruminations and resumed his own trek. Farther along the path, he heard footsteps and a collage of voices, one of them speaking English. Wary, but in no position to resist a British attack by himself, Le Mercier hoped for the best and waited. His heart skipped a beat when a thin, scraggly man in mud-caked and grass-stained clothes suddenly appeared before him. The filthy creature was as surprised as Le Mercier by the encounter, grunted an incoherent English complaint, and came to a halt. It was then that Le Mercier saw the barbed collar around the man's neck and the rope attached to it at one end and to the hand of the giant Shawnee called Striking Eagle at the other. With the Shawnee were Jolicoeur Bonin and a squat Delaware brave with splotchy, bronzed skin and a splay of crow feathers at the apex of his skull. The Raven was one of several multilingual Indians with the expedition: He spoke French, English, and several of the Iroquois dialects in addition to his own language.

"Private, who is this man?" Le Mercier demanded.

Bonin came forward, running his hand along the rope to increase its tension. The dirty man at the end of it—the prisoner—winced in pain as the barbs dug into his neck, forcing his scabbed lips to separate and expose an incomplete row of front teeth. Jolicoeur released the rope and faced the Captain.

"His name is John Ramsey, sir. He's a British deserter. We caught him—or, I should say, Striking Eagle caught him—after we spotted him hiding in a pond east of here."

Le Mercier looked John Ramsey over from his gnarled, chestnut hair to his substantial and callused feet, finding nothing remotely impressive. The prisoner returned the scrutiny in kind, whether in fear or mere curiosity the Captain could not tell. The Englishman was a foe thoroughly beaten. Exhaustion was his only sensation.

"I'm surprised he's still alive. Doesn't your friend have a passion for killing Englishmen?"

Jolicoeur smiled and said, "He wanted to but I talked him out of it. I told him you and Captain Villiers would want this one alive for questioning."

"Very good, Jolicoeur," Le Mercier replied with genuine sincerity. "You have a head on your shoulders. And your…friend," he added, extending a hand toward the Shawnee.

"Striking Eagle," Jolicoeur reminded.

"Yes, yes…Striking Eagle," the Captain blurted. "Striking Eagle, I want to congratulate you for capturing this prisoner. It was a brave thing."

Striking Eagle took the proffered hand and shook it vigorously.

"Thank you…It…was…my…pleasure," he said in clipped French, one eye on Bonin to make sure he had spoken the memorized phrase correctly.

Le Mercier's attention shifted to the Delaware.

"Raven, would you please tell Captain Villiers we have a prisoner?"

The dark, stocky Indian promptly vanished into the glen. A minute late, he reappeared behind a jogging and breathless Villiers. The aroused Commander searched the faces of his subordinates, his melancholy mood temporarily in remission.

"His name is John Ramsey, sir," Le Mercier said.

Villiers motioned the Raven forward to serve as interpreter.

"John Ramsey, what is your organization? Are you with Washington?" Villiers asked politely but expectantly.

Upon hearing the Raven's repetition of the question, Ramsey replied, "Yeah, Cap'n Mercer's comp'ny. Colonel Washington's the Commander."

"Where is Washington now?" Villiers shot back, hoping to shock Ramsey. But the Virginian, though fearful for his life, was wary. He said nothing. Villiers motioned the others aside, leaving himself and Ramsey standing in the middle of a triangle with vertices at Le Mercier, the Raven, and Bonin. Striking Eagle sat on the ground next to Jolicoeur, paying the rope out an extra two meters.

"M'sieur Ramsey, I am normally a patient man but I am, at the moment, in a hurry, as I'm sure you can understand," Villiers said, circling the prisoner circumspectly. When his path intersected the rope, he gestured for Striking Eagle to release it, then raised it to the level of Ramsey's neck and continued circling. After one orbit, the Commander faced the captive and pulled the rope tight. Once again, Ramsey responded with a cry of pain.

"Where is Washington?" Villiers repeated calmly.

Ramsey gasped, bug-eyed, but said nothing. Villiers resumed his cyclic journey, paying out the rope as he went.

"M'sieur, I need information which only you can give me. As honorable men, I can assure you that neither I nor the marines I command will reveal you as its source. But I must have it, and am prepared to reward you for your co-operation. If you will not tell me what you know..." Villiers said ominously, reinforcing his words with a yank on the rope as he stared into the prisoner's eyes. "...I will have to hang you."

"But...but, that's not honorable," the deserter sputtered. "I'm a soldier, not a criminal."

"You were found lurking about our encampment. How do I know you're not a spy?"

"I was trying to find my way home. I'm sick of working like an ox and starving," the prisoner blurted, unaware he had told Villiers half of what he wanted to know—that the British food supply was low.

"You're a deserter, not a soldier. You have no rights!"

By this time, Ramsey was beginning to panic, terrified that Villiers might be speaking the truth. He fell to his knees and nearly began to weep.

"I done you no harm, sir," he pleaded. "I done you no harm at all."

For Villiers, it was the perfect response. The Commander raised his arm and pointed back toward the glen.

"No harm? You say you've done me no harm, M'sieur Ramsey?" he barked testily. "My brother is lying back there with his skull split open, murdered by men completely devoid of honor. And, M'sieur Ramsey, I have every reason to assume you were one of them."

Ramsey tried to speak, to explain that he had not been present at the massacre, had instead been with the mission to Gist's plantation that day, but was intimidated by Villiers' personal involvement. The French Commander would have no mercy. John Ramsey was a dead man. Then he did weep, with soft, fatalistic tears, for himself and for the Sieur de Jumonville. Proximity to death had humanized him.

"I'm sorry...I...I'm sorry," he moaned beseechingly. "But I...I wasn't there. I really wasn't..."

"Tell me where Washington is now or you hang," Villiers insisted coldly. Still the man hesitated.

"Take him. Hang him," Villliers said dismissively, then made a move to leave.

"No, no..." Ramsey faltered, making a last call for mercy with his eyes. "Colonel Washington...is at Great Meadows."

"On his way back to Virginia?" Le Mercier asked.

Ramsey swung his head languidly back and forth while he murmured, "No...they've built a fort. A small one."

Le Mercier could sense the emotional ferment welling up in his commanding officer. Villiers tore into Ramsey with an icy vengeance, demanding answers or death. The prisoner's resistance collapsed totally under the barrage. How far was it to Great Meadows? *Five miles or thereabouts.* What kind of weaponry does Washington have? *Muskets, nine swivel guns.* What is the strength of the British force? *Three hundred Virginia militia and a hundred regulars from Carolina. The Indians and Civilians had disappeared into the night.* As Ramsey had feared, the Frenchman showed no mercy, but his rancor was aimed at the prisoner's will, not his life. When the interrogation was over Ramsey was led away, a broken man whose loyalties had now deserted him twice. As Bonin, the Shawnee, and the Raven marched the prisoner back to the Regiment, Villiers approached Le Mercier.

"Captain, you may now proceed with the other matter," he said distastefully, then added with a wrathful undertone, "Five or six men should be enough. I'll be within shouting distance when you return."

"Yes, sir. Do you intend to have a service for the men?"

Villiers' response was instantaneous: "No, just the officers. It will be brief."

Le Mercier saluted, begged his leave, and turned to go.

"Oh, and Captain..." Villiers said, hesitant.

"Yes," replied Le Mercier, spinning around. Shyly, the Commander approached the Captain, his hands hidden behind his back, his lips forming words without speaking. Finally, he managed to blurt out: "I wonder if you would do me a favor?"

"Of course. What is it?" inquired Le Mercier, anxious to relieve Villiers' distress in any way he could.

"My brother…" Villiers began reluctantly, pointing shakily toward the glen. "My brother is at the far end. His skull has been split open to the collarbone and his brains spilled on the ground. The animals…have been at them…Would you…"

Le Mercier waited patiently, thinking it best to let his Commander work through his grief. Villiers took the opportunity to compose himself, then said, "Captain, I know this will sound like a strange request but…I would consider it a great favor if you would put them back…the brains I mean…what's left of them…if you would put them back in his skull."

The stout regimental engineer said he would.

July 2, 1754, Great Meadows

It was the kind of situation that would normally cause his temper to flare, but Colonel George Washington could no longer afford such a luxury. Of the four hundred troops at Great Meadows, nearly a hundred were too sick or exhausted to work. Of the remaining three hundred, a third were Mackay's Independents, who wouldn't work. How in the name of all things holy was he supposed to prepare Fort Necessity for the inevitable assault without manpower and supplies? Why couldn't Dinwiddie, and Carlyle, and the comfortable stewards of the Virginia government who were supposed to be standing behind this mission understand that the need for men and supplies was *now,* not some arbitrary moment in time when the essential ingredients of money, availability, and political expediency chanced to meet in blissful congruence? In his saturated brain, this was the dominant thought driving George Washington as he gave the chestnut mare a hefty swat and sent Southy Hazlip on his way to Williamsburg to inform Robert Dinwiddie of their desperate plight and to plead, nay beg, for prompt assistance.

"Ha!" the voice of Robert Stobo gleefully commented. Washington turned to find his regimental engineer pointing at him and muffling the sound of his laughter with his other hand.

"What?" Washington asked, incredulous that Stobo should find humor in their tenuous circumstances. "What's funny?"

"George...George," Stobo said, struggling to contain himself. "George, you looked like you wanted to kill that horse."

Breaking into another fit of laughter, Stobo had to sit down at the table in front of Washington's tent where the engineering sketches were spread out. Although his temper told him to maintain the foul mood he was in, Washington found Stobo's merriment contagious and sat down to enjoy the moment.

"The horse be damned," he announced, chuckling profusely. "I wanted to kill Dinwiddie!"

"And Carlyle," Stobo added with a roar.

"And the damned Quakers!"

"And every charlatan who sold us a three-wheeled wagon or a crippled cow."

A passing Virginia Volunteer saluted and scurried on his way, mystified by the revelry.

"I don't think they love us anymore, George. I really don't...Ha!"

More laughter, more high spirits, fists pounding on the table. Washington scurried into his tent and came back with a bottle of corn whiskey he'd picked up in Winchester, pouring generous quantities for himself and Stobo. They toasted the anticipated battle.

"Look at it this way, Colonel," said Stobo. "The worst that can happen is that we'll be eaten by savages or shipped off in chains to Canada."

"It could be worse. We could win," Washington joked, downing a substantial gulp of whiskey. "And then we'd have to feed the prisoners. We can't even feed ourselves."

"No, no, you've got it backwards," Stobo interrupted, waving a corrective finger. "We don't *feed* the prisoners. We *eat* them. Kill two birds with one stone."

"Oh...good idea. We should invite the Half-King. He would certainly appreciate a dinner of French *pate* and *frog*-legs!"

Stobo acknowledged his Commander's wit with a snort and another toast, although neither man could think of anything else to toast. It was the first time Washington had relaxed since Wills Creek. Aided by whiskey and the affable Stobo, he found it a heady experience. For so long he had thought of nothing but the mission and its problems that the invasion of lighthearted repartee into his head was intoxicating even without the liquor. He wanted to go home, to visit a tavern or two and pat a few saucy barmaids in plump, precious places. Or, better yet, do nothing, say nothing, empty his mind of everything. To his own surprise, he found even the thought of Sally fraught with vexing entanglements.

"Robert, I think I may not be cut out for this kind of life," Washington said gloomily. "I think I'll go back to farming."

Stobo, still in an impish mood, said, "Colonel, what you need is a good night out with a couple of blithe spirits and a bevy of buxom barmaids…"

"Stop right there, say no more! I've already had that fantasy."

"Ha!…I'm sure you have," the urbane Scotsman gibed. "Nothin' wrong with that. Have it again. Why don't you and I fulfill your fantasy when we get back?"

Washington gazed at his friend over the raised rum glass. He almost wished he could be the wealthy Robert Stobo: slim, handsome, sophisticated even in work clothes, qualities he would never possess.

"I'd like that, Robert," he said wistfully.

"Seriously, George, I know you *are* a farmer, but I don't think you'll ever be completely content with that life," Stobo said provocatively.

"What do you mean?"

Stobo leaned back on his chair and looked out over the expanse of Great Meadows toward the miniature fort they had built together. From Washington's tent in the northwest, they could see the men of Virginia digging trenches and constructing breastworks on the north side of the stockade and affixing swivel guns to the raised platforms behind it, in accordance with Stobo's sketches. They could also see Mackay and his Independents in full regalia, drilling and honing their military skills as usual. Stobo pointed his finger at the leader of the Carolinians.

"I mean that *he* is what you want to be," the Captain said with a knowing grin at his commanding officer. "And you won't be satisfied until you are."

"I may have no choice in the matter."

"Perhaps...but you won't be satisfied. You'll come back and try again. You love it too much."

It was, Washington thought, an extreme way to describe his interest in the military life.

"I *love* it too much? Let me tell you, Robert. Right now I'd be happy to be a clerk in a general store," he objected.

"Yes, of course. So would I," Stobo acknowledged with a nod. "But that notion will pass as soon as you've had a decent bath, a good meal, a long night's sleep...or two, or three...or two years...or three years. It doesn't matter. Then you'll want to be James Mackay again."

Washington pondered his subordinate's words, wondering if they could be true. Then he lifted a sinewy arm and motioned toward the strutting Mackay, as Stobo had done.

"Tell me, Robert, how did he get where he is? Who is James Mackay that he should command a regiment of regulars? It's certainly not his personality that got him there."

The remark evoked another prattle of giggles from Stobo, who then got to his feet and approached the Virginian, a faint, whiskey-induced swagger in his step.

"That's where you're wrong, George. It *is* his personality, his boorish, anti-social disposition that got him where he is. He's a Scotsman and therefore he's a stubborn ass, just what the British want in a military leader."

Washington laughed politely, but was skeptical, commenting, "I find it hard to believe that being a stubborn ass is a qualification for entering the officer corps of the British army."

"Nevertheless, it is," Stobo retorted, energized by inebriation and beginning to look the part. "To be a stubborn ass—that is, to be a Scotsman—is an advantage in all professions, but to enjoy such an advantage one must be willing to be envied and thus to be despised. We Scots are good at it. In matters of finance, we are seen as miserly. In religion, our fanaticism converts us into drab, monomaniacal soldiers of Christ, marching in lock step to the Pearly Gates. And in the military profession..." Stobo teetered a bit as he once again pointed at his countryman across the field. "...we become James Mackay."

Finished with his exposition, the Captain flashed a sudden, unstable grin at Washington. His balance being equally precarious, he decided to sit down.

"If pertinacity is such a stalwart virtue, why haven't the Scots conquered the world?" the amused Colonel asked.

Stobo shook his head in commiseration and said, "Because each Scot is his own stubborn ass. He belongs to no one, to nothing but himself. It's a very limiting trait for anyone interested in world conquest."

"What about you, Robert? Surely you don't consider yourself a stubborn ass," Washington replied playfully.

"I most certainly do!" Stobo asserted, straightening himself in his chair, then slumping again. "It's just that I'm on vacation right now."

"You're on vacation? Here? Now?"

"Certainly, Colonel. This is an adventure," Stobo explained slyly. "In my real life, I'm a rich merchant. You will never catch Robert Stobo the importer selling his calicos, silk shoes, glassware, copper kettles, fire of brimstone, or Balsam of Life for any less than twice what he paid for it abroad. He can be quite obstinate in such matters. But this..." Stobo spread his arms to encompass all he could see. "...this is fun!"

It was Washington's turn to shake his head in disbelief. Stobo was joking of course, but there was an element of truth in the amiable Scotsman's perspective of unflagging, even eccentric diligence. How should he weigh this advice against Dinwiddie's cajolery, Gist's frontier stoicism, and La Peyroney's Machiavellian pretense? Which of these would best serve him in the coming conflict? The wisdom to know was a prize that was beyond his grasp. Perhaps the best counsel had been that of Lord Fairfax: Ignore Dinwiddie's flattery and stay home. But it was too late for that.

"Robert," Washington called, leaning over the sketches. "Come here a moment."

Stobo complied, moving his chair closer.

"What is it?"

Washington pointed to the battlements Stobo had sketched for the south side of the fort. They were essentially the same as those under construction on the north side: trenches and breastworks in a diamond shape shielding the stockade.

"No one is working on these," the Colonel pointed out.

"I know. There aren't enough healthy men. We've had to make choices. The north side is where the French are most likely to attack."

Washington let his gaze wander toward the Independent camp.

"Those men aren't working," he said.

"George, you know Mackay won't…"

"He's your countryman. Couldn't you use your considerable powers of persuasion on him? Surely, if you can sell goods for twice what their worth…"

"I…George, I don't…"

Washington played his trump card.

"Ask him to do it as a favor," he said, grinning with the same puckish delight that had invested Stobo. "As one Scotch jackass to another."

It was exactly the right way to appeal to the clown in Robert Stobo. The Scotsman stood, saluted and, with inflated pomp, said, "*Yes, sir! Sir*, may I be excused?"

"For what reason?"

Stobo released the salute so his hand would be free to point across the field again.

"To…to…ah…to…" he stammered, struggling with the laughter that wanted desperately to escape. "I'm going to…ah…go see the stubborn ass across the way."

With his intention stated, Stobo roared his pleasure to the world, nearly losing his already dubious balance in the process. He turned and aimed himself at the Independents' camp and started a cautious jog in that direction.

"Robert!"

Stobo halted. Washington cocked his head toward the flagon of corn whiskey sitting on the tabletop.

"Take that with you," he said. "And two glasses. Offer my compliments."

Like mirrored sunbeams, merriment danced in Stobo's eyes and in the glistening teeth of his broad smile.

"Scotch would be better, sir. A much more civilized concoction.

You wouldn't happen to have any, would you?" he kidded.

"No."

"I did'na think so. Well," the buoyant Captain shrugged as he inspected the level in the bottle. "I suppose this will have to do."

With a wink, Stobo resumed his journey, the whiskey he'd ingested giving him a meandering waddle. Once, he turned around to wave at Washington, who cheerfully waved back. By the time he reached the other side of the meadow his path had straightened enough that he no longer resembled a distracted duck, merely an intoxicated captain. Washington watched as Stobo approached his objective, wondering if it had been wise to send a drunken Scot to reason with another who was entirely too sober. It would be just his luck if Mackay turned out to be a teetotaler.

But his luck was good. Surprised by Stobo's visit, the haughty Captain of the Independents at first stood rigidly erect facing Stobo, as if shocked by such a blatant display of bribery. Then he relaxed, took a glass from his visitor, and hastily downed several offerings. This loosened Mackay's tongue. Even though he was too far away to hear, Washington could see Mackay jabbering incessantly with the equally garrulous Stobo for ten minutes. Then he turned his gaze to Washington and executed a formal bow of thanks. *Mission accomplished.*

Reassured, the Colonel rose to stretch his legs and shake off the soporific effects of the whiskey. Despite Stobo's encouragement, he remained unsure of himself and of his ability to command. Had he made a mistake in turning to arms? Was he temperamentally unsuited for the military profession? Could he ever hope to overcome the barriers against colonials that seemed to permeate the officer corps of His Majesty's armed forces?

Of more immediate moment was the question of what he should do: hold his position or withdraw. For the moment, it was La Peyroney's advice he would follow. Whatever his decision was, he would pursue it confidently, as if it were the only logical tactic. Emboldened, he made his final decision—to stay.

But from what direction will the French attack? The other battlefield, Jumonville's glen, is to the west. They'll go there first. Then they'll come.

𝕮hapter 𝕱ourteen

July 3, 1754, Fort Necessity

omething is moving out there, Michael Scully actually declared to himself as he chewed on a wad of Virginia prime tobacco and peered into the woods to the southwest. Seeing was difficult because it was early and the heavy overcast diffused the sun's rays, preventing them from penetrating the forest canopy in force. Hearing was not a simple matter either, with the noise of the drenching deluge pounding in his ears. With sight and hearing thus subdued, Scully decided he would simply shoot at the next movement he saw or snap he heard, which he did, the triggering incident being the swish of wet leaves rustling in the underbrush. But Scully was not prepared for what happened next: a return musket blast from the source of the disturbance that caught him a good one in the side.

"Sonofabitch!" the frightened Virginia Volunteer opined, then scurried east on the road to Fort Necessity and safety. Despite his wound, Scully would make it back in short order, the welfare of his scalp taking precedence over the discomfort of his wound. Halfway home, he realized the wad of tobacco was no longer filling his mouth. He had swallowed it.

* * *

"The frog-eaters are here! The frog-eaters are here!" came the barely audible cry from across what would more appropriately have been called Great Swamp than Great Meadows. The storm clouds that had been gathering all morning suddenly released their liquid load, filling the trenches and turning Great Meadows and Indian Runs into raging torrents of caramel-colored water.

"Sonofab…" Washington gasped, nearly mimicking Scully's impromptu reaction to the inauspicious arrival of the enemy. Having heard scouting reports that the French were near and strong, Washington had that morning conducted an *ad hoc* inspection of the Fort Necessity preparations. With galling obstinacy born of anxiety, he had harassed Stobo and, through Stobo, Mackay, to redouble their efforts to complete the trenches and battlements. Anticipating a conflict, he had the young Surgeon-Major, Dr. James Craik, set up a medical station at the storehouse inside the stockade. The tiny hut, with its bark and hide roof, was the only protection available for the Regiment's valuables: powder, medicine and, of course, rum.

The cries were coming from a man approaching from the southwest along the road to Gist's plantation, which the scouting reports said was now in French hands. He was doubled over, holding his side and limping. Recognizing the man as Michael Scully, one of the men who had been assigned to sentinel duty, Washington rushed past James Craik to the storehouse inside the stockade. Surprised by the intrusion, Craik, who was arranging his medical equipment just inside the doorway, hastily stepped aside.

"What's happening, Colonel?" the Doctor asked. "I heard…"

"It's Michael Scully. I think he's been shot," Washington replied, grabbing one of several muskets stacked at the far end of the enclosure. Before leaving, he looked directly at Craik and said, "We'll have to bring him back here, Doctor."

James Craik scanned the facilities, a veil of despair hanging heavy on his features. There was not enough room in the storehouse for more than ten wounded men and rivulets from the downpour were already snaking their way beneath and between the log walls. Still, it was the driest place inside the stockade. Heaving a bottomless sigh, he said, "Yes, I suppose you will."

Washington thanked him and rushed outside to discover to his relief that Matthew Nevison and John Biddlecome had already hastened to Scully's aid and were serving as crutches for what was clearly a wounded Virginia Volunteer. With the rain dispersing the blood, the stain on the left side of Scully's blouse was huge and, except for the crimson spot where the ball had entered, a pallid shade of pink.

"Michael, what happened?" Washington asked when he reached the bleeding man.

The pale Scully, his normally well-groomed hair covering his face in wet clumps, looked up as if he'd seen the gates of hell.

"Frog-eaters, Colonel, hunderds of 'em. Indians, too, some kinds I never seen before," he whispered, too deep in shock to speak forcefully. "I didn' see 'em at first, but then they shot me an' I run like the devil. Saw 'em comin' outa the woods in three lines. They was takin' their time about it. Tried to shoot me again but missed."

Scully's account of his escape was infused with a measure of pride. He had come face to face with the Gallic horde and survived. It soon became clear from his general composure and garrulousness that, despite being in shock, Scully was not going to die from the wound. There were other, more critical, things to attend to.

"John, Matthew, take him to the storehouse. Dr. Craik is over there. And if you see any of the officers, tell them to come to the southwest gate immediately."

Some of the Virginia officers, among them Robert Stobo and Adam Stephen, were already arriving, as were James Mackay and Christopher Gist, to find out what was going on. To a man, they were soaked through to the skin. Stobo was also caked with mud from digging in the trenches.

"Adam, sound the call to arms and get the men lined up in front of the trenches," Washington ordered with methodical circumspection, trying to calm everyone down, himself included. "Robert, there's no sense digging anymore. Just get your men in place."

Stobo nodded his concurrence, squeezed some of the mud out of his shirt, and joined Adam Stephen in a double time back to the stockade. That left Mackay and Gist. In his primary role as guide, Gist had no critical function in a military situation like this, but Mackay...Washington needed Mackay.

Hesitantly, the Commander of the Virginia Regiment drew himself up before the Commander of the Carolina Independents and said, "Captain Mackay, we need to come to an understanding..."

Mackay, in full uniform except for the coat draped over one arm, held up the flat palm of the other hand and replied, "Sir, there is no time for discussion. We'll take the front positions. It's what we do."

With that, the normally irksome Scot saluted Washington, slipped on the coat, and turned to join his troops, who had already begun to file into the most exposed trenches on the southeast and southwest sides of the diamond-shaped breastworks.

My God, I'm beginning to like this man, Washington found himself admitting.

"Christopher, why don't you go get your sons and find a place to shoot from inside the stockade?" Washington asked as he strode purposefully back to the stockade with Gist. From the corner of his eye he spotted Andrew Montour riding toward them from the northwest, where he had been on patrol duty. Montour was bedecked in his usual garish attire but the red paint and bear's grease on his face had been washed away by the rain. Without the disguise, he looked almost like a white man and could have passed for one but for his sweeping black hair. Few Europeans had hair both that straight and that long.

"What do you think I am, George, an old man?" the unflappable Gist objected.

"Yes," Washington replied bluntly.

In no position to dispute such brusque logic, Gist made an unpleasant smirk and replied, "Well, that may be, but it doesn't mean I can't shoot…"

"I didn't say you couldn't shoot. I just want you to do it from behind palisade walls," the Colonel declared with growing impatience, then forced himself to hold it in check. "Christopher, I don't want you killed. This is a job for young men. Please don't give me an argument."

Gist mumbled, cursed, and made generally unpleasant noises but did as his Commander wished. The last Washington saw of him, the guide was entering the stockade. It was then that Andrew Montour rode up alongside, his attention focused on the southwest perimeter of Great Meadows.

"Colonel, can you see them?" Montour asked, pointing to the tree line in that direction.

Washington looked but could see nothing but rain, mist and tall grass swaying in the storm winds.

"No, I can't," he said and then threw his tricorne to the ground, leaned the musket against the palisade wall and extended his free arm toward the half-breed. "Lift me aboard. Let's take a look."

Montour didn't hesitate. Leaning down to grasp Washington's arm in his own, he swung the Colonel around and onto the horse's rump. Saturated by rainwater, the black horsehair surface was too slippery to provide its new rider with much purchase, so Washington clung precariously to the saddle. Montour dug his heels into the horse's flanks and, with a jerk that nearly unseated its rear passenger, struck off to the southwest.

When they had gone a hundred yards, Washington spotted the three columns of French and Canadian troops and an irregular force of Indians, some of whom were marching with the columns, others out to the side in random groupings. Their war paint, clothing and embellishments were unfamiliar to Washington.

"What Indians are those? I don't recognize them."

Montour halted the horse three hundred yards from the approaching army and said, "Nipissings, Algonquins, Hurons, a few Abenakis and Ottawas. They're from the north. Some Shawnee and Delaware too, but you know them."

The Colonel scanned the invading infantry once more, trying to judge its strength, which, because most of it was still in the woods, was impossible to do with any accuracy. Most of the French marines were shouldering muskets and were dressed in the Canadian wilderness uniform he had first seen at Venango. Several men—or, perhaps, boys—were attired in uniforms of standard issue, and were wielding pikes and halberds, wicked-looking medieval weapons for spearing and chopping at close quarters. Such weapons were useless in a modern army except to intimidate, to send a message to one's opponent that *we intend to get close enough to use these.*

Although only a fraction of the *Compagnies franches* were in the open, the composed, deliberate pace of their march conveyed a sense of much more to come. The infantrymen were simply marking time, going through their paces, while the rear echelons moved into position. There were no frayed nerves, no panic. They knew they would win. Washington wondered apprehensively if they had brought siege guns. If they had, it would be a very short battle. While he was worrying about this and weighing his options, the French before him formed a skirmish line, several of whose members knelt down and began loading their muskets.

"They're going to shoot at us!" Montour said. The horse beneath him felt the tautness in the half-breed's thighs and became skittish, anxious to escape the danger its master was communicating to it.

"Then I suppose we'd better leave," said Washington with an embarrassing tremor in his voice.

By this time, the musketeers were taking aim.

"I suppose that's an order, Colonel," Montour said dryly.

"Yes, definitely."

Montour brought the horse around and reversed course, this time whipping it to a full gallop.

"Duck!" he yelled.

"What?"

The half-breed turned his head ninety degrees and said with insistence, "Get your head down."

"Oh," Washington replied, obeying immediately. But he couldn't execute the maneuver with total success because Montour's back was in the way. So he leaned to the left and hunched over, clamping the horse's haunches between his knees. It was an awkward maneuver but a stable one, the only discomfort being the repeated pounding to his buttocks and proximate parts as the animal cycled through its stride.

A musket discharged, then another, then a flurry of musket fire. A split second later, several of the musket balls whizzed by, leaving an acoustic buzz in the air like a swarm of hornets gone mad.

"Charming," Washington commented, not expecting to be taken seriously.

"Charming?" Montour replied, taking him seriously. "You wouldn't think so if a ball went in one ear and out the other."

I don't suppose I would. But then, I wouldn't be able to do much thinking at all under those circumstances.

Much to the Colonel's surprise, Montour and he arrived safely back at the southwest entrance of the stockade where the officers of the five Virginia companies were waiting, expectant and saturated.

Washington slid off the horse and let Montour go on his way to engage in further reconnoitering of the enemy, a skill for which this man of two worlds was instinctively well suited.

Approaching the officers, Washington shouted instructions: Stobo and his men were to continue occupying the trenches of the southern part of the diamond behind Mackay, and Hogg's men would be inside the stockade and would shoot through whatever cracks and prepared openings were available. The other companies would occupy the remaining positions inside and outside the stockade. A contingent of nine men, specially selected for their sharpshooting skills and headed by Adam Stephen, would man the swivel guns. After the officers had dispersed, Washington put the tricorne back on his head to shield it from the downpour, retrieved the musket he had left leaning against the stockade and headed toward the southwest breastworks. Through the mist churned up by the bombarding rain, he could make out the lead elements of the approaching French marines, still tramping along at a purposeful, deliberate pace. Feeling unnecessarily exposed, he moved to step into one of Stobo's trenches, slipped, and fell into muddy water a foot deep, the cumulus of the day's deluge.

"Sonofab..." he mumbled, then reprimanded himself for nearly cursing the second time that day, and it was only 11:00 AM.

One of Stobo's men, noting the lapse, looked at his prone and rankled Commander and said, "It's all right, sir. Go ahead 'n curse. We all been doin' it since we got here this mornin.'"

The soldier, grinning with a limited supply of front teeth, offered his hand to Washington and pulled the Virginia Commander to his feet. The Colonel gave his thanks, brushed himself off, and again scanned what would shortly be a battlefield. In addition to the French, it was becoming inundated with a myriad of spontaneous rivulets spilling into one another, a network of opaque, gushing liquid, whose ultimate destiny was to feed Great Meadows and Indian Runs, the banks of which were already overflowing.

What did I call this place? He tried to remember. *A charming field for an encounter?*

174

July 3, 1754, Late morning

"What are they doing?" a perplexed Striking Eagle asked his undersized colleague Jolicoeur Bonin as Captains Villiers and Le Mercier directed the lead elements of the French marines into a skirmish line. The Captains were frustrated and argumentative because the mud was making the marines' footing treacherous and the rain was limiting visibility. This was why Striking Eagle had, perhaps inelegantly, posed the question.

Again the Shawnee asked, "What are they doing, Jolicoeur? The British are so far away I can't even see their long noses."

As a European whose ancestry could conceivably include a trace of English blood, Jolicoeur became suddenly aware of the length of his nose but had the mental discipline to set the impertinence aside and reply, "I don't know. Maybe Captain Villiers is trying to make them think we have artillery."

"Artillery?"

"Cannons."

The Shawnee, his face streaked by crows' feet of bare skin where rainwater had eroded away the otherwise ubiquitous red paint covering it, stared skeptically at his friend. Neither Villiers' tactics nor Bonin's explication of them made sense to him. The marines had already fired at and missed the two men on horseback who had galloped away a minute ago. How could they possibly hit targets at twice the distance?

"It is stupid. The musket balls will not fly that far!" Striking Eagle muttered in disgust.

As the Shawnee was speaking, the line of kneeling marines exploded with musket fire. Involuntarily, Jolicoeur jumped. Striking Eagle did not, only shook his head in bewilderment. The volley accomplished nothing discernible. Not a single divot of soaked sod was kicked up on the far side of the field. The Indian, leaning on his musket, aimed an *I-told-you-so* look at his friend. Jolicoeur, who was using the lull in the action to squeeze his capot temporarily dry, shrugged and said, "It wasn't my idea."

Commander Villiers, whose temperament had assumed a cold detachment since finding his half-brother brained and scalped, finally saw the futility of firing at such long range. That he had given the order to do so in the first place was an indication of the fragile state of his nerves. Pacing anxiously, he ordered the marines back into the three-column formation, barked a command to double time to a more forward position, and mounted his horse, which had been brought up by an aide.

"What are we doing now, Jolicoeur?" the still doubtful Striking Eagle asked as he jogged with abbreviated strides to keep from overtaking the smaller Frenchman.

"I don't know. They don't tell me these things."

"But we are moving toward the fort! We should be spreading out into the forest, using the trees to shield us. If we keep moving like this, we will be like that row of ducks we shot at the other day."

"Dinner, you mean?"

The Shawnee grinned appreciatively at the gibe but couldn't quite bring himself to laugh aloud.

"Yes, dinner! I don't want to be eaten by a British general, do you?"

"No," Jolicoeur admitted, wondering what Villiers was up to and wishing his company was a little farther back in the line of march. "But there aren't any British generals over there. Besides, Captain Villiers knows what he's doing," he added with unconvincing ardor.

When they were fifty meters from the stockade and could see British eyes peering between the palisade timbers, British heads popping above the trenches and an array of Brown Bess muskets pointed their way, Captain Le Mercier brought the platoon to a halt and formed another skirmish line. Jolicoeur was assigned to its second rank. Mounted and vulnerable, Villiers stayed a hundred meters to the rear to observe. The Commander of the *Compagnies franches* was taking no chances. Risking his life was not the hand he wanted to play. As a veteran frontier soldier, his courage was beyond reproach, but a premature death would be a major setback to his immediate plans. His brother, the Sieur de Jumonville, must be avenged and Villiers was the only one who could be relied on to pursue the task with the necessary sense of commitment.

A sudden *bo-woomp* filled the atmosphere, followed by a rooster-tail of mud and sod that began ten meters in front of the skirmishers and continued until the cannonball that had created the spray emerged and rolled swiftly but harmlessly past the marines' left flank. Bonin shot a glance at the stockade in time to see a puff of smoke drifting like a lazy cloud away from one of the swivel guns. Its crew was already stuffing the next charge into the barrel.

"Jolicoeur, it is stupid to stand in an open field waiting to be shot at," an anxious Striking Eagle complained.

Neither Le Mercier nor the front rank of skirmishers flinched at the salvo. All muskets were loaded and leveled at the enemy. The Captain's arm was raised high in the air, ready to drop on the 'fire' command. Bonin finished loading his musket and turned to face his friend.

"It's called a fusillade—all muskets firing at once. When the first rank is done, the second rank—that's mine—steps forward and fires while the first reloads. It's a technique used by all the major armies. A well-executed fusillade will send the enemy scurrying to the rear."

The Shawnee, who had instinctively stooped down to reduce his target profile, mumbled, "It is a stupid way to fight. We will be the ones scurrying to the rear."

As if to silence Striking Eagle's protest, Le Mercier dropped his arm and shouted the order to fire. With near simultaneity, the twenty-four marines of the front rank fired their muskets and an equal number of musket balls splattered mud and splinters but no human flesh on the British side of the battlefield. The Englishmen then seized the opportunity to execute their own, not quite as orderly, fusillade, which was nevertheless more effective because the French marines—as Striking Eagle had pointed out—were sitting ducks. Two men in the front rank went down and a third in the second rank cried out in pain as a ball passed through his shoulder. Terrified but obedient, Bonin was readying himself for the second French fusillade when Le Mercier, realizing the futility of the tactic, drew his sword and made a command decision.

"To the woods!" he shouted, sword high above his head, running toward the northwest tree line as if his intent were to assault the flora and fauna residing there.

"I told you it was a stupid way to fight," the Shawnee said, racing alongside Bonin.

"You'll get no further argument from me on that score," Jolicoeur admitted, his short legs churning twice as rapidly as his friend's.

With some difficulty, they made it across Great Meadows Run and to their intended cover: a pair of old sugar maple trees framing the entrance to an ancient Indian trail. Bonin scooted behind the left tree before his scrambling marine colleagues could claim ownership. Striking Eagle was in less of a hurry and, instead of ducking behind the other tree, sat his musket and haversack on the ground beside it, then withdrew the tomahawk from his belt. He was still in the open. Twisting the weapon in his right hand, the tall Shawnee placed one foot ahead of the other and rocked back and forth as if preparing to sprint. An unholy alliance of pride and terror consorted in his cavernous eyes. Then Jolicoeur knew: He *was* going to make a run for it!

"What are you doing? Get down," a horrified Jolicoeur implored.

Striking Eagle raised himself to his full, considerable height, sucked in a deep breath, and tested his footing in the soft, wet earth. Then, with an unsteady, beguiling glance at Jolicoeur, he simply said, "Watch!"

Before the diminutive Frenchman could muster a contrary argument, the Shawnee was off and running toward the British fort, screaming blood-curdling war whoops. With the tomahawk clenched in his hand, his arms pumping as vigorously as his legs, he sprinted onto the field they had just evacuated, making of himself an easy if noisy and distracting target. Apparently spellbound by the Indian's weird flight of fancy, the Virginia and Carolina soldiers in the trenches could only gape in awe. Twenty-five meters from the stockade and floundering in the overflow of Great Meadows Run, Striking Eagle reared back and let fly the tomahawk. Wobbling as it flew, the hatchet climbed to a height of thirty meters, arched over, and nearly knocked the tricorne off a tall, lanky officer who did not have the good sense to avoid exposure. At the last minute, the surprised officer realized the tomahawk was headed his way and stepped aside. The weapon fell harmlessly into a neighboring trench, scattering the muddy water generously over its occupants.

His grand gesture executed, Striking Eagle felt suddenly naked standing in the middle of Great Meadows only twenty meters from the enemy and watching the barrels of a platoon of Brown Bess muskets lining up in his direction. But before they could be discharged, a volley of French musket fire blasted from behind him. Striking Eagle stared in fascination as the musket balls chewed up the earthworks shielding the trenches, terrorizing most and wounding several of the British. But the seduction was short-lived. With an almost religious conviction Striking Eagle realized he had to get away from that place. He turned and, with impossible acceleration, began a frantic retreat in a single, instantaneous motion. When he was halfway back to the tree line and safety, the British guns finally started delivering their bullets. One took a bite out of his left ear, another passed through the leather of his breechclout. But that was all. The scampering Shawnee dived behind the tree opposite Jolicoeur Bonin, landing in an awkward but well-protected heap.

"Ay-y-y! That hurts!" the big Shawnee cried, holding his injured ear.

Disturbed by what he considered Striking Eagle's irresponsible behavior, Jolicoeur's face was nearly as red as the blood splashed on the Indian's shoulder.

"What were you trying to do? Get yourself killed?" he scolded. "That was the most insane thing I've ever seen! How can you call *our* tactics stupid when you do something like that?"

"Your tactics *are* stupid," the Indian replied.

"And yours aren't?"

"I was attacking the big Englishman with the black hat," Striking Eagle answered, pointed toward the trenches in front of the stockade. "And I nearly got him too. Did you see?"

"You attacked with a tomahawk! They were firing back with muskets and cannon!"

"Yes, it was very brave, wasn't it?" the Shawnee said proudly, his grin still active and expanding. "I wish Old Smoke could have seen me."

With what Striking Eagle had told Jolicoeur of Old Smoke, the Frenchman had a different opinion to offer.

"If Old Smoke is as wise as you say, he would tell you what a stupid thing you did," said Jolicoeur.

Striking Eagle's grin abruptly vanished. Exchanging no further words, Jolicoeur Bonin and Striking Eagle attended to their primary duty of killing Englishmen, or trying to. For attackers and defenders alike, the battle had become a brawl. There were no more orderly fusillades on either side, only men briefly exposing themselves to discharge their muskets and then hastily returning to their shelter—trenches, stockade, or trees—to reload. It was a symphony of noise, with the orchestra of droning musket balls underscored by the occasional percussion of metal on bone. The swivel guns so cherished and nurtured by the British did little more than plow up real estate and crack a few tree branches, they were so inaccurate. Even with grapeshot, they were ineffective as killing machines.

The British troops in the trenches were getting the worst of it. The water-filled ditches simply had not been made deep enough to offer adequate protection. Jolicoeur could not directly see how many of the British had been killed or wounded but he could tell by the empty spaces along the trench front how many were no longer firing muskets. If each of the vacancies represented a casualty, the battle would be over in a few hours.

"Do you really think it was stupid?" the humbled voice of the Shawnee asked from the other side of the path.

Jolicoeur momentarily leaned away from his musket to look for his companion in arms. Although the rain falling between them and pelting the Shawnee's face distorted the expression on it, the Frenchman could sense Striking Eagle's distress.

"Sometimes brave and stupid are the same thing," he said kindly and, he thought, truthfully.

Chapter Fifteen

July 3, 1754, Late afternoon

hey're shooting the animals! The bastards! For reasons he did not have the time to sort out, Washington found the killing of cattle, horses, and dogs to be especially outrageous. They were *innocents*, particularly the dogs, who had no value beyond their service as pets to the men and boys of the Regiment. A small, white terrier, playfully engaged in a game of bite-and-run with a beagle twice his size, had just been hit in the neck by a French musket ball. The pathetic sight of the confused little dog yelping and running in circles as it sought to attack the source of its pain stirred in the young Virginian both a burning rage and a profound depression. From his vantage point in the southern outworks, the signs of agony and death were all too much in evidence: the contorted repose of the bodies in the trenches, the moans of the gut shot, the chorus of dying horses and cattle protesting their innocence, their disdain for humankind and for his infernal amusements. It was odd that the horses struggled so pitifully, always trying to stand up, always failing. The cattle were so much more tolerant of death, or so it seemed.

The terrier's frenzied self-pursuit brought it to the south shore of Great Meadows Run where it lost its footing on the embankment and fell into the swiftly moving current. Its yelps briefly intensified, then stopped as the water filled its lungs. Partially submerged, it washed downstream and was out of sight less than a minute after its fatal entry into the rampaging stream.

To take his mind off the terrier, Washington asked Robert Stobo, his current trenchmate, "Do you think they'll attack?"

"Why should they? We're not going anywhere," Stobo replied. In his present state, the Scotsman was possibly the filthiest man Washington had ever seen. Mud caked the skin of his face and arms and made his hair look like a pit of writhing vipers as the storm winds set it a-flutter.

"That big, bald Indian attacked me, nearly split my skull."

"A true, foamin'-at-the-mouth loony that one is," Stobo said, then kidded, "But you're invincible, Colonel. Everyone knows that."

The allusion was to Washington's growing reputation as the possessor of a charmed life. It was a distinction he was not anxious to nurture. Christopher Gist had spread the word of his and Washington's misadventures with the lone Indian called Nootimus and their winter dunking in the Allegheny River. Taken together with the horseback ride behind Andrew Montour and his apparent inability to get himself killed hopping from one trench to another during the battle, the young Virginian did seem to be Providentially advantaged.

Washington spotted a feathered head peering out from behind a dead tree, took aim, and fired. The ball dislodged a piece of the tree trunk but left the Indian behind it in one piece. Bracing the stock of his musket on a shelf of shale protruding from the trench wall to avoid immersing it in the pool at the bottom, he reloaded.

"How many wounded now?" he inquired.

"Lots, Colonel, lots. About half of them Mackay's people, brave lads. My own, too. Four dead, I think. Andrew Lewis got it twice but he's still fightin'. William La Peyroney is down, but alive. Poor Peter Mercier is dead, though. The bastards shot him again while he was bein' carried to the stockade. And your personal servant, of course."

Washington shook his head sorrowfully. The first bullet Mercier had taken failed to put him out of action, the second disabled him, and now he was dead. It was strange to think that a man he had known so recently no longer existed, could no longer face him across the dinner table and make bad jokes about apathetic burgesses and inept government officials. He was at even more of a loss to know how to feel about his servant Joseph. The Negro had been with him for years, had been loyal, and a good friend. Yet this fight did not belong to him any more than it belonged to the animals. Should he be as outraged by the murder of Joseph the innocent witness as he had been by the senseless killing of the terrier? Somehow that didn't seem quite right but Washington was too much of a southern aristocrat to understand why. He could love Joseph and mourn his passing, but he could not yet completely admit him into the fraternity of man.

"This is not the way I thought it would be," he sighed in dejection.

The Scotsman, thinking Washington was referring to the strategic shortcomings of their situation, replied, "They do outnumber us two or three to one. There's not much we can do about that…"

"I thought it would be a brisk, sunny day with two well-disciplined armies marching in platoons onto the field in full battle regalia, colors flying, each determined to annihilate the other. I thought it would be beautiful," the young man reminisced through daydreams past, then looked up at the teeming rain clouds. "I didn't imagine a storm, or a flood, or having to shoot at feathers and hats because the enemy won't give you any more than that…"

"And being picked off one at a time, and crawling through mud, and slipping in the blood of your own men," Stobo added.

"Yes, yes…"

Robert Stobo the businessman, the avoider of internecine conflict, the realist, crossed his arms and chewed his lip in contemplation, then said flatly, "I once knew a girl who thought with all sincerity that the heavens would break into music and song when she fell in love."

Washington easily deduced where his friend was going but played along.

"Did they? Did she?"

"She's married now, has two boys and a girl: a bass, a tenor, and a soprano. They serenade her constantly, not always to her delight."

The young Virginian smiled knowingly.

"I understand your point, Robert. I'm not *that* young."

"Ah, but you are, lad, you are," Stobo kidded mercilessly. "I myself am too young to be givin' you such advice. What am I, three years your senior?"

Washington could not help but laugh at the Scotsman's light-heartedness in the midst of such misery.

"I'll do better next time."

"We all will, George, we all will…assuming we have the good fortune to enjoy a next time…"

As Stobo was speaking, a sharp cry from above pierced the rain and mist. Washington looked up to see Godfrey Bomgardner of Adam Stephen's company kneeling beside the swivel gun he had been wielding, wounded but alive.

"We should have cut holes in the wall to fire those damn things," Stobo shouted, spitting the words out like expletives. "Not put 'em up in the air for the whole damn French army to take potshots at…"

Since the decision to mount the swivel guns on elevated platforms had been Stobo's, Washington did not comment. He had made his own share of bad decisions, not the least of which was the location of the stockade. James Mackay had been right: Fort Necessity needed to be at least fifty yards farther from the south woods than it was to force an attacking enemy into the open. As things stood right now, the French and their Indian allies could fire all week from behind their trees, stumps, and boulders without serious risk to themselves. *If only I had anticipated the possibility of retreat*, his mind hammered away at his judgment. The two innocuous words *if only* seemed to be the eternal lament of a military commander. The stockade had been intended as a warehouse, not as a full-fledged defensive fortification. How could he have known? Perhaps that was what made a good commander, the ability to anticipate all contingencies, to be thorough to a fault. It was clear now that he had focused too much on speed, on getting to Redstone at all costs, thereby leaving himself and his troops vulnerable to an attack by superior forces. The lesson was simple: Leave yourself a ready avenue for retreat if all does not go well. Easy words, less easy to implement and to know at what point caution itself would become an obstacle. There was so much he needed to learn, so many compensations he had to make for not being naturally clever.

Bomgardner was removed from his swivel gun and taken to Dr. Craik in the log cabin, where the seriously wounded were accumulating rapidly. To his surprise, Washington saw the swivel gun disappear from its platform into the stockade. He and Robert Stobo glanced at one another, each hoping the other understood what Adam Stephen was up to. Neither did. The unstated question re-emerged a few minutes later when the clamor of chopping axes reached their ears and several of the timbers from the southeast section of the stockade began to waver, and then leaned forward in a sequence of controlled falls. Stephen's men were deliberately creating a breach in the wall!

"What in the name of heaven is he doin'?" a perplexed Robert Stobo trumpeted.

Since he did not know the answer to Stobo's query, Washington declined to reply. But there was no need to. Two swivel guns suddenly appeared on both sides of the breach and began blasting away at the enemy gathered in the forest at the southern edge of Great Meadows. The swivel guns were no more or less effective than before but at least Adam Stephen had found a way to use them without exposing their operators to the murderous enfilading fire from the French. Each time the small cannons boomed, sending a hot swarm of grapeshot and a trailing cloud of gunsmoke across the battlefield, the Virginians and Carolinians voiced their approval. The swivel guns, if they achieved nothing else, had become morale boosters.

Without artillery of their own, the French were in no position to assault the British fortifications and were not inclined to. With superior numbers and better cover than the British troops in the trenches, they could afford to wait, picking off their adversaries one at a time. But, as both sides accommodated themselves to the prospect of a long siege, nature decided to become uncooperative. The floodgates of heaven suddenly swung full open, sending not drops but sheets of steamy rain plunging to the earth below.

"Is it enough water for you, Colonel?" Stobo gurgled as the waterfall at the end of his ridge-like nose splashed against his lips.

"I had my fill two hours ago," the Virginian muttered in disgust. To vent his disenchantment with the weather he had been given for his first real battle, he decided to fire a round in the general direction of the enemy. He leveled his musket, aimed, and squeezed the trigger. Nothing happened.

"Wet powder?" Stobo asked, then decided to check his own musket. A firm pull on the trigger produced the same result: nothing.

"Wet powder," Washington acknowledged with renewed and magnified concern: *How can we fight a battle if we can't use our muskets?* In the present downpour, they might not even be able to re-load. They would need to find some way to shield the powder from the deluge. In hopes of finding a solution to the dilemma, he glanced back toward the stockade, where the swivel guns were still arrayed and firing through Stephen's gap. He was troubled to discover that spillover from Great Meadows Run was creeping upward and around the stockade. Several cartridge boxes and empty barrels were drifting by the fort like a flotilla of miniature assault boats. Then the swivel guns fell silent—all of them, including the pair Adam Stephen had moved alongside the breach in the wall. Shortly thereafter, the sounds of musket fire on both sides diminished and then, along the British lines, fell completely silent. While gunfire from the French continued, there were no more fusillades, only scattered and occasional blasts whose echoes from the hills and trees gave them more respectability than they deserved. As he peered inside the stockade, The Colonel glimpsed a flurry of activity and heard the audible tailings of men speaking to each other in less than genteel tones.

"I'm going to the stockade to find out what's happening," he announced and awkwardly removed his drenched and dingy frame from the trench. With little to fear from the infrequent French musket bursts, he was quickly inside the stockade and surveying the debilitating situation the rain had caused. James Craik had moved his medical supplies, bleeding soldiers and operations out of the log hut, from which several men were busily removing kegs of rum and rolling them to their battle stations. The reason for Craik's action soon became obvious: Water completely surrounded the tiny structure.

The powder! My God, the powder!

"Doctor, have you…" Washington began, then realized that Craik, who was bandaging a man's neck, had important things to attend to. Hurriedly, he rushed inside to realize his worst fears: Abner Hazlip and John Biddlecome, both experienced militiamen, were lifting a barrel of gunpowder out of the water onto a table. Two younger men with guilty expressions on their faces whom Washington recognized as Jacob Morrow and Peter McClure were attempting to push a keg of rum out the door. Their Commander cast them a disapproving glance and turned to Hazlip and Biddlecome, who had managed to upright the barrel on the table and were peering inside. Biddlecome plunged a hand into the barrel, scooped a handful from its contents, and lifted it out for Hazlip and Washington to see. What should have been dry, coarse-grained black gunpowder oozed between John Biddlecome's fingers like swamp mud.

"Are they all like this?" Washington asked, unable to hide the desperation in his voice.

"I don' know, Colonel. Haven't checked 'em all," Biddlecome said, then pointed to the other barrels. "But they're all underwater. That's for sure."

Washington looked at Biddlecome's gaunt, stubbled face for some sign of hope. The older man merely stared back with neither hope nor despair in his countenance, waiting for Washington to tell him what to do next.

"John, you and Abner check the other barrels. Find some men to help you move them out of here to a dry place..."

"And where would that be, Colonel?" Biddlecome asked, rolling his bulging eyes first at the myriad leaks in the roof and then in the general direction of the heavens.

"I don't know, John," Washington snapped, then softened to more measured tones. "Pitch some tents, but *get this powder out of here.*"

Having received unambiguous orders, Biddlecome and Hazlip nodded, gave cursory salutes, and left, taking the just examined barrel of gunpowder with them. Washington then approached the two younger men who, correctly assessing their Commander's cold stare, had ceased their activities and were waiting sheepishly by the coveted keg of rum. Stopping directly in front of the keg, the Colonel glowered from one to the other.

"Did your officers tell you to come get this?" Washington demanded, pointing at the keg.

"No, Colonel, we..." Morrow stuttered.

"Gentlemen, we are in the middle of a difficult battle. This is no time for a party. Or were you planning to drink yourselves into a stupor and surrender?"

Still shamefaced, but with an undertone of resentment, McClure said, "Sir, the cows are shot, we got nothin' to eat...an' now we got no powder to shoot with..."

The perplexed young Volunteer didn't finish his rebuttal but didn't have to. Washington mentally completed it for him: *What else can we do?* Without moving a muscle, McClure's stance communicated his despair.

It was true, of course. Without gunpowder, they could not defend themselves. Even if the French guns also ceased firing, the besiegers had three times as many men and therefore three times as many bayonets with which to kill their enemy. Why not call it a lost cause and get drunk? That some of his men could behave so dishonorably was testimony to his shortcomings as a commanding officer. What he should do is put them before a firing squad, hang them, enforce discipline. But he was tired, disheartened and, in the middle of a torrential downpour with the enemy surrounding him, lacked the opportunity. It was just as well because he was not emotionally prepared for such extreme measures. *There is a final reason why a firing squad is inappropriate*, he sniggered grimly to himself: *There is no dry gunpowder.*

"Take it, but no more," he said, disgusted and weary, dismissing the men with a curt wave of the hand.

John Biddlecome and Abner Hazlip returned with four men to remove the remaining barrels of black powder to higher and hopefully dryer ground. Several of the officers—James Mackay among them—arrived simultaneously demanding to know why no powder was being delivered to their positions. Washington briefly explained the predicament, which, in any case, was obvious to anyone with one good eye. After the initial shock of the news had worn off, all pitched in to move the powder barrels into the two tents Hazlip and Biddlecome had pitched at an elevation high enough to be unattainable by the burgeoning flood waters. As he struggled against the still rising water in the hut, Washington had the feeling that they were not truly engaged in a desperate battle but were more akin to the players in a comic opera, complete with pranks, fools, and nature's whimsy.

When all the barrels had been placed in the tents and opened in the hope that, by doing so, the drying process would be accelerated, all returned to their posts except for two men assigned to keep watch over the powder. Before they dispersed, Washington directed the officers to have the troops under their command attach socket bayonets to their muskets and prepare for the inevitable assault. He then walked back to the trench where he had left Robert Stobo. The Scotsman was still there, every bit as filthy as he'd been before, in spite of the deluge from the skies whose intensity had not notably diminished.

"Robert, how do you manage to stay so dirty in the midst of all this?" he asked, reluctantly inserting himself into the foul ditch.

"I take a roll in the mud every half-hour or so," Stobo laughed heartily, then inquired, "What *is* our situation?"

"The powder is all wet."

"Wonderful."

Fatalistically, the two men took the bayonets from their slings and placed them on the barrels of their muskets. In an attempt to increase his comfort level, Washington removed his tricorne, squeezed as much water out of it as he could, fluffed his soaked hair, and put the hat back on. It was not long before the rain had once again filled the brim to overflowing and a steady downspout of water splashed against his chin. He looked sheepishly at his trench mate.

"This is ridiculous," he said.

Stobo gazed up at the relentlessly fecund black clouds and replied, "It is indeed, Colonel. Among other things."

July 3, 1754, Early evening

Captain Louis Coulon Ecuyer, Sieur de Villiers, unhappily peered out from the entrance of his tent into the dim light of the saturated forest and, parroting Washington's sentiment, said, "C'est ridicule!"

His remark was directed at Captain Francois Le Mercier, his second in command, who had just arrived with news of a significant turn of events, which he had not yet had a chance to report.

"What is it, Francois?" Villiers asked, remaining inside the tent. He had been resting, saving his mental energies, and had drifted off. The prospect of stepping outside into a raging tempest was singularly distasteful.

Le Mercier, who was sufficiently drenched that further inundation was irrelevant, saluted and said, "Captain, the English guns have stopped firing."

"Why?" Villiers queried, yawning, his brain not yet fully up to speed. He did notice that the musket fire from his own troops was rather sparse and found himself listening curiously to the sharp, hollow sounds and reverberating echoes that single gunshots make in the woods. It was a sound that had always fascinated him but now filled him with alarm. *This is a battle! It should not be possible to distinguish the fire of individual muskets!*

"Francois, why is there so little gunfire? Is the battle over?" he asked, his mind still not completely engaged.

Patiently, with rivulets slithering across his chin and mouth like water snakes, Le Mercier responded, "The answer to both questions, Captain, is that the rain has soaked through much of the gunpowder. At least that is why our fire has slowed. Since the English have ceased firing entirely, we assume their problem is more severe. It certainly looks that way."

Villiers almost reprimanded Le Mercier for not telling him earlier but then realized that his pudgy second in command was doing just that—informing him of a breaking event. He had to force his brain to consciousness.

"Just a minute, Captain," Villiers said, disappearing inside the tent.

When he re-emerged, the French Commander was wearing his standard issue *Compagnies franches* captain's uniform, distinguishable from that of the ordinary soldier by the quality of its material, the gold laced vest, and the gilded gorget at the neck. By contrast, Le Mercier, like most of the soldiers and officers, wore his wilderness uniform with its hooded capot, moccasins, and breechclout. To protect his finery, Villiers had covered himself, including the tricorne on his head, with a blanket. He did not plan to stay outside very long.

"This is absurd," he mumbled at Le Mercier and the stampeding downpour. "Captain, you said *it certainly looks that way.* Please show me what you are referring to so we can both get back inside."

The corpulent but competent Le Mercier led the way to a spot in the woods where the density of leaves between the meadow and the two of them was relatively low and a clear line of sight was available. The second in command pointed with undisguised pleasure in the direction of the British fort.

"It would seem they may all drown before we have a chance to attack," he said gleefully.

Villiers pulled the blanket around his head like a shroud to better protect himself and his uniform against the pounding rain, and stared out at the delightful spectacle before him. The British fort was almost an island, the only connection to Great Meadows being a narrow land bridge at the southwest corner. Anything small and buoyant that the British had not transferred to a higher place was afloat in the *ad hoc* moat, some of it washing downstream. Even a dead cow had begun to drift with the current and was pressing against the outer earthworks. The men in the northern earthworks were in the most precarious predicament: Their trenches were almost totally submerged and the men within them were having great difficulty maintaining low profiles without drowning. Villiers also noted that, while a considerable number of Brown Bess muskets were pointed toward the French lines, none were being fired. It was a feeble attempt at deception.

"Ha!" Villiers cried joyfully. "We have them where we want them, Francois!"

"We do, Captain," Le Mercier agreed, then removed his tricorne to shake it dry. "And yet there is the problem of the wet powder. If we attacked now it would have to be a bayonet charge across that sea of mud down there. Many would be killed. It is not clear if our troops on the other side of the fort could even support us, since they would have to cross that ugly stream the British are having so much trouble with."

As he spoke, Le Mercier pointed at the churning series of rapids Great Meadows Run had become. Villiers nodded in agreement.

"We should have brought at least the lighter cannon," he said regretfully.

Le Mercier donned the clammy tricorne and shook his head, saying, "No, Captain, if we had done that, we would still be hacking our way up the mountain slope and the British would be gone. Here, as you say, we have them, even if we cannot easily attack."

Villiers was grateful for the vote of confidence in his decision to travel light. Because of the dire consequences that often accompanied a flawed military tactic, commanding officers were a nervous, worrisome lot. To receive confirmation that one's judgment had been correct did not inspire joy as much as simple relief. Even so, the irony of "having them" without being able to administer a *coup de grace* weighed heavily on his mind.

"I think God wants us to achieve this victory, Francois. I only wish He would tell us how," Villiers opined, then turned his gaze upward at the persistent torrent plummeting from above. Speaking loudly enough that his maker was sure to hear, he added, "And I wish He would not throw so many obstacles in our way."

"God helps those who help themselves," Le Mercier mumbled sardonically.

"If only He would exercise a little restraint," the French Commander rejoined, maintaining the intensity in his voice. "I think God must have forgotten that rain falls on us as well as the British."

The two men relished the casual banter. It had been a while since either had engaged in witty, meaningless conversation. Attempting to stay dry, Villiers removed his tricorne, pulled the blanket over his head, and replaced the hat. It probably wouldn't work, but it was worth a try. Returning to real world sobriety, Le Mercier delivered an estimate of their status.

"Unfortunately, sir, I think we must attack soon. It would be preferable to simply starve them out but our provisions are low. We may starve ourselves instead. I don't think I need to tell you that morale is low. The men are tired and wet…"

"…and rebellious!" Villiers shot back, lamenting the fact that the *Compagnies franches* had to rely so heavily on undisciplined Canadian militia. There was something about the North American continent that made men unwilling to bend to authority. Maybe it was too much fraternization with the savages.

"Not rebellious, just…contrary," Le Mercier the diplomat continued, trying to remain on point. "I should also mention, sir, that the Indians are getting impatient. Some have already left."

"How many?" Villiers asked, unfazed. Indians were always coming and going for what seemed to white men the most trivial of reasons.

"About ten or twenty."

"Did they say why?"

"They don't like fighting under these conditions," Le Mercier explained with an impassive glance at his Commander. "I think they are apprehensive about the risks. Indians prefer the quick thrust and parry. The prospect of being bogged down in that quagmire terrifies them. They prefer to attack, scalp, and withdraw. If they can't do that, they would rather go home and wait for another day."

Villiers glowered at his Captain and was about to cast aspersions on the fickle Indian character. But he restrained himself, largely because he too was hesitant to get "bogged down in that quagmire," as Le Mercier had put it. The Indians might actually turn out to be the most judicious players in this murky drama. The Commander surveyed the forest, looking for his men. The first one he found was lying prone behind a boulder, his capot over his face, a musket resting at his side. A second sighting was of two men resting against adjacent tree trunks, engaged in casual, lethargic conversation. Another man nearby, propping himself on one elbow, was simply staring off into space. Everywhere he looked, Villiers found a decided lack of exuberance but no shortage of down-turned mouths and visages slumping with *ennui*.

"We cannot attack, Francois. There is no sense in it," Villiers asserted authoritatively. "We have only eighteen casualties now, three of them dead. If we attack, God knows how many more will die, especially if we have nothing to attack with but bayonets."

Le Mercier nodded his head, indicating that he understood Villiers' logic and sympathized with it. But he did not agree.

"There are also the reports of a large body of British reinforcements in the mountains to the southeast. And of cannon fire from that direction."

"Yes, yes, I know, and I do not believe a word of it! Indians will tell you anything for a flagon of rum," Villiers protested in frustration. The mission had been dogged with numerous reports of British troop movements in the near vicinity. He continued forcefully, "Do you not see the illogic of an invading British army firing off its cannon before they reach the field of battle? Who are they shooting at? We are *here*, not in the mountains to the southeast!"

The portly Captain was still nodding his head sympathetically—perhaps he had never stopped. Nevertheless, he was unswayed.

"Can we afford to *assume* that the reports are false?" was his curt response.

"So you are saying we *must* attack even though you agree we *cannot* attack," Villiers shot back, hoping his second in command would appreciate the irony and suggest a way out of the quandary.

But Le Mercier, with a hint of something akin to amusement, said only, "Yes, sir."

Villiers snorted his frustration. Le Mercier was clearly going to let his superior make the decision whether or not to attack. But he couldn't blame the man. It had been at Villiers' insistence that he be given the command of the expedition and Contrecoeur had enthusiastically agreed. Le Mercier had also agreed but only God knew whether the burly officer harbored any lingering resentment over his demotion to second in command. If so, it had not been a major obstacle in their relationship until now. And—Villiers chided himself for gratuitous fault finding—the decision *did* belong to him, not to his cousin Francois Le Mercier.

The French leader reconsidered his reason for demanding the command: the killing of the Sieur de Jumonville, his younger half-brother, at the hands of the British. Although he had been initially enraged at the news of Jumonville's murder, time and a better understanding of the events leading up to the British ambush had somewhat cooled his ardor, if not his intellectual commitment to vengeance and honor. He remembered the face of a small boy, then the adolescent at Green Bay where his father had served in the *Compagnies franches* until his violent death twenty years ago. Although the six sons of Nicolas Antoine, the elder Coulon de Villiers, had all served honorably with the French colonial forces, they had only rarely crossed paths. So it was with Villiers and Jumonville. *Le Grand Villiers* hardly knew his younger sibling. That had been the first thing to check the flame of his outrage: insufficient fuel. The second had been when he learned that Jumonville's mission included an element of espionage and employed a sizable contingent of armed marines. This did not make the mission a dishonorable one but it did change its character from a purely peaceful, diplomatic venture into one with unmistakable, martial overtones. The British could with some veracity claim that their attack, cowardly as its execution showed it to be, had nevertheless been a legitimate military action. This interpretation by the civilized world could not be allowed, but

Villiers had found it increasingly difficult to sustain the emotional commitment to the pledge he had made at Lake Chautauqua in the presence of his hundred and thirty Algonquins and Nipissings. He still sought vengeance for his brother but he could no longer comfortably wear its costume or coax its visage onto his face. Somewhat to his surprise, this had sharpened his wits and his cunning. He had an idea.

"Francois, it is necessary only that we achieve a clear victory, is it not?" he posited.

"Yes," the not quite comprehending Le Mercier answered.

"And that the blame for these hostilities be placed exactly where it belongs: with the British. Correct?"

Le Mercier again replied, "Yes."

"Then bring a scribe and paper to my tent," Villiers instructed, now fully awake and cogent. "We are going to compose the terms of the British capitulation."

A puzzled Le Mercier asked, "How do we know they will agree to these terms? Surely they will not readily admit to the murder of the Sieur de Jumonville without some…persuasion."

Already on the way to his tent, the animated Commander replied, "The terms will be very agreeable. They will accept them."

This Le Mercier found nearly impossible to fathom, but decided an explanation could wait until he was inside Villiers' tent and significantly dryer. He turned his attention to practical matters.

"Captain, do you want me to bring an English interpreter to translate the terms of surrender?" he inquired in perfect innocence.

Villiers stopped abruptly, whirled fully around, and paused thoughtfully before saying, "No. We are the victors. The articles of capitulation will be in French."

Le Mercier understood and accepted his Commander's insistence but wondered why a flicker of a smile had flashed on Villiers' lips as he hastened back into his tent.

*　*　*

The skies were free of rain and its parent clouds. The resident god, *Manito*, had squeezed them dry of every drop of moisture that

195

afternoon in one of His random fits of displeasure with the mortals below. Unblemished by overcast, a bright orange sunset crowned the endless forest beyond the western edge of Great Meadows. Though the skies were dry, the earth below was still recovering from the day's contribution to the effluent that would ultimately travel thousands of miles to the Gulf of Mexico and oblivion. Great Meadows and Indian Runs gurgled with complaint as late-arriving runoff dripped from the leaves of trees and languidly traversed the grass-covered dish of the pasture to fill their streambeds. Where there was no grass, there was mud, in some places a foot deep. In the air, the steamy remnants of the storm persisted, occasionally visible as smoky apparitions, everywhere oppressively humid. The men of Virginia and Carolina were surprised to find they could still make fires, even though the available wood and other burnables were soaked through. It was a simple matter of getting the *first* fire started—the rest followed easily from it. The members of the expedition were so pleased with the prospect of being dry once again that they drank like sailors and chattered like wives at a sewing bee. A passing traveler would have seen the fires dotting the landscape around the stockade, heard the friendly, often inebriated conversation, and been cheered on his way.

Angus Dexter and Bobby Chisolm had a fire, a cut of salt pork, and a bottle of rum in their trench on the southwest side of the fort. As sentries, it was their duty to keep their eyes peeled for hostile activity on the part of the French forces in their sector of the battlefield and to discourage, by their presence, the possibility of such hostile activity. Dexter, the more senior of the two by thirty years, was doing most of the eating and drinking while Bobby Chisolm did most of the watching. Bobby was jittery to the point of panic.

"Bobby, why don'cha settle down an' stop worryin'? The frog-eaters ain't gonna do nothin' tonight," chided the paunchy and, except for a horseshoe of ancient, frizzy and uncut hair, bald Angus Dexter. He was seated at one end of the trench alternating bites of salt pork and gulps of rum.

Bobby Chisolm raised his head above the trench to see the French campfires flickering between the trees. He brushed back his perfectly straight, russet hair, separating it in the middle of his forehead.

Except for casual conversation, there did not appear to be any discernible activity on the French side of the field.

"It's too quiet over there," he said in a whisper.

"Too quiet?" the older man boomed with cheerful sarcasm. "Hey, you frog-eaters out there, make some noise, will ya? Mr. Robert Chisolm thinks you're too quiet! Why are ya worried about it bein' too quiet, Bobby? It's noise you should be worried about—muskets, war whoops, things like that. A good attack is noisy as hell."

Bobby lowered his head and inched his lanky form toward Dexter, then shielded the right side of his mouth from French view with one hand.

"Angus, I hear them Indians can sneak up on ya in the dark and rip your scalp right off before ya know it," he said, still whispering.

Dexter bellowed, nearly ejecting the rum he had just poured into his mouth.

"Nah! They slit your throat first. *Then* they scalp ya. That way ya can't scream."

Taking the statement as literal truth, Chisolm fell back and sat himself on the soft clay of the trench wall, his eyes bulging in terror. As if to push them back in, he covered his face with his hands. Seeing his young friend was about to cry, Angus put the bell-shaped liquor bottle down and gave him a hearty pat on the back.

"I was only foolin' ya, boy. Don't take me so seriously. Nobody else does. Besides, Indians don't like to fight at night. Somethin' about their religion..." he said, having no idea whether or not Indians would fight at night and even less familiarity with their religious practices. It sounded plausible, though.

Bobby's fingers fell away from his face. "Really?" he beseeched, hopeful.

"Yeah, really," Angus barked, making himself comfortable again with his two consumable companions. "An' don't worry so much, Bobby. Jesus, God a'mighty, you're the biggest worry wart I ever seen."

"I ain't worried, Angus. I'm just..."

"Bobby, if I was you an' I was behavin' like a spooked mare an' I *wasn't* worried, I'd be worried."

The conundrum was about two qualifiers too many for Bobby to follow. He squinted from small, round eyes still moist with tears that had, to Dexter's relief, stopped bulging. This was about as calm as Bobby was likely to get until he was off sentry duty.

"I don't wanta get killed, Angus," he said, his lower lip quivering erratically. "Not out here with nothin' but a useless gun."

Angus Dexter's craggy face mellowed. He thrust the liquor bottle toward Chisolm and said, "Bobby, have a drink, please. It'll help ya relax. An' besides, your gun ain't useless. Ya got a pig-sticker on the end of it that'll stop any frog-eater, Indian, or half-breed tries to jump ya. Remember too, that's all they got—pig-stickers! They ain't shot at us in a coupla hours an' what that prob'ly means is their powder is wet, just like ours, an'..."

"*Anglais!*" an alien voice called from the expanse between the two camps. It sounded close. "*Anglai-is!*"

Bobby reflexively grabbed his musket and assumed a firing position.

"What was that, Angus?" he demanded in a desperate hiss, sighting down the barrel of the gun as if a real target existed.

Angus Dexter set his bottle aside and peered over the side of the trench in the direction from which the voice had come. For some reason, his face was covered with perspiration; droplets of sweat were blurring his vision. He brushed them aside with a quick hand stroke.

"Sounds like a frog-eater out there somewhere. Maybe he wants to join us and enjoy our lux-ur-i-ous accommodations."

Bobby was not amused but he did finally realize the futility of aiming an unloaded musket at an invisible enemy. He had cleaned it out after learning of the wet powder problem. Circumstances had dictated it remain empty. Bobby studied the emasculated weapon, then gripped it hard as he would if his intent were to disembowel an attacking enemy soldier.

"*Anglais! Voulez-vous parler?*" the voice said again.

This time it was Dexter's turn to say, "What was that?" but with less dread than Bobby had revealed.

"Something about a parlor..." Bobby offered, then shrugged his bewilderment.

"God-damn..." Angus muttered. He raised his head higher and

spotted an oil lantern with the outline of two men behind it at the edge of the meadow. It was dark enough that he couldn't see faces clearly but one of the uniforms, that of the man holding the lantern, was an officer's.

"Hey, frog…" he began, then caught himself. He tried again: "Hey, Frenchman, we don't know what you're sayin'. Could ya speak in English?"

Dumb thing to say, Angus brooded. *If he could speak English, he would've.*

Dexter heard some murmured chatter that ceased when the man without the lantern disappeared into the trees. He was back three minutes later with a third man, who took a position slightly in front of the officer with the lantern.

"Englishman, are you willing to talk? We think it would be good to have a parley," the new man said somewhat stiffly.

The question hung tenuous and haunting in the air like one of the vaporous apparitions the storm had given birth to. Dexter and Chisolm stared dumbly at one another, the matter of how to respond a void in their collective consciousness.

"Bobby, go get the Colonel," Angus Dexter finally insisted, an action Chisolm was happy and relieved to perform.

Angus dropped below ground level, licked his pallid pink lips dry, and cleared his throat of phlegm and salt pork, then popped up again to face the French silhouettes. With the best diction and grammar his negligible education would permit, he said haltingly, "Sirs, can you wait a few minutes? We have to get our commanding officer."

Prattle, then the third Frenchman said, "Yes, yes…of course."

Angus decided to say no more, fearing he might commit some subtle but critical error in diplomacy if he talked too much. He watched the three men suspiciously. Unlikely as it was, they *could* be the salient of a night attack. But the first two—probably both officers—did nothing but pace and converse in French while the third stood at ease, apparently waiting for orders.

As Bobby had done, Angus gripped his musket at the barrel and stock, capturing it between his body and the trench wall—just in case. Again sensing perspiration on his brow, he released one hand to wipe it away, then discovered when he did that a film of water began immediately depositing on the freshly mopped skin. It was not perspiration at all but a mist too fine to be called rain that wanted to cover every exposed surface and penetrate every nook and cranny of his abundant exterior.

"Sonofabitch!" he complained, glowering at the last rays of the sunset he had enjoyed fifteen minutes before. That sunset had promised clear skies and he was offended that the promise had been a false one.

It wasn't right for nature to be so fanciful and headstrong.

𝕮hapter 𝕾ixteen

July 3, 1754, Evening

s he struggled to make sense of the two sheets of paper Jacob Van Braam had brought back, Washington played back the episode with the French Commander in his mind's eye. In the emerging gloom of dusk, Villiers' form was little more than the blurred profile of a man, but the moist evening air carried sound with so little corruption he might easily have been no more than an arm's length distant. The taciturn French Commander was saying:

"Sir, let me introduce myself. I am Captain Louis Coulon Ecuyer, Sieur de Villiers, of the *Compagnies franches.* I am the Commander of the forces you see set before you. We are cold and wet, M'sieur, and so are you. As I am sure you have now come to realize, we will win this battle. There is no reason for killing more men. Is this not so?"

The words had been spoken reasonably, persuasively, from across the meadow as Washington and Mackay waited anxiously with Angus Dexter and Bobby Chisolm. Washington struggled to find the language to address a man whose brother's death he had been responsible for.

"Sir, I am Colonel George Washington of the colony of Virginia and this is Captain James Mackay of the colony of South Carolina. What terms do you offer?" Washington replied to the shape behind the lantern.

After a delay for translation, the response came back:

"Colonel Washington, the stipulation of your surrender is the removal of you and your armed forces from the lands of his Christian Majesty Louis XV of France. You will be permitted to return to your homes without fear of imprisonment or reprisal. However, if you refuse this offer, or delay your acceptance of it, I must warn you that we are anticipating the arrival of a body of four hundred of our Indian allies. While the armed forces of his Christian Majesty will conduct themselves with civilized restraint, we cannot guarantee that our allies will do likewise…"

Washington wondered if Villiers was making a less than subtle threat or merely speaking the truth. He recalled the behavior of his own Indians at the glen and shuddered at the thought of being at the mercy of four hundred French Indians. If Mackay's forces and his were obliged to surrender, the best time would be now.

"What do you think, James?" he said to the leader of the Carolina Independents by his side.

As he was wont to do as a prelude to speech, Mackay maneuvered a delicate elevation of his aristocratic chin and said, "I think we should learn the details of their terms, send someone over. Do you have any French speakers? I don't."

"La Peyroney, Van Braam, Montour. Montour isn't back yet. La Peyroney is injured."

"But he's French, isn't he? Van Braam is Dutch."

Washington saw Mackay's point. French was La Peyroney's native tongue; there would be a smaller chance of a misunderstanding if he acted as interpreter. Two weeks ago, Mackay would blatantly have insisted that Washington order the Ensign to perform that duty but now he knew such an approach was more likely to incite the Virginia Commander's ire than to achieve its purpose. James Mackay heaved an onerous sigh and pinched his lips together at the spiritual pain of subduing his authoritarian impulses.

"I'll send Van Braam and La Peyroney over," Washington said. "I don't want any Frenchman inside the stockade."

Mackay concurred with the soundness of Washington's judgment. The two British officers—neither of them remotely British—were sent on their way across the meadow to the French camp, Van Braam serving as a crutch for the ailing Huguenot. After an hour's absence, Jacob and William returned, La Peyroney's face several skin shades paler than when he'd left, his legs as limp as the neck of a just-killed deer. It was not long after Van Braam and he reiterated the terms of the French offer that Ensign William La Peyroney passed out and had to be carried to Dr. Craik, whose medical station now consisted of an *ad hoc* assemblage of tents and lean-to's along the eastern boundary of the stockade. The terms sounded fair and reasonable but Washington remained suspicious of French motives. There was also the embarrassment of ignominious defeat. He did not want to compound his humiliation by agreeing to vague and controversial articles of capitulation. He must perform as a professional soldier would in defeat, with dignity, honor, and steadfastness. It would have to be a good performance, an act of supreme will, to overcome the depression he truly felt. Washington ordered Van Braam to return to the French Commander with a demand for a written summary of the terms of surrender, or to reject the offer if the French would not comply.

That had been an hour ago and Jacob had returned once more. With him were the articles of capitulation, which had been scribbled in French and which Washington, Mackay, and their officers were now attempting to study in the not entirely waterproof tent hastily set up to shield them from the ubiquitous rain-mist. The papers were lying on the table for all to see, although, blurred and in a foreign language, they offered little enlightenment to anyone but Jacob Van Braam. Jacob was seated at the table, framed by Washington and Mackay, who were standing somberly at his side. The awkward bumps and inflections in Van Braam's diction kept his oration lively; it was the only element of the proceedings that was. The dim light of two candles flanked the articles spread in front of the Dutchman, creating an atmosphere perfectly compatible with the temper of those present: gloom. The rhythmic undulations of the black candle smoke and its shadows on the walls of the tent had the quality of dawdling poltergeists come to observe what was afoot in the world of men.

If gray was the color of their collective mood, it was dappled in several shades and individually accented. Andrew Lewis's depression was the deepest, his buoyant Irish temperament intolerant of failure. Seated opposite Van Braam, Lewis's big-boned frame and neckless head were weighed down by a melancholy as grim as the storm clouds that had presaged their defeat and ultimately guaranteed it. On Lewis's left sat a stiff-backed and tight-lipped Adam Stephen, who was less humiliated than provoked by defeat. Peter Hogg rested, nearly prone, on the sod in one corner of the tent, fighting sleep, and Robert Stobo was busily puffing the sleeves and bodice of his blouse trying to dry them out. As co-commanders, Washington and Mackay displayed appropriately stoic exteriors.

Supporting himself with outstretched arms, Jacob Van Braam droned:

"...Of his most Christian Majesty, to those English troops actually in the fort of Necessity which was built on the lands of the King's dominions July the 3rd, at eight o'clock at night, 1754.

As our intention has never been to trouble the peace and good harmony which reigns between the two friendly princes, but only to avenge the...death which has been done on one of our officers..."

"Wait a minute, Jacob. Something is wrong with that sentence. It doesn't make sense," Washington interrupted.

Van Braam turned and glanced up at his commanding officer, his raised eyebrows twin question marks.

"What doesn't make sense?"

"The part about avenging the death done on one of their officers. You can't *do* death on anyone. It's not good English," Washington said.

"It's not English. It's French. And I am a Hollander," Jacob replied, providing some welcome comic relief to the morose proceedings. "Maybe it means *killing.* I'm not sure."

Washington leaned over the table, squinting in the soft candlelight as he tried to make out the alien text.

"Jacob, how can you read any of this with all these blurs and blotches?" he asked.

Van Braam bent forward to peruse the section of the text Washington was pointing to. As he scanned it, his mouth contracted into an orifice-like hole and he sighted down along his long nose instead of tilting his head forward to get a better view. It was a pose of concentration. Jacob, too, was having trouble reading the French words, half of which had been smeared into illegibility by rain and careless fingers.

"Show me what you were reading," Washington said.

Van Braam underlined a passage with his forefinger, then swept the finger lightly across the page.

"Where's the word we're having trouble with?"

Jacob pointed at a word that began with *l*, had an *s* in the middle, and a *t* at the end, but was completely blurred in the interstices between the three letters.

Washington looked at his colleague with a new respect and said, "I'm amazed you can make anything of this."

Visibly pleased by the compliment, the Dutchman replied, "It's the context. As you can see, only certain words will fit in dat sentence."

"Nevertheless, I'm impressed," Washington responded with a smile, straightening himself. "But it's getting late, Jacob. Why don't you look over the text and give us your interpretation of the important items. Then we can get some sleep."

Encouraged by the prospect of imminent repose, Van Braam returned to his work with renewed vigor.

"Dis part is about allowing us de honors of war," he said, his comically angled features assuming a doll-like solemnity.

"And what *are* the honors of war?" Robert Stobo called sarcastically from the other end of the tent. He had stripped to the waist to get its grimy texture away from his body, and had been surprised to find at least as much dirt cached on his skin.

Van Braam briefly reviewed the section, then looked up and said, "We can beat our drum and take one cannon when we leave."

Some tittered at the Dutchman's clumsy translation; others did not.

"One cannon? What good is one cannon?" the rueful Andrew Lewis interposed.

"It shows dey want to be our friends," Van Braam said.

"How do you know that?" asked Peter Hogg from the east end of the table.

"It says so," Van Braam replied, then quoted, "... *We...treat dem as friends*. Dat's what it says."

"Odd thing to put in a surrender document," Hogg mumbled, frowning.

Over his extended chin and crossed arms, James Mackay gave the explanation in his stilted English.

"Gentlemen, no war has yet been declared and it is by no means obvious one will. The French are taking care not to be seen as the aggressor."

"They attacked us!" Andrew Lewis bellowed.

"We attacked them first," Mackay retorted sharply, first bouncing a deferential glance off Washington. "Killed their Commander, *permitted* our savages to mutilate their dead. That will be their story."

Heads nodded in agreement. It made sense, as did most things military coming from the mouth of the haughty Scot.

Feeling like a man being given his last rites, Washington said, "Go on, Jacob, what else does it say?"

Jacob decided to sit on one of the stools around the inner periphery of the tent. He took one of the candles with him, holding it close to the paper in his other hand and gazing down at it with the peculiar expression that was apparently his reading countenance.

"Ve will be allowed to take our belongings except for…" he said, tripping over a particularly battered word, then continued, "…munitions."

"No munitions? You mean no weapons?" Washington cut in, startled.

"Yes… *munitions de guerre*…yes."

The Colonel shook his head violently, then began pacing.

"You'll have to get them to remove that passage, Jacob. We will not surrender honorably only to be massacred by their Indians, which they themselves admit they can't control."

There was general agreement with Washington's judgment. Jacob Van Braam made a note in the margin and sighed deeply. He was beginning to weary of his role as diplomatic tennis ball. Finished, he looked up to his commanding officer for further instructions. Washington noticed the Dutchman's eye contact and continued down his mental checklist.

"The part about the two hostages. Read that again."

Van Braam found his place and started, *"We on our part declare dat we shall give an escort…"*

"No," Washington interrupted. "Start earlier, maybe a paragraph back."

Jacob read: *"Since the English have in their possession an officer and two cadets whom dey took when dey…"*

Noting the discontinuity in the Dutchman's speech, Washington asked, "What is it, Jacob?"

"The words are smeared again."

"Do the best you can," said the young Virginian, once again dismissing a clause in the articles of capitulation that, in the eyes of prominent Europeans, would ultimately make of him either a villain or a fool, depending on their worldview.

Van Braam backed up and started over.

"*...All the prisoners whom dey took when dey...*" he said, pausing again at the uncertain scrawl, then plowing through with: "*...When dey killed Sieur de Jumonville, dey now promise to send dem with an escort to Fort Duquesne...*"

The paragraph that Van Braam read in French, understood in Dutch, and repeated in English was essentially an exchange of prisoners, the twenty-one Frenchmen captured at the glen for two British officers. What had not been settled or yet discussed was who the two English prisoners—hostages—were to be. Because the duration of their detention would be no more than two or three months, the hostages were to be selected only after all other issues had been resolved.

"What else, Jacob?" Washington said as Van Braam's soliloquy abruptly ended. The Colonel was anxious to accelerate the proceedings and put the unpleasantness behind them.

Van Braam's eyes darted over the page. Then he said, "Ve vill be permitted to cache our property and return for it later."

"If the damned Indians don't steal it first," Adam Stephen snapped.

"Aye!" Several Scotch voices chimed in.

Raising a hand to quell the commentary, Van Braam continued, "To guard our property, we can leave as many troops behind on the condition dat..."

Jacob paused to study the text, unaware he had left his audience hanging in suspense.

"Come on, Jacob, what's the condition?" Andrew Lewis asked with a doleful frown. His face was beaded with sweat.

With an abashed "Oh!" of acknowledgment, Jacob read on: "On the condition dat we give our word of honor not to make any establishment on dis side of the mountain for one year."

The expanse beneath the canvas covering of the tent momentarily fell silent. The muted conversations of the soldiers sitting around their fires outside seemed like the embarrassed rumblings of an audience confronted by an actor who has forgotten his lines.

"Can we accept that?" Adam Stephen asked.

"No," Washington answered without hesitation.

The curt reply raised some eyebrows, enough that the Colonel saw a need to explain himself. Fortunately, he didn't have to. Robert Stobo came to the rescue.

"What our adversaries really mean to say is that they don't want us trespassing on the lands of his Christian Majesty Louis XV for a year. I see no problem with that," Stobo said glibly, with a smile to match.

A pause ensued while the others waited for Stobo to elaborate. He didn't, but it was obvious from the roguish expression on his face that something was up his sleeve.

"But there *is* a problem. The Colonel just said we can't accept that," Adam Stephen mulishly insisted.

It was Peter Hogg who finally cackled like several hens in concert and declared, "We're not on King Louis's property, Adam!"

Stephen stared at Hogg as if his colleague had gone prematurely mad.

"What? Of course we are…"

"It's *not* King Louis's property we're on," Hogg interjected, lifting one eyebrow to emphasize the shrewdness of the argument. "It's King George's."

"Oh…I see," Stephen said, suitably humbled, enlightenment sprouting on his face like spring blossoms on a dogwood. "Robert, you're not a Scotsman, you're a Greek Sophist. Do you think the French will accept that interpretation?"

"Not if they know about it," Stobo said with a wink his colleagues immediately understood and acknowledged with wry grins and sly snickers. There would be no requests for the French to clarify the passage.

Having for the third time reviewed all the items on the two pages, Washington sent a rapidly tiring Van Braam back to the French lines once again to negotiate a revision to the article refusing them their weapons. Jacob returned with a smile: *munitions de guerre* had been crossed off the list of items the Englishmen could not take with them. Without ceremony, Washington and Mackay signed the surrender document and its twin. It remained only to select the two men who would be held hostage until the twenty-one Frenchmen of Jumonville's ill-fated party had been released and returned. Washington eyed Van Braam as the now relieved and effervescent Dutchman packaged the documents for transport.

"Jacob," Washington called.

Van Braam ceased his preparations and turned to face his Commander, hoping Washington would not have another nuisance task for him to perform.

After a moment's hesitation to gauge Jacob's reaction, Washington said, "Jacob, you speak French and you have no family…"

Washington hesitated, looked away, then back again, unsure how to ask a man to volunteer for jail time. Van Braam's face became a parody of puzzlement as he tried to comprehend what the young Virginian was trying to say. Then it came to him.

"You mean you want me to…" the Dutchman stammered hoarsely. After three readings of the French papers he had worn his unprepared vocal chords to a frazzle.

Washington raised his arms in supplication.

"It's only for two or three months, Jacob," he pleaded. "You'll eat and certainly drink better than we will…"

Washington's decision to ask Van Braam to volunteer was based not only on the Dutchman's French language skills and bachelorhood but on Jacob's view of himself as a non-British immigrant in an English-speaking society. Jacob generally went out of his way to please and would often go further for a friend like Washington. As he watched Van Braam stand flat-footed, rubbing his dimpled and stubbled chin in ungainly consternation, Washington was sure Jacob would come around to his point of view. But before the Colonel could finish persuading the deliberating Dutchman, another figure suddenly appeared: the half-naked physique of Robert Stobo, grinning with all his perfect white teeth, his slim torso resplendent with curly black hairs individually topped by beads of dried mud.

"Bachelor Robert Stobo reporting for hostage duty," Stobo said, snapping to attention and popping off a mock salute. As handsome a figure as Stobo cut, he successfully managed to make himself look slightly ridiculous.

Taken aback by the offer, Washington sputtered, "You, Robert? Why would you want to volunteer?"

"For my God, my country and..."

"...and the adventure," Washington said with dawning comprehension.

"Exactly, and don't forget..."

"The food and the drink?" Washington added. He should have known. An odyssey with the enemy. A real life melodrama written and performed by Robert Stobo of Petersburg and Edinburgh for the world to enjoy. A lark.

"Your appeal to Jacob was quite convincin', sir," Stobo gibed, his grin extending upward and outward on his carefree face. "I couldn't resist and...I could use some decent clothes..."

With a deft twist of the forearms, Stobo wrung the dingy blouse he'd removed earlier. The water it had absorbed fell to the ground like a whimsical rainstorm. Then he unwrapped it, scanned it suspiciously, and scowled: it was still unwearable.

"Colonel I'll have to be gettin' somethin' better to wear in the mornin'. This just won't do for travelin'."

"Robert, you'll probably have to go tonight," Washington pointed out.

The scowl remained, accompanied by surprise. "Really? Why?" the Scotsman asked.

"You'll be a prisoner," Washington explained, as if to a child. "You may not have a choice."

Stobo wore the scowl a while longer, trying the word *prisoner* on for size. *Hostage* had more character, was a cut above *prisoner* in the pecking order of military detention, but *prisoner* still retained an honorable status. While the French might think of him in such terms, he was sure his fellow citizens of Virginia would see him in the more elevated role of *hostage.*

"You're right, Colonel. I've got to go and pack my things, just in case," The Scotsman said, tossing the wet blouse to the ground and heading for the exit. He had been gone no more than a second or two when his engaging grin and unkempt locks of bronze hair reappeared between the tent flaps. "Oh, and Colonel, would you be kind enough to find Will Poulson and tell him he'll have to be takin' over for me? Tell him we'll have a little ceremony."

With that and a nod of self-congratulation for thinking of the ceremony, the enigmatic Stobo disappeared again, leaving his colleagues shaking their heads in disbelief. Washington wondered if Stobo would try to convince the French to let him take his coach and servants along with him to Fort Duquesne. Given Stobo's unflagging charm, he might even succeed.

With everything more or less settled, a pall seemed to lift from the room. Conversation stirred once more. Some of the men from the campfires entered bearing rum and ruddy complexions and, after a proper interval, laughter. A few were polite enough to glance at Washington to gauge his reaction but they needn't have been concerned. He understood their need to release the unbearable stress of the last few days. They weren't indifferent to defeat. They were simply exhausted and happy the fight was over. Even with only the light from two candles and the few oil lamps the newcomers had brought with them, they would celebrate life, especially their own, which, much to their surprise, they still had. The defeat was not theirs. It was his, and he would bear it.

Suddenly, Washington remembered Jacob. He had asked the Dutchman to be one of the hostages and Stobo had interrupted. Making a quick scan of the room, he found Van Braam seated at the table to his right and rear, the candle he had used to read the surrender document beneath his chin, its light illuminating the hills and casting shadows into the valleys of his facial terrain. Jacob's twisted knob of a nose, crudely sculpted features and gangling limbs made him look and move like a giant marionette. Even his moods were puppet-like caricatures. In joy, his grin and eyebrows rode high on the cliffs of his cheekbones and brow ridges like those of a jack o' lantern. In anger, his narrowed gaze and pinched lips could have been those of a terrified baboon frantically warding off predators. But they were real moods nonetheless, like the one possessing him now: a mix of pride, apprehension and anticipation. Pride because his friend George Washington had asked of him a great favor, apprehension about being held hostage by the French, and anticipation for the adventure ahead. In Jacob's brain, this alchemy of fluid emotions bubbled like an overheated boiler, sending out impulses to fuel his drumming fingers, his tapping toes, and his fluttering lips, whose erratic movements could have been interpreted as speech, except for the absence of accompanying sound.

Washington sat down beside his friend.

"Jacob, are you all right?" he asked.

Van Braam's fingers stopped drumming. As he emerged from his fidgety reverie his eyelids popped open like those of a raccoon caught stealing forbidden trash.

"Colonel, I would like to volunteer to be the second hostage," he said with fitful alacrity.

"You don't have to, Jacob."

"No, no, Colonel, I will be fine. Robert and I will have an interesting time...an interesting time, I am sure," he said, putting on another wide grin. Then his gaze centered on Washington as he declared, "But I would like to ask you a favor."

"Certainly, Jacob. What is it?"

"I would like to buy your uniform."

Prepared for a more momentous request—like writing to Jacob's friends and relatives in Holland if he should die in captivity—Washington was caught unawares. It was so trivial! But, as he thought about it, trivial as it was, having a decent uniform to wear in the presence of the enemy was a consideration that would have been in the forefront of his own meditations were he to be in Jacob's position. Jacob was only two years older than he was and, to men of such an age, military adventure meant an opportunity for glory and, if not glory—clearly unavailable in the present circumstances—then honor. And honor, while theoretically attainable even by a naked man, looked much better in fine clothes.

"Do you mean my new one with the silver fringe?"

"Yes. I will pay you for it," Van Braam said hopefully.

Washington leaned back in his chair, thoughtfully rubbing his chin. He had not yet had a chance to wear the new scarlet vest and broadcloth coat in a military situation and was reluctant to part with it until he had. But here, now, the only chance he would have to do so would be in abject defeat. Jacob's was the greater need.

"And of course I will replace the insignia and make it to be a captain's uniform," Jacob added.

"It might not fit," Washington said, still searching for a rationale to keep the uniform. Van Braam was a tall man, over six feet tall, but Washington was notably larger in all other directions.

"I will try it on," Jacob retorted, sensing victory.

"Robert will still be prettier," Washington joked, caressing, with his mind's touch, the image of Stobo's magnificent blue broadcloth coat with its scarlet cuffs and waistcoat.

"Robert will always be prettier," said Van Braam with a mirthful cock of his head. "And it has nothing to do with his uniform."

They laughed and agreed on a price to be taken out of Jacob's next pay, which would, in any case, be of little value to him in his pending role as hostage. Van Braam followed Washington to the latter's quarters. The rain had stopped but avoiding puddles of rainwater and swamps of mud remained a delicate task. Once there, Washington lighted a lamp, rummaged through his chest for the uniform, found it, and held up the coat for Jacob to see.

"Oh...my," Jacob moaned in a mellifluous tone not far from ecstasy. He touched the coat lovingly, then said, "It's beautiful!"

Pleased by Van Braam's reaction, Washington said, "Try it on."

Jacob did as suggested, entranced by the feel of the fine material as his arms entered each sleeve. It was too long in the sleeves and too broad in the shoulders and hips but not enough to make him look ridiculous, at least not any more ridiculous than he normally looked. The fit was entirely appropriate for a man whose gangling frame gave him the appearance of a string puppet. But the expression on his face had changed: It was no longer a cartoon of a man but had taken on a detached, dreamy aspect, like the face of a small boy with a new toy.

"You look wonderful, Jacob," Washington said sincerely. "Why don't you wear it now? I'll wait with the others while you change."

Jacob happily agreed to the proposal and was removing his befouled buckskin breeches before Washington turned to depart. Back at the council tent, more men, noise and lighting were in evidence, most of the latter in the form of oil lamps, which, along with the rum, gave the scene a festive quality. When he saw Robert

Stobo, Washington realized there was more to this impression than just a mood. There were, indeed, actual festivities taking place. Stobo had attired himself in his glorious blue, scarlet and silver-laced regimentals and was marching with stiff, martial, steps to the beat of the Virginia Regiment's only drum. In front of him stood Abner Hazlip with what looked like a buckskin shot pouch on his head. From the chatter, Washington deduced that Stobo was giving a dramatic demonstration of how he intended to surrender to the enemy. Abner Hazlip was playing the part of Villiers, the pouch on his head a crude imitation of the French capot.

Stobo stopped before Hazlip-Villiers, gave him a crisp salute, then barked: "SIR! Do I have the honor of addressing the Commander of the frog-eaters, SIR?"

Hazlip glanced around as if searching for the object of Stobo's query. Then he looked the Scotsman over skeptically as he might inspect a horse, circling to Stobo's right. When he had made a complete circle, he placed his hands on his hips and pushed a square chin to within an inch of Stobo's face.

"Yeah, I guess that'd be me. What'd you say your name was, son? Stupo?" Abner said, freezing the chin in place.

Stobo nearly lost his composure. Others in the crowd did as the sounds of random belly laughter filled the confined space.

"Stobo, SIR! The name is Captain Robert Stobo," the Scotsman forced himself to declare.

"All right, all right. Don't get excited. I believe ya," Hazlip said, nodding in affirmation. "What is it you want, son?"

"SIR! I wish to surrender and become a prisoner of his frog-eating Majesty King Louis XV, SIR!"

"Now why would ya wanta do a silly thing like that?"

"I'm told there's no mud in Canada, SIR, only ice. I've developed an intense dislike for mud, SIR, and ice goes well with Scotch!"

Stobo and Hazlip continued their farcical improvisation, each trying to outdo the other in evoking the stronger audience response. Robert Stobo was truly amazing, Washington concluded. Within the hour he would become a French prisoner, totally subservient to the whims of his keepers, and yet here he was laughing and joking as if he were anticipating nothing more than a night out at the local tavern.

It was not as if Stobo was behaving irresponsibly. He had been among the most vigorous Virginia defenders. But once it became clear that victory was not in their grasp, he simply let go of his passion and went on to the next logical step in bringing this misadventure to an end. Washington admired this ability but could no more emulate it than he could soar like an eagle. The defeat at Fort Necessity would remain in the being of George Washington for a very long time.

While Stobo and Hazlip were playing out their impromptu comedy, Jacob Van Braam arrived, caught Washington's eye, and tried to approach his commanding officer without fanfare. He looked better than presentable in the new uniform but not much. Cut for Washington's height and large-boned frame, the coat hung low beneath Jacob's knees like a dress and the silver-trimmed tricorne was so undersized it dropped nearly to his ears and leaned forward, forcing the Dutchman to peer out from under the front corner. Jacob looked like a homely gentle-matron dressed for a ball, indiscriminately batting her eyelashes at potential dance partners. The resemblance was not lost on Robert Stobo who, when he spotted the Dutchman surreptitiously entering the tent, destroyed any chance for blessed obscurity that Jacob might have hoped for.

"Ma-dam!" Stobo exclaimed, breathless and staring, seemingly enraptured by the as yet oblivious Van Braam. The Scotsman executed a deep bow and, offering an outstretched arm, said in his best French accent, "My buxom beauty, my princess of perpetual precipitation, my mistress of the murky meadow, my quaintly querulous queen of the quintessential quagmire…"

"Five Q's in a row! Stobo, you've gone too far…" a critic groaned from the audience.

The Scotsman, unfazed, finished his entreaty: "…may I have this dance?"

Even though Robert Stobo was looking directly at him, Jacob Van Braam thought that he must be speaking to someone else. The Dutchman looked around, confounded, trying to determine at whom the Scotsman's odd query might have been directed, but found only faces that were either already laughing or were puckering up to do so. Jacob gazed with envy at Stobo in his splendid, form-fitting uniform, then looked down at his new coat flaring below the knees like a petticoat, and realized the joke was on him. Without missing a beat, he bunched the material of the upper part of his coat into a passable pair of breasts, approached Stobo, and curtsied, extending one delicately fingered hand toward the Scotsman.

"Enchante', M'sieur," he said in a raspy falsetto. "Permittez-moi de me presenter. Je m'appelle Jacque-*line* Van Braam."

Stobo understood none of what Van Braam had said except that Jacqueline Van Braam had agreed to dance with him. He stood erect, snapped his fingers, and barked, "Maestro, music please!" The regimental drum and a wood flute started up, providing an acceptable rhythm but no discernible melody. Fortunately, the happy couple was blissfully unperturbed by this musical shortcoming. Stobo held out his arm for Jacqueline and, with a polite nod, said pointedly, "Madam."

"*Madamoiselle*, s'il vous plait," the lovely and unattached Jacqueline replied, her eyelids aflutter with possibilities.

The pair danced a minuet of sorts, consisting mostly of Jacqueline circling the enchanted Stobo as if he were a maypole. The aloof but subtly flirtatious lady grasped her partner's hand as she might an over-used handkerchief—loosely and with a minimum of contact. Bawdy remarks filled the air as Jacqueline wriggled her hips and assumed various feminine but highly suggestive poses. To everyone's surprise and delight, Jacob Van Braam not only resembled but was turning out to be a born clown.

"He's certainly having more fun than he had at Venango, isn't he?" Christopher Gist's voice resounded from behind Washington. Gist was wearing the same clothes he had that afternoon, with an added layer of grime. Like everyone else, he looked bone-tired with exhaustion, though his alertness belied it.

"Yes, he is. As a matter of fact, Jacob is having more fun than I thought him capable of," Washington said wistfully.

"Don't worry too much about him, George. Jacob knows how to live among strangers."

Washington glanced at the man with whom he'd begun this troubled adventure, both pleased and disturbed that his thoughts could be read so easily. Gist acknowledged the look with a quick darting of his eyes toward, then away from, the younger man, but did not expand on the remark. Washington's attention returned to the entertainers.

"They both do. I'm actually more worried about Robert. This is too easy for him. I think he may get himself in trouble…"

Since he had no substantive evidence on which to base the remark, the Colonel let the sentence hang in the air, like sunlight at dusk, until it no longer piqued the senses.

"How are your sons, Christopher?" Washington asked, meaning: *Have your sons been wounded?*

"They're fine," Gist answered, meaning: *No, they haven't.* "And how are you, George?"

It was a casual question but Washington knew there was substance behind it. Christopher Gist was his friend but, at moments when the younger man was vulnerable, their relationship seemed to transform into something more akin to a father-son affinity.

"I'll be all right. Defeat is not supposed to feel good," said Washington, managing a half-smile.

"What will you do when we get back?"

"Explain it to Dinwiddie after I've explained it to myself." Washington said, then gestured toward the captives-to-be. "and make sure the Governor doesn't forget about those two."

"Do you think he'll understand?"

"No. With all his bluster, Dinwiddie is a civilized European who's never been farther west than the Shenandoah Valley. He thinks *Fredericksburg* is the backwoods. How could he understand?"

Stobo and Van Braam ended their *ad hoc* promenade, largely because the flautist's limited talent for extemporaneous musical composition had run its course and a single regimental drummer could not produce viable dance music, even for two buffoons. The audience applauded and hooted its appreciation loudly and vigorously. The performers bowed and, after the shy Jacqueline refused a kiss to her doting consort, resumed their true identities. The hour was late. The real Robert Stobo, if such a creature could be said to exist, appealed for calm with raised hands, then called for Lieutenant Will Poulson to join him at center stage. Waiting until absolute quiet reigned, Stobo said a small prayer, then unbuckled his sword and handed it to Poulson.

"Take it, Will. I'll have no use for it now," he said sullenly, a perceptible quiver in his chin. With set jaw and resounding conviction he added, "And don't be sparin' it when you've the opportunity to draw it on behalf of your country."

This provoked wild cheers and ovations even though, if asked, few of the revelers could have named the country to which Stobo referred. Was it Virginia? But Virginia was a colony, not a country, and there was still considerable debate whether or not the land on which they stood *was* Virginia. It might be Pennsylvania. Was it British North America? That was an even more nebulous concept. Was it Great Britain herself? Not likely, especially with rebel Scots and assorted immigrant malcontents among the celebrants. But it didn't matter. What was important was to exude pride and patriotism and, by doing so, cast out the hobgoblins of ignominious defeat, to feel good about oneself, one's colleagues and the noble quest. There was no higher motivation for creatures that collectively referred to themselves as humanity.

Jacob Van Braam was the first to say good-bye. Still red-faced from his performance and a little embarrassed by it now that he had transmogrified back to himself, the maladroit Dutchman gave a tentative salute and said, even more tentatively, "Adieu, mon Colonel."

"Au revoir, Jacob," Washington offered, exhausting one third of his repertoire of French expressions.

The meaning of his Commander's reply was not lost on Van Braam. Lifting a grin onto his rude features, he replied, "Thank you," leaving Washington to wonder what in the name of heaven the Dutchman had to thank him for.

After a final round of drinks with his admirers and looking a little out of context without his sword, Robert Stobo sauntered over and anchored Washington's hand between both of his as if securing himself to a dock in a raging sea. Now that the time had come to actually depart, the Scotsman was less sanguine about his impending captivity. He was not having second thoughts, only first emotions, about his decision.

"I'll be back," he said. Stobo, too, had run out of adequate expression.

"Of course you will," Washington said, eschewing the usual repartee. "Don't do anything foolish, Robert."

For the moment, at least, this brought Stobo out of his funk. Spreading his arms in supplication to the whims of fate, he said, "It's a little late to tell me that, Colonel!"

Then, after packing away the articles of capitulation and executing the mandatory handshakes on the way out, Captain Robert Stobo and Captain Lieutenant Jacob Van Braam, with Ensign William Broraugh tagging along to return one copy of the document after Villiers had signed, were gone. The spiritual void they left in their wake seemed to suck all the sound from the air and all the vitality from the faces of men who, a moment before, had been celebrating the wonder of their existence. Washington made his way outside, feeling a strange, inexplicable compulsion to watch the men cross the meadow even though it was now eleven o'clock in the evening and there was only the background of the smoldering French campfires to illuminate the scene.

Washington felt a hand on his shoulder.

"They *will* be back, Colonel."

Although Washington recognized the voice, he turned his head to verify its owner's identity. It was James Mackay. Of all the things Mackay's gesture might have evoked in his mind, Washington found his thoughts focused on the most trivial: It was the first time the Captain of the Independents had acknowledged his rank.

Chapter Seventeen

July 4, 1754, Midnight

here were too many of them to fit inside the tent, so Captain Le Mercier had the folding table and three stools set up outside Villiers' quarters. Van Braam, Stobo, Broraugh, and their *Compagnies franches* attendants stood at ease opposite the three French Captains, Villiers, Le Mercier and de Longueuil, with the Commander, Villiers, in the middle and peering alternately over his *pince-nez* at his captives and down at the documents before him. A single lantern illuminated the scene like a harvest moon in a sky dotted with the glowing embers of French and English campfires. In the true sky, there were no moon and stars, only the blackness of residual overcast that, too weak to wring its moisture out of the air into droplets, expressed its serous nature as a clammy humidity whose oppressiveness wrung beads of sweat from the brows of the weary humans. A hoot owl, equally disenchanted with the weather, screeched its protest from the deep bowels of the woods.

Villiers studied the three Englishmen—or Virginians, as they called themselves. He already knew Van Braam from the surrender negotiations. The man had obviously washed himself and found new clothes. Of the other two, one was dirty and restless, the other well attired and reticent. Villiers looked over the copy of the capitulation document in front of him and searched, using his finger as a guide, for the sentence containing the names of the British prisoners. After bringing the lantern closer, he found it and gazed directly at the well-attired and reticent Englishman.

"You are Captain Robert Stobo?" he asked, confident of his surmise.

"I am," Stobo answered through Van Braam.

"This is your signature?" Villiers asked again, pointing to the line in the document.

"Yes, of course," Stobo replied, glancing down at the paper but making no effort to confirm Villiers' statement. *Why would anyone but a designated hostage put himself in the hands of the enemy?* Villiers' question was gratuitous and time wasting.

If Villiers detected irritation in Stobo's tone, he blithely ignored it and pressed on. Alternately glancing at Stobo and Van Braam, he said, "You understand that by affixing your signatures to this document you become my prisoners?"

"Hostages!" Stobo corrected.

Jacob struggled for a French term to make clear the distinction. With abounding hems and haws, he tried various phraseologies and finally found one that conveyed the correct meaning. Then he nodded to Stobo to indicate that Villiers understood.

The French Commander went on: "And you understand that you will remain hostages until such time as our people are freed..."

"Sir!" Stobo interrupted sharply. "We comprehend all of it. It is not necessary for you to challenge our intelligence. We are to be your hostages and you are to permit our troops to return home with their property and small arms in hand. There is no ambiguity. We can only hope that you will genuinely abide by the terms agreed to..."

The pugnacious Scotsman argued with the fervor of a barrister trying not so much to make a point as to deflect an opponent from making his. The topic Stobo sought to avoid was the proscription in the terms of surrender against British bodies trespassing on the lands of 'His Christian Majesty' for a year. The British argument—his own—that these lands were not those of 'His Christian Majesty' Louis XV but the rightful property of King George II of England was intended for an international forum, not for a French field officer with the power of life and death.

Villiers did not jump out of his stool but might have had he not so firmly gripped the table before him to restrain his indignation. The muscles of his brow tightened over narrowed eye slits, giving him the predatory mien of a cat ready to pounce.

"Captain Stobo, your remarks are most insulting! You forget that we, not you, are the victors. Our terms are quite generous, as you must know. As for your suggestion that we would fail to abide by those terms, this is especially outrageous!"

Enjoying the Frenchman's trepidation, Stobo relaxed and drew back a barb or two. "Sir, I did not say you would. I only said we would be anticipatin' a rigorous enforcement of the agreed-to terms. And we would expect that enforcement, Captain, to include your savages as well as yourselves," he said, catching Villiers' glare and throwing it back at him.

It was a fair point. Neither side was able to exercise as much control over its Indian allies as it would have wished. The Scotsman had accomplished his objective: diverting attention away from the textual details of the capitulation. What he did not know was that, although Villiers' current mood of fuming consternation belied it, the diversion suited the French Commander's purpose just as well as Stobo's. Villiers was reminded of that purpose by a nod from Le Mercier, who had been studying the second copy of the articles during the squabble. What Le Mercier's gesture meant was that he had finished his review and found the document to be an honest summary of what both parties had negotiated. The English had not surreptitiously altered anything. When he realized this, Villiers' distressed condition instantly dispersed into the ether.

"We will do our best, Captain Stobo," he said with an unctuous articulation that betrayed, even to the non-French speakers present, a hint of mendacity. Villiers stood and transferred his attention from Stobo to the third Englishman, Ensign William Broraugh.

"M'sieur..." he said with a virtual shrug to indicate his ignorance of Broraugh's identity.

"Ensign William Broraugh," said the apprehensive Englishman.

"You will be returning directly to your camp?"

"Yes."

"In that case..." Villiers began, affixing his signature to the document in front of him, then doing the same to Le Mercier's copy. To dry the ink, he waved the second one in the air several times, then handed it to Broraugh. "Please give this to your Commanding officer— Colonel Washington, I believe it is. Is that correct?"

"Yes," Broraugh replied, then glanced at Stobo and Van Braam for instructions.

"You can go, Ensign," Stobo said, puzzled by the sudden mellowing of Villiers' mood. He would have preferred to argue with the Frenchman a bit longer, for fun and to establish a modicum of dominance, which could be useful later on.

Ensign Broraugh hastily departed, having not a clue to the meaning of the interplay that had just taken place between Villiers and Stobo. Jacob Van Braam, currently revisiting his fears of imprisonment, understood the interchange only slightly better than Broraugh and had no appreciation of or interest in political gamesmanship. From Villiers' evasive reaction, Stobo suspected something pernicious was in the offing, but had no idea what it was and, in any case, was in no position to do anything about it. His ruminations on the subject were soon cut short.

"M'sieurs, it is time to sleep," Villiers announced. "Tomorrow will be a long day. Do you agree?"

Without waiting for an answer, the Frenchman barked a few commands to the attendants and the two hostages were soon being nudged, gun butts first, deeper into the woods, presumably to their new quarters. Despite the haste of their departure, Stobo managed to extract an agreement from Villiers to discuss the disposition of the horse-drawn coach he had arrived in: He did not want it to be sold, intentionally or inadvertently, to some Montreal livery. Villiers' assent was promptly forthcoming. He did not want any complications with the hostages and assured the Scotsman that Canadians were too honest and God-fearing a people for such a thing to occur. Stobo, with no access to the appropriate French enforcement institutions, grudgingly accepted the promise and marched off without further complaint to his destiny. With the hostages disposed of, Villiers turned to Le Mercier.

"Has the message been prepared, Francois?"

"As soon as I saw the English signatures…" Le Mercier said with a tiny smile that revealed vestigial dimples on the barren topography of his bulbous cheeks. "…it came into my mind like a revelation. I will write it down and send it with a runner tonight."

Villiers gave a curt wave of dismissal.

"Use the rest of the evening to write it well so that there will be no ambiguity as to its significance. France and Europe must be made to understand that we have done nothing more than our rightful duty and that we have done so honorably. I'll sign it tomorrow morning and we can send it to Contrecoeur then."

"He will be pleased, I'm sure," de Longueuil commented. He had risen from his stool and was gazing over Villiers' shoulder at the document. Laughing, he added, "With that miserable itch of his, Captain Contrecoeur has little enough opportunity for pleasure."

The two others shared in de Longueuil's gaiety. Because his infirmity, though severe, was not life threatening, Contrecoeur's incessant scratching was the source of much mirthful commentary at Fort Duquesne. The fort's Commander had, on several occasions, been seen attacking his rump with the vigor of a bear with a tick bite.

Circling round to view the document over Villiers' left shoulder, Le Mercier shook his head and said, "It's still difficult to believe the English actually signed this document without modification."

"But it's a true account of the assault on my brother's party. You heard Mouceau's story," Villiers pointed out.

"Still, they could have insisted on a revision of the text, made themselves appear less culpable," Le Mercier argued.

"We defeated them. They had no choice but to sign."

"It's much simpler than that," de Longueuil interjected. Knowing the statement would arouse their curiosity, he waited until they turned toward him, their faces burnished with anticipation, then explained, "They didn't *understand* what they read."

Le Mercier's eyebrows shot up, reached an apogee of one centimeter, then fell. The face of Villiers remained blank, not a stray tic disturbing its composure. Neither man spoke, leaving de Longueuil with the impression that they failed to grasp what, to him, was intuitively obvious. Disappointed that his comrades could not see the truth, he stepped back and swung his gaze from one to the other, hoping to energize the powers of reason in at least one of their brains.

"Van Braam, the Dutchman," he said, almost stammering in frustration. "His French is not that good. Don't you remember how often we had to repeat to make ourselves understood? And there are a number of places in the document where the text is so blurred not even a Frenchman could read it. Why…"

At this point, the speaker became animated, leaned over the terms of capitulation, and began running an index finger over its surface as he searched for something. Le Mercier followed the roving finger with a curious stare, his lips moist and slightly parted. Villiers' head turned toward the front, but his gaze focused not on the paper but on some phantom point ten meters beyond.

"Look, look, right here. Read that, Francois," de Longueuil insisted, lightly tapping the searching finger on the first word of the sentence it had been seeking.

Le Mercier projected himself forward, squinting to see better, and recognized the passage.

"I know what it says already," he muttered.

"Pretend you don't. Imagine you are seeing it for the first time, like the Dutchman. Read it out loud," the confident de Longueuil appealed.

Le Mercier could not see the purpose of the exercise but, to placate his colleague, sighed and began reading.

"As our intention has never been to trouble the peace and harmony which reigns between the two friendly princes but only to avenge the…"

"Why did you stop, Francois?" de Longueuil asked. He was smiling.

"Because I *am* the Dutchman and I can't make out the next word," Le Mercier said with a sharp edge of sarcasm. "Those were your rules, were they not?"

"Exactly, but do you know the word?"

"The word is *assassinat,*" Le Mercier said.

"Good, now read the sentence as you know it to be," the pedagogue instructed.

Le Mercier started in the middle of the sentence instead, reciting, *"…But only to avenge the murder which has been done on one of out officers…"*

"A damning statement, don't you agree? The most damning statement in the document. The English would never have signed anything containing such an admission."

"But they did just that…"

"No, they didn't, Francois," de Longueuil chided, shaking a long, curling finger in front of his comrade's nose. "I think when the Dutchman had to choose a substitute for the illegible word, he simply examined the context and picked one that suited his own purposes. For instance, he might have read: ...*but only to avenge the assault which has been done on one of our officers.* It is not nearly so incriminating a statement. Do you not agree?"

Le Mercier saw at last. "O-o-o-oh!" he sang, shaping the sound in the circle of his lips as he nodded in affirmation.

With Le Mercier a convert to his theory, de Longueuil turned his attention to Villiers. Surely the French Commander would now recognize the compelling logic of his argument, would appreciate the purity of its intrinsic irony as he did. But when he saw the ebullient visage of de Longueuil radiating self-congratulations, Villiers showed no surprise, only a smug politeness.

"Very clever of you, Charles. I would never have thought. *Amazing*," the French Commander said, in a voice conspicuously free of amazement.

July 4, 1754, The battlefield

The dawn was God's apology for the day before. Striated with reds, yellows, oranges and medleys thereof, it appeared on the horizon as a streak of brilliant gold on the dark canvas of night. As the sun rose and its radiant brush strokes penetrated the sky, the blackness of the void was transformed to deep, then shallow blue, an altogether more suitable background for exhibiting the foibles of man. But it was a tentative, superficial apology that God offered. While white stratus clouds soared overhead and the streaming sunlight made a myriad of rainbows in the mist captured by the leafy fingers of trees, earthbound things retained their worldly attributes. The cattle carcasses strewn about Great Meadows among the tents and campfires of the Virginia and Carolina troops did not yet smell of death but were beginning to attract flies and were already under the keen surveillance of an advance squadron of turkey buzzards lazily circling overhead. Great Meadows and Indian Runs were no longer raging torrents but had settled down to more sedate existences as cascading rapids. Tomorrow, the turbulence of their churning flows would be audible to a distance of no more than a hundred feet. As legitimate streams, now contained completely within their established banks, they no longer posed a threat, but the floodwaters of the third of July had left a gelatinous layer of silt in the backyards of the tent dwellers. Dogs and men skirted the slime when they could and cautiously tiptoed through it when necessary. A less fastidious species, the horses plodded recklessly through the stuff, scattering swarms of mud beads over everything within five feet of their hooves.

With coffee mug in hand, Colonel George Washington surveyed the scene of his first military disaster with at least as much interest as the turkey buzzards but with a less carnal focus. For reasons he could not explain, a compulsion to commit it all to memory had taken hold of him. Later he would record his impressions in the daily journal he kept but now, as he picked his way among the dead and the debris outside the northwest wall of the stockade, he simply wanted to take it all in, to paint a picture of it in his mind. For future reference, he convinced himself, an educational device, a learning tool, a visual essay to study and critique. In fact, his fascination was not entirely without its seamy side. *So this is what the aftermath of a battle looks like,* he found himself musing. Then a more outrageous thought: *There is even beauty in it, of a sort. But is it really beauty or is it merely awe-inspiring, this weird mixture of chaos and rebirth? If it is not truly beautiful and I think that it is, is there something wrong with me?* He wondered.

"Look!" said a voice behind him. Peter Hogg's.

Hogg had not changed his clothes for three days and, Washington judged from the stubble on his chin, hadn't shaved for at least that long. He looked old. He *was* old compared to the other officers of the Virginia Regiment, in his fiftieth decade, a period during which men usually died if they made it that far. Peter seemed healthy enough but his complexion was a wan, milky hue, the fold of loose skin below his chin and jaw more like a pouch of ancient leather than it had been at the beginning of the expedition. He should have stayed home with his new wife instead of marching out here seeking glory and Dinwiddie's free land. There would be no land grants after this journey, perhaps never.

Washington followed Hogg's gaze to the south woods. Many of the Virginia Volunteers inside and outside the stockade were doing likewise, some having spotted the two lines of French marines emerging from the tree line, others reacting to the monotonous but steady beat of the drummers leading the twin processions. Both wore King's livery blue coats trimmed with crimson and white lace and carried blue drums ornamented by a ring of *fleur-de-lis*. The bulk of the men of the *Compagnies franches* were attired not in the wilderness uniform they'd fought in, but in the standard issue gray-white uniform with blue facing. They were marching with muskets mounted on their left shoulders, their tricornes cocked to the right so that any manipulations of the weapons would not send their hats flying off in all directions like startled ducks. Among the regulars were scattered a few marines in blue and red uniforms like those of the drummers, but sporting distinctive white metal buttons and absent the exotic lace. These were the artillerymen. They were few in number because the French had not brought any artillery with them. One of their number, Jolicoeur Bonin, a convoluted wooden pipe clenched between his teeth, struggled to force his short legs into a stride matching those of his taller comrades.

Aside from the natural fascination aroused by a parade in progress, what interested and mystified Washington was that the entire multitude of French soldiers, weaponry, and equipment passing before him was spotless. Where, in any section of Great Meadows or Indian Runs or their nearest tributaries, could the French have found water clean enough to wash themselves?

"I think they're gonna give us a show, Colonel," Hogg murmured. As if on cue, an entourage of officers—Stephen, Poulson, Lewis, and Gist—arrived to ogle the performance.

A performance is precisely what it was. Upon reaching a point just outside the last trench, the two columns of marines halted. A French officer between the two lines barked a sequence of commands, the last of which must have been a signal to execute the ones preceding because it was at this point that the two columns abruptly faced each other, snapped the muskets from their shoulders and, with a deft series of maneuvers, brought their muskets to rest, butt first, on the ground. All of this was done in near perfect unison.

"Beautiful!" Andrew Lewis exclaimed. "Absolutely lovely!"

It was a thought Washington had also entertained with some trepidation. He was happy to hear it expressed by someone other than himself. There was no doubt about it: beauty, not just magnificence, was involved.

"What are they expectin' us to do, run the gauntlet?" Adam Stephen commented, not bothering to conceal the brooding hostility he had been working on since the night before. The twin line formation of the French did, intentionally or unintentionally, resemble a gauntlet, and was clearly intended to define a pathway, both tangible and symbolic, for the victors to usher away the vanquished from the field of battle.

"It's no gauntlet. It's a reception line with tables covered by roast pheasant and home-brewed ale at the end of it, served by pretty maids with big tits risin' up out a' their corsets like ripe melons," joked the big man, Andrew Lewis. The look of anticipation on his face and the moist tongue lubricating his dry lips suggested that Andrew might also be entertaining a fantasy or two. There was no sign of the previous evening's melancholy.

"And what are you plannin' to feast upon, Andrew, the pheasants or the maids?" asked Will Poulson.

"I don't have to make that decision 'til I get to the other end a' the line," Lewis rejoined merrily, pulling his tongue back inside his mouth so the musings of his mind wouldn't be so transparent, then smiling like an angel to assert his aloofness from such impure ruminations. The tactic didn't work, nor had Andrew expected it to. Except for Adam Stephen, the officers kidded him mercilessly about how he intended to peel the melons and whether he preferred the nimble nibble or the grand gulp approach to melon consumption. Lewis gave as good as he got in a raucous interplay of ribald witticisms completely devoid of meaningful content. Though vacuous, it was not difficult to draw a proper conclusion from the inelegant conversation: These men had been out of the presence of women far too long. Their instincts and their manners needed some serious attending to by the gentler sex.

Adam Stephen was the lone holdout. Whether the former surgeon was of too earnest a disposition to enjoy the levity or was simply distressed by the circumstances, Washington couldn't decide. A mood that, the evening before, was merely disagreeable had been transformed into a rancorous distemper. Adam could not bring himself to laugh. His spirit seemed to vacillate between anger and despair, manifesting itself in his body as a dull paralysis interrupted by bursts of nervous energy.

"They're probably positionin' their muskets so they can beat us with them when we march by," Stephen said, imagining the remark to be humorous. The unresponsive faces of his colleagues then inspired him to even greater transgressions. "Let's hope they don't attach the bayonets. Ha!"

The *Ha!* was included to make it clear a joke was intended but Stephen's delivery was laced with too much cynicism. The message arrived—stillborn.

"Well, that's a nice thought, Adam," Andrew Lewis finally said to grease conversational gears that had suddenly seized.

It was not a nice thought and Adam Stephen knew it. Rather than be patronized, even in jest, he turned on his heel and headed for his company's campsite, which, like those of all the Virginia and Carolina companies, was on the western slope of Great Meadows. His compatriots could do nothing but shake their heads in bewilderment.

"Wait, Adam," Washington called, cutting the distance between the two men with long, purposeful strides.

Stephen halted, turned to face the Virginia Commander, his face a dark, silent cry of anguish. It was an expression both deferential to Washington and guardedly defiant, the expression of a principled but practical man. He said nothing, waiting for his Commander to speak. Without knowing its source, Washington found himself hesitant to confront the discontent that was consuming his subordinate.

At thirty years, Adam Stephen was in the middle of the age range of Washington's officers, but looked younger. This was perhaps an attitude rather than anything the years had or had not done to his physiology, supplemented by a lock of sandy brown hair that corkscrewed down his forehead to the broad bridge of an unremarkable nose, there to be flanked by bushy, Celtic eyebrows. The lock was the only stand of hair on his scalp with any curvature; the rest lay flat against his skull like stacked timbers or jutted in arbitrary directions like trees in a logjam. When he was in good spirits, Adam Stephen let the lock of hair dance and twist with the movement of his head. Under duress, he was constantly brushing it back with spread fingers, trying to make it adhere to the rules passively obeyed by its siblings. Today, Adam was wearing a gold-trimmed tricorne cocked over his forehead, a disposition that effectively captured the rebellious lock of hair. The tricorne was not his only affectation. Although his blue breeches were as grungy as those of any member of the Virginia Volunteers, he had put on a clean white linen shirt.

"Adam, what's wrong?" Washington finally asked, placing a firm but friendly hand on the other man's shoulder. "Why are you so upset? We've all lost this battle. It's not just you."

His vexation barely in check, Adam Stephen struggled within, unsure whether or not he should speak. Finally, he decided he would.

"Colonel, it's not my business to tell you how to run the Regiment…"

"Everyone else does. Why shouldn't you?"

Stephen smiled politely but was not amused. As he dropped his chin to his chest, the smile vanished and with it the last vestiges of good cheer in him.

"Have you never been beaten before, Colonel?"

"I've hardly fought a battle before. But no, I'm embarrassed to say this is my first defeat."

Adam was not about to let his Commander raise the temper of the conversation above melancholy. His lips had a serrated shape that made his p's and b's hiss when he spoke. Somehow, the effect of this quirk was to give his speech a shadowy, subterranean quality that he used to advantage.

"I've lost nearly every battle I was ever in, and the ones we didn't lose, we decided we couldn't win and withdrew. We marched all the way to Derby in England, then turned around and came back. It was stupid, the way we fought, like thick-witted barbarians…"

Washington assumed Stephen was talking about his experiences ten years earlier in Scotland.

"You mean the Jacobite rebellion in forty-five? I don't know much about that," he said, *except for what I learned the other day from my officer corps.*

"And you're not likely to. It's not a war the British would be rememberin' fondly. It's not a war the King or his foul issue, Billie the Butcher, want anyone to know about."

Stephen spat the foul-tasting name of the Duke with a special vehemence.

Billie the Butcher, Washington recalled, the Duke of Cumberland, youngest son of King George II, hero of Great Britain. He considered interrupting the vitriol flowing from the gnarled mouth of his colleague, but found no opportunity as Adam warmed to his subject.

"Culloden. Do you know about Culloden Moor, Colonel? We touched on it the other day—his eminence, Captain Mackay and I."

As he spoke, Stephen cast a furtive glance toward the tents of the Independents, where Mackay's regulars were breaking camp with their usual military efficiency.

"Culloden Moor was the last battle. Our tactics—if you can call them that—were abominable. Prince Charlie wasn't much of a general and you've got to have good generalship and discipline to keep a savage band of Scots from gettin' themselves killed. They did that, you know. Thought they were damned invincible, wavin' their battle axes and screamin' as they charged only to have their throats drilled with British arrows before they got halfway across the field of battle. Stupid bastards were too dumb to know any better..."

As he embellished his portrait of the battle, Adam's voice broke. He might be critical of his former cohorts, but he loved them still.

"We lost the battle and the war. No surprises in that," Stephen continued, disguising the fact that he was wiping tears away by swiping at his brow with a forearm. "But Billie wasn't satisfied with just a victory. The *good* Scots were already on his side and he didn't want any more clan rebellions. There'd already been too many to suit his fragile Hanoverian temper. So he sent his soldiers out to kill the survivors."

Stephen paused to gather his thoughts and to let what he'd said sink in. While his interest lay primarily with the relevance of this story to the current situation, Washington was shocked by the charge that the King's son was a cold-blooded killer.

"You're saying that the Duke of Cumberland murdered those men?"

"Hunted them down, one by one or in small groups and had them killed like rabid dogs," Stephen confirmed.

It was hard to believe and Washington was not sure he did. He certainly didn't want to. The fine points of European warfare was not a topic dear to the heart of an American colonial, let alone a Virginia farmer. But George II was the King of England, Washington's sovereign, and William Augustus, Duke of Cumberland, was the King's son and servant. Suppose he had gotten his wish to become an officer in the British regular army and had been ordered to exterminate Scots after they'd already been defeated. Would he have done it? Suppose, just for the sake of placing the hypothetical in a more relevant context, that they'd been Virginians instead of Scots. What then would he do? But that was too farfetched. Virginians were too complacent for rebellion. It was difficult enough rousing them to fight the true enemy: France.

Sensing that he now had Washington's full attention, Adam Stephen softened the edge of his sullen scowl. His anxiety still showed in his feet, which kept kicking the ground like the hooves of an angry bull, but he folded his arms to prevent them from taking on lives of their own.

"If they'd been French or Dutch or Spanish, they'd have been spared," Adam said, continuing his narration. His tone had softened too. "But Billie didn't see the clan Scots that way. To him they were not quite human and they had the audacity to be inhabiting *his* island. They were savages with no more right to be treated by the rules of civilized society than those beggars over there."

The *beggars* were the French Indians, some of whom had drifted in with the French parade, others filtering in later, to form two more rows parallel to and behind the rows of French marines. They did not march in like the French, with a rhythm governed by the cadences of European martial music. Their rhythm winced like muscle spasms and their singing was a sustained moan that, to the European ear, sounded discordant and not quite musical. If it was music at all, it was the music of the dead, or the disembodied, or the spirit world.

Washington's gaze settled on a tall Indian near the front of the left row. A long queue of hair emanating from the center of his skull like a decorative plant wriggled as he rocked back and forth on his feet to the peculiar rhythm. The Indian was simultaneously trying to converse with a short French marine in front of him and chant his mournful song with the rest of his band. The man looked familiar. Then he realized it was the man who, the day before, had launched the tomahawk at his skull during the opening phase of the battle. *No beggar this one*, Washington thought to himself, although several alternative expletives came to mind. While he watched, the Indian intercepted his gaze and flashed back a grin that would have been broad if his mouth had been three or four tooth widths wider. *Yes, I tried to kill you yesterday,* the tall Indian seemed to be saying, *but I'm not trying to kill you today so let's be friendly.* The Indian's smile was so engaging that Washington's impulse was to return it in kind, but then he remembered the tomahawk arcing across the battlefield toward him and averted his gaze. It came to rest on Adam Stephen, who was waiting expectantly for Washington to reply. Adam wore the self-satisfied smirk of a pedant who has just scored a debating point. Maybe he had.

"Maybe you're right, Adam. Maybe the Duke of Cumberland murdered your countrymen in cold blood as you say. And maybe history will curse him for it," Washington said. "But I don't see what that has to do with our circumstances right now, today, here..."

Adam Stephen had seen the grinning Indian and strolled a few paces toward the enemy lines, fixing a steady glare on the man all the way. He stopped, facing away from Washington, maintaining his focus until the Indian decided that making peaceful overtures to the English was not worth the aggravation and quit the eye contact. Adam continued staring at the man for a full minute, then made a half-turn toward his Commander.

"I don't intend to be shot, or have a hatchet buried in my skull while I'm not lookin', Colonel," he said calmly, then extended a pointing arm at a French officer. The man was distinguished by the quality of his dress, with its distinctive gold-laced vest and gilded gorget, and by his position to the left and rear of the two lines of French marines. Villiers was the officer's name, Washington recalled, the French commanding officer, and he was the brother of one of the officers who had been killed in the attack at the glen. Strangely, and sadly, he couldn't recall the dead man's name.

"That man is not Billie the Butcher," Stephen said, in a rhetorical manner that guaranteed a 'but' was coming. "But he could be if he wanted to. He's defeated us without much effort and it would not surprise me if he sees us as nothing but a mob of ignorant colonial rabble."

Adam paused to let his words register and to formulate his next declaration.

"If that *is* the way he sees us, Colonel, I think we're as good as dead. Look at those savages! There's not a one of 'em wouldn't like to relieve us of our scalps."

"That may or may not be, Adam, but the surrender terms specifically permit us to keep our small arms and go home. Are we ourselves to ignore those terms?"

"It wouldn't be hard to pry a useless piece of paper from the fist of a corpse and burn it at your leisure."

"Adam, I understand your concern," Washington replied, annoyed. "No one is more aware of our vulnerability than I am. But the most sensible thing for us to do—given the circumstances—is to get as far away from here as possible. What would you have us do? Attack?"

The direct challenge took some of the steam out of Stephen's pugnacity. It did not take a great deal of military acumen to know that an attack against a force of two to three times their number with no reliable weaponry but bayonets was out of the question. But he was determined to remain skeptical. In many ways, he was afraid not to.

"Just be wary, Colonel, be wary," he said, turning on his heel to go. "The French and the British are tigers of the same stripe. Can't trust either one with the lives of men like us. I, for one, intend to pass between those two rows of French *gentlemen* with my head held high and my musket at the ready. And if any mother's son decides he wants a piece of me, he'll damn well feel a rifle butt in his teeth or the cold steel of a bayonet in his gut, by God!"

The primal glint in his colleague's gray eyes reminded Washington that Adam Stephen was a Scot and that this was no bluff. It occurred to him that he ought to be worried that, in Adam's present frame of mind, the man might provoke an incident whose consequences could prove disastrous. Instead, he was refreshed: The contentious Scotsman's attitude of defiance was much to be preferred over the chilling gloom that had descended on his own soul. Was this how defeat always felt? If so, victory must be euphoric, an experience comparable to entering the Kingdom of Heaven without mortal sin. Was membership in a profession that so recklessly aroused the extremes of human passion something to be coveted?

Stephen saluted. Washington returned it.

"We're going to form up soon, Adam. Have your men ready," Washington reminded.

"We'll be ready, Colonel…" Adam replied, then pulled the bayonet from his belt and held it up for viewing as he walked away, a confident bounce in his step. "…for anything."

Washington shook his head in dismay as Adam Stephen headed for his company's encampment. How a man could be simultaneously high-spirited and irritating he couldn't fathom, and yet Stephen was just that. Adam seemed able to boost his spirits by the simple device of, literally and figuratively, spitting in the eye of the enemy. Washington wondered if it was a talent that could be learned and concluded it must be. Otherwise, no commander would ever get past his first defeat. The emotional devastation would be too much for him to bear. Was there an equal and opposite device for quashing the elation of victory? There was at least one tangible benefit of defeat: It forced the vanquished to face his shortcomings. Triumph, on the other hand, could lead to vainglory and vainglory to flights of fancy. The historical record was replete with imaginative but dead generals. Maybe the best military campaign was one that neither suffered nor imposed a major defeat until the last battle, which, of course, had to be a stunning victory. If that was so, then he was still in dire straits because the Battle of Great Meadows—or whatever history might call it—*was* a major defeat. And for George Washington, it was already too late for intellectual trickery: He had permitted the ghouls of despair to kill his spirit. Only time could revive it.

Enough.

Washington turned to see his officers chatting amiably where he had left them, but otherwise indolent. *Yes, you are disheartened,* he told himself. *But you don't have to behave that way. You may need these men in the future, so give them a decent memory.*

"Andrew, Peter, come here, and bring the other officers," he called, waving them over. When they arrived and gathered round, he said, "We have to leave now. And we have to do it well."

Then he told them how.

§hapter Eighteen

July 4, 1754, Late morning

he two-abreast line of Virginia and Carolina troops stretched from Great Meadows Run in the northwest to Indian Run in the south. Between these extremes, the line snaked around the trenchworks of the stockade and cut sharply to the west before anchoring on the bank of the southern stream. It ended a hundred yards from the tree line where the French and their Indian allies had, the day before, crouched behind trees, bushes and boulders while laying down a decimating hail of fire. The line was to be a parade, with the drummer, the flautist, the Union Jack, and the flags of Virginia and South Carolina in the lead rows, and was to proceed symbolically between the two rows of French marines to a point distant enough to be called 'outside.' After first discussing it with his officers, Washington presented the idea to James Mackay, who embraced it eagerly. A messenger was then sent to Commander Villiers, who embraced it with somewhat less passion, but who appreciated the need for a formal ceremony and replied with such lavish courtesy that the Americans nearly had second thoughts about producing a spectacle so pleasing to their conqueror.

An hour had passed since Washington had conceived the notion of a parade. When informed by their officers of the Colonel's intention to march formally out of camp with drums beating and flags flying, the men of Virginia and Carolina waxed enthusiastic as well. Most had never been in a parade before and this was not only an opportunity to march in one but, in doing so, to remove themselves from a place where they had been mostly miserable and sometimes terror-stricken. In the nascent sunshine of a sky that showed signs of thoroughly dispersing its clouds, they chattered, joked, and attempted to clean their clothes by various means. The most common was to remove an item of clothing, shake it vigorously, put it back on, and go on to the next, never, in the process, frolicking in complete nudity. Without complaint, they did what parade participants have always done and will always do: They waited for the parade to start. In the bliss of this perspective, they differed from their French counterparts, who had been instructed to stand at ease and had been doing so for more than an hour. More than a little cranky, the marines scowled at the proceedings on the British side of the field, at their own officers, and at each other. This was no way to celebrate a glorious victory.

"Peter, where are the powder barrels?" Washington asked Hogg as the Captain scurried about to form his company into an evenly spaced, double row of marchers in the brief space allotted to his segment of the parade.

"Over there, Colonel," Hogg said impatiently, pointing to the intersection of the two mounds of earth bordering the southernmost trenches.

Washington stretched his neck trying to see between the men of Stobo's company who stood directly in front of the trenches. Eventually he spotted Horatio Bomgardner standing next to the barrels, ax in hand, looking like an executioner at his first beheading.

"Who's got the cannon?" he asked, risking another peevish glare from the preoccupied Hogg. The terms of the surrender permitted them to keep one swivel gun.

"Adam has it," Peter said with a faint grin. "He says he's going to mount it on a wagon. Wouldn't be surprised if he fires it at the frog-eaters as he goes by."

Hogg smiled generously to show he wasn't serious but Washington wasn't as confident of Adam Stephen's good sense as Hogg was. He knew the hot-tempered Scot would not fire at the two rows of French marines, but he was perfectly capable of firing over their heads and bursting a few eardrums…just for fun. It was the first time Washington had been grateful the powder was still damp.

"If you see Adam, tell him I'll have him court-martialed if he fires that damn cannon," he told Hogg, trying not to break into open laughter. *Odd how effortless cursing has become, almost like normal conversation.*

Washington bade his busy company commander farewell and made his way along the parade-to-be toward the powder barrels. There were only three horses that hadn't been shot by the French; each was hitched to a wagon. Both were abnormally jittery, which was understandable in view of the horrors of the previous day.

"Colonel, when do we go?" a boy with a gaunt face called out.

"Soon...maybe ten minutes," Washington replied, striding off again.

The fact was that they had not yet decamped and would not until after the parade was over. All knew the parade was to be a strictly ceremonial event, but spirits and egos were more content to think of it as an ending.

As he approached Stobo's company, Washington called to Lieutenant Will Poulson, its new commander, to meet him by the powder barrels. Poulson was already enjoying his new promotion by buckling the sword Stobo had given him around his waist. With the red backdrop of Poulson's surprisingly unsmudged uniform behind it, the sword lent the young man a militant bearing his unassuming personality did not.

"Will, do you have all the barrels?" Washington asked curtly, taking in Poulson's new look with an approving eye. The only problem with the costume was the unrelieved, ripened tomato color stretching from neck to knee. *Even tomatoes are adorned with green leaves*, Washington noted, and vowed once more to fix the uniform problem when he got back to Williamsburg.

"Yes. Do you want Private Bomgardner to..."

"No, no, I'll do it," Washington said, then looked up at the doleful Bomgardner standing atop one of the mounds beside the trenches. "It doesn't look like Private Bomgardner is of a mind for it anyway."

"He's not comfortable dumping the powder, even if it *is* wet," Poulson explained.

"I know, I know. Neither am I, but it has to be done," the Colonel muttered. With a purposeful stride, he squeezed between the men in the two columns and bounded to the top of the pile of clay and shale occupied by Bomgardner.

"I'll take it now, Horatio," he whispered to the Private.

Relieved, Bomgardner handed over the ax to his Commander. As he took the long, curved handle in both hands, Washington realized the ax was larger and heavier than he had expected. Tentatively, he swung it back and forth, gauging its balance, enjoying the raw power it exuded and that he projected through it. *It almost feels like a weapon,* he mused. *Probably could behead a man with one swipe.* Delicately, he rested its iron head on the ground, unbuttoned his shirt cuffs, and rolled up his sleeves. It was then that he noticed all eyes in the parade were turned toward him and that the incessant babble of four hundred restless men had dwindled to an erratic buzz. With his six foot, three inch frame elevated three feet above the crowd by the mound, he could see their expectant faces. They were waiting for him to act. When Lieutenant Poulson and several of the men under his command started hustling nearby spectators away so his activities could easily be viewed by everyone in the south meadow, Washington knew he was at center stage. His first reaction was embarrassment. Then he decided embarrassment was such a trivial emotion compared to the others plaguing him that he would simply play out the scene and see how it was received.

"Private Bomgardner, the first barrel please," he said in a louder than a conversational level to make sure at least the proximate members of the audience heard.

Bomgardner dutifully rolled a powder barrel into place, then stepped back. Washington spread his feet, not quite straddling the mound but firmly securing his stance, and leaned forward on the ax handle. He eyed the barrel a moment longer like a foxhound aiming itself for the kill. Meticulously, he raised the ax overhead, keeping a steady gaze on the barrel as if it might try to escape, and swung it swiftly in a downward arc. There was no contest. The top barrel surface split precisely in half and the force of the blow blasted the staves out of the upper barrel hoop. The crushed barrel, its staves splayed like the petals of a giant flower, could no longer serve to contain. Moist gunpowder spilled out like diseased pollen, stuck to the staves, or otherwise settled into a clump at the center of the space where the barrel had been. A rumble of animated voices rose above the buzz, beginning in the circles of men nearest Washington and spreading like a wave to both ends of the parade. The Colonel looked up, stunned: He hadn't anticipated this. Shyly, he smiled and nodded his appreciation, then went back to work.

"Private!" he said, his eyes indicating his readiness for the next victim.

Bomgardner cleared the debris and replaced it with a fresh barrel. Washington repeated his performance. The barrel and its contents scattered, bouncing off several of the astonished onlookers. The acclaim was immediate and impassioned, only the closest spectators showing any hesitancy, and this out of concern for those who had been struck by the flying staves or segments thereof.

No one was truly injured, but Washington was beginning to feel the heat and humidity of July's stagnant air. Already coatless, he removed his tricorne and placed it on the ground. Even for this he received a mild ovation. It was as if he were the ringmaster of the only show in a town starved for entertainment and then realized this was not an analogy at all but an accurate description of what was actually taking place. These men were hungry for good cheer and would seize any moment that promised to lift their spirits. He could be chopping firewood and would still get a hefty round of applause. He scanned the faces in the crowd, hoping to absorb some of the excitement radiating from them. Some men had not washed or shaved since his announcement of the parade, but most had their shirts tucked in and their hair combed, if short, or brushed, if long. There were even wigs here and there, probably family heirlooms dusted off and mounted only for ceremonial occasions. Only a few had taken the trouble to don the red Virginia militia uniform.

"Again, Mr. Bomgardner," he said.

Another louder and more sustained cheer went up as the detritus of destruction flew in all directions.

Washington and Bomgardner finished the obliteration of the powder barrels in less than twenty minutes, by which time the melodrama of violence had begun to cloy and the intensity of the crowd response to fade. Soon the melding of multiple conversations into random babble submerged all else. Great Meadows took on the aura of a vast garden party, or a horse race, or even a slave auction, but definitely a grand social event. The crushing of the powder barrels had released pent up frustrations, and loosened spirits and tongues.

Washington returned the ax to Horatio Bomgardner, then leaped back onto the mound and raised his hands high in the air. Poulson and Bomgardner cast quizzical looks at each other, wondering what the Colonel was up to, speculating whether a long-winded speech might be in the offing. Washington noticed their puzzlement, offered only a reassuring smile in reply, and waited for silence. A few noticed the solitary figure on the mound reaching for the heavens and passed the word to their neighbors, who did likewise. Soon, a hush fell over the meadow.

"Gentlemen of Virginia..." Washington summoned, speaking as loudly as he could without shouting. He let his gaze drift languidly along the line of soldiers from south to north. All were gazing back at him, attentive and still. When his eyes alighted on Mackay and his Independents at the northwest end he quickly added, "...and South Carolina."

James Mackay tipped his hat and grinned effusively at the speaker as the others, aware of the early animosity between the two men, laughed politely.

"Gentlemen of South Carolina and Virginia..." Washington repeated to assure the Independents equal billing. "...show your pride!"

As he voiced his entreaty, Washington swung his right arm forward in a prearranged signal for the parade to begin. The flags of Great Britain, Virginia, and South Carolina snapped to attention, the drum and flute struck up a martial tune, the lead rows of marchers took up the cadence, and a deafening roar of voices burst forth like a cannon salute into the wet morning air. The parade was alive and thrusting itself toward the waiting lines of French marines whose faces, while not fearful, displayed a greater anxiety than they had five minutes before.

Poulson and Bomgardner set off to join their companies, saluting their Commander sharply as they left. Washington stood cross-armed for a while, transfixed by the passing marchers and by the knowledge that it had taken so little to rejuvenate them, make them whole again. Military leadership, he decided, was not just directing men in a fight. A good leader had to maintain the support of his men for the next battle. Whether or not he would participate in that battle depended to a large degree on whether these men would follow him and that would depend on how they perceived his actions. He had lost a major battle. That would always count against him whether or not the blame was entirely his. How would he be seen ten days from now, he wondered: as a man who, burdened by the torment of defeat had taken the time to inspire his men with fresh zeal, or as a clown who foolishly thought he could buy their loyalty with a parade?

At the sight of a familiar face, Washington descended from his mound and greeted Thomas Patton. The sparse diet of the last month agreed with Thomas. Formerly round and red like the two halves of a beefsteak tomato, his cheeks were actually sunken. The pudgy lines where the flesh of his chin and nose met were subdued, diminishing his resemblance to a suckling pig. Thomas was marching alongside Ezekiel Richardson, a man whose height and girth challenged those of Andrew Lewis. But where Lewis loped like a bear, Richardson waddled like a landed sea beast.

"May I walk along with you?" the Colonel asked, placing a hand on Thomas's shoulder.

"Surely," Thomas spoke first. Richardson flashed his concurrence with a glance.

"How are your men? Any injuries?"

Both said no.

"We'll be glad to get home though, sir," Patton said, assuming the burden of conversation.

Washington nodded but didn't answer. His own feelings about going home were mixed. He would have much to answer for. His thoughts were distracted by a flock of magpies descending to feed on the hordes of juicy earthworms that had been forced to the surface by the flooding of the two creeks. How strange it was that the birds could be so oblivious to the death and destruction that had occurred here. *They don't even know we're here*, he thought as he watched a pair of tapered beaks maneuver, then clamp around one of the plump pink bundles.

"We'll get them next time, sir," a voice that did not belong to Thomas Patton said. Washington emerged from his reverie to see Richardson offering a sympathetic countenance beneath the battered straw hat he wore to protect his bald pate from the July sun.

"Yes, yes, thank you," Washington stammered, then hastened to add, partly out of unrequited wrath and partly to prevent Richardson's sympathy turning to pity, "There *will* be a next time."

* * *

"I don't like this, Jolicoeur. They still have their guns!" a restive Striking Eagle complained as the parade of Englishmen passed before him.

Standing in front of his friend, Jolicoeur Bonin could only glance sideways and upward but could see a scowl so tight and tense it might have been made by a drawstring in the Shawnee's neck. Bonin was sufficiently acquainted with the big Indian to know that indignation, not fear, was what motivated the question. A defeated enemy should show the proper embarrassment or, if he failed to do so, suffer death or at least disgrace, the choice depending on the victor's penchant for mercy. But he should not be allowed such a provocative display of military pomp, especially since the British had lost the battle so miserably. In Striking Eagle's code of ethics, abject humiliation was the proper milieu for a conquered enemy.

"It's a parade, a formality," Jolicoeur explained patiently. "There is no danger. They have no gunpowder."

"There are knives on their guns," Striking Eagle pointed out.

"They won't use them. They would be killed if they tried. It's always a good idea to let your enemy save face. If he feels he has been honorably treated, he won't have something to prove in the next battle."

"*Save face,* what does that mean?"

Bonin explained. Striking Eagle was appalled.

"A beaten enemy should not be saving his face. He should be screaming as burning stakes are thrust into his eyes or holding his tongue if he is brave!"

The diminutive Frenchman shook his head, both amused and saddened. Striking Eagle was such a refreshingly primitive fellow! They could like each other but would never understand one another's ethics. It was becoming clear to Jolicoeur why the Jesuits and

Recollects were so anxious to convert these people to Christianity: Martyrdom and its heavenly rewards were never more than a bad sermon away.

Bonin heard a sharp command from somewhere nearby and saw Striking Eagle's attention distracted by something in the British parade. He turned in time to see at least twenty ranks of marchers raise their muskets to the vertical *make ready* position and grip their firelocks as if preparing to shoot. Jolicoeur heard himself and several nearby colleagues gasp and felt his hands reflexively tighten on his own musket. Had Striking Eagle been right? Were these Englishmen readying themselves for an attack? They would be slaughtered to a man, of course, but not before taking a substantial number of marines with them of which, Jolicoeur realized to his chagrin, he was sure to be one. But as suddenly as the threat had come, it vanished. Another sharp command brought the musket of each marcher to within a centimeter of his nose in an emulation of a sword salute. Then the right hand gripping each firelock was released to snap a hand salute. All in unison. It was a breathtaking display.

As a final command to return each musket to the appropriate shoulder was given, Bonin spotted the officer in charge. It was the same man who had glowered at Striking Eagle not fifteen minutes before, the man with the mischievous tuft of hair that would not stay on his head. He was staring back at them, an insolent grin framing his well-aligned teeth.

"I hope you are not going to tell me the English were just saying hello!" Striking Eagle exclaimed with undiminished consternation.

"No, it was a provocation," Jolicoeur sighed. "But well done, don't you think?"

The single-minded Shawnee was not about to yield anything to his adopted enemy. His gaze followed Adam Stephen as the Virginian marched defiantly alongside his men in the narrow space between the parade and the left row of Frenchmen, occasionally colliding with the misplaced hip or foot of some hapless marine.

"He has good hair," the Shawnee said like a pubescent child, flourishing a broad grin not unlike the one Adam Stephen had brandished. "Some day I may take it from him!"

July 4, 1754, Early afternoon

Adam Stephen knew his anger was self-induced but didn't care. He didn't like losing nor did he much care for its accouterments: humility, resignation, and an endless litany of laments beginning with "If only…" There had been too much losing for his sensitive nature to abide, from Culloden Moor to this, which had hardly been a battle at all. It was a special embarrassment for a proud man like Stephen, who could not be easily mollified by appeals to moderation. To him, an opinion not passionately held was not worth expressing. Whatever wrongs had been done to Adam Stephen would only grudgingly be forgotten or forgiven.

The parade was over and he had derived little satisfaction from it. He *had* stepped on several enemy toes and had actually bowled over a few inadequately braced French marines, but these were minor pleasures that could not supplant the fact of defeat. His smoldering anger giving way to depression, he left the small clearing where the parade had reached its anticlimax and, nearly as dirty and unkempt as he had been after the battle and the flood, headed back to his tent in the west meadow. On one shoulder he rested his musket, holding it by the socket bayonet at the end of the barrel. Stepping cautiously around the miniature swamps in his path, he climbed the slight grade to the camp, where the men of Virginia were already collapsing tents and packing away their belongings, supervised by clusters of French marines and northern Indians. To his right, Stephen watched as another squad of French marines set fire to the stockade, some of whose posts had been extracted from the ground to serve as kindling. Wagons were burning too. In the center of the stockade, high up on the flagpole, a white flag emblazoned with a field of *fleur-de-lis* languished in a frail breeze.

Feeling the bile rising in his stomach, Adam averted his eyes and resolved to focus his efforts on the matter at hand—getting as far from Great Meadows as possible. Making a leftward correction to his heading, he spotted his tent and, shortly thereafter, a man coming out of it carrying Stephen's suitcase on one shoulder. The thief was wearing a red *toque* pulled down to his eyebrows and glancing around surreptitiously as he scurried away.

"Hey! Hey, you frog-eatin' sonofabitch!" Adam cried, breaking into a trot and bringing the musket forward to the ready position. "Come back here with that! You can't outrun me, you frog-eatin' bastard! Don't you try! Don't you try to outrun me!"

Whether or not the thief understood English, he clearly understood the hostility in Stephen's exclamation and the deadly glare that accompanied it. Seeing the larger Scotsman bounding toward him at a full gallop, the Frenchman forgot that his side had won the battle and broke into a full retreat. Howling a series of "Come here you…" punctuated by imaginative epithets summarizing the man's likely parentage and sexual proclivities, the Scotsman easily closed the distance between them. The Frenchman panicked, tossed the suitcase to one side, and headed directly for the south woods where his fellow marines were diligently breaking camp. Adam Stephen unburdened himself of excess weight by removing the socket bayonet from the musket barrel and hurling the gun aside. It was then a simple foot race for which the Frenchman, barrel-chested and bow-legged, was not physically well-adapted. Stephen reached out with his left arm and hooked the man around the neck, using his size advantage to bring them both to a halt. As Stephen's forearm dug into the thief's esophagus, the Frenchman choked, coughed and, eyes bulging like blood blisters, desperately tried to call for help as his air was cut off. Ignoring the man's protestations, Stephen brought the bayonet point against the soft tissue beneath the jaw, pressing hard enough to open a wound and spill blood onto the weapon. A steady rivulet flowed down the blade to pool in the crease of the Scotsman's grip.

"So, you would have my possessions, thief? How would you like my knife through your gullet?" Stephen growled, pressing the bayonet farther into the skin of the man's throat. What had been a trickle of blood doubled in width. A small animal noise somewhere between a squeak and a squeal emanated from the thief's lips, but he kept his body rigid for fear the bayonet might penetrate even farther. With a deft motion, Stephen abruptly released his grip and withdrew the bayonet, then dropped back to a position where he had room to execute his next maneuver. With considerably more than symbolic force, he kicked the thief in the rump, landing the blow not on the fleshy muscle of the buttocks but between them, so that the toe of his boot caught the underside of the recipient's testicles. A better placed kick might have seriously diminished the Frenchman's opportunities for fatherhood but Stephen was satisfied to hear the man cry out in agony. Then, seizing his crotch with both hands, the thief fell to the ground where the vocal expression of his pain degenerated to a pathetic whimper. There was little chance for Stephen to enjoy the spectacle as two pair of hands grabbed his arms from behind. The hands belonged to two young French marines who, when he could see their faces, looked more bewildered than angered by his actions.

"You ...you are violate the capitulation!" one of them stammered in clumsy English, releasing one hand to wag its index finger in the face of the wild man. "You...strike him. That is not to permit."

"Damn the capitulation!" Stephen roared, shaking his arms free and pointing an accusing finger of his own at the figure writhing on the ground. "That sonofabitch has already violated the capitulation by stealing the suitcase from my tent!"

Unprepared for a hostile confrontation, the English speaker listened intently to the raging Scot, but came up short on comprehension.

"Son of...bitch? Suitcase?" he murmured, then put the question into a shrug.

"The bastard tried to take my suitcase," Stephen bellowed in frustration, then walked to where the suitcase had landed in a bog of wildflowers.

"Bastard...ah, yes...bastard. We know bastard," the English speaker said to his companion, nodding and gesturing toward the thief, who had recovered enough to release his crotch and was now gingerly stuffing the red *toque* into his breeches. Without the *toque*, the thief's curled ebony tresses flowed sumptuously over his shoulders and down his back. Adam Stephen gazed at the man with renewed contempt. The man was a fop! Worse, he was a French fop! *I'm glad I kicked you in the balls, you obscene pansy!*

The non-English speaker whispered something into the English-speaker's ear as Stephen righted his suitcase and worked the latch free. He concluded that the two young men were probably officers and probably Canadians because, while both were as olive-skinned and dark-haired as their felonious cohort, there was a casual vigor to their deportment that bespoke of a North American birthright. The thief, on the other hand, had the furtive eyes of a sewer rat, useful only to those who have practiced the low art of pilfering in the back alleys of urban Europe. While Stephen was opening the suitcase, the English-speaker detached himself from his companion and approached.

"Yes, yes, we agree. Pierre is the…uh…*a* bastard," he said, grinning nervously and casting a corroborative glance at the squatting thief. "But you are not to strike him. You come to us…Yes? Do you agree?"

Knowing only that he had been saved from the clutches of a mad Englishman and unperturbed by the *bastard* appellation, which was, after all, accurate, Pierre offered a squeamish grin of conciliation. Stephen ignored the gesture and rifled through the clothing in his suitcase. When he found what he was looking for, he put it on, stood up, and presented himself to the young Frenchmen in his flaming, tomato red regimental coat.

"I am Captain Adam Stephen of the Virginia Regiment," he said stiffly without saluting, then knelt down to pick up the bayonet he'd stuck into the ground by the suitcase. "And if I catch *that* sonofabitch or any other frog-eatin' sonofabitch with my property, I'll cut his throat."

The statement was followed by a symbolic swipe of the bayonet across his own throat.

Still eschewing direct confrontation and oblivious to the meaning of the 'frog-eating' reference, the English-speaker offered a wan smile and stammered, "Perhaps you would like to take the two of *us* hostage. We understand there are some very pretty ladies in Virginia."

Adam Stephen was the wrong man to approach with an appeal tainted by Gallic debauchery, even one made in jest. Beneath a freshly furrowed forehead, making no attempt to hide his repugnance, he watched the raised eyebrows and surreptitious glances pass like lewd remarks from one man to the next. Sheathing the bayonet, he closed the suitcase, hoisted it to one shoulder, and turned away to retrieve his musket.

"I wouldn't introduce you fine gentlemen to a herd of Virginia heifers," he muttered under his breath, or at least thought he had, then decided he didn't give a damn whether the sons of bitches heard him or not.

𝕮hapter 𝕹ineteen

July 4, 1754, Mid-afternoon

The worst part of captivity is the boredom, a half-naked Robert Stobo concluded as he lay propped on one elbow in front of the tent assigned to him and Jacob Van Braam at the French camp south of Great Meadows. The food was, if no improvement, at least more abundant, and the shade of the endless forest kept the air relatively cool. The two sentries resting their bodies and muskets against the ancient, moss-laden oak trunk to his left could speak only French and, in any event, did not look like conversational material. He knew their names—Patrick and Rolland—and nothing else. Both were unshaven, grimy and, except for the occasional verbal exchange between themselves and the more frequent scratching of their perspiration-induced itches, virtually lifeless. As was he, Stobo had to admit, the humidity of summer having taken its toll on his vitality. The only proximate signs of life were the morning song of a mockingbird in the branches above and the Dutchman's incessant snoring, the tonal variations of which were a source of either amusement or amazement to the sentries. Their languid faces defied further clarification. Like the turkey buzzards at the battlefield, the mockingbird was oblivious to the men below. They were of no more significance than grass, and certainly not as important as the tree in which she was perched.

"*Wu la pan... Wu lan de u!*" a nearby voice grunted, accompanied by the shuffling sound of feet on pebbles. The sentries heard it, as did Stobo. He rose to his feet to investigate; they preferred to conserve their limited energies. From the northeast traipsed a procession of northern Indians jabbering gaily and carrying pots, jewelry, clothing and other paraphernalia from the English camp. Stobo's first reaction was intellectual: The articles of capitulation clearly specified that the Virginia and Carolina troops would be permitted to keep their belongings. They could not very well do that if their belongings were in the possession of these savages. While he was deliberating on the best way to lodge a protest, the issue became more personal. One of the Indians—a short, chunky man with a nose ring and huge ears made larger by slits—was carrying Stobo's valise!

"Sir...Sir!" he began, moving toward the Indian. When the man merely shot him a hostile glance and failed to stop, Stobo decided it would be well if he enlisted the support of the sentries.

"M'sieurs...please. Come here please. I am being robbed," he called, pointing an accusing finger at the band of Indians.

The sentries indicated their incomprehension with a succession of hand gestures, shrugs and facial contortions but otherwise failed to respond. The Indians were their allies. Their orders proscribed interference with Indian activities except in unusual circumstances. A disgruntled Englishman was not an unusual circumstance.

Frustrated by the sentries' inaction and the double language barrier, Stobo decided to take matters into his own hands by confronting the squat Indian bearing his valise. Surely, if he chased after the thief, the sentries would chase after him rather than risk letting him put himself into a position where an escape attempt could be made. He would make no such attempt, of course; he was honor bound not to. But the sentries were obviously simple men and might not appreciate such gentlemanly imperatives.

When he broke into a trot, Stobo's audience responded as he had hoped. With pained "What now?" expressions on their simple faces, the sentries got off their petrified arses, onto their feet, and began stalking Stobo as they might a wayward farm animal, irritated with the pesky beast for disrupting their torpor. The Indians slowed, studying Stobo as if fearful he might attack. To show his peaceful intentions, he raised a reassuring hand and pointed at the valise with the other.

"That's my valise," he said, pointing to himself, then to the valise again. "*My* valise. You must give it back."

The Indians held a spontaneous conference. Whether or not they understood what he had said, they did understand that he wanted the valise because the squat man grunted a series of protestations, pointed at himself and, after shaking his head vigorously, clutched the valise to his bosom. The sign language was unambiguous: He did not intend to give it up.

"Does anyone speak English?" Stobo asked, struggling to keep his good humor.

Another conference followed, with an ebb and flow of chatter among the participants, most of it accompanied by hand gestures and exclamations peppered with either indignation or laughter. Except for the laughter and the prevailing state of nakedness, it could have been a session of the Virginia House of Burgesses. Finally, a gruff Indian with full, frowning lips and straight, black hair contained by a green and white wampum bead headband stepped forward. When he was directly in front of Stobo, he casually pulled back his leather cape to reveal a ball-headed club stuffed between a quilled belt and his breechclout. It was a not-so-veiled threat.

"Nest-Eater say he will keep box," he said firmly, indicating the squat Indian holding the valise.

Nest-Eater! How appropriate.

"But it's my box. My valise," Stobo insisted. "Where did he get it?"

Bad-tempered and imperious, the sentries finally arrived wanting to know what was going on. The gruff Indian, on whom Stobo had decided to bestow the *nom de plume* 'Frowning Man,' was apparently fluent in French as well as English and took responsibility for translating the explanations, Stobo's included. Troubled that his demands were to be presented to his captors by a potentially hostile intermediary, Stobo's mood deteriorated. Frowning Man was looking at him quizzically and pointing at Patrick.

"...Says what do you want? Says you cannot go with us," said Frowning Man in his chronically peevish tone of voice.

"I don't want to go with you. I just want my valise," Stobo said curtly, pointing at the valise. Pointing a finger at one thing or another seemed to be the greater part of sign language, he concluded.

The firmness of the response incited another conference, this time restricted to the sentries, Nest-Eater and Frowning Man, leaving Stobo off to one side to sizzle under the acrid stares of a dozen, cavernous Indian eyes. Separating himself from the huddle, Frowning

Man approached Stobo hesitantly but purposefully.

"...Says why do you think box is yours? Many boxes are in English camp."

Although Frowning Man's question suggested the sentries might be its source, Stobo suspected it had actually been posed by Nest-Eater.

"Because it *is* my valise," Stobo declared with studied calm, then directed his statements directly to Patrick. "If you open it, I'll..."

He was about to describe a plan to identify himself as the owner of the valise by giving an accurate description of its contents and insisting that the terms of capitulation be enforced. But Frowning Man distracted him by turning to his colleagues and beginning a dialogue, some of which was supplemented by gestures and sign language at eye level. The action first caught Stobo's attention because he was trying to interpret what Frowning Man was saying, but then he spotted the gold ring on the Indian's finger. *His* ring!

"That's my ring!" he exclaimed, incredulous, then grabbed Frowning Man's hand for examination. Again he shouted, this time at Patrick, "That's my ring! I must insist you force this man to give it back."

Patrick listened, as did his partner, Rolland, but exhibited either incomprehension or a strong dose of apathy. It was hard to tell which. Rolland shrugged; Patrick shrugged; Stobo stewed. He was not about to continue making demands through a man who had stolen from him. Releasing Frowning Man's hand, he placed himself directly in front of Patrick.

"I must speak with your commanding officer. I must speak with Captain Villiers," he demanded, trying his best to pronounce the French name as he had heard it the previous evening.

"Villiers?"

"Yes...Villiers...*Oui.*"

Patrick replied unintelligibly but made himself understood by repeating the sound 'Vill-yeh' and pointing toward Great Meadows. Villiers was at the battlefield.

"Then I must speak with one of your officers," Stobo said, then tried, "Off-i-sare!" in hopes the French and English words differed only in pronunciation.

No luck.

An idea dawned. Stobo fingered the silver trim adorning the cuffs of his regimentals, coaxing, "Off-i-sare. Off-i-sare. Cap-ee-tan."

A fleck of comprehension appeared in Rolland's eyes.

"*Capitan?*" he asked.

Stobo sighed, "Yes, yes, Cap-ee-tan."

"Non," Rolland replied, shaking his head. "Sergeant."

What does that mean, that there are no captains available, only sergeants?

"I don't care. Captain, sergeant, it doesn't matter. Just get me an officer!"

Startled by Stobo's vehemence, Rolland jumped and hastily made his departure, muttering, "*Je vais…Je vais…*"

Before he had gone too far Stobo shouted, "And try to get one who speaks English. *Anglais…parley Anglais.*"

To Stobo's relief, Rolland appeared to understand, indicating as much by raising his hand and beating its fingers and thumb together like a pair of flapping lips and repeating, "*Anglais, Anglais…*" Then he was off.

Rolland returned in ten minutes with one Sergeant Julien Penisseau in tow. The Sergeant was every centimeter a non-commissioned officer: burly, impatient, with a graceless athleticism that inspired fear rather than admiration. His uniform, regulation issue with the telltale gold lace of the *Compagnies des franches* on his cuffs and coat pockets, appeared to have been purchased thirty pounds ago. The flesh acquired since threatened the integrity of his breeches at the waist and of his blouse at the neck and shoulders. Immediately after his introduction to Stobo, Penisseau expressed his displeasure at being called away from the far more important activities of breaking camp and making sure all the captured British equipment had been secured for transport or destroyed. Stobo had the feeling Penisseau was deliberately trying to disqualify himself as a suitable sounding board for his complaints and ignored the diatribe. Penisseau spoke English and represented French authority. Those were the only qualifications Stobo cared about.

"I am sorry, M'sieur, I can do nothing," Penisseau lamented dolefully. "The Indians are not under my command."

It was a predictable first parry: Avoid the issue by disclaiming responsibility.

"Are you telling me, Sergeant, that your allies may violate the terms of surrender and you can do nothing about it?"

Penisseau, anxious to be elsewhere, squirmed and snorted like a wild boar snared in a net. Angrily, he shouted at the unsuspecting Rolland, who scurried off in the direction of Great Meadows to obey whatever orders the Sergeant had given him.

"Of course you may have your possessions back, M'sieur," the Sergeant replied in a more civil, but still petulant, tone. An adamant glower at Nest-Eater and Frowning Man was followed by a nod to Patrick. The sentry confiscated the valise and ring from the woeful Indians and handed them to Stobo. His integrity re-established, Penisseau gazed with satisfaction at his tormentor and added, "Is there anything else you require?"

The question was dripping with palpable sarcasm, the only weapon available to the trapped Sergeant. Penisseau might prefer to let the Indians violate the agreement but he could not overtly sanction such an action. Stobo breathed more easily. His insistence on speaking to an officer had been a wise one.

"Yes, I do. I would like to return to my tent," he said.

"And why do you need to do that, M'sieur?" the Sergeant groaned, disguising it as a sigh. Great Meadows was more than a kilometer away.

"I have other valuable possessions. I want to safeguard the ones that haven't been stolen and catalog those that have," Stobo replied.

Penisseau winced as if afflicted by a sudden headache. He understood why Stobo wanted to identify which of his possessions were missing: so that he could lay his findings before what would serve as an international court to demonstrate French non-compliance with the articles of capitulation. This was something Penisseau definitely did not want to happen, so he was not inclined to comply with the request.

"Come here," the Sergeant commanded Patrick, who was standing with the Indians. When Patrick obeyed, Penisseau repeated the command, said something that sounded like an Indian name, and began waving at someone in the group. A dark, wiry Indian wearing nothing but a deerskin breechclout, a circle of turkey feathers attached to a queue of silky dark hair, and diagonal stripes of black and red paint on his face and torso, fell in step behind Patrick.

"M'sieur Stobo, this is…" Penisseau began, then realized he didn't know the man's name in English.

"Moses the Song," the man said, arching his eyebrows in punctuation and drawing air into his lungs in anticipation of further speech.

"Yes, yes…Moses speaks English," Penisseau stated the obvious. "Private Saliere and he will take you to your camp."

It was a second or two before Stobo realized that Private Saliere was Patrick. He gazed with curiosity at the Indian, who stared back from sockets so deep that his eyes were like two subterranean creatures peering warily out from their caves.

"Haven't we met before?" Stobo asked.

Moses the Song smiled and said, "Yes, at your Mr. Gist's plantation." Then he fell silent, his eerie gaze still fixed on Stobo.

Stobo nodded, remembering that the man was a relative of Monacatoocha and had attended a conference at Gist's plantation, one of several failed attempts by Washington to keep the Indians on the British side. He avoided the temptation to criticize the man for deserting and joining the enemy. Desertion was a white man's notion. The Indians had their own priorities, chief of which was survival. Any Indian tribe that could not be supplied with muskets and powder by one of the two white combatants would find itself at a severe disadvantage. Making peace with the probable winner of that contest was not simply desirable. It was essential.

As if intruding into Stobo's mind, Moses the Song said plaintively, "I did not fight against you. I am Mohawk."

A Mohawk. An Iroquois. A keeper of the eastern door who has absented himself from the conflict. It was a simple statement of fact. The cavernous eyes of Moses the Song were insistent: his honor was intact.

Wisely, Robert Stobo offered his hand. Moses the Song took it and mutual respect was established.

"M'sieur, I must go," an impatient and increasingly apprehensive Sergeant Penisseau declared. "Private Saliere will take you where you want to go. Please obey his instructions or you will suffer the consequences."

Stobo could tell by Penisseau's tone of voice that the Frenchman did not really expect him to attempt an escape. But the Sergeant was a military man and, as such, believed threats to be a more effective way to control human behavior than reasoned discourse. The Sergeant moved off in the direction from whence he had come, his bulky torso and head swaying like the pendulum of a metronome.

Patrick led the way through the labyrinth of overgrowth, vines and undergrowth that constituted the path to Great Meadows. Moses the Song fell in behind Stobo, whether at Penisseau's instigation or on his own initiative the Scotsman didn't know. Since Patrick was not conversant in English and Moses the Song was not, at the moment, inclined to be, Stobo found himself pondering his circumstances and making a mental checklist of things to do if opportunities arose. It was a habit that had served him well as a merchant and factor in Petersburg.

He was grateful his manservant had not been killed as Washington's had. Hopefully, the French would permit all of his servants, mechanics, and his carriage a safe return. The carriage had cost him dearly. Somehow, he would have to run his business from Fort Duquesne and wasn't sure how he would do that or if, indeed, it could be done. Surely, his French captors would be decent enough to let him post letters to his business associates. After all, he was not a prisoner but a hostage. He *was* looking forward to the respite: Fishing in the rivers surrounding the fort, improving his French language skills. There should also be plenty of time to hone his Scotch accent. Stobo had found a mild accent to be an asset for a businessman in the colonies. It endowed a man with a certain sophistication unless it was too heavy. Then it made him seem alien. When he got back, he fully intended to play the role of heroic figure to the hilt, showing off his French and spicing it with a dash of Scotch brogue. It should not be difficult. The only competition was Jacob Van Braam and Jacob was certainly not cut out for the role of a heroic figure.

By the time the incongruous party of three reached Great Meadows, Robert Stobo, businessman and adventurer, had talked himself into a buoyant frame of mind. It was, perhaps, because of this that his mood plummeted to the depths of melancholy when he saw the havoc that had been wreaked on his regiment. As he stepped out onto the dense grassland from the embrace of the forest his jaw crept downward in mounting astonishment. The stockade and the hut within were nothing but charred ruins. A pall of listless smoke hung over them like a poltergeist admiring its handiwork. Inside the circle of black stumps that had been the palisade wall, French marines were spiking the swivel guns and destroying supplies, wagons, and anything else they and their Indian allies could wrap fingers and palms around. Where the camps had been in the east and west meadows, the exhausted men of the Virginia and Carolina Regiments were packing whatever equipment they could salvage or fighting for their possessions. One Indian was pulling the shirt off a man's back and laughing while another held a knife to his throat. For the most part, the French marines present gathered together in small conversational clumps, the better to ignore the activities of their felonious allies. As a grim backdrop to this nefarious conduct, the slain cattle and horses—bloated and caked with mud—lay like harvested sheaves of wheat randomly strewn over the devastated landscape.

This is defeat? No, this is humiliation.

"Take me back," Stobo said, not entirely sure whom he was addressing.

Patrick looked at him dumbly, then at Moses the Song for the translation. After Patrick had spoken, the Indian turned to Stobo and said, "He wants to know why you changed your mind."

"Can't you see?" Stobo rejoined angrily. "Your people are ravaging us. They are stealing everything. There is no point in going back!"

Caught in Stobo's hostile stare, Moses the Song felt compelled to respond.

"They are not *my* people. I am Mohawk," he said, then turned and strolled casually back into the woods.

July 4, 1754, Late afternoon

Of all the depredations they had suffered, the most embarrassing to

Washington was the loss of the one swivel gun owed them by the honors of war and guaranteed by the terms of surrender. A regiment needed a cannon to distinguish itself as a serious fighting force as much as it needed a drum to bring order to the battlefield. Without a cannon, and with only every third volunteer possessing a proper uniform, a regiment might be mistaken for an unruly mob. But a keen sense of the practical was also an essential component of an army and of its commander, and practicality demanded that those who were not too exhausted to travel assist the wounded and the lame. The count as of 10:00 AM was thirteen killed, fifty-five wounded, nineteen unaccounted for or deserted, and ten men overlooked. This last was another embarrassment: A commander simply did not forget to take men home with him.

"Rider coming up, sir," said Peregrin Williams from behind. Williams, one of Stobo's men, was serving as an *ad hoc* aide.

Walking at the head of the two columns of soldiers, Washington and Mackay turned to see the mounted figure urging his dappled gray mare, one of the three surviving horses, along the left column in the narrow space between it and the forest. The mare's flared nostrils and spittled mouth told of a sustained gallop of several miles. The rider, standing in his stirrups and stroking the horse's perspiration-soaked mane and neck was Solomon Batson, the leader of the rescue party sent to retrieve the neglected men. Doing his best to steer the mare away from the tired marchers, Batson made his way to the two commanders, dismounted, and saluted. Coincidentally, Peregrin Williams gave a sharp command for the procession to halt.

"We got 'em, sir," Batson announced with weary pride. Solomon was a man of average height, with thick-lensed glasses, burgeoning gray hair that wanted to grow around or into every topological feature of his head and face, and a figure that was long on flesh and short on bone. But he was known to be a man of dogged determination, which was why he had been chosen for the mission.

"Where are they? Do they need our help?" Washington asked with a lingering apprehension.

"About a mile back. No, no help necessary. If we can wait a half-hour, they'll catch up. We did have some trouble…"

It was not difficult to tell from Batson's animated expression that he had a story to tell. Mackay gave him the opening.

"What kind of trouble?" he asked.

"The Indians had 'em, sir," Batson said, letting his robust body relax into an *at ease* posture. "But we made 'em take us to the frog captain...what's his name?"

"Villiers," Washington offered, pronouncing the name with the 'r' intact, as a man with Batson's rural Virginia dialect would.

"Villiers," the portly soldier repeated with the same pronunciation. "Vill...*yers. H*mpph! Them French names are hard to say. Yeah...he talked to us, then to the Indians, and finally told 'em to hand our boys over. Which they did."

"Was there any trouble?" Washington inquired.

"Nah!" Batson crowed, waving a dismissive hand. "Just a lotta grumblin', that's all."

Washington nodded, still cautiously skeptical. The ability of the French to restrain their Indian allies was by no means absolute. Just after dawn, he had lodged an angry complaint with Villiers after a series of incidents involving the Indians, which included breaking into Dr. Craik's medicine chest and the accumulated pieces of baggage that had to be left behind for later retrieval. One of the trunks contained the Regiment's enormous Grand Union flag, of no practical significance but endowed with great symbolic value. Villiers had responded to the complaint by drawing his sword and taking a couple of half-hearted swipes at the perpetrators while dressing them down in French. The Indians reluctantly obeyed, drifting off without replacing the booty already pillaged. It *was* an absolute certainty that they would be back to pillage again when the French departed.

"Take care of them," Washington said. "If we have to stop to let the wounded rest, we will. But you have to tell us *when* to stop, Solomon. Otherwise, we'll keep going. Do you understand?"

Batson said that he did, then re-mounted the mare and returned back the way he had come. Washington watched as horse and rider retreated alongside the twin columns to the cheers and adulation of the men of Virginia and Carolina. The rescue could hardly be called a victory but it was as close to one as they would get. The close confines of the trail and the faint illumination of the filtered, diffuse sunlight—more like a tunnel through the forest than a simple roadway—lent the occasion a singular intimacy. When Batson finally disappeared around a distant bend, Washington signaled Peregrin Williams to sound the order to march. With a lethargy born as much of spiritual as physical weariness, the survivors of the opening engagement of the French and Indian War plodded eastward toward Wills Creek.

"We can't stop too often," James Mackay said with some trepidation. Though now on friendlier terms with Washington, Mackay still did not consider himself subordinate to the Virginian, but had learned to eschew confrontation with his short-tempered colleague.

"I know, James, I know," Washington sighed deeply, sensing what was coming.

"All we have left are our muskets and not enough men or powder to use them effectively," Mackay continued for emphasis. "The French will leave us alone, but their Indians won't."

"I know, James, but we can't leave sick men behind to die," Washington said, silently pleading with his eyes. "We'll survive."

We'll survive. Mackay rolled the words over in his mind like dice because that's what they were: articles of random chance. *We certainly can leave them behind if it means jeopardizing the rest.* If Washington insisted on making decisions devoid of military logic, he would never achieve his goal of becoming a British officer or, if by God's will he did, would not last long at the post. Mackay gazed wistfully at the young man who had finally become his friend, still surprised by the fact of that friendship. A month ago, the gaze would have been a glower and would have been accompanied by harsh and, he now had to admit, improvident words. But there was no way around it: He liked George Washington. The battle at Great Meadows had been a debacle and Mackay was content to let the young Virginian willingly shoulder the responsibility for it. It was another military dictum that Washington had naively chosen to violate: *Take credit for victory and blame others for defeat.*

Still, he could not help feeling sorry for the man at his side who looked less like a warrior than an overfed farm boy. Tall, big-boned, blue-eyed, with a head shaped like a gourd and a physique that swelled at the hips and narrowed at the shoulders, Washington might be mistaken at a distance for a simpleton. But one could not look into his face—the firm chin, the wide, narrow mouth, the slightly hooked, aquiline nose and the thoughtful brow line—without knowing that intelligence governed this awkwardly majestic frame and the soul residing therein. *All right, George, we'll survive if you insist,* reflected James Mackay, *but I can't help wondering how.*

"George, tell me, do they have taverns in Alexandria?" Mackay asked, hoping to lighten the conversation.

"Yes, of course," Washington answered. It was a half-truth. There was one *small* tavern in Alexandria.

"Why don't you and I find one when we get back? Have a fine night of drinking and…pleasant interplay with the ladies?"

He had almost said, "carousing with the ladies" but thought better of it. The lad seemed a little too strait-laced for such loose talk.

"I said we had taverns. I didn't say the taverns had ladies in them."

"What, taverns without women?" Mackay roared in protest. "What kind of town has taverns without women?"

"A small town," Washington retorted, letting himself be carried along in Mackay's mirthful wake. "whose women are all wives."

"By God, George, I don't want them to have *children* by me. I just want them to sit on my lap and tell me how brave I am," Mackay chortled as he wagged a scolding finger at his companion. "Surely there must be at least one patriotic tavern owner in Alexandria willin' to lend me his buxom wife for an evenin' of innocent flirtation!"

For the next ten minutes the two men enjoyed themselves talking and joking about women and the pleasures of aristocratic life denied them by their hapless journey to the west. Washington was pleasantly surprised by the mellowing of the Scotsman's personality. Apparently, Mackay was transformed into a stubborn jackass only in his role as a regular officer. He had even lost his British accent, as he'd done during the *Billy the Butcher* discussion at Gist's plantation.

Mackay looked directly into his young friend's face and asked, "Do you have someone, George? A lady, I mean?"

The question caught Washington off guard, as had the one about taverns in Alexandria. But this one was personal.

"Why do you ask?"

Mackay glanced away, scratched an itch, then turned to Washington again and said, "Because I think you need a woman. I think you need to be a husband."

Once more glancing away, loosening the buttons of his coat while he summoned his rhetorical skills, Mackay paused thoughtfully. Then, gazing into the depths of the forest, he said, "You brood too much, George. A woman can take your thoughts to other places."

Perhaps sensing his statements had become too personal, James Mackay suddenly stopped speaking and jogged ahead, allegedly to exercise his cramping calves. Washington was left with a myriad of inchoate thoughts stirring in his brain. The similarity between Lord Fairfax's admonition to ease his "manly frustrations" and Mackay's advice was striking. What was it about him that caused these two men to decide he was ripe for marital bliss? In Fairfax's case, he knew it had to do, at least in part, with the great Lord's concerns for the perceived virtue of his cousin's daughter-in-law, but Mackay knew nothing of this. Was it because his temperament was so complaisant that he might as well be married? He didn't think so. Even his overbearing mother had not been able to deflect him from charting an independent course through life. Did they see him as some sort of Lothario who needed reining in by a strong-willed woman? But even as he posed that question to himself, Washington knew such a notion to be ludicrous. George Washington was the most willful person he knew. He could no more indulge in debauchery than smite the French army with the jawbone of an ass. For him, discipline was a self-imposed mandate that could not be withdrawn. Without it, he could achieve nothing.

"No, James, there is no woman in my life," he answered as casually as he could but a bit too loudly. It *is* the truth. *Why does it feel like a lie?*

Mackay shot a sly glance over his shoulder.

"None? Ever?"

"A few. Not many," Washington replied, remembering the Low-Land Beauty of the poem he'd written when he was sixteen. He was not going to mortify himself by mentioning that. "I haven't had time. Too busy earning a living as a surveyor and…"

"…and conquering the French army in North America," Mackay

gibed as he jogged ahead, made a quick circuit around a stand of white pines and returned to his place in line alongside the young Virginian.

Washington took the ribbing in stride. "Maybe I should refuse to accept my pay for a month or two," he replied, only partly in jest.

Wiping his drenched face with a linen kerchief, Mackay shot his companion a critical glance.

"George, don't ever refuse money from your patrons," he admonished. "A professional soldier never refuses to be paid. Remember that if you remember nothin' else. More often than not you'll be beggin' for what's rightly yours…but let's get back to the more inspirin' topic of your love life. You say you have no lady friends so we're goin' to have to remedy that. First thing I figure we'll do after we dry up the taverns in Alexandria is take a good look around the town, see if there are any unattached lasses about. Who knows…You might've overlooked one or two…"

Mackay's ebullient mood was infectious and Washington found himself laughing in spite of himself. The Captain of the Independents was a completely different man leaving a fight than he had been entering one. Maybe that was how professional soldiers balanced the heavy odds against their continued survival: by heartily celebrating life when they could in case the next battle took it from them. If that was the case, Washington feared he could never be a professional soldier. Mackay was right. He brooded too much. Even now he felt the lightness of the moment slipping away, the strident echoes of failure reverberating through his brain.

What should a commander do who has lost his first major battle in so abjectly humiliating a fashion? Resign? It was not the same for Mackay. He had more experience in dealing with defeat and, for that matter, victory. For him, the knowledge that one ultimately followed the other tempered the euphoria or the despair of the outcome. No such accommodation was possible for Washington. He had no true victories to look back on except for the skirmish at the glen, and the French were calling that a crime.

What should he do? For the moment the question was an easy one to answer: Get his men back to Wills Creek. That would be no simple task with the large number of wounded and the shortage of supplies, wagons, and horses. But once that was accomplished, what then? Surely Robert Dinwiddie would support another expedition, better organized and better funded than this one had been. Surely the British could no longer ignore the encroachments of the French on their territory and would supply whatever military aid was necessary. By the articles of capitulation, no Englishman could return for a year, but that time could be used to create an overwhelming military force.

Where would George Washington fit into such an expedition? Would the British want him? Or would they reject him for the usual reasons, supplemented by his involvement in the disaster at Great Meadows? When he juxtaposed his dream to become a British officer against the record of the past two days, the despair he felt was like a poison violating his stomach, the nausea as tangible as if he had ingested a charge of black powder.

He turned around and walked in reverse, watching the double column of colonial soldiers snaking its way through the tunnel of vines and branches back to Wills Creek. Except for the collective thud of feet on packed earth, the marchers were silent. Except for the occasional winces of pain as sharp pebbles pressed against poorly protected arches, their faces were impassive. After these men left, there would be no one to defend the Ohio lands or even the Virginia frontier against whatever incursions the French chose to make.

Will this humiliation be avenged? As comforting as it would have been to think so, he couldn't quite convince himself it would.

𝔊hapter 𝔗wenty

July 7, 1754, The Allegheny River

or his own arcane reasons, Stump Neck was wearing the fur hat with the figure of a running man stitched into it, the one that had puzzled Old Smoke at Venango. From past experience, Gabriel Menard had found it wise not to speculate on Stump Neck's motivations for anything he did. But Michel Gagnon, the messenger from Villiers who had arrived earlier that evening with the news of the British defeat at Great Meadows, was both fascinated and disturbed by the man who had been Pariah West and who was sitting across the campfire from him on one of the pine logs. Except for his fur cap, Stump Neck was as naked and almost as dark as any of the Indians in his band of what Menard had begun to think of as outlaws, because they obeyed no higher authority, white or Indian. Gabriel Menard could no longer control the whimsical maniac and had returned to the more legitimate pursuits of trapping and trading to support himself, Bright Dawn, and the baby who was beginning to make his wife's belly swell like a melon in the moist, rich soil of her womb. But he was a loyal Canadian and so had agreed to summon Stump Neck to the meeting Gagnon had asked for.

"We want you to attack the English settlements west of the mountains," Michel Gagnon said with infinite patience for the third time. Gagnon looked more like a fur trapper than a soldier, wearing light linen and burlap clothing with no military markings and a wide-brimmed black felt hat pushed back on his head. He had a gnarled scar that started on his forehead, jumped the chasm of his left eye socket, and continued on his left cheekbone down to the jaw line. It looked like a gash that might have been made by the downstroke of a hatchet, which, thrust forward ten centimeters more, would have split his skull.

"I don't want to stay here. I don't like it here," Stump Neck snarled with the petulant whine of a willful child. Then he took a gulp of the rum that Menard—reasoning that liquor was a better drink on a hot, sultry night than coffee—had brought out for the occasion. It was, but Stump Neck, like the Indians he wanted to emulate, did not react well to the liquor's influence.

Gagnon cast a long, pleading glance at Menard, then said to Stump Neck, "Why don't you finish the work we want you to do and *then* cross the mountains. We don't care..."

"Who the hell is this *we?*" the madman howled with a start, rising to his feet and circling round the fire toward the messenger. At first it seemed to Menard that he intended to attack his *provocateur*, but then he turned away, chugged another gulp of rum, and stared angrily at the heavenly bodies in the night sky as if they were the bars of a jail cell. While the madman was rooted in place, Bright Dawn emerged from the tent behind Menard bearing two fired clay plates holding corn meal, yellow lotus, and broiled trout that her husband had caught by rowing out into the river at midnight with a bark torch and a spear. She handed the plates to Menard and Gagnon, let her inscrutable gaze rest briefly on Stump Neck, and returned to the tent.

"Commander Villiers," Gagnon answered stiffly. "...who speaks for the Canadian government."

"So *we* is the Canadian government?" Stump Neck queried, his angular profile projecting from powerful shoulders like an outcropping of shale from a riverbank. "And who runs that?"

Gagnon sighed at the pointlessness of the exchange, but replied, "The Marquis Duquesne is the Governor General of Canada."

This caught Stump Neck's attention. He turned around to face the Frenchman.

"Duquesne? The same one they named the fort for?"

"Yes."

"Must be an important man," the madman said, upending his cup to illustrate its emptiness. Menard paid no attention. "But this ain't Canada."

"It will be if you help us."

First pausing to glower at Menard for not offering a refill, Stump Neck strolled with casual disdain back to the pine log and sat down.

"Make me a captain in your army," he demanded with a grin like death in caricature.

"M'sieur, we cannot do that. To be a member of the *Compagnies des franches* you need to have specialized training…"

"Then why should I help you?"

"We have already supplied you with much weaponry and equipment. We can get you much more."

Since Stump Neck had not the slightest interest in becoming a soldier, he did not argue. The madman had his own agenda.

"But, of course, if we do you must help us to persuade the English back to the other side of the mountains…by whatever means," Michel Gagnon inveigled. The messenger did not smile but he might have: The three men all knew what was meant by "persuade."

Bright Dawn returned with a plate for Stump Neck. Surprised by the gesture, he stood, took it, nodded his thanks, silently but incoherently moving his lips at the same time. He looked at her puffy pink cheeks, then down at her swelling stomach, an uncharacteristically genteel but otherwise unreadable expression on his face. It was as if a human emotion, like longing or envy, had briefly possessed him. For her part, Bright Dawn maintained her physical and spiritual distance, diverting her gaze downward. Then she returned to the tent, the flickering firelight playing on her taciturn face like waves on a bay-shore.

Stump Neck seated himself and began gobbling down the food, any budding signs of humanity now extinguished.

"Where is it you want us to attack 'zactly? *This side of the mountains* is a big place," he said between swallows.

"There are a number of settlements. I will show you on the map. When you have disposed of these, you can do anything you wish."

Stump Neck grunted a comment about those who thought they could restrict his actions, then muttered, "When do we get the guns?"

Gagnon smiled, tossed his head back and tried to wink at Menard as he did. The gesture didn't quite work because of the improperly healed tissue beneath the scar.

"We can have them here within days. Not only guns, but powder.

We have just received a big shipment from Colonel Washington of the English!"

Gabriel Menard understood the jest and returned a polite grin. Gagnon would provide Stump Neck with the gunpowder Washington had left on the battlefield at Great Meadows. What could be scraped up from the detritus of destruction, that is. But the irony, whether or not he understood it, was lost on the madman.

"Did you say Washington?" he asked.

"Yes, do you know him?" Gagnon replied.

Stump Neck hesitated, picturing in his mind the young Virginian with the heavy jaw and the skinny shoulders, only a few years older than himself, who had come to take him back to tidewater Virginia. No feelings of loss or sorrow welled up in him, only a mild curiosity that the fool had managed to stay alive. He then considered whether the truth or a lie would better serve his purposes, concluding it didn't make much difference but that deceit was the safest course.

"Nah! Just heard the name somewhere," he shrugged it off, then came bluntly back to the subject at hand. "Why do you want to kill settlers? What diffr'nce does it make to Doo-kane whether they stay or go?"

Stump Neck was in one of his rare, rational moods, the kind that made it difficult for men like Michel Gagnon to see the cesspool of perversion that lay beneath the surface.

"We do not *want* to kill settlers, M'sieur," Gagnon explained, looking somewhat discomfited as he removed the felt hat, exposing a bald spot whose polished surface caught the moon's light and proclaimed its presence. "We want them to go back to their British colonies across the mountains."

"Like I said, what diffr'nce does it make whether they do or not?"

"It is no good to defeat their soldiers and leave their agents in place. It is a bad example."

Stump Neck finally found some humor in Gagnon's words and giggled like a small boy with a new bag of hard tack.

"They ain't nobody's agents, you fool! They're just people. They don't give a damn who per-sides over the real estate!"

For once Menard found himself in agreement with the madman. He had no particular desire to dislodge the English settlers—there was no shortage of land—and could not understand why his government felt obliged to adopt such a hard line. He eased his disquietude by assuring himself that, had the British won the Battle of Great Meadows, they would be behaving as badly as the French were.

"As I have said, M'sieur, it is a bad example. If the English settlers are not removed, the fact that they have not been will attract more. And then we *will* have a problem," Gagnon said, patiently elucidating the official position, which, Menard had to admit, made a modicum of good sense.

"Why don't ya kick 'em out yourself?" Stump Neck growled peevishly.

Gagnon paused, choosing his words, then said, "We cannot do that. The activities of the *Compagnies des franches* must be seen as above reproach. There remains the question of right of possession. Our recent action at Great Meadows was a justifiable response to the murder of the Sieur de Jumonville. If we send our armed forces against British settlers, it could be seen as a hostile and illegitimate strike against innocent civilians who may conceivably have lawful claims…"

If Stump Neck had ever heard a barrister speak, he might have concluded Gagnon was one. But there was no ambiguity about what the voluble Frenchman had in mind, and the madman knew it.

"So you want us to kill English settlers for you?"

The patience and the rhetoric of Michel Gagnon had about run its course and, while it was his job to do so, he was tired of framing his arguments euphemistically. It was he who rose this time, staring in the direction of the Allegheny River. The stream on whose bluffs they were encamped flowed into the Allegheny a mile to the west.

"Will you help us or not, M'sieur?" he said without further elaboration.

"Let's look at the map. See where you're talkin' about," Stump Neck suggested plaintively.

Taken slightly aback by Stump Neck's abrupt concurrence, Gagnon retrieved a sheet of paper from his pack, which lay at one end of the pine log on which he and Bushy Bear had been sitting, and spread it on the ground between the Shaman's feet and the campfire. Then he told Menard to extract one of the partially burnt logs from the fire to use as a torch. Bushy Bear obeyed and knelt on one knee, holding the working end of the torch over the meter square map as Gagnon squinted to make out its markings and Stump Neck finished his meal.

"There are settlements here, here, here…" Gagnon said, pointing to locations mostly west of the Allegheny and Monongahela Rivers but never far from them. Realizing he needed a marker, the messenger probed for and found a suitably cooled piece of charcoal near the fire and place an 'x' at each of the designated spots.

"What about Chiningue?" Stump Neck asked, setting his plate to one side and aiming a finger at a section of the Ohio River running almost directly north from the forks.

"There are no English at Chiningue," Gagnon responded with undisguised satisfaction. "Even the Iroquois are gone."

This was news to the other two men. Bushy Bear found himself exchanging a look of surprise with the disturbingly composed Stump Neck.

"This is where we want you to start," Gagnon finished, smashing a soiled finger on a point thirty miles up the Allegheny from the forks where the river began a lazy turn to the southwest.

"Why?"

"Because it is fortified. They go there, the English do, when they are threatened by hostiles."

"I know the place," Bushy Bear said, breaking the silence he had granted Gagnon to let the messenger make his case. *I even know the man who built it,* he said in his mind. To the others, he said, "It's called *Kid Han Nunk.* The Indians go there too, the ones the Moravians have converted."

"How do you know so much?" the madman chafed testily, the thin veneer of control falling away momentarily. The response, like most of the madman's interfaces with reality, was impatient, bathed in the hot pool of resentment that had been gradually filling his soul since childhood.

"I live here," Menard replied.

The simplicity of the answer elicited only a confirmatory grunt from Stump Neck. He looked querulously at Gagnon through cat-like eye slits and said, "When do we get the guns?"

Gagnon paused, performing a quick calculation in his head.

"Three days," he said tentatively. "We can meet you where this stream joins the river."

"Ammunition, powder?"

"Yes, of course," Gagnon nodded, folding the map. "But we can't guarantee the powder. You'll have to make sure it's dry."

"Good. Three days. Three days," Stump Neck said as he rose and held up the three good fingers of his left hand for viewing. "Three days. No delays. Three days."

The madman grinned boyishly, pleased by his crude if unintended poetry, and began the walk back to where he had camped near the horses.

"M'sieur Stump Neck, there is one other condition," Michel Gagnon called.

Stump Neck halted, turned, and looked at the messenger with an unreadable expression that could have been anything between disgust and resignation.

"What's that?"

Gagnon's feral eyes darted from Bushy Bear to Stump Neck and back again.

"We want you to take M'sieur Menard with you."

The appearance of a hungry predator poised for the kill might have disturbed Bushy Bear's composure more, but accompanying the madman on his next mission was definitely on the top ten list of things most likely to disrupt Gabriel Menard's tranquility. But Gagnon's statement came as no surprise to the French trader. Bushy Bear and the messenger had spoken about the possibility of his joining Stump Neck's band for one final series of attacks to push the English out for good and all. Unwilling to present a blatant refusal, Menard had danced around the issue, pointing out that he could better serve as an intermediary between the official French presence, in the form of Villiers and Contrecoeur, and the less conventional auxiliaries, like Stump Neck's bloodthirsty band. The rotund Frenchman now regretted his pusillanimity.

"Why, don't you trust me?" Stump Neck demanded.

"We don't know you, M'sieur," Gagnon said, businesslike. "We do know M'sieur Menard. And we trust *him*."

The madman maintained his equivocal stare, shielding from view the workings of the mind behind it. Then, the germ of a grin broke the stalemate.

"You sure Gabriel wants to go?" he challenged, speaking to Gagnon but holding Menard in his cryptic gaze. "Gabriel, you wanta come along with us and kick hell out of the English?"

The madman's face had turned cold and menacing, like a frozen remnant from an earlier, more frigid season, sending a chill through Menard. But it was also laced heavily with mockery, and it was this that caused Bushy bear to make an unwise decision.

"Certainly, I will be...honored to serve in whatever capacity Commander Villiers might wish..." he said, never quite completing the reply as his heart sank to his bowels.

Stump Neck's budding grin transformed to a broad half-moon, glee sparkling in his eyes like contained hellfire.

"Good. Good. Be just like old times," he crowed merrily, applauding with an unnatural stiffness that made it clear to Menard that mockery was still the entree being served. Then the madman turned hastily on his heel and disappeared into the blackness.

July 10, 1754, Redfield's fort

It was bigger than he remembered and bristling with long-barreled muskets and rifles at every portal. Gabriel Menard lay prone in his deerskin hunting clothes fifty meters from the broad palisade wall on the river side of the home-made fortress Michel Gagnon had made the first target in the madman's campaign of terror against the English. It was early evening of the steamy, mid-July day. A fat orange sun was preparing to pack it in for the night while a chorus of crickets sang a tuneless opera celebrating its imminent if temporary departure from their universe. In the light summer breeze, the inconsonant smells of sweetly rotten pears and washed clothes hanging out to dry competed for dominance.

Bushy Bear had already loaded a charge and ball into his musket, but had not primed the pan. He would wait a little longer before doing that to make sure the priming powder was fresh, dry, and exactly where he wanted it to be to detonate the charge. Stump Neck had said sunset and his signal would be simple and unambiguous: He would howl like a rutting wolf and fire the first shot. Then the irregular force of Indians, *coureurs de bois*, and half-breeds under his spell would rush through the thick grass to the fortified enclosure screaming anything they damn well pleased at the extremes of their vocal power and shooting at anything that looked vaguely human and unfamiliar. It was the most elemental of plans, free of guile and surprise, relying only on the combined firepower of the forty or so men who would be staging the attack and whatever panic could be induced in the fort's inhabitants by their blood-curdling cries. Gabriel Menard gazed skeptically at the tall palisade wall with its sturdy timbers hacked to jagged points at the tops and the high, diagonally-opposed log buildings at the corners that served as bastions. From these, the defenders could view the fifty-meter wide void that Stump Neck's band would have to rush across before they could even reach the walls.

It was a terrible plan. It couldn't work. The people inside—he had no idea how many there were but the number of guns pointing their way was seventeen—knew how to defend a piece of territory. They had food, water, virtually impregnable walls, and a three hundred sixty degree field of fire that their enemy would have to enter somewhere before he could even attempt scaling the walls with ladders. That tactic would be hard to execute successfully because of the height of the walls and the ring of defenders crouching behind them on raised platforms. *Stump Neck must be mad*, he thought, and then found himself laughing out loud at the absurd morsels his overwrought brain was offering up. *Of course he is mad*, he corrected, *but he has lost not only his sanity but his cunning as well!* That was new, and disturbing, and, though Menard could not put his finger on the why of it, not quite believable.

"Marcel, how many do you count?" he yelled to a nearby colleague, a thief and perhaps a rapist but an otherwise decent man, as Stump Neck's retinue went.

"Seventeen," a hoarse bass voice replied.

"Can you tell if they all have men behind them?"

"No."

"Do we have a count on the other side?"

A pause, then the voice said, "No."

"We should try to find out."

A murmur of assent, then a rustling of branches as Marcel, or an appointed surrogate, left to count musket barrels on the opposite side of the fortification. If there were as many on that side as this, it would mean there were almost as many able-bodied defenders as attackers, not a propitious ratio for the assaulting organization. Two-to-one would be tolerable, three-to-one acceptable, four-to-one preferable, but one-to-one, ridiculous. At that moment, Bushy Bear decided that, based on his age, impending fatherhood, and generally cautious approach to violent altercations, he would *not* be in the forefront of those leading this charge. That decision made, he sat up, adjusted his position so that he could not easily be seen or shot at by one of the seventeen visible guns, and reflected on his tenuous situation, which he was beginning to regard as a predicament. The sense of foreboding had begun earlier that day...

* * *

Bright Dawn and he had been waiting for Michel Gagnon at sunrise that morning at the mouth of the creek that eased uneventfully into the Allegheny River from the east, the only evidence of its penetration a trail of lazily swirling eddies, yellowish-brown on one side and olive-hued on the other. The shallow tributaries that tumbled down from the mountains were always of a more jaundiced, opaque cast than the verdant rivers to whom they gave their life's substance. The Menards had crossed the river amid the myriad wisps of fog rising like evanescent morning glories from its surface, with the sun's early rays grasping for purchase over the treetops. At that hour, the silence was nearly absolute; the only sound was that of the paddles bending the waters to their will. Gabriel had not wanted to bring Bright Dawn with him, insisting that her condition and the madman's desultory mood swings precluded her leaving the camp Bushy Bear had established precisely for its remoteness and inaccessibility. But Bright Dawn had been as adamant as he—explaining that her womanhood, Chippewa heritage, and shaman father had given her special insights her husband could not possibly fathom. It was an argument Bushy

Bear had never won so he finally consented to let her come to the meeting place if, afterward, she would leave with Michel Gagnon. Even this she resisted, an indefinable but genuine panic infecting her eyes and voice. But this time his will was stronger, and she relented.

They lingered on the south shore of the creek mouth for a half-hour, strolling in the brisk coolness of the morning and watching the river wisps lose their corporeal forms as the sun rose higher above the eastern horizon. Then Bright Dawn—her far vision was much better than Bushy Bear's—spotted the two bateaux and accompanying canoes approaching from the south, their bows undulating in the gentle waves kicked up by a light breeze.

Gabriel Menard waved first and called "Over here!"

A man standing on the bow of the lead bateau responded in kind. It was not long before Bushy Bear, Bright Dawn, Michel Gagnon, and his men were standing in the shallows shaking hands and chattering about the exigencies of the journey from Great Meadows to Fort Duquesne and from thence to this place. Michel Gagnon inquired as to where Stump Neck and his men were, to which Menard could only shrug and reply that he did not know.

While they waited for the madman to arrive, Gagnon had his men unload Washington's discarded gunpowder from one bateau and the muskets—several of them were of the exquisite Tulle marine design made at Saint-Etienne—from the other. The firearms, ammunition, and powder were moved up from the shore to the base of the low bluff that marked the boundary of the river basin. Gagnon broke open one of the new powder barrels to show Menard that the gunpowder had dried and was therefore usable. Bushy Bear nodded, said something to the effect that everything seemed to be in order and, although he secretly wished the madman would vanish from the face of the earth, fretted inwardly at his absence. After three hours, the sky was a hazy blue behind a luminous maize sun that had successfully dispersed the apparitions of the dawning hours. Michel Gagnon announced that he could wait no longer.

"Will he come, do you think?" the troubled soldier asked.

"I don't know."

"You have said he is mad. Is this an example of his madness?"

Bushy Bear watched Gagnon nervously rub the scar on his cheek, which seemed to be unnaturally inflamed by his anxiety.

"I don't know that either," Menard said. "With Stump Neck, madness cannot be measured by a single incident."

The messenger's features contorted in puzzlement; he had no conception of Menard's meaning.

"If he does not come, hide the arms and we will get them later," Gagnon instructed, walking back into the water to the lead bateau, which had already been prepared for departure. When he reached it, he climbed aboard, turned, and said to Menard, "I have to say, Gabriel, this has not been an entirely satisfactory day for me."

"Nor for me," Bushy Bear replied, bristling at the implied criticism but declining to mention that, whether or not Stump Neck appeared, his day was bound to be fraught with more unpleasantness than Gagnon's. Even if all went well, he would be separated from Bright Dawn for an indefinite period, which he had had to do before, of course, but never while she was pregnant and with such a gnawing sense of uncertainty gripping his nerves.

He looked to his wife, who was standing at the river's edge, her head slightly bowed, waiting for him to come and bid her *adieu*. Her silky black hair descended in twin braids onto her shoulders and the white broadcloth dress embroidered with a serrated black trim fell loosely over her torso without revealing the budding protrusion at the waist. Bright Dawn had, it seemed, lost her brightness. She would not plead with her husband to let her stay. That had already been resolved between them. It would certainly not be compatible with her upbringing to shed tears over something so trivial as the temporary separation of her and her husband. But she was desperately unhappy. How he knew this Bushy Bear could not say, but he did, and painfully regretted he could do nothing about it.

He walked to her, smiled, and offered his arm. She took it, returning his smile with a thin, ethereal smile of her own, a poor substitute for the mirthful exuberance her delicate lips were capable of celebrating. With a single motion, he took her under the arms and lifted her aboard the same bateau Michel Gagnon had boarded.

"I'll see you soon," he said.

"Yes," she said, a bit too quickly, and averted her gaze.

As the bateaux and canoes pushed off, Gabriel Menard strode out of the water to stand on the rocky beach and turned to watch their departure. Bright Dawn was standing stiffly at the bow of the bateau, her hands clenched as if in prayer, her lips pursed together into a single, horizontal line. The unblinking gaze she had affixed to him seemed to be drawing his very being toward her.

"Au revoir," she whispered, raising one hand in a limp wave.

"Au revoir," he responded, lifting a hand in reply, but for some reason, finding himself unable to complete the gesture.

* * *

"Gabriel, there are thirteen. Thirteen muskets on the other side," the gruff voice of Marcel said from Menard's left.

"Thirteen! Thirteen what, did you say?" Menard stammered, his mental image of Bright Dawn suddenly shattered.

"Muskets," Marcel growled impatiently. "There are thirteen muskets on the other side."

Bushy Bear paused to collect his thoughts. Marcel had cut short his reminiscences and forced the present back into his awareness, a rude thing to do. Finally managing to recall what and where constituted his present existence, he said, "Thirteen. That's not a good number, Marcel."

"It's only thirteen on one side. The whole count is thirty," a humorless Marcel grumbled, revealing that he had already thought about and rationalized away the insidious number's appearance.

"Forty of us, thirty of them. That's not good either, Marcel."

The *coureur de bois* must have agreed with him because Menard heard only a grunt emitted with the tonality of acquiescence and a cyclical snorting, as if Marcel had a plug of mucous lodged in each nostril. The labored breathing attested to a certain restiveness as well.

Bushy Bear risked exposing his woolly face to the thirty-four eyes behind the seventeen muskets to take a quick look around, hoping to identify Stump Neck's position so that he could anticipate the onset of the assault. Although he saw and recognized half of the attacking force behind trees, squatting in the muck, or kneeling in the grasses, he could find no sign of the madman. But that was not particularly worrisome. As the commander of the strike force, Stump Neck could be anywhere placing his troops and setting them up for the attack. So Bushy Bear sipped from his rum horn and let the remaining history of the day wash through his mind like a wave probing a beach, then fleeing back to the sea from whence it had come...

* * *

They appeared on the shallow bluffs at nearly the same moment that Bright Dawn and the bateaux disappeared from view.

"Gabriel!" the tenor voice of the madman beckoned.

When he saw Stump Neck to the east of and above him, the first thing that struck Gabriel Menard was that the leader of the barbarian horde assembled behind him was still wearing the fur hat with the figure of a running man stitched into it. Otherwise, Stump Neck was gloriously bedecked for battle. The upper right and lower left quarters of his bronzed face were smeared with a mixture of black charcoal and bear grease. Beneath a red blanket cape draped on his shoulders and edged in scalplocks, his bare torso was festooned with painted red and black figures of serpents, snakes, scorpions, and even a pair of hawk's wings centered over his heart and spread for flight. A white buckskin breechclout and moccasins decorated with intricate beadwork completed the war costume. In his right hand, with a pride that was evident in the taut muscles of his arms and neck, he clutched the traditional symbol of the war chief: a *coup stick*, this one arranged with three fans of hawk feathers along its two meter length. With a bemused grin whose cocked angle seemed to betray some secret and evil intent, the madman descended the steep but short path to the beach. As he approached, Menard got a better look at the blanket-cape. The scalplocks sewn along its edges consisted mostly of silky, black strands of hair but, interspersed among them at regular intervals were browns, blonds, and red-oranges with varying degrees of curl.

"You were here all the time. You were hiding, waiting for them to leave," Bushy Bear charged.

"Yeah," Stump Neck admitted, so unfazed by the implied criticism that his smile remained, unabated.

"Why? What purpose does it serve?"

"The fewer who know me, the better."

"Better for whom?"

"For me, naturally."

The members of Stump Neck's band filtered down the path and gathered around the cache of arms. Gleefully, they lifted the weapons, jostled them to gauge their weight, and playfully sighted each other along the barrels.

"Is the powder dry?" the madman asked.

"Yes. Do you want to check it?"

"No, Gabriel, no need," the would-be chieftain replied, the weird smile and the desolate eyes taking on a taunting mien. "I *trust* you."

Using the *coup stick* to stabilize himself on the loose sandstones covering the beach, Stump Neck joined his colleagues in examining the weaponry and making his own choices among the several varieties and generations of French musketry. In every external aspect but the wheat-colored hair and the green eyes that betrayed his European ancestry, the madman had become what he wanted so dearly to be: an Indian. No, not just an Indian, a savage. And yet in his obsession to be something he was not and to have that which he was not entitled to, he was indeed still a white man.

So this is what we become when we release ourselves from the laws of God and man, Gabriel Menard mused. *It is no wonder he thrives out here.*

* * *

It did not really sound like a wolf howl at all, but like a child's imitation of one: shrill and clamorous, with none of the rich texture of the wild beast lamenting its solitary existence. But it was enough to shake Menard out of his second reverie. Hastily grabbing his musket, Bushy Bear brought the butt against his right shoulder and aimed it in the general direction of the seventeen-barreled palisade wall. To his left and right, he heard the rustling of grass and branches as the outlaws of Stump Neck's band responded to the first of the prearranged signals and prepared for the impending assault. It was odd, Menard thought as he fished in his powder horn for the gunpowder to pour into the musket's priming pan...odd, now that he thought of it, that the madman's inanimate screech sounded so near, almost as if it were coming from directly behind him.

A roar, so intense inside his ears and skull that it sent urgent calls of distress to his brain, exploded somewhere above him. Almost immediately, musket fire erupted around Menard from behind every rock and tree trunk as the attackers heeded the second of the two signals their master had given them. Menard's response was the exception. When the blast momentarily disabled his senses, he reflexively dropped his musket. Enraged, he rolled over to find Stump Neck standing over him, an Ojibwa-style crown of hawk and duck feathers perched on his granite head and an iron tomahawk of the kind made in British factories in his right hand. He had dropped his musket too and was clasping the fur hat with the running figure in his left hand.

"What the hell?" Menard sputtered, aghast. "West, what are you trying..."

"How do you like my new hat, Gabriel?" the madman said in a voice so unctuous with sincerity that Menard almost answered. As he spoke, Stump Neck's pupils rolled upward toward the feathered crown, disappeared inside the eye sockets, and descended again to fix on the prone Frenchman. It was then that Bushy Bear knew he was going to die.

"This one is yours," the madman said almost melodically as he tossed the fur cap at his mentor. Frantically, Menard tried to reach for the musket at his side, then remembered he had not yet primed the pan. There was no time to pray, or even to form a coherent thought. So Bushy Bear simply closed his eyes and did his best to summon forth an image of a smiling Bright Dawn cradling a baby in her arms as the madman leaped on him and sunk the ax blade deep into his brain.

Richard Patton

Chapter Twenty-One

July 11, 1754, Redfield's fort:

One of the men in the westernmost of the two towers spied her in the middle of the river, paddling her canoe toward the docks at the far end of the clearing that served as a buffer between the fortifications and whatever threats—man or beast—might be lurking in the forest. Because she was an Indian, some raised the possibility that she might be part of the lead element of another attack force like the one they had repulsed the previous evening. But this was dismissed as unlikely. It was obvious the woman was alone and the lethargic, almost lugubrious character of her movements revealed a soul filled with dread, not malevolence. They watched her as she beached the canoe, took note of their presence, ignored it, and started searching the woods, shrubbery, and grasses around the clearing. The dead man, the only casualty of the brief battle on either side, was down there, of course. The defenders were still gathered within the protective walls of the enclosure and had planned to remain there until midday, when a party would be sent out to bury the body and to assure themselves that the woods were free of evil-doers. That the woman would find the body was a certainty. It was not well hidden and a telltale swarm of horseflies hovered hungrily over the spot. She did, fell to her knees, and launched into one of the seemingly endless, discordant songs that those of Indian heritage within the compound knew to be a chant of grief and woe, but which their white neighbors found only to be ominously nerve-wracking. Jasper Redfield was among those who watched and listened and, as the leader of the defenders within the compound, quickly decided it would not do to let the woman exorcise her demons alone. Christian

284

rectitude demanded that misery have company.

Since there was no apparent threat, an *ad hoc* party was formed to approach the woman, determine how they could help her, and find out who she was and why she was here. The possibility of further violence was judged to be so remote that Redfield included his whole family in the excursion: his wife Charity, his daughter Felicity, and Cornpicker. Along with ten or eleven of the others, Redfield and his family cautiously made their way across the field and halted, waiting for the grieving woman to acknowledge their presence. When she ceased her chanting and gazed quizzically up, somberly studying each of the faces surrounding her, Jasper Redfield decided the time to speak had come.

"Who are you?" he asked and, although the dead man looked vaguely familiar, also inquired, "Who is he?"

"My name is Bright Dawn. I am Chippewa. He is my husband, Bushy Bear. His white name is Gabriel Menard."

She spoke in a rush, as if anxious to resume her mourning, or possibly because she was not entirely comfortable with the French language she had used to deliver the statement. Redfield was proficient enough in French to follow her words and instantly remembered the dead man: a Canadian trader he had met at Logstown more than a year ago, when the tensions between French and English had not been so venomous. He could not call the man a friend, but they had conversed with each other about their lives, their occupations, and the peculiarities of their respective worlds, as decent men do in such circumstances.

"We did not do this, Mrs. Menard. He and the Indians and the other Frenchman were attacking..."

"I know you did not do it. It is not the way you kill," she interrupted, letting her gaze drift to the chasm in her husband's skull and the oozing gray matter it exposed. Only part of the mortal wound was visible because of the fur cap with the figure of a running man, which had been crudely propped on the corpse's head. With meticulous care, Bright Dawn lifted the fur cap from Bushy Bear's head and sat it on the ground. With the hat off, they could all see that the scalp had been removed, leaving a pulpy, irregular surface of exposed flesh and dried blood.

"But it is *his* way," Bright Dawn added cryptically.

Upon seeing the grisly spectacle close up, Charity Redfield and the other mothers in the group sent their children off to play, which all but Cornpicker were happy to do, having spent the greater parts of the last two days within the confines of Redfield's fort. But Cornpicker stayed, partly out of fascination with the violated carcass of Gabriel Menard, and partly because he did not want to be perceived as squeamish.

"Who is this man you speak of?" Redfield inquired.

She glanced up at Redfield to watch his reaction when she said, "Stump Neck."

A buzz of conversation among the members of the delegation filled the air. Although none had had any interaction with the notorious Stump Neck, they were all acquainted with the unsavory reputation of the man who, with his band of Indian and Canadian miscreants, had been indiscriminately murdering British traders and settlers in the Ohio country and on the western slopes of the Allegheny Mountains. His victims had been put to the most unspeakable kinds of torture and death: burning at the stake, amputations of fingers and toes, infecting of raw wounds with maggots and spider eggs. Only the most cruel and inhuman acts were contained in Stump Neck's repertoire and he seemed to be broadening his perspective with every vicious foray. No one seemed to know who he was or where he had come from, although many had opinions. Some thought him to be a shaman from an especially primitive Algonkian tribe living somewhere in the wilds of Canada, or perhaps Florida. Others had heard he was a local chieftain who had turned bad because of an uncontrollable blood lust. But there was no evidence, no certitude, only speculation.

"But your husband was with the attackers. Why would Stump Neck kill him?" Jasper Redfield wanted to know.

"Stump Neck is mad," she spat at the air. "He only wants to kill, nothing else. And he wants no one telling him when or how. He is death walking as a man."

"Do you mean to say your husband was one of the leaders?" Nathaniel Stewart, a round-featured, barrel-chested farmer with a tendency to apoplexy rumbled angrily. Redfield held up a calming arm. The thin lips of the red-faced man sputtered to an abrupt and unanticipated halt. For an instant, Stewart's glower and its strident overtones were directed at Redfield. Then he reeled in his temper, humbly bowed his head, and yielded to his host. The shaggy leader squatted down on his spindly legs in front of Bright Dawn, his wispy gray hair cascading like a waterfall over his arms and shoulders.

"*Was* your husband directing the attack on us?" he asked in a disconcertingly civil tone.

Bright Dawn shook her head.

"No. He was here because the man from the fort wanted him to be."

"The man from the fort?"

"The man who brought the guns. From the fort where the rivers meet."

"Fort Duquesne?"

"Yes…yes…the French fort," Bright Dawn nodded, any tenuous loyalty she might have felt to her husband's nation perishing with his death.

Redfield paused to ponder the increasingly precarious situation of the settlers. Several days earlier, a rider had brought news of the British defeat at Great Meadows. That news was the reason why he and his neighbors had been so well prepared for Stump Neck's abortive onslaught. This woman's words seemed to indicate that the French were behind the recent wave of attacks on British settlers in the Ohio country. This in itself was not news, only a confirmation of what all had suspected, that the French were playing an active role in the attacks, at least picking the targets to their own advantage and supplying the weapons. But if this Chippewa woman was right, the French—intentionally or unintentionally—were not exercising much control. Redfield was not sure what was more insidious: a French-Canadian government that could not restrain its bloodthirsty mercenaries, or one that *chose* not to. Either way, it meant that the rules of 'civilized' warfare were not likely to be fastidiously observed. Scalps would be taken, women and children killed with no more hesitation than if they were battle-hardened veterans. What was worse, the settlers might be tempted to adopt similar tactics rather than be wiped out. That would be a terrible calamity for their souls.

Jasper Redfield felt his wife's long fingers kneading his shoulders. He looked up and saw her moist eyes, like mountain lakes, sparkling down at him, drawing him toward her. As he stood she cupped her hand around his ear, whispered into it, then withdrew, her lips poised in a knowing smile.

"Mrs. Menard, my wife says you are with child," Redfield said, amused by his own stupidity. "Is that true?"

"Yes," Bright Dawn blurted. Then, when the whispers among those in the delegation intensified, she became apprehensive, cast a beseeching glance up at Redfield and said, "Will you kill me?"

"No, we won't kill you," Redfield bellowed, incredulous that she should ask such a question. Again he felt his wife's fingers touching his own, telling him to subdue his ire and show kindness.

"We will not harm you. My God, Mrs. Menard, you're pregnant. That would be the most depraved of abominations," he continued in a state of vexation.

Bright Dawn stared blankly at Redfield, puzzled as to why her condition should make any difference. In the world she had come from, a pregnant woman was as worthy of slaughter as anyone, perhaps more so. Bewildered, she simply fixed her eyes on the man who, in physical appearance at least, somewhat resembled her husband, except that Bushy Bear's hair grew in tight, brown spirals while the milky white hair and beard of this man fell in fine, sinuous strands. Both Redfield and Bushy Bear had more hair covering their bodies than any of the males among her people could hope to grow in a lifetime. Perhaps there was something wrong with white people, some sickness that made such a useless growth spread so abundantly over their pallid bodies. But when she thought of the living Bushy Bear and then compared the image to the dead body lying in front of her, tears nearly came to her eyes. She successfully fought them back, as she usually did.

"Do you have a place to go?" Charity Redfield asked, kneeling down to Bright Dawn's level. "Where are your people?"

"My people?" Bright Dawn murmured, unprepared for the question. "I don't know...we have wandered much."

"Would you like to stay with us?" the other woman asked.

Bright Dawn could not answer. She was uncertain what to make of these strange people, especially of this woman, whose high cheekbones and attire identified her as an Indian, but whose clipped manner of speech was like that of a white. Why were they asking her to stay? She was the enemy. Vengeance was their privilege, their right.

"Why don't you think about that and tell us your decision later?" Jasper Redfield suggested, folding his arms as he pondered the situation. "We would like to know more about this Stump Neck. Can you tell us who he is, where he came from? His tribe?"

"He has no tribe. He is a white man. A boy."

This inspired an abrupt wave of shocked commentary. When it dissipated, Bright Dawn told them how the white boy who would become Stump Neck had wandered into her village, had been recruited by Bushy Bear, and how she and her husband had instructed him in the ways of a shaman.

"What is his name?" asked Nathaniel Stewart, his earlier hostility transformed into an intense curiosity.

"I do not know. My husband did, but he did not tell me," Bright Dawn said, risking another glance at the dead body. She pointed at the fur cap still sitting near Bushy Bear's decimated skull and added, "That belongs to him. That is the madman's..."

"Madman?" Redfield queried, taking the cap in hand.

"It is what we called him to ourselves."

He wanted to ask her the reason for the appellation but his curiosity was suddenly struck by the figure on the cap. His brow furrowing in fascination, he held it up to her view and asked, "Do you know what this is? What it means?"

She shook her had, answering, "No."

Redfield inspected the cap for further clues, found none, then handed it to his wife for safekeeping. Through the wisps of hair that kept drifting with the breeze from the river across his leathery face, Redfield watched the Frenchman's woman, wondering what should be done with her. She returned his gaze impassively, as if it didn't really matter to her what they did as long as she remained alive.

"This white man who became Stump Neck. Was he a French soldier or a trader? Do you know how he got here from Canada?" Redfield asked, determined to extract as much information from Gabriel Menard's wife as possible.

The question had the unexpected effect of energizing the woman. An expression of incredulity, almost amusement, consumed her fine-featured face and she began urgently shaking her head. Suddenly, she rose to her feet and waved her hands in front of Redfield's befuddled face.

"No, no, you do not understand," she explained. "He is not a Frenchman. He did not come from Canada!"

"But you said he was not an Indian…" Redfield protested in confusion.

Bright Dawn hesitated, struggling to find a way to explain. Finally, she dropped her arms, abandoned her frantic gesticulations, and came to the point.

"He is an Englishman," she said bluntly.

There was another moment of shocked silence followed by a spirited, verging on violent, series of verbal exchanges among the members of the delegation, many of them punctuated by hostile glares at Bright Dawn. Placing her hands on her swollen stomach in an unconscious, protective reaction, she silently prayed to her God, *Gluskap*, and to her husband's white God, whose name she could not remember, reasoning that He would have the greater power under the present circumstances. She prayed that these strange people would not change their minds about her. She did not want her baby to be killed. If necessary, she would plead with them to let her live until the child was born. Then they could kill her if they wished, as she fully expected them to do.

Seeing Bright Dawn's distress, Charity Redfield went to the Chippewa woman, smiled, and guided her back to the fort. Expecting the worst, Bright Dawn was surprised to learn that she was to be fed rather than burned alive. It would be the first of many such lessons.

Chapter Twenty-Two

August 1, 1754, the Belvoir Plantation, Virginia

How can she possibly be angry with me? It was a question that had plagued Washington since he'd read Sally's note after returning to Mount Vernon. He had brought the note in his waistcoat pocket but had no need of it. The words were seared into his memory: "I must accuse you of great unkindness in refusing me the pleasure of seeing you this night." *How did she even know I was back? Someone must have told her, one of the servants, perhaps.* What really bothered him as he guided the sorrel through the woods separating Mount Vernon and Belvoir was Sally's insensitivity. The note was a callous reproach. There were no words to assuage his wounded pride, no soothing reassurances that he would eventually recover from the depression that had consumed him since the humiliation at Great Meadows. *Doesn't she know how it's affected me? No, of course she doesn't,* he sadly concluded. Sally could not extend herself that far, not even for him. Her most ascendant emotion was a keen sense of fun. She had to laugh. Depriving Sally of laughter was like depriving a hungry man of food; she wouldn't tolerate it. If she found herself in a group of sober-minded merchants or damnation-minded zealots she would beat a hasty retreat. If a friend showed signs of excessive sobriety she would tickle, joke, and prod until he or she—usually he—emerged from that unfortunate state into the light of good cheer. Sally was always upbeat. It was her nature. It was her gift. It was her most ingratiating and exasperating character flaw.

As the horse emerged from the forest shadows onto the broad meadow immediately outside the mansion grounds, Washington's mood lightened a notch. The hot, white August sun was an improvement over the gloom of the woods but pummeled his eyes and face with its brilliance and drew crisp shadows beneath the huge oaks guarding the bluff above the Potomac. An ephemeral breeze smelling of manure and cut grass titillated his nostrils but did nothing to mitigate the sensation of being broiled alive. Sweat would be pouring from his brow soon but he had prepared for that by bringing a kerchief and wearing a simple brown, cotton suit and a broad-rimmed felt hat: the clothes of a farmer. Gently, he convinced the horse to accelerate to a brisk trot. There would be none of the melodrama of his last visit: no dramatic gallop to the bluff and back, no ostentatious new uniform to strut in, no false pride. He just wanted to push the bad feelings to some place far from the center of his consciousness and get on with what life had in store for him.

Comfortable with the feel of the sorrel's striding rhythm against his thighs, Washington's thoughts filled with Sally. She was near. Somewhere under the gabled roof of the mansion or on the grounds surrounding it, she stood, walked, sat or labored. It didn't matter which. It was odd and not a little disturbing that another person could consume his being so thoroughly, could plunge him into a state approaching despair with nothing more than a note of haughty, childish pique. Wistfully, he recalled the episode at Gist's plantation when he had chastised God for inflicting Sally on him. Had he meant it? Were these unpleasant emotional tribulations God's punishment for his presumptions? *No, God wouldn't do that. But Sally would, if she knew. Of course, she doesn't know,* Washington reminded himself, feeling a little foolish for even entertaining such an absurd thought. *This thing has really set my mind agog.*

In the driveway, James, the Fairfax's ancient black servant, was waiting for him with his habitual aplomb.

"Afte-noon, Mar'se Washington," he said in languorous greeting as he steadied the sorrel.

"Good afternoon, James," said Washington, dismounting. "And how is your grandson Uriah?"

The pupils of James's coal black eyes expanded gaily as he replied, "He's fine, fine. Almost five months old now. He's a strong boy. Got him a pair 'a lungs like a preacher."

Washington laughed and said, "Maybe he'll be one some day."

"I hope so. I hope so. That's my dream," the full brown lips proclaimed. His tone turned suddenly somber as he said, "I was sorry to he-ah about your man."

He's referring to Joseph, Washington realized. But they'd hardly known one another—Joseph and James. There had been few opportunities for them to meet; they were slaves on separate plantations, after all. Yet they were both black men. Perhaps that blackness had forged a bond that no white man could appreciate or even comprehend. Washington studied James's eyes for meaning but found only the shimmering gleam of unshed tears.

"Thank you, James. It was a tragedy, a random bullet that somehow found him."

James nodded meekly but Washington sensed something more substantive beneath the surface. Not anger—slaves could not afford anger—but a restive sadness, the stoic acceptance of man who has no choice but to accept his plight, but with an undertone of disquiet. "How could you do this?" James might have demanded. "How could you let your man die for something he had no part of?" James might have said it, but he didn't. Instead, he turned toward the coachery his graying head slightly bowed, and led the sorrel away.

"Is Sally in the house?" Washington called.

Slowly, James shook his head. Bringing his glassy gaze up to meet Washington's, he said, "Miss Sally down by the big oak."

As he spoke, the servant kept the horse's reins in hand but lifted them to point toward the summerhouse. Washington looked and did, indeed, see Sally sitting in the pinewood swing one of the other slaves had built a few years back. With one foot she was keeping the swing in motion, kicking against the ground once each cycle. Dressed for a hot summer day in a straw milkmaid hat and a beige cotton dress with a white muslin apron and bib, Sally nevertheless appeared to be uncomfortable. Impatiently, she fidgeted with the parasol in her hand trying to find the angle that gave the most shade. He hadn't seen her on the way in because the swing faced the Potomac and was partially hidden by the giant oak. He wondered if she'd seen him. She heard him coming and turned.

"Hello, Sally," he said, removing his hat.

"Hello, George," she said with a curt smile.

"You look pretty."

"Why, thank you," she crooned demurely, then gave him an inquisitive look. "Are you all done with soldiering now?"

The remark might have contained a hint of sarcasm or might simply be Sally's blunt, self-absorbed way of expressing herself.

"Yes, we're all done with soldiering for the time being," he said.

"I thought so. You don't have your soldier uniform on like you did last time."

Washington wondered how Van Braam was faring with that uniform. It would not be comfortable in this heat, especially with the humidity from the three rivers at Fort Duquesne to contend with. Even the light cotton stock around Washington's neck chafed, and his feet felt as if they were immersed not in leather but a bed of hot coals. How much worse would it be wearing the heavy broadcloth and all the accouterments of that uniform? *Oh, to go barefoot and bareassed again,* he mused, recalling his summers at Pope's Creek as a boy.

Hoping to communicate the grimness of his mood he murmured, "I don't feel like a soldier. None of us does. Besides, I sold it."

"You sold it!" Sally crowed. "You sold that love-ly blue suit? Why did you do that, George? You looked so good in it, so hand-some…Come here, George, sit by me. Don't look so hangdog…"

Sally was patting the empty space to her left and smiling effusively. She *had* noticed his depression and, true to her calling, was doing her best to remedy the situation.

"I didn't bring anything with me. I thought we'd…"he muttered as he eased onto the swing beside her.

"Oh, don't worry about that. It's too hot to read or play act. Let's just sit and talk and try not to drip on one another. Esther will be bringing lemonade soon."

"Have you read anything interesting lately?" he asked. *Small talk.*

"George William got me a book of Moliere plays in Williamsburg. Lord Thomas brings me one of his classics to read from time to time…"

She sounded bored and looked the part, staring up at the sky above the Potomac, which, except for a pair of hovering seagulls, was empty, even of clouds.

"Sally, I'd like to talk to you," he said tentatively, leaning forward and away from her.

Sally's only immediate reaction was a tiny, but unmistakable, sigh of petulance. When finally she faced him, it was with a quick, dismissive motion and a projecting, censorious lower lip.

"George, are you going to be serious again?" she snapped. "I hate it when you get serious."

"Sally, you sent me a note..."

"I sent you a note because you just simply totally ignored me when you got back! I declare, you didn't even stop by to say hello! I would've thought you'd at least want to say hello after being away for such a long time."

With that eruption Sally returned her gaze to the 'eyes-front' position, accenting her peevish posturing with an elevated chin and a tight-lipped frown.

"Sally, I was tired," he said with greater intensity of feeling than he intended. "We were beaten, humiliated. Men were killed..."

"You can't blame me for that," she complained with histrionic incredulity.

Of course I can't. I don't.

"I thought you would understand how I felt. It's important for a man to do well at what he aspires to in life. In my first real engagement as an officer, I failed miserably. Your note made me feel even more disgusted with myself, more...wretched."

She leaned forward so they were abreast of each other and covered his hand with hers.

"I'm sorry, George. I didn't know it meant that much to you..."

You should have.

"...It's just that nothing ever happens at Belvoir. There's no one to talk to but the servants, and what can they talk about? Feeding the chickens and having black babies? Colonel William is too busy to pay attention to anyone. Lord Thomas hates women—he does, honestly—and he doesn't visit here that often. And George William...George William..."

"Your husband."

"Yes, George, I *know* he's my husband," she whimpered, fixing an icy stare on him. "But he never talks to me...not really. We go places together but it's like being with someone I've only just met. We talk about the weather, about our friends in Williamsburg—mine mostly—and about the slaves, the horses, lots of subjects. But none of it is personal. Talking to George William is like talking to someone on the other side of a wall. He's not like you, George. He's not like anyone here…"

She had been staring at him, a mien of despair corrupting her pretty face, but tore it away and rose quickly to her feet. Seizing the parasol, she raised it overhead and began walking toward the Potomac. Sally was right, of course—George William *was* different. He had spent ten years of his boyhood at Leeds Castle in England going to school. How William Fairfax could send his son away for that long a period was difficult to comprehend. There was speculation that it had something to do with the uncertain ancestry of the Colonel's first wife, George William's mother, who had come from the Caribbean. The Fairfaxes were, after all, members of the British aristocracy. Upon his return to Virginia, George William and Washington—seven years younger than Fairfax—had become fast friends. As far as anyone knew, no major disasters had befallen George William in England, but the trauma of extended separation from his family had clearly taken a toll—that and the virtual adoption by Lord Thomas of the strapping lad from Mount Vernon. George William must certainly have interpreted some of this as rejection and his spirit processed it accordingly.

Hat in hand, Washington caught up with Sally. She was still fidgeting with the parasol's orientation.

"This awful thing just doesn't work," she fumed, swinging it around as if to smash it against something. "The sun shines right through it. George, what am I to do? It's so hot!"

Washington took the gold parasol in hand and examined it. He could see through it, even around the edges where the muslin was overlaid with white lace.

"You need a heavier material, like canvas."

"That would be lovely, wouldn't it?" she said, arching her perfect eyebrows into the ivory skin of her forehead. "Then I would *really* look like a farmer's wife."

"But it would work," he said with an uplifting grin, placing the parasol so it rested on her shoulder. "Why don't we walk in the shade?"

She returned his smile with a coquettish upturn of the lips. When they were directly beneath the oak's umbra Sally stopped, lowered the parasol to her waist, and gazed up at the vast, serpentine network of boughs and leaves overhead. As a tropical summer wind rustled through the labyrinthine pathways, the pawing shadows of the oak leaves danced on the grass below like the crude appendages of a marionette.

"I love this old tree, don't you?" Sally said, her voice wistful with reverence. "I think this old tree, and the view of the river from here, and the way the road leads past the mansion...I think it's why I decided to marry George William..."

For a mystical moment, Sally did nothing but turn her head, absorbing the grandeur of the surroundings with her eyes. A faint, faraway smile played on her lips, as if she were enjoying a pleasant daydream. It was obvious to him that she loved this place. He felt, but could not define, a pang of jealousy. Then her eyes settled on him and the spell was broken.

"But it isn't enough," she sighed, dropping her gaze. "In Williamsburg, we had parties, social events, politics, lots of reasons to have a good time. I may not have been a grand lady, but I felt like one. I could imagine myself being one. That's the kind of woman I am, George. I think you know that."

He did, and gave a nod of acknowledgment when her eyes posed the question. Then, as if afraid he might withdraw his sympathy, Sally raised the parasol overhead and drifted away toward the Potomac.

"Here we don't do anything. I *am* just a farmer's wife," she began, then scolded herself. "Oh, I don't mean that. We do have guests. We do entertain. I am the mistress of Belvoir, or will be when Colonel William is gone. That should be enough, shouldn't it, George? To be the mistress of a grand place like Belvoir: What woman wouldn't be green with envy to have what I have? It should be more than enough for anyone...but it's not."

As she spoke, Sally turned her head to look at him over her left shoulder. The parasol on the right shoulder framed her face like a painting.

"You probably think I'm spoiled, don't you?" she asked, a pout weighing on her lips.

"If I did, it wouldn't matter."

She understood, letting him know by reinstating the smile, but without its usual effervescence. "I need you, George," she murmured. It was more than an admission. It was a plea.

They stood with their eyes locked on one another, not knowing how to escape safely from the moment, less sure if they wanted to. How long the rapture lasted neither could have said, but the sense of timelessness came to an abrupt end when her eyes released his and shifted their focus to the woods. Then Washington heard the steady padding of hoof-beats. He turned to see a rider on a piebald mare approaching at a fast trot, his blue breeches identifying him as a member of the Regiment. The horse's flanks were lathered in perspiration, as were the wedge gusset armpits of the rider's linen shirt. Washington recognized the youthful visage and russet forelocks of Private Robert Chisolm. Bobby vaulted from his saddle before the mare came to a complete halt, snapped to attention, and gave Washington a brisk salute.

"Sir, I have a message from Governor Dinwiddie," he said in clipped, military English.

Washington returned a less flamboyant salute and noticed that Chisolm's other arm was extended toward him. In it was an envelope. He took it.

"Did you come all the way from Williamsburg?" Washington inquired, extracting the folded paper inside the envelope.

"Yes, sir. I stopped at Mount Vernon first, but you weren't there…"

Suddenly embarrassed at the inanity of what he was saying, Bobby stammered an indecipherable sentence or two and then regained control of his tongue.

"…One of the servants told me you were here, sir," he finished with an anxious flourish.

Washington nodded as he studied the opening remarks of Dinwiddie's letter, then plunged into the text. As his eyes scanned the page, he was at first irritated and then enraged by the dispatch. *Robert Dinwiddie at his very best*, he thought. By the time he reached the mocking words "Your Humble and Obedient Servant, Robert Dinwiddie" his face was red and his temper boiling over.

"Do you know what this is all about, Bobby?" he barked, taking a swipe at the letter as if challenging its author to a duel.

Taken aback by Washington's intemperate reaction Chisolm gave a start, then said, "Uh…yes, sir, a little."

Cutting the Private some slack, Washington mellowed his timbre and said, "Good. You go back to Mount Vernon and get something to eat. I'll join you shortly and give you a reply."

Before he could stop them, Bobby's eyes took in a quick glimpse of Sally, who was strolling lazily toward the bluff. Washington saw the reflexive gesture.

"That's Mrs. Fairfax. She's my neighbor," he said, resisting an impulse to elaborate further.

Forcing his eyes to the front, Chisolm said "Yes, sir," saluted again, and galloped away on the piebald mare. Washington folded the letter along its creases and joined Sally. She was watching the two seagulls hovering over the water, waiting to scoop up any fish careless enough to swim too near the surface.

"What did he want, George?" she asked tentatively.

"The Governor wants us to attack," he answered, making no attempt to hide the disdain in his voice.

"But you just got back!"

He handed her the letter and said, "Read it yourself. He wants me to bring the Regiment back up to strength, join Colonel Innes and his three companies in Wills Creek, and march on Fort Duquesne."

"Can you do that?"

Washington felt like he wanted to explode. If anyone but Sally had asked the question, he thought he could have.

"No, I can't do that!" he shouted, flinging his hands wildly in the air. "It's insane! Where am I going to get the men? And if I could, where would I get the supplies, the horses, the wagons, and the weapons to take an army over the mountains again? The French took our swivel guns. What do I do for artillery? You can't attack a fort without artillery! We had trouble getting all that together the first time out. With settlers fleeing the frontier, it will be virtually impossible! The man has lost his senses!"

Sally was looking at him with a mixture of apprehension and concern. Although others had, she had never really seen him angry before, and it frightened her. Snatching her eyes away, she laid the parasol on the ground and unfolded the letter. Realizing his self-control was not all it should be, and regretting his outburst, Washington took in a long gulp of humid air and sauntered to the edge of the bluff. He wanted to give Sally time to peruse Dinwiddie's letter and himself time to calm the raging storm inside him.

Behind him, he heard Sally gasp.

"George, it says here you murdered someone. A Frenchman!"

He turned to find Sally staring at him, dismay and disbelief twisting her features.

"It says the French are *claiming* I murdered an officer named Jumonville," he corrected.

Sally looked down at the letter again, then back up at him, and said in a quavering voice, "It says you admitted it."

"That's a lie! The only thing we admitted to in the articles of capitulation was that Jumonville was killed in an engagement between his party and ours..."

Then it dawned on him. The articles of capitulation were in French and there had been more than a little smearing of the text due to the heavy rainfall on the day of the battle. The only Frenchman in the Virginia Regiment—William La Peyroney—had passed out from his wound and was unable to translate. The Dutchman, Jacob Van Braam, had done all the translating. Had Villiers tricked him into a confession of murder? *Yes*, his mind said with absolute certitude, *he had*.

"I didn't murder anyone, Sally," he said, the anger draining from him, replaced by a sickening sensation of being sucked down by a whirling undertow of self-doubt. "Jumonville was killed in a legitimate military engagement. They had guns. We had guns. We just got the better of them, that's all."

And our Indians scalped their commanding officer, Washington recalled, the memory sending a chill down his spine.

Turning on his heel, he started back to the path he had come by and said, "I have to go. I have to give Bobby my reply."

"What are you going to tell the Governor? Are you going to do what he wants?" Sally asked uneasily.

"No."

Sally might have felt relief except for his abruptness. It was not a good omen. She accelerated to stay abreast of him.

"Can't you stay awhile, George?" she said uncertainly. "Look, Esther is here with the lemonade! Stay and have some lemonade with me, George. Please."

Esther was indeed coming down the path toward the swing, a pitcher and two glasses perched on the tray before her, a mouthful of dazzling white teeth accentuating the darkness of her skin. But it didn't matter. Washington turned to face Sally, resting his hands on her shoulders.

"I can't do it anymore, Sally," he said, searching for understanding in her lovely eyes.

Did he understand himself? He remembered with fond nostalgia the pride he felt when Robert Dinwiddie had published the notes from the Venango expedition, his first journey to the west as a representative of Virginia and the British Crown. The notes had received wide and favorable distribution in both the colonies and England. As Dinwiddie had predicted, he had achieved a certain, satisfying degree of fame. Now, because of the French charges, he would be famous again. This time there would be no plaudits. Some would call him a murderer. The rest would brand him a fool, which, in many ways, was even worse.

As always, he was pleased to be staring into Sally's pretty face, but, as always, saw not one whit of comprehension in it.

"I'm resigning my commission, Sally," he said, fatalistic. "I won't be a soldier any longer."

She tried to conceal her reaction but Washington could see that Sally was pleased. Had he been capable of it, he might have despised her.

𝔓review of 𝔅ook 𝔗hree

𝔗he 𝔏ion's 𝔄pprentice

In *The Lion's Apprentice*, the third book of the *Neophyte Warrior* series, the British are finally alarmed by the French dominance of the North American frontier. The Duke of Cumberland and his allies in the British government enlist the services of Major General Edward Braddock to lead an expedition to dispossess the French of Fort Duquesne, then turn north and east to seize French fortifications on the Great Lakes. Braddock is an old soldier with a reputation as a disciplinarian but has only a smattering of battlefield experience, all of it in Europe. He is not familiar with the North American wilderness, nor does he know or appreciate the fighting tactics of its inhabitants.

Smarting from his humiliation at Fort Necessity and the French charge that he has, in the terms of surrender, admitted to the murder of the Coulon de Jumonville, Washington decides to pursue a life as a gentleman farmer. His retirement from the military is short-lived. A letter from Edward Braddock entices him to join a new Ohio expedition as an *aide-de-camp* with the brevet rank of captain. For the adventure, he borrows a black stallion from Sally Fairfax but his quixotic love affair with his neighbor's wife is beginning to show signs of strain. To make matters worse, Washington contracts the 'bloody flux' but refuses to stay out of harm's way. He sees his participation in Braddock's expedition as a springboard to what he has always coveted: a King's commission in the regular army of Great Britain.

At the instigation of his uncle, Buffalo Hair, Old Smoke joins the French at Fort Duquesne. His friend, Striking Eagle, is already there.

The fort's commandant, the Sieur de Contrecoeur, assigns both Shawnee to a company led by two of his men with the mission of conducting raids against English settlers. Old Smoke quickly becomes disgusted by the murderous behavior of his colleagues and withdraws, but remains at Fort Duquesne. He will fight alongside the French against the British when that common foe inevitably arrives. He has promised his uncle that much.

Meanwhile, Stump Neck and his band of cutthroats lurk in the dark recesses of the endless forest waiting to see who will win the prize. Although loosely allied with the *Compagnies des franches*, the madman's fortunes do not require a French victory. He has his own bloodthirsty agenda, the first item of which is to track down a preacher who knows precisely who and what he is.

The stage is set for another violent confrontation in the wilds of North America. This time a British general and the army he has brought from England will challenge the French. Will it make a difference?

ABOUT THE AUTHOR

Richard Patton is a six-fold grandfather with a Ph.D. from Case-Western Reserve University and several lesser degrees from other institutions. Except for a lifelong desire to be one, contributions to college literary magazines, and a creative writing course at an ancient academy called Carnegie Tech, his credentials as a writer are restricted to numerous but esoteric technical papers and Book One of *Neophyte Warrior—His Majesty's Envoy.* His true credentials lie in an abiding interest in early American History and the patience to root out some of its lesser-known tidbits. He has had some success in little theater where, among other things, he learned the dynamics of dialogue and an important lesson also mastered by the young George Washington: A good actor must be able to persuade his audience that he knows what he's doing until such time that he actually does.

Dr. Patton lives in the South Hills of Pittsburgh with his wife, Jo. *Neophyte Warrior: The Reluctant Commander* is his second novel.

THE MAIDEN'S SONG by Debra Tash   ISBN: 1-894869-25-7

THE PINECROFT THOROUGHBREDS by Selwyn A. Grames
ISBN: 1-59109-054-7

THE VANDALIANS by Thomas Cater   ISBN: 1-894869-47-8

HIS MAJESTY'S ENVOY by Richard Patton   ISBN: 1-894869-38-9

THE RELUCTANT COMMANDER by Richard Patton
ISBN: 1-894869-57-5

THE MOTHER'S SWORD by Dr. Bob Rich   ISBN: 1-894869-45-1

MAINSTREAM FICTION

YESTERDAY'S TEARS, TOMORROW'S PEARLS by Martine Jardin
ISBN: 1-59109-167-5

MANIPULATIONS by Shrinivas Sharangpani   ISBN: 1-894869-32-X

PARADOX OUTPATIENT by Bernie Schallehn   ISBN: 1-894869-16-8

MYSTERY

TRACETRACKS by Larry Rochelle   ISBN: 1-894869-14-1

BEN ZAKKAI'S COFFIN by Harley L. Sachs   ISBN: 1-894869-20-6

DEATH AND DEVOTION by Larry Rochelle   ISBN: 1-894869-30-3

DANCE WITH THE PONY by Larry Rochelle   ISBN: 1-894869-18-4

FANTASY

CRYSTAL DREAMS by Astrid Cooper ISBN: 1-59109-065-2

THE BLOOD CIRCLE by Ellen Anthony ISBN: 1-894869-34-6

EROTICA

SEA ORPHAN by J. Kramer ISBN: 1-59109-062-8

SCIROTICA by Cameron Hale ISBN: 1-59109-063-6

WHY SHOULD GUYS HAVE ALL THE FUN by Cindy X. Novo
ISBN: 1-894869-40-0

HORROR

THE CHRONICLES OF A MADMAN by Michael LaRocca
ISBN: 1-59109-068-7

GOTHIC

ECHOES OF ANGELS by Caitlyn McKenna ISBN:1-894869-41-9

YOUNG ADULT

FIVE DAYS TILL DAWN   ISBN: 1-894869-51-6

NON FICTION – SELF HELP

HOW TO MANAGE ANGER AND ANXIETY by Dr. Bob Rich
ISBN: 1-59109-064-4

EDUCATION
PROF RAP by Professor Larry Rochelle   ISBN: 1-894869-53-2

Made in the USA